2

PRAISE FOR *TAKE DOWN*

"No one in the world does this stuff better than Jim Swain. No one knows it better or writes it better. Satisfaction guaranteed."

—Lee Child

"James Swain is one of my favorites. His books never fail to entertain, teach, and surprise. *Take Down* is his best yet, with his knowledge and experience dripping off of every page, and a character like Billy Cunningham to lead the way. Great stuff."

—Michael Connelly

"James Swain is the best at writing fast-paced thrillers about Las Vegas thugs and conmen. I can't put down his newest, *Take Down*."

—R. L. Stine

"Nobody knows the dazzling reality of cons and capers in Las Vegas better than James Swain, from the luminous illusions of casinos to the dark side of buried bodies in the desert night. *Take Down* is a unique portrait of this universe."

—John Langley, executive producer and creator of *COPS*

BAD
ACTION

ALSO BY JAMES SWAIN

Billy Cunningham Series

Take Down

Jack Carpenter Series

Midnight Rambler
The Night Stalker
The Night Monster
The Program

Tony Valentine Series

Grift Sense
Funny Money
Sucker Bet
Loaded Dice
Mr. Lucky
Deadman's Poker
Deadman's Bluff
Wild Card
Jackpot

Peter Warlock Series

Dark Magic
Shadow People

JAMES SWAIN

THOMAS & MERCER

This is a work of fiction. Names, characters, organizations, places, events, and incidents are either products of the author's imagination or are used fictitiously.

Published by Thomas & Mercer, Seattle

www.apub.com

Amazon, the Amazon logo, and Thomas & Mercer are trademarks of Amazon.com, Inc., or its affiliates.

ISBN-13: 9781503935211
ISBN-10: 1503935213

Cover design by David Drummond

Printed in the United States of America

To Kjersti and Kevin

ONE

-THE KILLING-

Billy Cunningham had never wanted to kill anyone in his life. He was a lover, not a fighter, and liked to believe he could talk his way out of any jam. Only this time, he didn't have a choice. He'd told the man in the bedroom how he felt, and the man had drawn a switchblade. Right then, Billy had known that it was not going to end until one of them was dead.

Billy retreated from the bedroom and walked backward down the hallway with the man following him. The condo's layout was unfamiliar, and he kept bumping into walls. Upon reaching the living room, he drew the Sig Sauer P220 semiautomatic tucked in the small of his back, steadied his arm, and took aim. If he didn't pull the trigger, the man was going to kill him—probably slowly, certainly painfully—and would have no second thoughts about it.

His enemy put on the brakes and broke into a smile.

"You think I'm kidding?" Billy said.

"Your arm's shaking," the man said.

No surprise there. Billy wasn't fond of guns. He'd been scamming the casinos of Las Vegas for a decade and never felt the need to carry heat. His weapon was his wits and his ability to stay one step ahead of the law. That wasn't true for most cheats. Most cheats carried guns and would use them if necessary. They didn't care if they capped a victim during a job, and they certainly didn't have a problem killing another thief who crossed them.

Billy was different that way. He didn't possess a killer's instinct. Never had, never would. The man with the switchblade sensed that. He had sized Billy up and decided he liked his chances pitting his blade against Billy's gun.

"You don't have the balls to shoot me," the man said.

"You're not a very good judge of character," Billy said.

"You've never shot a gun in your fucking life."

"That doesn't mean I won't shoot you."

The man's eyes were filled with contempt. He wasn't scared of Billy at all.

"You're bluffing," the man said.

"Call my bluff and see what happens," Billy said.

Eight feet, maybe less, separated them. The adrenaline coursing through Billy's veins had caused a surreal slowdown of events, and he saw the tip of the knife flick back and forth in the man's hand like a serpent's tail. His enemy's smile vanished as he lunged forward.

Billy squeezed the trigger. As he did, he had an unsettling thought. He didn't know whether the Sig was loaded. It wasn't his gun, and in the heat of the moment he hadn't bothered to check the chamber. Only when the gun barked in his hand did he know. The bullet slammed into his enemy's chest and the man melted to the floor.

"Rot in hell," Billy said.

The life seeped out of the man's body, his eyes shutting a few centimeters at a time. It didn't seem real. A few short days ago, Billy had been preparing to pull the biggest heist of his life. Twelve months of planning had gone into it, along with weeks of rehearsals at a rented house in Lake Tahoe. It was such an ingenious piece of larceny that

Billy hoped to someday write a book about it, just so the world would know what he'd done.

So how had he ended up in a strange house, killing a man he hardly knew?

Billy thought he knew. He'd let his feelings for a beautiful woman cloud his judgment. He'd been a thief for most of his life, and he never let his emotions interfere with a job. But this situation was different. He'd fallen in love, and love did strange things to people.

Voices carried from outside. At the living room window, he parted the curtains. A police cruiser was parked in the street, its bubble flashing. A pair of uniforms stood behind the cruiser pointing their guns at the house. One of the uniforms was on a walkie-talkie, calling for backup.

He stepped away from the window and tossed the Sig onto the couch. He'd dug a deep hole for himself. The question was, could he climb out of it, or would he spend the rest of his life in prison, hustling his cellmates at penny ante poker? Taking out his cell phone, he called Travis, the number-two man in his crew. He told Travis that he was not going to be at the casino that afternoon for the heist, and for his crew to proceed without him.

"Where are you? We're all getting nervous," Travis said.

"Change of plans. You're now officially in charge," Billy said.

"Are you coming back?"

"Not right away. I'll explain later. Just follow the script, and we'll all end up rich."

"For the love of Christ, Billy, this is insane."

"Have I ever steered you wrong before?"

"That's not the point. You're not here, and you're the whale. What do I tell DeSantis if he asks me where you went?"

"I told DeSantis I had to bail a friend out of jail. Use that story."

Travis went quiet, and Billy wondered if he'd lost him.

"I sure hope you know what you're doing," the big man said.

“Keep the faith,” Billy said.

His next call was to his defense attorney, a silver-haired fox named Felix Underman. Billy paid his attorney a fat monthly retainer for situations just like this, and the receptionist patched him through without asking what the call was about.

“Hello, Billy, how are we today?” his attorney asked.

“Not so good,” he replied.

“I’m sorry to hear that. What seems to be the problem?”

“I just shot a guy, and the police are going to arrest me.”

“Is he dead?”

“Yeah, that’s why I shot him.”

“I’ll meet you at the jail in an hour. Whatever you do, don’t say a word to the police.”

“I wasn’t planning on it,” the young hustler said.

TWO

-WEDNESDAY, THREE DAYS EARLIER-

Lake Tahoe was for lovers of the great outdoors. Snowcapped mountains ringed the twenty-two-mile-long body of water, the scenery around the lake so breathtaking that it wouldn't have been a surprise to find the von Trapp family sharing a picnic.

The employees who worked Tahoe's casinos were equally attractive, with athletic dealers and pit bosses who spent their off hours hiking or burning down the slopes.

Tahoe was also a good place to plan a heist. The locals were friendly but minded their own business. There were also fewer cops and hardly any gaming agents snooping around. Billy felt comfortable here, so he'd rented a five-bedroom house on the south side and set up shop.

His crew had spent two weeks rehearsing in front of video cameras. Each member was about to take on a new identity as part of their role in the scam. It was no different than performing in a play, and at night they'd sat in the living room and watched videos of their performances while critiquing themselves the same way acting students would.

By the end of the second week, Billy decided it was time to try out their new identities. Their target was the Montbleu Casino on the southern tip of the lake. The eighties rock group Styx was performing in the casino's theater, and the joint was packed.

The blackjack table had seven chairs. Billy sat in the chair to the dealer's immediate left, called first base. Next to Billy sat Travis, the crew's mechanic. Beside Travis sat a comely brunette named Misty. Misty had recently gotten a face-lift to avoid arrest and gone back to using her real name on her driver's license and other ID, but the crew still knew her as Misty.

Beside Misty sat Pepper, a stunning redhead who'd acted in porn movies with Misty before joining Billy's crew. Rounding out the table were two college-age hustlers named Cory and Morris, and a master forger named Gabe, who happened to be the oldest member of the crew.

The dealer was a tanned stud named Evan. Evan removed the six decks of cards from the discard rack and shuffled them on the table.

"Place sure is busy for a Wednesday night," Billy said.

"The old rock acts bring out the geezers," Evan said. "They sit in the audience stoned out of their minds and sing along."

"Hey, I resemble that remark," Gabe said.

Evan continued to shuffle. Decks of cards in a prearranged order were every casino's worst nightmare. To prevent this scam from happening, dealers were required to shuffle under the watchful eye of a surveillance camera directly over the table. The shuffling was recorded and would be scrutinized by security if the table lost a large sum of money. Evan was a veteran dealer, and his nimble fingers made the cards purr.

"So what brings you folks to beautiful Lake Tahoe?" Evan asked.

His crew went into their spiels. Lying about your past wasn't easy, and Billy was pleased at how effortlessly each of them had slipped into their new roles.

Evan slid a yellow plastic cut card toward Billy. Billy had decided to steal three grand from the Montbleu, which would pay for the rented house and their meals.

"Let one of the ladies do the honors," Billy said.

Evan slid the cut card toward Misty.

"What am I supposed to do?" she asked innocently.

"Stick the plastic card somewhere in the middle," Evan said.

Misty smiled flirtatiously. It was the perfect distraction, and she let the cut card fan through a slug of six cards, slightly separating their edges as a fiber-optic lens hidden in her fingertip recorded their values. The lens was concealed by flesh-colored plastic that ran into her sleeve and down into a hidden receiver in her purse. From there, the information was transmitted to an LED display stitched into the rim of Gabe's baseball cap.

Gabe stared into the cap's rim, spying the six cards' values. His next task was to communicate to the crew what each of their first cards would be during the round. Gabe accomplished this by toying with his chips. Each player got two cards in blackjack. By knowing the value of one of those cards, the player gained an enormous edge over the house.

Based upon Gabe's secret signals, Billy was about to get an ace, Travis a ten, Misty a four, Pepper a five, Cory a king, and Morris a jack.

Billy made a large bet, since the odds of him winning with an ace were high. Travis, Cory, and Morris also made large bets, since their odds of winning were also good. Misty and Pepper made small bets, since their odds of losing were high.

The scam took five seconds to execute. Had Evan been paying attention, he might have spotted the optic fiber in Misty's sleeve. But Evan could not stop looking into Misty's bedroom eyes, and as a result, he completely missed the play.

Evan cut the cards at the spot Misty had made with the cutter, and slid the six decks into the dealing shoe. "Good luck, everyone," he said.

Evan dealt the round.

Billy, Travis, Cory, and Morris won their hands, while Misty and Pepper lost their hands. This put them ahead three thousand bucks on a single round of cards.

It was a sweet scam, and it didn't get old. Like Billy's mentor Lou Profaci was fond of saying, it sure beat working. Billy decided to end the scam early so they could return to the rented house. In a few short days, they were going to take down a casino for many millions of dollars, and that was worth celebrating over.

- - -

Some people get caught in a time warp from which they never escape. The owners of the rented house were stuck in the eighties, and the house's interior was a tribute to chintz. Sitting at the dining room table, Billy gave his crew a final pep talk.

"For the next three days, we're going to be given access to a make-believe world called Comp City," the young hustler said. "It won't seem real, and that's because it isn't. Incredible hotel suites, the most delicious food you've ever eaten, servants at your beck and call, shopping sprees, and all of it's going to be free. Whatever you do, don't act impressed. Understand?"

"Will we have to sign for anything?" Misty asked.

"No. But you are expected to tip generously. Remember, I'm going to be impersonating a whale, and you're all my friends."

"Got it."

"Are the suites wired?" Cory asked.

"They might be. To be safe, don't say anything out of character," Billy said.

"My lips are sealed."

"I'm confused," Pepper said. "Our reservations are at the Rio, but we're planning to scam the Carnivale Casino, which is on the other side of Vegas. How does that work?"

"We're going to be lured from the Rio to Carnivale by a VIP host," Billy explained. "Carnivale has the most aggressive VIP hosts in Las Vegas, and they're known to hit their competitors' casinos and steal away their whales."

"Steal how?"

"With incentives. If a whale has a history of losing a million or more a weekend, a Carnivale host might offer him a hundred grand to play with, just to make him switch."

"Free money?"

"That's right. Carnivale knows they'll make it back. They also give whales rebates on their losses as high as twenty percent. Say a whale blows a million bucks in a weekend. In reality, the first hundred grand is free, and he gets rebated another hundred and eighty grand on the back end."

"Rich people have it made."

"Yes, they do. Any other questions?"

"You still haven't told us how this scam at Carnivale's going to work," Travis said. "Hell, we don't even know what the scam is."

"Yeah, why the secrecy?" Cory asked.

"Don't you trust us?" Morris chimed in.

His crew was the closest thing Billy had to family, and he would have trusted each of them with his life. But when it came to stealing, loose lips sunk ships, and there was no good reason to add another element of risk to the heist, which was why he hadn't told them exactly how the scam would go down on Saturday afternoon at Carnivale's casino.

"If Billy didn't trust you, you wouldn't be here," Gabe said, coming to the defense.

"Do you know what the scam is?" Cory asked.

"Of course I know what it is. I built the gaff to make it work," Gabe said proudly.

"So why won't you tell us?" Cory asked.

"Because if more than two people know something, it's no longer a secret," Gabe replied. "Would you be happy if I told you it's going to make us really rich?"

"Stratosphere rich?" Morris asked.

"Close enough."

"I can dig that."

"I'd still like to know what I'm getting myself into," Travis said. The big man had a new wife and two young stepsons and was less risk tolerant than the other members of the crew. "You know, just to put my mind at ease."

Billy understood where Travis was coming from and said, "What's the hardest part of ripping off a casino?"

"Getting the money out of the joint," Travis replied.

"That's right. If the casino suspects a scam, they won't pay off until they review the surveillance tapes. It's ruined more than one heist. Well, I figured out a way around that."

"How?"

"I can't tell you that. But it's rock solid."

"They won't feel the loss?"

Billy shook his head. "Not until we're long gone," he added.

"This is sounding better all the time," Travis said. "Can you tell us the haul?"

"It will be more than ten million."

"How can they not feel ten million?"

"I can't tell you that. But they won't. At least not right away."

"What's our cut?" Travis asked.

"The usual."

Travis rocked back in his chair. The rest of his crew looked equally stunned. When Billy had recruited them, each member had been up to his or her eyeballs in debt. He'd helped all of them climb out of the financial hole they'd dug for themselves and get back on solid ground. Now he was going to take them to another level and make them rich.

"Let's celebrate," Billy said.

- - -

Billy grabbed a bottle of Cristal from the fridge along with seven plastic champagne flutes he'd bought at a local party store, and upon returning to the table filled each flute until exploding bubbles were cascading down the sides. They raised their glasses in unison.

"Here's to taking down Carnivale," he toasted.

They knocked back the drinks. Cory was fidgeting in his chair and his facial expression said something was eating at him. Billy had recently cut Cory and Morris loose because they liked to smoke weed on the job, then had a change of heart and brought them back into the fold. They were still on probation, and Cory wasn't going to speak unless spoken to.

"What's wrong?" Billy asked.

"Carnivale is the newest casino in town," Cory said. "I've heard they're using facial recognition software and anticheating techniques that are second to none. They're light-years ahead of everybody else."

"Who told you that?"

"Remember Johnny March the blackjack hustler?"

"Is he the guy who used a hidden laser in a cigarette pack to mark cards during the game?"

"That's him. Johnny's used his cigarette pack to scam every casino in town. Johnny tried to scam Carnivale the first week the joint opened and it didn't go so well. I talked to Johnny's sister, Suzie, and she said Johnny got busted and is facing ten years in the pen."

"They got the goods on him?" Billy said.

"Caught him red-handed. The eye-in-the-sky at Carnivale has a filter designed to detect lasers. No other casino in Vegas has that. Johnny's screwed."

"Yipes. Maybe we should scam another casino," Misty suggested.

"Can we do that at this late date?" Travis asked.

All eyes fell on the boss. Billy leaned back in his chair and considered their options. In the old days, casinos had factored a 5 percent loss to cheating and inside theft. Times had changed, and the new owners of casinos, mostly large corporations, did not tolerate stealing, and they installed elaborate systems to prevent it. His crew was worried, and for good reason. Carnivale's casino was the best protected in town.

Normally, that would have been enough incentive for him to call off the play. No job was worth getting arrested over. Except maybe this one. Carnivale's management was so focused on drawing in whales that they'd lost sight of the damage a whale could inflict upon the company's bottom line. That damage could make Billy more money than anything he'd ever tried. The risk was huge, but so was the reward. And those jobs turned him on the most.

He looked each of them in the eye. When he spoke, his voice was quiet but firm. "I'm not going to let Johnny March's screwup ruin this score, and neither should you. Every casino can be ripped off, including Carnivale. It's all about preparation, my friends, and I've been planning this heist for a long time and have scrutinized every angle. If you don't believe me, just ask Gabe."

"Billy's done his homework on this one," Gabe said.

"Yes, I have. So here's the deal," Billy said. "I'm going outside on the deck to do a little stargazing. If you want in, come outside and join me. If not, pack your suitcase and leave tonight. No hard feelings."

And with that, Billy rose from the table and walked out of the room.

- - -

The temperature had dropped twenty degrees, and Billy hugged himself to stay warm. It was a flawless night, and he found himself wishing that a cheater named Maggie Flynn was huddled up beside him. He'd been carrying a torch for Mags since he was a teenager, but when the opportunity to seal the deal had presented itself, he'd gotten cold feet and run out on her. It had seemed like the right thing to do at the time, yet now he regretted treating her so poorly. He'd heard Mags was back in Vegas ripping off suckers, and he'd decided to call her when the Carnivale job was done, to see if he could patch things up.

Gabe joined him at the railing holding two bottles of beer.

"I'm in," Gabe said.

"I already knew that. What about the others?"

"They're talking it over."

"Think they'll stay?"

"I told them they'd be idiots not to."

They clinked bottles and Billy took a long pull. "That's nasty tasting. What is it?"

"It's a local IPA. Real hoppy," Gabe said.

"I hate IPAs."

"You'll like drinking them in twenty years when your taste buds fade."

"Did I handle it right in there?"

"You're the boss. You can handle things any fucking way you want."

"That's not what I asked you."

"You handled it fine. Cory should have kept that story about Johnny March to himself and talked to you about it later. Now the girls and Travis are spooked, that dumb shit."

"I told Cory to speak his mind, and he did. Don't hold a grudge."

"Me hold a grudge? Never. But he's still a dumb shit."

His crew trailed out onto the deck. Each shouldered up next to Billy and said they wanted in. Billy had expected each would stay, but the vote of confidence was still worth hearing. Pepper remained by his side and snuggled up against him to keep warm.

"I sure hope you know what you're doing," she said.

"Have I ever been wrong before?" he asked.

"No, but there's always a first time. I'm ready to get back to Las Vegas."

"So am I."

Pepper turned her head and stared at him. "Still pining over that girl, aren't you?"

"Is it that obvious?" he asked.

"Yes. Think you'll ever hook up again?"

"Could happen. She's back in Vegas, running with a black hustler named Jimmy Slyde."

"Somebody you know?"

There wasn't a hustler in Las Vegas that Billy didn't know. Most were stand-up guys who did their business and kept their mouths shut. But there was a handful that were nothing but trouble. Pepper was still staring at him, and he nodded.

"What's Slyde like?" she asked.

"He's a real scumbag," Billy said.

THREE

Jimmy Slyde had been a fixture in the Las Vegas underworld for twenty years.

Slyde was a hard guy to miss: his Armani suits, eighteen-karat-gold jewelry, and polished Gucci loafers would catch your eye in a room full of people, as would his neck ringed in gold chains. Sometimes the suit was pin-striped and sometimes it was gray, but he always wore a suit.

Slyde had started out pimping prostitutes on Fremont Street, all of whom had gone to jail. Later he'd graduated to peddling drugs via a network of female cab drivers, who'd also ended up in the slammer. Every successful criminal had a special talent. Slyde's talent was finding desperate people willing to do his dirty work for him. Vegas was filled with hard-luck stories, and Slyde was a master at recruiting them.

Slyde's latest recruit was Maggie Flynn. Every casino in town had Mags's mug shot tacked to a bulletin board in their surveillance room, forcing Mags to wear a cheap blonde wig and shades whenever she was scamming a casino.

Slyde had discovered Mags at Jerry's Nugget, painting cards at blackjack using a substance called daub. Daub was the cheat's favorite substance as it was invisible to the untrained eye. Mags had been pounding G&Ts, and her play had reeked of desperation.

Later, he'd found her eating scrambled eggs in the coffee shop and had introduced himself. When she hadn't told him to fuck off, he'd pulled up a chair and made his pitch.

Slyde had a poker scam that could make them rich. The scam was foolproof, in that it required no confederates or crooked dealers. With this scam, Mags would know when her opponents were strong or when they were weak. With that information, she could not lose.

"Is this something new?" she'd asked.

"Brand new," Slyde replied.

That was a lie. The scam had surfaced a few years earlier at the World Series of Poker Main Event, allowing the cheat using it to walk away with the eight-million-dollar grand prize.

The WSOP had seen plenty of cheating. Players had been caught using confederates to peek at their opponents' hands and signal the information to them with cell phones. Other cheating players had brought extra chips into the game to gain an edge. But these scams were nothing compared to a swindle pulled by a punk out of LA named Garvey Jenkins.

Jenkins was an average player who took perverse pleasure in needling his opponents. While playing in the Main Event, Jenkins had correctly guessed when his opponents were bluffing time and again. His stellar play had led to the final table, and eventually the championship. Everyone had thought Jenkins was cheating, but no one could prove it.

When the tournament was over, Jenkins dumped his girlfriend. Out of revenge, she'd told one of Jenkins's opponents how her boyfriend had used drugs to enhance his play and hustle the other players. The poker world was a small one, and word had quickly spread.

When Slyde learned of Jenkins's scam, the gears had started turning. The scam required the cheat to take a cocktail of powerful drugs that altered the landscape of thought and alertness and was the equivalent of an athlete competing on steroids. The first drug was Modafinil, which kept the cheat awake while enhancing his short-term memory;

the second was Adderall, a mixture of amphetamine salts that enhanced the cheat's vision and hearing and overstimulated his brain; the last was good old-fashioned speed, which kept the cheat running longer than he should. Over time, these drugs would have a disastrous effect on the cheat's health, and Slyde knew he had to pick his accomplice carefully.

His accomplice had to be someone without a family or loved ones. A person who'd run out of road. Someone who wouldn't quit, even when the drugs took over.

A loser.

Mags was the perfect candidate. She had few friends or people who cared about her, just a daughter back east whom she rarely saw. The gaming board was after her, and it was only a matter of time before they caught her and threw her into the slammer.

Mags had no future, and a person without a future was just what Slyde was looking for.

- - -

Slyde knew the concierges of every Strip casino on a first-name basis. During the holidays, he sent them cans of peanut brittle stuffed with hundred-dollar bills. In return, the concierges got Slyde invited to high-stakes poker games held in private suites in their hotels.

Tonight's game was being played in a Salon Tower suite at the Wynn. The game was No Limit Hold 'Em with a thirty-thousand-dollar buy-in. There were four players at the table: a real-estate magnate named Harvey Grubbs, two of Grubbs's childhood chums, and Mags. Mags cleaned up well, and she wore a fetching low-cut purple dress and diamond earrings. Her hair was done up in a bun, exposing her cover-girl cheekbones and sensual neckline.

"Raise," Mags said.

"You're raising me?" Grubbs said.

"That's right, Harvey, I'm raising you. You got a problem with that?" she asked.

Grubbs was getting clobbered. Because he was good at selling real estate, Grubbs thought he knew how to play poker. Sitting at the bar in the suite, Slyde had determined that Grubbs was actually a lousy player, his knowledge coming from bad commentary he'd absorbed watching TV poker shows. Mags went for the kill and shoved two monster stacks into the center of the table, which the hired dealer counted with a bank teller's precision.

"The raise is fifty thousand dollars," the dealer declared.

"You're raising me fifty grand?" Grubbs asked.

"Do I hear an echo?" Mags deadpanned.

"You haven't lost a hand," Grubbs whined.

"What can I say. Beginner's luck."

"If I didn't know better, I'd think you were cheating me."

"I'd tell you to go fuck yourself, but something tells me you've already tried."

Grubbs had been an ugly little boy, was now an ugly middle-age man, and would age into an ugly old man. The remark cut to the bone and Grubbs's face turned red.

"Get the strongbox," Grubbs said to his friend Big Mike.

"Come on, Harvey, we're done," Big Mike said.

"No, we're not. Go get the strongbox."

Big Mike was a working-class guy from Grubbs's hometown. Judging by his haircut and threads, Big Mike probably made ten bucks an hour slicing mouth-watering cold cuts at the local Piggly Wiggly. Big Mike was out of his league, yet he still knew more than his friend.

"Come on, Harvey, you're drunk. Let's cut our losses," Big Mike said.

"The bitch's bluffing. Get the strongbox."

"How about I take you to a strip club, get you a lap dance. Like the good ol' days."

"Get the strongbox."

Big Mike shook his head. He had the gravitas of a man fully grounded in life's realities.

"You sure about this, Harvey? We were going to play with that money."

"I'm not going down without a fight."

"Whatever you say."

Big Mike rose and shuffled into the adjacent bedroom. Upon his return, he placed a metal strongbox onto the poker table and lowered his massive body into his chair. Grubbs popped the clasp and removed several thick stacks of newly printed hundred-dollar bills.

"I'll call your raise, and raise you another fifty thousand." Grubbs tossed the money in the center of the table and crossed his arms triumphantly in front of his chest.

"I can't cover your raise," Mags said.

"So get it from your boyfriend," Grubbs said.

Slyde didn't like the direction the game was heading and hopped off the stool. Grubbs was a jerk and might cause them trouble by complaining to the Wynn's concierge. Slyde came up behind Mags's chair and leaned over.

"Let's blow this joint," he whispered.

"Fuck no. Give me the money," she whispered back.

"It's too much."

"He's holding rags. Give it to me."

"What if you're wrong?"

"I said, give it to me, or I'll scratch your eyes out."

The drugs had turned her into a raving bitch. She'd be awake all night, talking a mile a minute, and would need plenty of weed and Valium to come down.

"You sure he's got rags?" Slyde whispered.

"Have I ever been wrong? Don't go sideways on me, Jimmy."

Slyde's jackets were tailored with extra-deep pockets that allowed him to carry a great deal of cash. Out came enough money to cover Grubbs's raise. Mags's eyes danced as the stacks hit the table. She slid them across the green felt.

"Call," she said.

"What have you got?" Grubbs said.

"A set."

Grubbs choked. "You've got three of a kind?"

"It's called a set."

"Show me."

Mags flipped over her two cards to reveal a pair of red sevens. There was a black seven on the board, giving her a set. Laughing under her breath, she began to rake in the monster pot.

"Don't you want to see what I have?" Grubbs spouted angrily.

"All you've got are dreams," Mags said.

- - -

Grubbs cursed under his breath. The real-estate baron knew he'd been had, even if he didn't know how. Slyde grabbed Mags and got the hell out of there with their winnings before Grubbs's anger got the better of him. Mags laughed all the way down in the elevator.

"You shouldn't rub it in their faces like that. It ain't healthy," Slyde said.

"Screw healthy," she said.

"You got a death wish or something?"

"Whatever gave you that idea?"

The elevator landed and they headed across the lobby to the front entrance to grab a cab. Every casino was designed to part suckers from their money, either at the green felt tables or the outrageously priced high-end stores in the lobbies. The Wynn was no exception and featured stores with names like Givenchy, Rolex, and Penske Ferrari. Mags stopped to drool at the Italian sports cars parked behind the glittering display window.

"I want that," she purred, pointing at a bloodred beauty.

"Get serious," Slyde said.

"I am serious, big boy. Give me my share."

"You going to drive home in that?"

"That was the idea."

"But you're messed up."

"That's never stopped me from driving before. The money."

Arguing with Mags was a losing proposition. Slyde slapped her winnings onto her outstretched hand and watched her march into the store. Slyde knew how much a brand new Ferrari cost; Mags couldn't cover it with her share. So he waited.

Five minutes later, his cell phone came alive.

"Get your sorry ass in here," she said.

Slyde looked through the glass. "Where'd you disappear to?"

"I'm in the basement of the store. I just bought a car."

The basement was where the trade-ins lived. Slyde went inside and took the stairs down. He found Mags sitting behind the wheel of an '08 Spider smiling like the devil's daughter.

"Get in," she said.

Mags was his current meal ticket, so Slyde obliged her. She raced up a narrow ramp and was soon on the street burning rubber like a hot-rodder.

"You sure you can drive?" he asked.

"Let's find out," she said.

- - -

Driving like a lunatic through a strange neighborhood on the north end of town, Mags made the unexpected acquaintance of a Toyota Corolla parked in front of a house.

Pulling his face off the dashboard, Slyde checked his nose and found it wasn't broken. Then he got out to inspect the damage while adjusting the knot in his tie. The Corolla's rear end had shrunk a foot, while the Ferrari's hood sported an ugly accordion pleat.

Mags also climbed out. Her face was a mess, and Slyde wasn't sure if her tears were ones of joy or anger at her own foolish behavior. She had a death wish, that was for sure, but so did most folks who overstayed their welcome in this crazy town.

"We need to get out of here," he said.

"I agree," she said.

Slyde guided her down the sidewalk. If the Metro LVPD showed up and took one look at her, they'd know Mags was flying high and throw her pretty ass in jail. Mags had a few more good hustles left in her, and he cleaned her face with a silk hanky as they walked.

"I told you I could drive." She laughed.

They came to Las Vegas Boulevard where Slyde hailed a cab. Her nose had stopped bleeding and the tears had stopped as well. As they climbed into the cab's backseat, a thought occurred to him, one so obvious that Slyde wondered why he hadn't asked himself it before.

"I've got a question," Slyde said.

"Questions are free," she said.

"Why did you come back to Las Vegas? I mean, the gaming board is looking for you. Why not another town? There are plenty of casinos out there where your face isn't known."

"Why do you care?"

"Because it doesn't make sense."

"I came back because a hustler I was soft on screwed me over, and I want to return the favor. You may have run into him. His name's Billy Cunningham."

"You have a score to settle with that guy?"

"You know him?"

"Everybody knows Cunningham. What did he do to you, if you don't mind my asking?"

"That's none of your business."

They rode in silence. Mags sounded more hurt than angry, and Slyde suspected she still harbored feelings for Cunningham. Miss Maggie needed to be focused on the job at hand, and not thinking about ways to be settling an old score. Slyde rarely confided in the people who worked for him, preferring to leave them in the dark about certain things, but now he saw the need to make an exception.

"I'm going to tell you a little secret," he said. "Some powerful people in town want your friend out of the way, if you know what I mean. I don't expect Mister Billy Cunningham will be among us for much longer. So stop worrying about him."

"These people want him dead?"

"They most certainly do."

Along with the string of concierges on Slyde's payroll, there was a rogue homicide detective with the Metro LVPD who Slyde paid top dollar for information. Word on the street was that Cunningham had a bull's-eye painted on his forehead the size of a dinner plate.

Mags sat up straight. "Are you sure this information's good?"

"It's good. Cunningham's going down."

"When?"

"Soon. Like I said, stop worrying about the guy."

"Who said I was worrying about him?"

"I did. It's written all over your face."

Mags's expression turned to stone. Slyde thought he understood the situation. Cunningham had wounded her, the pain so searing that it had driven Mags back to the neon jungle in search of revenge, but in reality, all Mags wanted was to get back together with the guy.

"You're imagining things," she said.

FOUR

Nemo's Locker was a swill-slinging saloon on the north end of the Strip. As Junior Haney and his father Wilmer came in, Junior stopped to read the hand-painted sign that served to remind patrons why they'd chosen this bar over thousands of others in town.

NEMO'S, GETTING VEGAS SHIT-FACED SINCE 1961.

Two patrons sat at the water-stained bar swilling beer: a fat boy wearing a deliveryman's uniform and a sharp-dressed guy sporting a fancy gold watch. It was two o'clock in the morning, and they were the bar's only customers.

Junior and his father took a corner table. They could have been identical twins separated by thirty-odd years. Each sported a faded denim jacket, two-day-old stubble, and a limp ponytail—Junior having dyed his silver because he enjoyed passing for his old man. Both men's eyes were soulless and unrepentant. They'd done their business in bars before and Junior knew the drill. Soon the bar's jukebox was spitting out blaring surf-punk rock.

Wilmer frowned his displeasure at his son's choice of music.

"It was either that or country western. I ordered drinks," Junior said.

Ruben the tattooed bartender served them whiskey shots. When Ruben wasn't slinging drinks, he did odd jobs for hoodlums, and he was the reason the Haneys had come to Nemo's.

"Which one's Cunningham?" Junior asked under his breath.

"Pretty boy," Ruben replied.

"You sure?"

"Uh-huh. Paid with a credit card. When I saw the name, I called you."

Junior knocked back his shot. "Ever fix the bathroom wall?"

"What's wrong with it?"

"Last time me and my daddy were here, it was covered in writing by some guy who just got fired from his job. My daddy hates seeing that shit. He thinks it's disrespectful."

"It's called a virtual wall. Anyone can write anything they want," Ruben said.

"You let people deface your john? That's stupid."

"I'll tell the owner."

"You sure Pretty Boy's the one?" Junior asked again.

"Of course I'm sure. Don't you trust me?"

Junior and his father didn't trust another soul on the face of the earth. Most people who did business with them soon figured that out. Ruben went behind the bar and returned with a credit card receipt, which they both checked to make sure they were going to kill the right guy.

"What's Chubby's deal?" Junior asked.

"Fat Boy's harmless. He can't hurt anyone unless he sits on them," Ruben said.

"Are he and Pretty Boy together?"

"Nope. Chubby's been here a few hours. Pretty Boy arrived a little while ago."

"So they're not together."

"That's what I just said."

"Just making sure. Can you draw Chubby outside?"

"Sure thing."

"What about the security camera over the cash register?"

"I unplugged it."

"You're smarter than you look. Nice talking to you."

Ruben returned to his post and refilled the mugs of the two men at the bar, neither of whom were feeling any pain. The song on the jukebox had reached its painful conclusion, and Junior heard Ruben tell the chubby guy that he had a hot stereo in the trunk of his car for sale. The chubby guy hopped off his stool and followed Ruben out the back door.

Junior and his father approached the bar. They had done this enough times that verbal communication was no longer necessary. Wilmer believed that silence was the fence around wisdom and that the spoken word corrupted the soul. Junior played along because arguing with his crazy father was a waste of time. They took stools on either side of Cunningham.

"How you doing?" Junior asked.

"Doing great. Anyone ever tell you that you look like twins?" Cunningham asked.

"Come to mention it, yeah."

"Have you heard the one about the suicidal twin? He killed his brother by mistake." Cunningham slapped the bar, clearly a fan of his own humor.

"We're looking for a guy named Billy Cunningham. Is that you?"

"The one and only. What can I do for you?"

"We heard you were the slickest guy in town and knew every trick in the book."

"Trick? You want to see a trick?" Cunningham extracted a ten-spot from a pile of bills laying on the bar. "Ten bucks says I can tie a cigarette into a knot and not tear the paper."

"Is the cigarette wet? I've seen that one before."

"Nope, it's dry."

"Will you be able to smoke it when you're done?"

"You bet."

"Okay, smart guy, you're on."

Cunningham grabbed a pack of Marlboros off the bar, carefully removed the cellophane wrapper, flattened it out, then tightly rolled a cigarette in the cellophane. Done, he tied the cigarette into a knot without tearing it.

"Shit, I didn't see that coming. Guess I owe you ten bucks," Junior said.

"I'll let you win your money back," Cunningham said. "Another ten bucks says I can light this cigarette, take four puffs, and it will be the same length as when I started."

"How you going to do that?"

"Put your money down and I'll show you."

Junior's curiosity was gnawing at him and he tossed down the money. Cunningham removed the cigarette from the cellophane and rolled it on the bar so it looked like a cigarette again. Then he lit it with a paper match. Only he didn't light it on the end, but instead lit the cigarette at the center and took four puffs.

"Hah, that's a good one," Junior said.

Wilmer was balanced on the edge of his stool. Reaching into the sleeve of his denim jacket, the older man ripped away the ice pick secured to his forearm with electrical tape. The ice pick had a piece of cloth wrapped near the tip, called a blood arrester. When stuck into the victim, the cloth would stop the blood for a good minute.

"You're a clever guy," Junior said.

"Who did you say gave you my name?" Cunningham asked.

"Jack Shit."

"Who?"

"You heard me. Jack Shit."

"What is this, some kind of joke?"

Wilmer brought his hand around Cunningham's head as if giving him a hug. The ice pick was pointing inward, and Wilmer plunged the tip into the soft flesh of Cunningham's ear until he reached the brain. Blood spurted out of the wound and was soaked up by the cloth. Cunningham pitched forward and hit the bar with his face, instantly dead.

"Thanks for the tricks," Junior said.

- - -

They scooped Cunningham's personal items off the bar and together dragged him through the front door and outside to the gravel parking lot beside the building. Not a drop of blood had hit the bar or made its way to the floor. Their ride was a beat-up 1998 Cadillac Seville that Wilmer refused to part with. They dumped the body into the backseat, which they'd covered with sheets of plastic. Then they got in and drove away. To anyone watching from the street, they appeared to be giving a drunk friend a ride home.

Of all the neighborhoods in Vegas, the area east of the freeway and directly south of Nellis Air Force Base had the highest crime rate and was considered the town's worst place to live. The chances of being raped, burglarized, or murdered were off the charts. You took your life into your hands every time you came home and unlocked your front door.

Junior and his father didn't have a problem with that. In fact, they liked it. Living in a killing field afforded them a level of privacy that a respectable neighborhood didn't have. Their neighbors rarely showed their faces and ignored Junior and his father's strange hours.

As they pulled into the driveway, Wilmer used the Magic Genie to open the garage door. They entered, and Wilmer lowered the door behind them, thrusting the car into darkness.

Junior's breathing grew accelerated. As a child he'd regularly seen monsters spring from the ceiling of his bedroom. As he'd grown up, those monsters should have departed but instead had grown more pronounced. Junior tried to get out, and his father grabbed his sleeve.

"Let go of me," Junior said.

Wilmer grunted no.

"You know I hate the dark."

Wilmer did not let go. The fear passed and Junior became himself again.

Wilmer's cell phone hummed. His father hated cell phones, and owned one only because their clients demanded it. The cell phone was tossed into Junior's lap.

"Hello?" Junior answered.

It was the client who'd hired them to kill Cunningham, asking how the job had gone.

"It's done."

Their client wanted proof of death. The smart ones usually did.

"I'll send you a picture," Junior said.

Their client said that worked and hung up.

They got out of the car. Junior turned on the overhead light and, with his father's help, pulled the stiff out of the backseat along with the plastic sheeting and laid his body onto the concrete floor. Junior snapped a photo on his father's cell phone, which he sent to their client via text.

Moments later, the cell phone hummed.

"Are we good?" Junior answered.

Their client read the riot act to him.

"You're kidding me. I'm sorry, man. We'll make it up to you," Junior said.

Junior ended the call feeling like the world's biggest idiot. Kneeling, he took the stiff's wallet from his pocket and found a business card. The guy they'd whacked was a water softener salesman, not a cheat. Junior showed the card to his father. "We took out the wrong guy. I guess there's more than one Billy Cunningham in town. Our client said he'll come by tomorrow with Cunningham's address. He wants us to take Cunningham out where he lives."

Wilmer's eyes flared in anger.

"I don't like it, either, but what the hell else can we do?"

They went inside the house. Junior headed straight for the kitchen where he fixed himself a roast beef and pickle sandwich. The first time he'd killed a man, he'd vomited. Now killing produced different sensations, and all he wanted to do was stuff his face with food.

Junior went into the living room where he switched on the TV. They didn't subscribe to cable, and the few stations they got were crap. He settled on *America's Funniest Home Videos* with the sound muted. His father pulled up a chair and Junior gave him half the sandwich.

As Junior ate, he thought about the job. He wasn't thrilled about the idea of going to Cunningham's home. Better to do the job inside a dark bar or a parking lot; that was where most contract killings took place. But the client was demanding it, and there was the matter of their reputation. You were only as good as your last job in their line of work.

The Haneys made their living killing undesirables for the town's casinos. They'd been doing this for so long that Junior had lost track of the number of victims. Then the local CBS affiliate had done an exposé about all the unmarked graves being found during new home construction around Clark County. More than eighty graves so far, and Junior was pretty sure that he and his father were responsible for most of the stiffs lying in them. It sounded like a lot, and maybe it was. But as Junior was fond of saying, they rarely killed anyone who didn't deserve it.

FIVE

-THURSDAY, TWO DAYS EARLIER-

Gulfstream Aerospace's sleek corporate jets were the airplanes of choice for the world's über rich. Billy had decided to rent the company's top-of-the-line G550 for the journey from Lake Tahoe to Las Vegas. It was expensive, but first impressions were important when landing at McCarran, where dozens of private aircraft landed every day.

Billy stood on the tarmac beneath a bleached blue sky and soaked up the scenery. It had been a good two weeks, the mix of beautiful outdoors and gambling to his liking, and he made a promise to himself to return to Tahoe soon.

He boarded the G550 with his crew. Soon they were bouncing high in the clouds. The G550 had Wi-Fi and multiple TVs, and everyone stared at a different screen, except Travis. The big man knelt on the carpeted floor in the center of the aisle, polishing his dice switch. Travis's right thumb waved when he switched, and the big man had become obsessed with losing this tell.

"Billy, how do I look?" Travis asked.

Billy sat in the last row, examining his appearance in a handheld mirror. While in Tahoe he'd grown a goatee, moved the part in his hair, and started wearing glasses. By altering three areas on his face, he could dupe the facial recognition software the casinos used to catch cheats. Rising from his seat, he stood behind Travis and watched the switch from above.

"Do it again," he said.

Travis's hands were the size of cow udders. Before Billy's eyes, the red pair of dice in the big man's right hand magically became a green pair.

"That's pretty. Your thumb's hardly moving."

"I've been working on it."

"It shows."

The pilot's voice filled the cabin. Within minutes they bumped down and taxied to a small terminal. McCarran was always busy and provided most of the tourists who fed the town's casinos. Without it, Vegas was nothing more than a bus stop in the desert.

As Billy and his crew disembarked, a uniformed driver from the Rio named Kevin greeted them. Limo drivers were expected to treat every customer the same. Most could ignore wealth or even fame, and Kevin was friendly without being over the top.

Kevin pulled their luggage out of the belly of the jet and loaded it onto a cart. They followed Kevin to a stretch limo parked at the tarmac's edge.

"No Leon?" Pepper asked under her breath.

Leon was their regular limo driver. His crew liked Leon, and Leon often partied with them after a job was finished.

"Not this time. Keep your eye on Kevin. He's our ticket into Carnivale," Billy said.

"I thought he worked for the Rio."

"He does. He's also on Carnivale's payroll. So are the rest of the Rio's drivers. They get paid to alert Carnivale when whales hit town who Carnivale might want to steal."

"Like us."

"Right, like us."

"Is that why you hired the private jet? To make us worth stealing?"

"You catch on fast."

Kevin made small talk during the drive to the Rio. Were they planning to see any shows during their stay? Kevin rattled off the different productions at the casinos' theaters while doing a nice soft sell.

"We were going to see Bruno Mars tomorrow night at the MGM Grand, but our tickets fell through," Billy said. "The ladies are really bummed."

"I'll say." Pepper pouted.

As he drove, Kevin scribbled down this piece of information. As part of his deal with Carnivale, Kevin passed along valuable tips that could be used to lure Billy away from the Rio.

Billy brushed the sleeve of his sports jacket, signaling Gabe to start the conversation they'd rehearsed for this very moment. Gabe fitted on a pair of reading glasses and opened the MacBook Air on his lap. His nimble fingers deftly played on the keyboard.

"Just got an e-mail from Ned Bryant at Morgan Stanley," Gabe said.

"Ned Bryant's a moron," Billy said.

"I think your opinion of old Ned is about to change."

"How so?"

"Ned got an offer from Synergy Health Systems to buy your shares of the company."

"Tell him no."

"You haven't heard the offer."

"Tell him no anyway. All good negotiations begin with no."

"Whatever you say, boss."

The limo had a fridge stocked with miniature bottles of Dom Pérignon. Billy found the glasses and poured bubbly for his crew. "What's Synergy offering?"

"Twenty-four bucks a share. You paid seventeen," Gabe replied.

"Refresh my memory. How many shares do I own?"

"You own twenty percent of the company, roughly five million shares."

Billy faked a yawn. A thirty-five-million-dollar profit on a stock sale would have gotten most people doing cartwheels in the street. But for billionaire venture capitalist William Cummins, which was the alias he was using, it was just another deal.

"Should I stay or should I go?" Billy asked.

"The health-care industry is fickle. My advice is to get out now," Gabe said.

"I like your advice. Sell all of it."

"Yes, sir."

Gabe made an imaginary call to Ned Bryant on his cell phone and okayed the sale. In the windshield's reflection, Billy spied Kevin making another notation on his pad.

- - -

In Vegas, whales ruled. Whales didn't have to wait in line, or make reservations, or engage in any of the mindless day-to-day activities of the unwashed masses. The world was their oyster, and whales took advantage of that oyster every chance they got.

Billy and his crew waltzed past the Rio's check-in and were soon eating breakfast at the Hash House A Go Go. Billy ordered the house hash and flapjacks, while Cory and Morris got black skillet pork ribs. Gabe and Travis settled on farm-fresh sandwiches while Pepper and Misty got salads. The lunch crowd had yet to appear and the place was a tomb.

"I'm not understanding something," Misty said. "Why does the Rio think you're a whale? Don't whales need to be really rich to get that status?"

Billy blew the steam off his coffee. He liked when his crew questioned an aspect of a particular play. It told him that they were thinking.

"To the Rio, I am rich," he said.

"How'd you swing that?" Misty asked.

"Every casino is hooked up to a casino credit-reporting agency called Central Credit. It's the TRW of the gambling industry. I hacked the Central Credit site and created a profile of a fictitious billionaire named William Cummins. Cummins has a big line of credit in Atlantic City and the Caribbean islands. That's why the Rio's giving us the star treatment."

"I didn't know you were a hacker."

"An expert hacker," Gabe corrected her.

"That, either," she said.

Knowing how to hack gambling industry sites was integral to casino cheating. Before the play was attempted, the cheater's identity needed to be established with the casino. There was no better way to accomplish this than to hack a database like Central Credit and create a false identity. Using a knowledge of HTML coding and JavaScript, nearly any password-protected website could be compromised, as Billy had learned.

"How much is William Cummins worth?" Misty asked.

"A little over a billion dollars," Billy said.

"Marry me."

"Me, too," Pepper said.

"Keep it down. Our VIP host just walked in."

A raven-haired woman approached the table with the purpose of a cruise-guided missile. The VIP host's job was to cater to his or her clients' every whim and desire, no matter how outlandish or illegal it might be. She stopped at the table, breathing hard.

"Mr. C., there you are. My name's Kenna Davies, and I'm going to be taking care of you during your stay at the Rio," their VIP host said.

"Hello, Kenna. Is our suite ready?" Billy asked.

"Yes it is. And your luggage has already been delivered. Shall I take you upstairs?"

"Let us finish our meals."

"Of course." Kenna walked to the other side of the restaurant where she stopped to check her cell phone for messages.

"What's with the Mr. C. crap?" Misty asked.

"The VIP hosts are trained to call their customers by the first letter of their last name," Billy explained. "To call them by their full name might compromise their privacy."

"What should we call you?" Misty asked.

"Billy. Same as always."

They finished their meals and rose from their chairs. Kenna pocketed her cell phone and made a beeline for the table.

"Ready to go upstairs?" their VIP host asked.

"I believe we are," Billy said.

Their waitress appeared and, clearly not aware that Billy was a whale, slapped down a check. Kenna shot the waitress a look that would have turned most people to stone. Stricken, the waitress removed the offensive piece of paper from the table.

"I think I'm going to like this," Misty said under her breath.

SIX

Las Vegas had more hotel rooms than any other city in the world, and those rooms ran the gamut: some deserved the wrecking ball, while others were among the most luxurious accommodations ever created. The Rio Presidential Suite was at the high end of the spectrum, with three thousand square feet of decadent living space that included a sparkling baby grand piano, twenty-four-hour butler service, and a kidney-shaped pool on a private balcony with a panoramic view of the Strip.

"Oh, look, our very own swimming pool," Misty said.

"Hey Billy, can we go skinny-dipping?" Pepper asked.

"Only if I can watch," Billy replied.

Going onto the balcony, Misty and Pepper proceeded to peel off their clothes. They sunbathed in the nude daily and did not sport a single tan line. They dove headfirst into the pool even though a sign warned not to, and splashed water around while screaming in high-pitched voices.

"Your friends aren't the bashful type, are they?" Kenna said.

"What happens in Vegas stays in Vegas," Billy replied.

Kenna gave him a tour of the suite. The rooms went on forever, and Billy tried not to act impressed. He'd grown up in a tract house that wasn't a third the size of the suite. Those memories were always in the back of his mind, reminding him of what happened to people who didn't take chances. Stealing was wrong, but it was a hell of a lot better than being poor.

The tour ended where it had started. On the bar was a gift basket filled with fresh fruit and goodies. Kenna removed two envelopes from the basket and presented them to him.

"For the ladies. Our compliments," the VIP host said.

"Much appreciated," Billy said.

"What time should we expect you in the casino?"

"I'll be down later this afternoon."

"Will you be playing blackjack? I can hold a table for your party, if you like."

"Sounds good."

"Wonderful. Let me give you my card. Don't hesitate to call if you need anything. I'm here to make your stay as enjoyable as possible."

Billy walked Kenna to the door. In return for the comped suite and goodies, he was expected to play a certain number of hours of blackjack with minimum bets of $5,000 per hand. His expected loss would be between 1 and 2 percent, more than enough to cover all the free crap and leave a tidy profit for the house. There was no such thing as a free ride in Las Vegas. The corporations that ran the joints made sure of it.

It hadn't always been that way. Once upon a time in a galaxy far, far away, casinos had suffered losing nights and even losing weeks. It was the risk you took running a casino. Then the corporations took over and the landscape changed. Corporations didn't believe in risk, so they'd rigged the games by shaving the odds. A player might win over the short run, but over the long run a player couldn't win and would eventually get busted. It was a form of cheating, no different than dealing off the bottom of the deck.

Misty and Pepper came inside wearing pink bathrobes they'd found by the pool. Billy presented them with the envelopes. "These are for the shops downstairs. Have fun."

They tore the envelopes open and squealed with delight.

"Ten grand in free stuff?" Misty said. "I could learn to like this."

"Spend it while you can," he said.

"We'd better get moving, then. Where's our luggage?" Misty asked.

"In your room."

"Where's that?"

Billy led them to their room, which had a pair of queen beds and an oversized bathroom. During the tour, Kenna had described the suite's accommodations as if reading off a script, and it had made Billy wonder if the suite was bugged, and that Kenna was fearful that a slip of the tongue might affect her job. He decided he'd better find out, and he shut the door behind him. Thinking he had something else in mind, Misty and Pepper undid their robes and let them fall to the floor.

"I've always wanted to sleep with a billionaire," Pepper said.

"To hell with sleeping. Let's screw," Misty said.

Billy shushed them with a finger to the lips.

"Something wrong?" Pepper whispered.

"Maybe. Where's your cell phone?" he whispered back.

"In my purse on the bar."

"Go get it."

Pepper slipped on her bathrobe and left. She returned holding her iPhone. Billy called her on his Droid.

"Answer it," he whispered.

"But you're standing right here," she whispered back.

"Do it anyway."

Pepper answered the call. Billy pressed the volume button on his Droid to its highest setting, then walked around the bedroom waving it at the wall hangings and light fixtures as if it were a magic wand. Twice he heard distinctive clicks, which indicated his cell phone had detected an electromagnetic field in the room.

"Not good," he whispered. "Follow me."

They followed him into the bathroom. Billy shut the door and repeated the test with his Droid. There were no clicks this time. In the belief that he could never be too careful, he turned the spigots in the sink to their highest volume.

"Your bedroom's bugged," he said. "You need to watch everything you say. One crack out of turn, and this whole thing will blow up in our faces. Got it?"

Pepper and Misty turned serious and they both nodded.

"Are they watching us, too?" Misty asked. "You know, with hidden cameras."

"I'm about to find out," he said.

"How you going to do that without them seeing you?"

"Watch and I'll show you."

He removed the roll of toilet paper from the dispenser and unspooled the paper until all that was left was the cardboard tube. He powered up the flashlight app on his Droid so a bright yellow beam was emanating from the back of the cell phone. He returned to the bedroom with the girls, shut the blinds, and then turned off the lights so the room was pitch dark.

"This is getting creepy," Pepper said.

"Shhh," he said.

Casinos went to a great deal of effort to catch thieves, and smart thieves went to a great deal of effort to avoid being caught. He placed the tube over his right eye like a telescope and shut his left eye. He slowly swept the flashlight beam over the room, paying attention to any small glimmers that reflected back at him. A pinhole camera often had a charge-coupled device called a CCD sitting behind a wall or object that could be spotted this way.

"No cameras," he whispered.

"Like strange men haven't seen us naked before," Misty whispered back.

He turned the lights back on and tossed the paper tube into the trash.

"Shop till you drop," he said.

- - -

Cory and Morris sat at the baby grand in the living room playing a "Chopsticks" duet. They'd grown up in a foster home and were as inseparable as Siamese twins. They also shared a bad reefer habit, and Billy instinctively sniffed the air. Doing drugs had ruined more than one cheater's career, and he'd warned them the next time it happened, they'd be on the street.

"What's that funky smell?" he asked.

They sprang off the piano bench and stood in front of him.

"We started smoking e-cigarettes to help kick the habit," Cory explained. "We're really into the specialty flavors. Mango, clover, dragon berry. They're really tasty."

"You're not mixing it with dope, are you?"

"No, sir. We kicked the habit for good."

"Show me."

Cory's e-cigarettes were called Joysticks. Cory took a drag and puffed out a bluish cloud that swirled mysteriously above their heads before evaporating. It had an artificially sweet smell, and Billy could only imagine the number it was doing on their lungs.

"Does it get you high?" Billy asked.

"Nope," Cory said.

"We won't let you down again, and that's a promise," Morris added.

Billy dropped his voice. "The suite is bugged. Watch your mouths."

Their eyes grew wide. It made them look like little kids, and it reminded Billy of how young they were. If any members of his crew were liable to screw up, it was Cory and Morris, and he made a mental note to keep his eye on them.

- - -

Billy found Gabe and Travis in lounge chairs by the pool with their shirts off, sunning themselves. Both men picked up their bottles of beer and saluted him.

Billy got a bottle of Evian from the fridge by the pool. Then he bellied up to the guard railing and gazed at the Strip. It was quiet, and would not come alive until the sun dropped and the night creatures came out to play. He'd spent a long time planning this heist, analyzing every angle and trying to anticipate every situation that might occur. Only when he was certain the scam would work had he brought his crew into the fold and begun the necessary preparations. Nothing had been left to chance.

Except one thing.

Every scam he'd ever pulled in Sin City was short and sweet. Get into the casino, rip off the game, get the money, and get the hell out. No scam he'd ever tried had put him inside a casino for longer than a few hours. It wasn't safe to hang around too long.

The Carnivale scam was different. Billy and his crew were going to be inside Carnivale's hotel for several days. During that time, they'd be watched by security and taped by surveillance cameras and have their rooms bugged. If Carnivale's security people figured out they were up to no good, they'd be arrested and hauled off to jail.

His crew was vulnerable, and so was he. He hadn't mapped out an escape because there was no way to escape from Carnivale if things broke bad. The security was as tight as Fort Knox. Thinking about it gave him the willies, so he tried not to.

Gabe edged up beside him and clinked his beer bottle against Billy's water.

"The joint's bugged," Billy said.

"Out here, too?" Gabe asked.

"No, we're safe out here. Too much other noise."

"You and I need to talk about that asshole Cory."

"What did he do now?"

Gabe glanced over his shoulder into the suite. Billy did as well, and through the glass spied Cory and Morris horsing around on the piano. Gabe turned back around and sipped his beer. Billy looked at Gabe's profile and saw a simmering rage hiding below the surface.

"Tell me."

"Cory took advantage of my daughter."

"You're kidding me."

"No, I'm not kidding you."

Gabe's two beautiful daughters meant the world to him. For Cory to be getting horizontal with one of them was a serious transgression, and it needed to be dealt with.

"Let's go find a bar where we can have some privacy," Billy said.

SEVEN

Every Strip casino was a destination unto itself, filled with bars, restaurants, and live entertainment. The Rio was no exception, and it featured a recreation of New Orleans's Bourbon Street called Masquerade Village. A musical performance had just ended with lip-synching singers, overhead floats, and gyrating dancers tossing beads and confetti to the crowd. Billy and Gabe entered the Masquerade bar and grabbed a booth. Gabe ordered a draft beer, which Billy nixed.

"Bring us both coffee," he told the waitress.

"I can't have a beer?" Gabe said.

"You're steaming. You need to calm down."

Gabe's face turned sour. Gabe was old enough to be his father and Billy hated talking down to him, but he didn't have much choice. He needed to get this situation under control before Gabe did something rash like smash a chair over Cory's head.

"Which one of your daughters is Cory seeing?" he asked.

"Alexis. Her mother called me this morning with the bad news."

"How old is Alexis?"

"Eighteen. She came to visit three weeks ago and we went to UNLV to tour the campus. Cory came by the house that afternoon and they started talking about a business course he's taking at the school. When I wasn't looking, the little fucker made a pass at her."

"You saw him make a pass?"

"No, but that's what happened. My ex told me the whole story. After I went to bed, Alexis slipped out of the house, and she and Cory went to an under-twenty-one club called Frozen75. Then Cory took advantage of her in his car."

"Did Cory force himself on her?"

"That's what my ex thinks."

"But you don't know for sure."

"My baby wouldn't sleep with a jerk like that."

The waitress brought their coffees, which Gabe spiked with artificial sweetener. Gabe was big on diet drinks and fake sugars, yet he never seemed to shed any weight.

"How did your ex find this out?" Billy asked. "Did your daughter come crying to her?"

"No, it wasn't like that."

"Then what happened?"

"Alexis got a phone call from Cory this morning. She went into the other room to take it, and my ex stuck her ear to the wall with a glass and overheard the whole conversation."

"Your ex-wife spies on your daughters?"

"You would too if you had kids. The shit they get into these days is incredible."

"Did your ex say that Cory forced himself on her?"

"She didn't have to. Alexis isn't a little slut who has sex with every guy who makes a pass at her. She wasn't raised that way. Cory took advantage of her."

"You're sure about this."

"Damn straight I am."

Billy took out his Droid. "Let's call your kid and ask her what happened."

"No!"

"Why not? Afraid of what you'll hear? She's eighteen, for Christ's sake. Old enough to vote and drive and make adult decisions. For all you know, she might be in love."

"Don't say that."

"You can't go around being pissed off at Cory because you don't like your daughter's taste in boyfriends."

"What are you saying? That I need to act like it never happened?"

"I'm saying you need to deal with it."

Gabe stared into the depths of his mug. He'd once owned a fancy jewelry store inside a Strip casino that had afforded him a beautiful house, several nice cars, and a country club membership. He'd lost it all betting on college sports, and his wife had divorced him. Now, slowly, he was building a bridge back to his family, one brick at a time. You don't know what matters until it's taken away, and Gabe had learned that what mattered most to him were his kids.

"I have an idea," Billy said.

Gabe looked up expectantly. "What's that?"

"Tell Alexis you know she's seeing Cory, and you think it's cool. Tell her how much you dig Cory for going to college and trying to make something of himself. Employ a little reverse psychology. She'll dump him in a week."

"My ex suggested the same thing."

"It's worth a try, man."

"A week's too long. What if Cory decides to pay me back, and tells her."

"About the cheating? Alexis probably knows."

"You think Cory told her?"

"No. Cory wouldn't do that. But kids are smart. Alexis probably figured out you're doing something illegal. You haven't worked in years, yet you put a hundred grand in a bank account for her college education. The money had to come from somewhere."

"Alexis knows I'm a thief?"

"Probably. I figured out my father was cheating when I was seven years old."

"How'd you know?"

"I caught him."

- - -

Billy had learned that his father was a cheat after his mother went to prison. Money was tight, and his father had started holding Friday night poker games in their living room with a bunch of hard-drinking guys from the neighborhood. His father put out a spread of food, and there were always guys wanting to get in to the game.

One Friday night, Billy stole downstairs and crawled under the table to listen to the men tell stories and dirty jokes. It was great fun until a guy named Sammy had accused Billy's father of cheating. Sammy worked in a warehouse and was built like a gorilla. The table had grown still.

"Stand up," Sammy said.

"Screw you," his father said.

"You're hiding something," Sammy said accusingly.

In his father's lap was a deck of cards. Cards were supposed to be on the table, not in a player's lap. It had instantly clicked. His father was switching decks and fleecing the other players. The next few moments had passed in a blur. Billy had snatched the evidence and crawled out from beneath the table. Not slowing down, he'd scurried up the stairs to his bedroom, where he'd hidden under the bed, shaking uncontrollably.

The voices had carried from below.

"You're accusing me of cheating?" his father said.

"Damn straight I am. You've got another deck in your lap," Sammy said.

"All right, I'm standing up. You want me to take my clothes off, too?"

Sammy's voice changed. "Jesus, Frank. I'm sorry."

"To hell you're sorry. Get out of my house!"

Later that night, after the game broke up, Billy's father had come into his son's bedroom and coaxed him from his hiding place. His father had hugged him so damn hard that Billy had thought his ribs might crack.

It was an important lesson. There was no such thing as a free lunch, or a complimentary cocktail, or a free beach blanket. Everything had a price tag attached to it. And if your host put out a spread of food at a card game, it meant he was going to rob you blind.

They were on their second cup of coffee. Gabe had calmed down and no longer appeared bent on harming Cory. But that didn't mean Gabe wasn't harboring a grudge, and grudges were dangerous in their line of work. To run with a crew, you had to trust your partners.

"I know this situation with your daughter is rough. Let me talk to Cory and set him straight. It won't be the first time I've done it," Billy said.

"What are you going to say to him?"

"I'll tell him that if he doesn't treat Alexis like a princess, I'll have Travis throw him down a flight of stairs. That should put the fear of God into him."

"That's it?"

"What else can I do?"

"I want Cory to stop seeing her."

"That's your daughter's call. All I can get Cory to do is treat her right."

Gabe shook his head and glanced away. Then he looked at Billy.

"All right."

Billy's cell phone did a slow revolution on the table. Caller ID said it was Pepper.

"What happened? You run out of money during your shopping spree?" he answered.

"You anywhere near a TV?" Pepper asked.

The bar had several flat-screen TVs showing sporting events.

"I'm looking at one right now," he said.

"Go take a look at channel twenty-one."

"Why? What's going on?"

"Someone just murdered you," Pepper said.

EIGHT

"What does Pepper mean, someone just murdered you?" Gabe asked.

Billy ended the call. "Beats me. I thought everyone in Vegas loved me."

He threw down some bills onto the bar, causing the bartender to snap out of his daydream and hustle over. Working in a Vegas casino was as mind-numbing as fitting parts on an assembly line, and the only way to get an employee's attention was by flashing some cash.

"What's your pleasure?" the bartender asked.

"I need one of these TVs turned to channel twenty-one," Billy said.

"You got it."

The flat-screen TV hanging over the bar turned from college baseball to local news. A sun-kissed blonde reporter stood in an empty field conducting an interview. The only real action in Vegas was inside the casinos, only the TV stations weren't allowed to film in them because it was bad for tourism. As a result, to boost ratings, the local news focused on gruesome traffic accidents and street killings committed by the town's drug-dealing gangs. With the reporter stood an elderly man clutching a carved walking stick. The reporter asked a question and the elderly man pointed to a mound of earth behind where they stood.

"My dog found the body over there," the elderly man said.

"Do you walk here often?" the reporter asked.

"Yes, ma'am. Never found a body before."

The camera lowered to show a panting dog with different colored eyes heeling by its owner's side.

"What's wrong with its eyes?" Gabe asked.

"It's a blue merle Australian Shepherd. It was born that way," Billy said.

The camera returned to the reporter. "The victim has been identified by the Metro Las Vegas Police as William Cunningham, age thirty, of Las Vegas. According to police, robbery does not appear to be a motive. The police are asking anyone who might have seen Cunningham before he was murdered to call this special hotline."

A toll-free number for the police flashed across the screen. After a few seconds it faded away to a commercial for a local car dealership.

"You look like you could use a drink," the bartender said.

Billy glanced at his ashen reflection in the bar's backlit mirror. "You're right, I could use a drink. Give me a rum and Coke. Same for my friend."

The bartender moved away to fix their drinks. Billy remained standing with his stomach pressed against the bar. Gabe dropped his voice. "You know that guy who got murdered?"

"Never seen him before."

"Then why do you look so pale? He's just a dead guy with the same name as you."

"Do the math. A guy with my name and who is my age got whacked and dumped in a field last night. What do you think the odds are of that happening?"

"You've got a common name. It could be a coincidence."

Vegas had been built by people who knew the odds. People who didn't know the odds ended up broke or dead. Billy took out his Droid and got on the Internet. He typed in his own name along with Las Vegas into Google. A link to a site called White Pages appeared. By clicking on it, he was taken to a page showing every single person with the name William Cunningham with a Las Vegas address. He handed Gabe his cell phone.

"Here's a list of all the guys with my name who live in Las Vegas. Count them."

Gabe ran his finger down the screen. "There're fifteen."

"Each listing shows the guy's approximate age. How many are my age?"

Gabe studied the names on the site. "Two."

"And now one of them is dead. That's not a coincidence."

"It could have been a robbery."

"The reporter said the police ruled out a robbery. Know why? Because the victim had his wallet with him. That's how the police knew his name. Otherwise the stiff would sit on a slab in the morgue for a few days until a next of kin came and identified him."

The bartender served them. There was nothing to toast over and they knocked back their drinks. Billy liked to think he was one of the better-liked cheats in town. He'd lent money to other cheats when they were broke and had been respectful to the police the handful of times he'd been busted. He'd never shot anyone or critically injured anyone, and outside of the stealing, had kept his nose relatively clean. He didn't have any known enemies, yet obviously there was someone out there who wanted him in the ground. He needed to figure out who it was, because there was no doubt the person would try again. Vegas was funny that way. People had long memories and they held grudges. There was no such thing as unfinished business.

- - -

That afternoon as Billy was playing blackjack in the Rio's blackjack pit, he got introduced to the pair of guys who wanted him dead.

The word *pit* was a misnomer. There was no dip in the floor where the blackjack tables were located, and as far as Billy knew, there never had been. It was simply an area of the casino where the blackjack tables were assembled like a circle of covered wagons. As the dealers dealt the game, the stone-faced pit bosses lurked behind them, watching the cards, the bets, and the players at the table the way a fox watches a henhouse.

The pit was noisy and filled with cigarette smoke. Billy liked neither, yet had chosen to play here rather than the more refined high-roller salon. His purpose for coming to the Rio was to be stolen away, and that wasn't possible if he were hidden inside the salon.

His crew filled the rest of the seats at the table. They were horsing around and having a good time, and it was all an act. Cory, Morris, Travis, and Gabe were chugging on bottles of beer, only the beer had been poured down the drain in the john and replaced with sparkling water. Misty and Pepper were drinking vodka tonics, which had also been replaced with H_2O.

Their dealer looked like he'd just stepped off of the cover of the Latino edition of *GQ*. His name was Eduardo, and Pepper and Misty pretended to be smitten. There were more than twenty thousand dealers in Vegas, and they ranged from seasoned veterans to rank beginners. Billy decided to find out which category Don Juan fell into.

Billy tossed a five-thousand-dollar gray chip into the betting circle. The move was practiced, the chip landing so it straddled the line. Eduardo dealt the round and snapped the cards out of the shoe. Billy's first card came to him faceup. It was a six. Sixes usually produced sixteens, which were stiffs and lost the hand for the player.

"Change, please." He pointed at the gray chip.

Eduardo hesitated. The right call was to say, "Sorry sir, this is your bet." Only that might cause a scene. So Eduardo played nice and made change.

Billy placed a black hundred-dollar chip into the betting circle, saving himself four thousand nine hundred bucks. Some of the best scams ever invented had nothing to do with winning, and were designed to minimize a player's losses. "Change please" was such a scam.

Billy cleared his throat. The sound made his crew snap to attention.

"So where are you from?" Pepper asked.

"I grew up in San Diego," Eduardo replied, dealing the cards.

"You always work afternoons?"

"Yes, ma'am."

"Ever play football? You look like a tight end," Travis said.

"Soccer," Eduardo replied.

"Do you deal blackjack only, or do you work other games as well?" Travis asked.

"Just blackjack."

The questions alternated between innocent and personal so Eduardo wouldn't recognize that he was being pumped for information about his work habits. This information would be entered into a software database that Billy kept on his computer and traded like baseball cards with other cheats who'd give Billy equally valuable tips in return.

Billy's cell phone vibrated. Caller ID said the call originated from Turnberry Towers, where he lived. He excused himself and left the table.

- - -

He found an empty slot machine and took the chair. "Hello?"

"Mr. Cunningham, this is Jo-Jo at Turnberry Towers. Sorry to bother you, but two guys are here from the cable company to replace the box in your unit. I know you told me the cable people were coming, but these guys look like a couple of creepers. They're sitting outside in a van. Want me to let them into your unit?"

"What's a creeper?"

"Someone who acts weird and keeps doing it after you notice."

“How are they doing that?”

“It’s an old guy and a young guy. The old one doesn’t talk and kept staring at me like he was trying to drill a hole into my soul. The younger guy pretended not to notice.”

“Do they have credentials?”

“Yeah, they checked out. It’s your call, Mr. Cunningham.”

Billy lived in a penthouse unit that he’d won off a Texas oilman in a rigged poker game set up by the concierge at a Strip casino. The concierge owned half the unit and the lease was in his name. Billy lived there invisibly, or so he liked to believe, but there always was the chance that the Nevada Gaming Board had run him down and sent over a pair of techs to bug the place.

The gaming board was not his friend. He’d been playing a game of cat and mouse with them for years and wouldn’t have been surprised if the two strange-acting guys in the van were in their employ. Unlike the cops, who didn’t care one bit if the casinos got swindled, the gaming board made it their duty to run down every hustler who popped up on their radar.

If these guys had been sent to bug his condo, then Billy could start giving the gaming board all sorts of false leads and make their lives hell.

“Let them in,” he said.

“You sure? They’re really weird,” Jo-Jo said.

“Positive. Thanks for the heads up.”

“Anytime, Mr. Cunningham.”

Billy ended the call and got on the Internet. Turnberry’s management had installed CCTV cameras in each unit to stop the cleaning people from stealing. He could access the cameras in his unit by going to a website and typing in his username and password.

His unit’s interior appeared on the Droid’s screen. The picture was sharp as a bell.

He waited for the gaming agents to show their faces.

Cory took an empty chair beside him. "There's a guy hanging around the pit who I think's a VIP host from Carnivale."

"I'll be right over," Billy said. "So what's this about you and Gabe's daughter?"

Cory nearly fell out of his chair. "Who told you?"

"Gabe did. What were you thinking? Or were you high when you asked her out?"

"I swear, Billy, I quit smoking dope. Morris, too."

"That doesn't mean you're not getting high. You and Morris took a trip to Colorado. Did you stock up on edibles? I hear they don't leave any traces on your breath."

Cory swallowed hard. *Busted!*

"Did you have to screw her?" Billy asked.

"Who told you I screwed her?"

"Her mother told Gabe and he told me. Is this thing serious?"

"We're sort of in love."

"Jesus H. Christ. Get out of my face."

Cory slipped away and Billy resumed looking at his Droid. His unit at Turnberry got plenty of sunlight and the rooms took on a rusty hue in the late afternoon dusk. The front door opened and the creepers entered the condo accompanied by Jo-Jo. The creepers were mirror images and wore work overalls and carried toolboxes. Vegas attracted plenty of driftwood, and they didn't look any different than the aliens hanging out at the mall. Jo-Jo led them to the living room and pointed at the cable box. The older creeper extracted a hammer from his toolbox. The cable company had promised to replace the box, yet the creepers didn't have a new box to make the switch.

The older creeper bonked Jo-Jo on the back of the head and knocked him out cold. The younger one checked to see if Jo-Jo was breathing while the older one searched the unit. Not gaming agents, Billy suddenly realized, but hired killers. Were these the same killers who had taken out the other Billy Cunningham? His gut told him they were.

The older one returned to the living room and stood over Jo-Jo while wielding his hammer. The younger one spoke. The older creeper hesitated but did not lower his hammer. They were arguing about whether to kill Jo-Jo. The older one was obviously for it, the younger one against it. Billy should have called 911 but didn't. His condo was filled with enough incriminating evidence of his casino scams to put himself and his crew in prison for the rest of their lives. He liked Jo-Jo, but he didn't like him that much.

But that didn't mean he couldn't help him. The creepers looked like the type of guys who would run at the first sign of trouble. He called the landline in his unit and kept calling until one of the creepers answered.

"Cunningham? Hey, it's me, Paulie," Billy said. "The police have a warrant and are coming over. Get out of there, man."

Billy ended the call and hit an icon on his Droid that took him back to the CCTV in his unit. The creepers were heading out the door, and he took a screen grab of the video on his cell phone so he had a picture of what they looked like, certain it wasn't the last time he'd be seeing them.

Jo-Jo had been spared and sat upright on the couch, rubbing the back of his head. He looked dazed and did not appear to have any idea how close he'd come to checking out. A happy ending, Vegas style. The town was not known for those. People died here with a chilling regularity and were almost immediately forgotten, their memories blown away by the desert breeze. There was no warmth in the neon city, and he would go to bed tonight knowing he'd helped keep Jo-Jo from joining the unliving.

- - -

He returned to his chair at the high-stakes blackjack table. It occurred to him that if the creepers were bold enough to visit his condo, they might track him down inside the casino and try to kill him. It was a possibility, but not a likely one. Casinos afforded some of the tightest security in the world, especially for whales. He and his crew were safe here.

He spotted the VIP host from Carnivale: a dashing Italian guy wearing a tailored sport coat and a starched white shirt. VIP hosts could make or break a casino's bottom line, and the good ones knew how to present themselves to their rich customers.

The VIP host from Carnivale approached the table. The whale hunt was about to begin.

"Mr. C.? May I talk to you?"

"Who are you?" Billy asked.

"My name's Edward DeSantis but everyone calls me Eddie. I work as a VIP host for Carnivale. I hear you're looking for tickets to Bruno Mars's show at the MGM tomorrow night."

"You've got tickets to Bruno Mars?"

"I sure do. Third row center, seven tickets along with backstage passes. I can arrange for you and your friends to meet Bruno, if you'd like."

"You've got that kind of juice?"

"Yes, sir. They don't call me Fast Eddie for nothing."

Billy rose from his chair and stuck out his hand. "This sounds like the beginning of a beautiful relationship," he said.

NINE

The Double Down billed itself as a clubhouse for the lunatic fringe. Psychedelic murals covered every inch of wall space while disturbing videos of car crashes and people getting shot ran on TV screens bolted to the ceiling. Junior was at a table with his father when their client came in. Their client was double ugly, with connected eyebrows and curly black hair sprouting out of the wrong places on his head. Junior didn't know much about the guy except that he worked security for one of the casinos and that he wanted Billy Cunningham dead in the worst way.

"You guys aren't living up to your reputations," their client said after he'd sat down. "Everyone in this town says, you want someone whacked, hire the Haneys. So far, I'm not impressed."

Wilmer Haney stirred in his chair. Clutched in his hand was a half-finished Manhattan made with VO. The stuff was like rat poison and made him extra mean.

"Uck u," Wilmer said.

His old man hadn't said a thing in days. A crazy dog had bitten off his tongue a long time ago and reduced him to speaking in unintelligible grunts. Junior was the only one who could understand the barnyard sounds that came out of his father's mouth.

"Don't get me wrong, part of the blame falls on my shoulders," their client said. "I should have given you a photo of Cunningham so you wouldn't whack the wrong guy. But you know what they say, shit happens."

"That wasn't the only mistake you made," Junior said.

Their client swiveled in his chair to face him. "What did you say?"

"Going to Turnberry Towers was a bad idea. Cunningham wasn't home and we nearly got nailed by the cops," Junior said.

"Don't tell me the cops saw you."

"We got out of there before they showed up. Look, if you're going to send us to a guy's condo to whack him, first make sure he's home, okay?"

"My mistake. But I still need him whacked. You know what they say—third time's the charm. I'll make sure my information's right this time."

"There ain't going to be a third time if you don't pay up," Junior said.

"Whoa. I already paid you."

"Yeah, and we whacked a guy in a bar named Billy Cunningham, just like we agreed. Not our fault it was the wrong Billy Cunningham. If you want the real Billy Cunningham whacked, you're going to have to pay for it. We don't work for free."

"That's bullshit," their client said.

"Take it or leave it."

"I'll pay you half. That's fair."

"The full amount or we don't do the job."

Their client cursed loudly. Heads snapped at the bar, hoping for a fight. That wasn't unusual in the Double Down. Fights happened, people got bruised and bloodied, and new friends were made at the hospital ER.

"Pay us the full amount and we'll throw in a bonus," Junior added.

"What kind of bonus?" their client said.

"My father found some incriminating evidence in Cunningham's condo."

"What are you talking about?"

"You told us Cunningham made his living cheating casinos. We figured you ran security at a casino and that Cunningham is giving you problems. That's why you want him dead."

Their client fell silent, his eyes never leaving Junior's face.

"You're smarter than you look, you know that?" their client said.

Junior took this as a compliment. People assumed that his father was the brains of the operation and Junior the executioner. Nothing could have been further from the truth. It was Junior who did the thinking, his father the killing.

"My father found stuff in Cunningham's place that we think is his next big scam," Junior said. "Who knows? Maybe he's planning to rip off your casino with it."

"What do you know about scams?"

"Just what we've learned from the cheaters we've whacked."

"You've killed cheaters before?"

"Plenty of times. Casinos get sick of guys stealing their money, they call us. Last month we took out a yo-yo man scamming slot machines at Palace Station."

"A what?"

"Guy was playing a slot machine using a coin with a thread tied to it. He dropped the coin into the machine and pulled it out so he could play for free. Slot machines have a razor in the coin chute, but this guy used unbreakable nylon thread. We made him tell us what he was doing before we whacked him."

Their client digested this piece of information before speaking again. "You're right, I do run security at a casino, and Cunningham's been stealing from us. That's why I want him gone. So what did your father find in Cunningham's place?"

"Give us the money, and we'll show you."

Their client fell silent. Junior leaned back in his chair to wait him out. Their client could always hire another pair of killers to do the job, but he'd never find out what Cunningham's scam was. The hook was in the water; now the fish needed to take the bait.

"All right, I'll pay you," their client said.

"Right now," Junior said.

"Don't you trust me?"

"We've been fucked by better people than you."

"I bet you have."

The wallet came out. It was big and fat and filled with folding money. Five grand in crisp hundred-dollar bills was counted onto the table in a neat pile.

"Your turn," their client said.

Wilmer removed a handful of tiny screws from the breast pocket of his denim jacket and placed them on top of the bills like they were precious diamonds.

"My father found a bowl of these screws on the desk in Cunningham's study," Junior said.

"So?" their client said.

"The computer was turned on, and my father saw an e-mail that Cunningham had gotten from a guy named Gabe Weiss. You know this guy?"

"Gabe Weiss works for Cunningham. He's a master forger," their client said.

"My father guessed as much by reading the e-mail. He printed it off the computer."

"Let me see it."

Wilmer made another trip to his pocket. A sheet of paper was produced and unfolded. It landed on the table so the writing was facing their client.

Billy, we're set. I fitted the screws like you told me and did a thousand simulations. It ran like a charm. We win 65 percent of the time, enough to take the place down and give management heart attacks. Too bad we can only pull this once. Come over so we can celebrate.

"Can I have this?" their client asked.

"It's yours," Junior said.

"What about the screws?"

"Keep 'em. Do you know what the scam is?"

"They've rigged a machine and are going to sneak it into a casino with an employee's help. Probably a slot machine or maybe video poker. If they ran a thousand simulations, it means they're planning to bleed the game slowly so the loss isn't too obvious."

"Ehhh," Wilmer blurted out.

"What did he say?" their client asked.

"My father said that isn't it."

"How the hell would your father know *that*?" their client said.

"Cunningham lives like a king," Junior explained. "Penthouse condo, fancy furnishings, closet with more damn clothes than you've ever seen. We've whacked slot cheats and they were a bunch of two-time losers. Cunningham isn't a slot cheat."

"Then what's the scam?" their client asked.

"We thought you'd know," Junior said.

"Afraid not. But I'll figure it out eventually." Their client picked up the screws and slipped them into his jacket pocket. "You good with addresses?"

"Mind like a steel trap," Junior said.

"14235 Carmichael Lane. That's where Gabe Weiss lives in Silverado Lakes."

"I know the area."

"Good. I'm guessing Cunningham's staying there while plotting his next scam."

"We'll get him this time," Junior said.

TEN

To catch a whale, you needed a big piece of bait.

One hour after meeting Eddie DeSantis, Billy and his crew were standing atop a twelve thousand–foot peak northwest of Las Vegas called Mount Charleston, sipping hot toddies and nibbling fresh chocolate chip cookies while admiring the panoramic views.

Sometimes getting to a destination was half the fun. A sleek Sikorsky S-76 chopper had picked them up from a helipad outside the Rio and brought them to the top of the mountain in twenty minutes flat. Upon touching down, DeSantis had passed out fleece-lined jackets while explaining how temperatures on the mountain were thirty degrees cooler than the desert.

Billy had tried not to act impressed, but beneath the surface he was bubbling with excitement. Carnivale's management had checked out his credit rating and decided to put him on the top of their leviathan ladder, which was the internal rating system for whales that the casinos subscribed to. No expense would be spared to lure Billy to Carnivale.

DeSantis stood on the edge of the cliff and described the landmarks, which included a quaint village of pitched-roof houses nestled in the valley below. DeSantis had his spiel down pat and could have charmed the skin off a rattlesnake.

"What's that big building down there?" Pepper asked. "It looks like that scary hotel in *The Shining*."

"That's the Mount Charleston Resort," DeSantis said. "It's a great place for skiing. Carnivale has a special arrangement if you're interested."

"Oh, that sounds like fun. Billy—can we come back in a few months and go skiing?"

"It all depends on the accommodations. Do they have a spa?" Billy asked.

"A very nice one, plus a gym," DeSantis said.

"Are the restaurants any good?"

"They're okay, nothing great. However, I can arrange for a chef from Carnivale to be brought to the resort to prepare your meals."

"Our own chef? This is sounding better all the time. Is there a private dining area?" Billy asked. "I don't like public restaurants."

"That can be arranged as well," Eddie said.

"How about ski lessons? It's been a long time since I hit the slopes. Don't want to fall down and break my neck."

"That can be taken care of as well."

"Can I bring a few extra people?"

"Name your number, Mr. C."

"I think a party of sixteen would fit the bill."

"Consider it done." A cell phone appeared in DeSantis's hand. "What dates would you like? I'll reserve a block of suites for you right now."

Billy threw out some dates and DeSantis booked a block of rooms. It seemed too good to be true, and in a sense it was. DeSantis was a hustler, no different than Billy and his crew. DeSantis stole whales from the Rio and brought them to Carnivale, where they were sure to lose lots of money. If for some reason the whale couldn't or wouldn't pay up, DeSantis would turn the markers over to the Bad Check Unit at the Clark County District Attorney's office, the official collection agency for Vegas's casinos, and the whale would go to court.

Eventually, the whale would lose his house, his cars, and his business, all in the name of paying off his debts. That was DeSantis's scam, and it was perfectly legal.

Not every Vegas casino worked this way. Most were content to make money off slot machines and daily poker tournaments. Carnivale was a different breed of cat. It had cost a fortune to build and could not survive on chicken feed. For Carnivale to survive it needed whales, and it needed a lot of them. And it needed those whales to lose.

- - -

"I could get used to this," Pepper whispered during the flight back.

"Enjoy it while it lasts," Billy said.

They sat in facing leather seats in the back of the Sikorsky. Soft rock was playing over the hidden speakers and champagne was flowing. DeSantis had gone up front to talk to the pilot. Billy used the opportunity to reach in his pocket and remove a pair of matching jewelry boxes, which he handed to Misty and Pepper.

"For me? You shouldn't have," Misty said.

"They're on loan. You don't get to keep them," Billy said.

"Spoilsport."

Misty flipped open the lid of her box and gasped at the diamond necklace with a pear-shaped jade stone. The stone was of a vibrant emerald green color and nearly translucent.

"It's beautiful. Can I put it on?" Misty asked.

"That's what it's for," Billy said.

Misty fitted the necklace on and admired it in the window's reflection.

"How much is this little baby worth?" Misty asked.

"Half a million big ones. One of Gabe's buddies owns the Tesorini jewelry store inside the Bellagio. The necklaces are on loan," Billy said.

Pepper's box also contained a jade necklace, the stone carved as a leaf and encrusted with sparkling diamonds. She followed Misty's lead and put the necklace on.

"These look too perfect," Pepper said. "Are you sure they're not fakes?"

"Of course they're not fakes," Gabe said. "The stones are called jadeite. They come from Myanmar and are the most sought-after jewels in the world. The royal court of China once had a standing order for all available jadeite. The Chinese believe jadeite brings good luck."

"Let me guess. These necklaces are part of why we're here," Misty said.

Billy picked up the remote from the armrest of his chair and raised the music inside the cabin. He didn't think the pilot was eavesdropping from the cockpit, but there was no such thing as being too careful. He leaned forward in his seat and dropped his voice.

"Yes, they are," he said.

"What do Pepper and I have to do, beside wear them?"

"Nothing yet."

"Why won't you tell us more? I'm dying to know."

"Me, too. You can't keep us in the dark forever, you know," Pepper said.

Pepper's powers of persuasion went beyond that of most beautiful women, and Billy knew that she and Misty would have little trouble in extracting the desired information from him, if they chose to. He'd slept with both of them, and at the end of their lovemaking he would have recited the alphabet backward if they'd asked him to.

"All will be revealed. Just be patient," he said.

"Can we try to guess?" Pepper asked.

"You won't figure this one out, trust me," Gabe said.

"You'd be surprised at what Misty and I can figure out. Bet you we do."

"What's the wager?" Billy asked.

Pepper slapped her hand on Billy's knee and gave it a squeeze. "I'll think of something," she said.

- - -

DeSantis returned from the cockpit a few minutes later. He'd been gone too long, and Billy didn't think their host was schmoozing with the pilot. More than likely Fast Eddie had been on the phone with his boss at Carnivale talking over their strategy of how to reel Billy in.

"How about if we stop at Carnivale before I take you back to the Rio?" DeSantis suggested. "We have some fantastic accommodations that I'd like to show you. People say there's nothing like them in all of Las Vegas."

The invitation sounded forced. The boss had told DeSantis to go for the kill.

"Nicer than the Rio?" Billy asked.

"I would have to say yes. Much nicer," DeSantis said.

"We have a dinner reservation at the Rio. We'll have to take a rain check."

"I'll comp you to dinner as well. Carnivale's gourmet restaurants are considered the finest in all of Las Vegas. Name your pleasure and you'll be eating it in an hour."

DeSantis wasn't going to give up. It was bush league and lacked class. DeSantis was smarter than that, which meant it was his boss's doing. DeSantis's boss was a bean counter and wanted an immediate return on the investment Eddie had made on Billy and his crew.

"Italian," Billy said.

"La Madia," Eddie shot back.

"Is it good?"

"It's considered the best Italian food in town. I'll make the reservations right now."

DeSantis got on his cell phone and booked a table at La Madia. It was playing out exactly as Billy had hoped. Every casino had a flaw that could be exploited. Some printed their own playing cards to save money. A great idea, unless the cheats went to the printing plant and altered the presses so the cards were marked during the printing process.

Other casinos didn't properly train their dealers on correct table etiquette, allowing players to add chips to their bets after a game's outcome was known.

And some casinos even let security guards on the casino floor take private phone calls during working hours. Cheats would call these guards' cell phone numbers and talk to them while their crews were working scams in the casino.

These flaws cost casinos millions in losses every year and happened because someone wasn't doing his or her job right.

Carnivale's flaw was more serious. The owners were letting accountants run the show, and accountants didn't know jack about operating a casino. Because of the accountants, Carnivale was dependent upon whales to make their nut. That was fine, unless a whale got lucky. If that happened, the casino could suffer losses so catastrophic they'd go into the red.

It had happened in Monte Carlo a hundred years ago when eight Italian aristocrats had taken the fabled casino down. And it had happened in Biloxi, Mississippi, twenty-five years ago when a party of rednecks had gone on a tear and had owned the joint by the time their incredible run was over. It was going to happen again, only this time it would take place on the Las Vegas Strip, where it had never happened before. History was about to be made, a new chapter written.

Billy's haul would be in the neighborhood of ten million. But Carnivale would lose much more. He got excited just thinking about it.

ELEVEN

The next few hours passed in a blur for Billy and his crew.

They landed atop the roof of Carnivale's hotel and were whisked by private elevator to La Madia where a table in the special guest dining room awaited them. DeSantis had pulled out all the stops, and they were treated to a wine tasting by a dashing sommelier before starting their meal. The menu had every Italian delicacy and was missing only the prices.

Billy's idea of Italian food was pasta with plenty of red sauce. The food in La Madia was over the top, and he savored every bite of his lobster-stuffed ravioli while keeping an eye on his crew. They had settled down and were enjoying the star treatment just like any guest might do. A foot kicked him beneath the table.

"Did you talk to him?" Gabe asked under his breath.

"You mean Cory," Billy whispered back.

"Yeah, Cory."

"We talked. He got the message, loud and clear."

"But will he listen?"

"If he doesn't, I'll talk to him again. How's the roasted pig?"

"Is that what I'm eating? I thought it was eggplant. My daughter's in love with him."

"You talked to her?"

"She texted me the bad news. Fucking kids don't know how to talk these days."

"You sound pissed."

"That's because I am."

Flaming desserts and more alcohol followed. Billy sipped a brandy while keeping an eye on Gabe. Gabe was a bear when it came to protecting his kids, and the last thing Billy wanted was for Gabe to punch Cory's lights out in a public place.

"Is everything to your satisfaction?" DeSantis asked as the meal was winding down.

"The ravioli was too salty. I couldn't finish it," Billy said.

DeSantis's face crashed. "My apologies, Mr. C. I would have been happy to take it back to the kitchen and have the chef prepare you another meal."

"Your chef's supposed to get it right the first time. Is he new?"

"As a matter of fact, he is."

"It shows in his cooking."

The table went quiet. The ravioli had actually been delicious, but Billy was not about to tell DeSantis that. Billy had done his homework and discovered there were two types of whales: pricks and really big pricks. It came with having too much money, and for Billy to act any differently would have tipped off management that Billy wasn't who he said he was.

DeSantis knew better than to throw fuel on the fire and said nothing. If Billy and his crew went back to the Rio, DeSantis would have a lot of explaining to do to his boss, and he might lose his job.

Billy threw his napkin onto his plate and stood up. "I believe in second chances, Eddie. When are you going to show us the furniture of love?"

"The what, Mr. C.?"

"Your high-roller suites. I've stayed in them all—villas, bungalows, palazzos—and every other highfalutin architectural wet dream you casino guys can come up with. Let's see what Carnivale has to offer. And you'd better pull out all the stops if you expect us to stay."

DeSantis swallowed the lump in his throat. "Right this way," he said.

- - -

In Vegas, nothing succeeded like excess.

The top of the line for any Vegas hotel was its penthouse suites. Every major joint on the Strip had one, with the penthouse suite at the Hilton where Dustin Hoffman and Tom Cruise hung out in the movie *Rain Man* probably the most coveted suite in town.

Carnivale had pulled out the stops in creating their penthouse suites. They were so over-the-top opulent that they even had a special name—sky palaces. DeSantis keyed the door and ushered them through a foyer into a spacious living room with a working fireplace.

"You guys hang here," Billy told his crew. "Okay, Eddie. Wow me."

"Stay close behind me. It's easy to get lost," DeSantis said.

Eddie wasn't exaggerating. Part carnival barker, part museum tour guide, he escorted Billy through a labyrinth of lavish rooms that included a living room, a dining room, a media room, a billiards room, six bedrooms, an outdoor deck with lap pool, and a putting green. The amenities weren't anything to sneeze at, either, and included a steam room, a sauna, a Jacuzzi tub, plus towel warmers, floor heaters, and solid-gold swan-curved faucets.

"You need a bike to get around," Billy said.

"We've had guests use roller skates," DeSantis said.

Last stop was the master bedroom. It boasted a sitting room and wet bar and was large enough to drive a car through. Having grown up in a house as narrow as an alleyway, Billy felt his anger boil up and realized how much he was looking forward to scamming the owners of Carnivale, whoever the hell they were.

"So what do you think?" DeSantis asked.

"You've redeemed yourself. Let's talk money. The Rio is giving me a hundred grand in free play along with a ten percent discount on my losses based upon my playing BJ a minimum four hours a day at five grand a hand. Cover that, and I'm your man."

"We can cover that, Mr. C."

"Then I'm in. How soon can we move in?"

"Right now, if you'd like. I can arrange for your belongings to be transferred from the Rio to here. In the meantime, your friends can make themselves at home while we go down to the cage. I'll need to introduce you to the cage manager and establish your credit line."

"Which is how much?"

"Does five million sound about right?"

"You strike a hard bargain, Eddie."

"Nothing's free in Las Vegas, Mr. C."

"Five million it is. Let's go tell the troops."

Back in the living room, they found Cory and Morris using the iPad concierge to adjust the lights, lower a movie screen from the ceiling, choose a film from the hotel's private library, flick on the fireplace, play music, and order chocolate banana splits from room service.

"Having fun?" Billy asked.

"This place is better than Disneyland," Cory said. "Are we staying?"

"We are. Gather the troops; we're heading outside for a drink."

The sun was doing a slow fade as Billy went onto the deck, the sunlight replaced by five million watts of burning neon. The real day was starting, the casinos popping alive with the frantic urgency of a baby chick cracking its shell. Billy pressed himself against the balcony railing. Vegas never got old. It pulsed with a life all its own, fed by money and sex and more scores than a cheat could make in a lifetime, and the day he got tired of the place would be the day they laid him to rest in the ground.

His crew followed him outside. DeSantis came last, balancing a tray he'd taken off the bar containing a bottle of Chivas and seven glasses. He did the pouring and passed out the drinks.

"Welcome to Carnivale," their host said.

They clinked glasses in a toast. Billy didn't think it could have gone any better. Not only were they about to take down Carnivale's casino for a major score, they would be wined and dined and treated like royalty by their victim while they did it.

Pepper lowered her glass. "There's a strange man standing over there."

All eyes turned to the opposite end of the deck. An Asian man with a movie actor's good looks clasped the railing with both hands, eyes tightly shut, lips moving as if reciting the lines to a play, the words in what sounded like Chinese. He wore black slacks and a black shirt and was shoeless. He appeared to be sleepwalking and looked as if he might toss himself over.

Out of concern, Pepper stepped toward him. "Hey—are you okay?"

The Asian broke free of his trance and pushed himself away from the railing.

"Who are you? What are you doing here?" he demanded in accented English.

"We're staying here. Or at least I thought we were," Pepper said.

"My sky palace, not yours," the Asian said.

"Well, excuse me," she said.

Eddie stepped forward and tried to make peace. "I'm so sorry, Mr. W. Reservations said you were staying in the other sky palace. I was just giving these guests a tour."

"You promise me peace and quiet. Not working out that way," the Asian said.

"Forgive me, Mr. W. We'll leave right now."

Eddie began to herd Billy and his crew off the deck. Pepper acted put out and did not move from her spot. Mr. W.'s eyes grew wide as he stared at her chest.

"You don't have to be so obvious about it," Pepper said.

Mr. W. raised his eyes and gazed into Pepper's face.

"Your necklace is beautiful. May I look closer?"

"Look all you want. What's your name? Or should I call you W.?"

"My name is Tommy Wang," he replied.

"Nice to meet you. I'm Pepper and this is Misty, and that's Cory and Morris, Gabe, Travis, and that handsome little devil is Billy. Looks like we're going to be neighbors for a few days."

Tommy Wang was all smiles now. His anger had evaporated and he bowed graciously to Billy and his crew. He spotted the necklace adorning Misty's neck and fell all over himself again.

"Your necklace is equally beautiful," he gushed to Misty. "May I look closer?"

"What a pickup line," Misty said. "Sure, go ahead."

Tommy Wang's eyes were the most interesting part of his face. They were sad and soulful and filled with dark memories yet still danced with the promise of life's infinite possibilities. They were the eyes of an older man trapped in a younger man's body.

Billy went inside and got an eighth glass from the bar. Another round was poured and a toast made to their new neighbor.

"Nice to meet you," Billy said, raising his glass.

"And you as well," Tommy Wang replied.

- - -

The sky palace across the hall was equally spectacular and Billy's crew settled right in. The arrangement now needed to be finalized, and Billy agreed to go downstairs with DeSantis, where his credit line would be established with the casino cage manager and he could begin losing money hand over fist to pay for these fine digs. Before Billy could leave, Pepper asked to speak with him. DeSantis said he'd wait in the hall.

Pepper pulled Billy into a bedroom and shut the door. "I want to talk turkey with you."

Billy used his cell phone to check for bugs. "They're listening," he whispered.

Pepper pulled him into the bathroom and turned on the water in the sink to its highest volume. She rested her forearms on Billy's shoulders and looked him straight in the eye.

"Our meeting that Asian guy was a setup, wasn't it? The jade necklaces, us meeting him on the deck, you arranged that, didn't you?"

"Guilty as charged."

"How'd you do that? Do you have a mole in the hotel?"

"Uh-huh."

"Are you going to tell us who it is?"

"No."

"Why are you manipulating us like this?"

"I want your reactions to be genuine. It helps sell the play. The less you guys know, the more genuine your reactions will be when stuff happens. It's part of the con."

"I don't like it. Neither does Misty."

"It's only for a couple of days."

"Will you level with us after that?"

"When have I not leveled with you? I've thought this out. It's the best way."

Pepper took a hard look into Billy's face to make sure he was being straight with her.

"What about Tommy Wang?" she asked. "How does he play into this?"

"Remember the scams you and Misty practiced in Lake Tahoe? Well, Tommy Wang is your victim."

"So he's the mark."

"Correct."

"Do you expect me to bang him? Is that part of the deal?"

The words hit him like a slap in the face. The fact that Pepper had done porn had never lessened Billy's opinion of her or made him think of her as a whore.

"I'd never ask you to do that," he said.

"Not even if millions of dollars were on the line?"

"Not even for that. Just con him like we practiced back in Tahoe."

"Got it. So what's his deal? Where does his money come from?"

"Tommy Wang is the most fortunate man in China. He's also our ticket to the big time."

"Why's he the most fortunate man in China? What did he do?"

"Let him tell you."

She let out an exasperated squeal. "I hate you."

"Like I told you, I'll explain everything in a few days."

DeSantis was in the hall waiting to take Billy downstairs to the casino. The pieces were starting to fall into place, the players lining up in proper order, the year of planning finally paying off. Every heist Billy had ever pulled had been a dime store rip-off compared to this one, and he whistled to himself during the rapid descent in the elevator.

"Are you enjoying yourself, Mr. C.?" DeSantis asked.

"Having the time of my life," Billy replied.

TWELVE

The city of Havana had once boasted the most beautiful casinos in the world. None was more renowned than the famed Tropicana Club at Villa Mina. Located on a six-acre suburban estate on the outskirts of the fabled city, the building that housed the casino featured parabolic concrete arches and dozens of cut-glass chandeliers.

Carnivale's casino was a replica of the Tropicana Club and oozed class. It featured antique gaming tables, tuxedoed dealers, and old-fashioned cigarette girls who walked the floor handing out free smokes while a five-piece band played show tunes. Next to the casino was a theater where voluptuous showgirls called Flesh Goddesses appeared in a musical cabaret.

If Cuba had popularized any one game, it was roulette, the white-jacketed croupier's handling of the little ivory ball a joy to behold. To make their roulette game authentic, Carnivale employed a dashing Cuban croupier with a pencil-thin mustache and slicked-back hair. During their jaunt to the cage, Billy stopped to admire the croupier's elegant routine.

"You play the wheel?" DeSantis asked.

"Blackjack's my game. I just like the way he handles the ball," Billy said.

"Raul's a master. I'll introduce you, if you like."

"Not necessary, but thanks."

The cage was in the rear of the casino. Introductions were made, and the cage manager wrote up paperwork for Billy to sign. With a stroke of the pen, Billy was given $5 million in credit to gamble with.

"How much would you like to start with, Mr. C.?" DeSantis asked.

"Half a million," Billy replied.

"Give Mr. C. a half million in chips," DeSantis told the cage manager.

The cage manager passed the chips through the bars. Billy had studied whales and learned that they tended to carry their chips around in their pockets and rarely partook of the cheap plastic chip trays the casino provided. He filled the pockets of his sports jacket with his chips.

"Are you sure you wouldn't like to play in our salon?" DeSantis asked.

"Too stuffy. Point me in the direction of a lucky dealer," Billy said.

"You got it, Mr. C."

Billy followed DeSantis to the blackjack pit while having a look around. Vegas casinos lost 5 percent of their profits to cheating, and he would not have been surprised to see a familiar face on the floor. As a courtesy, he would not sit down at a game where another cheat was doing business but would move to another table.

He didn't see any familiar faces, but he did see familiar heads of hair. Dark, wavy hair, a genetic trait so prevalent that every member of the family shared it. They were spread out around the casino, scamming different games. Shit, he thought. This was a problem.

"Here you go, Mr. C. Twig's the luckiest dealer around."

DeSantis pulled back a chair at the blackjack table with a thousand-dollar bet minimum. Billy's eyes fell on the young guy sitting to the dealer's right. It was one of the Boswell clan, and Billy struggled to remember the kid's first name. He decided it was Nico. That's what happened when you lived in your old man's shadow. No one remembered you.

Billy took the seat and began pulling chips from his pockets.

"Good luck, Mr. C. I'm a call away if you need me," DeSantis said.

"Thanks, Eddie," Billy said.

Billy placed a gray five-thousand-dollar chip in the betting circle. The other players at the table placed their bets as well. Nico Boswell bet an orange chip worth $1,000.

Billy knew he was being watched by the eye-in-the-sky. All whales were watched when they gambled. The house didn't have a choice. If they weren't careful, a whale could go on a lucky streak and ruin them in the amount of time it took to smoke a cigarette.

Billy wasn't cheating, but Nico Boswell *was*, and the eye-in-the-sky might pick up the scam. If that happened, Nico would get busted, and the gaming board would review the video of the play and, with their trained eyes, spot Billy in his disguise.

And then Billy would be royally screwed.

It didn't take him long to figure out Nico's scam. Every high-valued chip in the casino had an RFID microchip hidden beneath the label. Installed in the player's betting circles were devices that detected pulses sent out from these RFID microchips. If a player placed a counterfeit chip into the circle, it would show up on an LED display in front of the dealer.

Nico was playing with counterfeit orange chips. He got away with this by having a real orange chip strapped to his knee. Each time Nico slid a fake chip into the betting circle, his knee touched the bottom of the table, tricking the detection device.

Playing with the house's money didn't work every time, nor did it have to. When Nico won a hand, he pocketed the winnings. When he lost, the house got the fake chip.

When Nico was up ten grand, he rose from the table and left.

Billy breathed a sigh of relief.

- - -

Nico made for the elevators, which made Billy think the Boswells were staying in the hotel while ripping off the casino. That took nerve, but so did most of the heists the Boswells pulled. They were known as the Gypsies and were legends in the cheating world.

Billy assumed the family patriarch, Victor, was running the show. They'd met months ago after Victor was shot in the leg by a gaming agent named Frank Grimes. Victor had nearly bled to death, and Billy had saved the older man's life.

Billy and Victor had traded phone numbers and promised to get together, but like the best-laid plans, it hadn't happened. Now Billy needed to talk with Victor, and it wasn't going to be an easy conversation. Billy couldn't pull his scam on Carnivale while the Gypsies were ripping off the joint. Someone had to leave.

Billy played a few more hands before quitting. He tipped the dealer and walked out of the casino, his destination a row of high-priced stores by registration. In keeping with the casino's Latino theme, one of the men's shops sold pastel-colored guayabera shirts and Panama hats. He changed in a dressing room, and a minute later he was back on the casino floor, looking much different than the whale who'd just left.

- - -

Finding the other members of the Boswell clan wasn't terribly difficult. Their thick manes of dark hair made them easy to spot.

The Boswell clan had a dozen members. Victor and his wife, Victor's brother and wife, Victor's two sons and two daughters, and his brother's four kids—one girl and three boys. It was a lot of mouths to feed, and the family was always stealing.

Tonight, there were seven family members in the casino along with Nico. All smart cheaters did their homework, and Victor Boswell had recognized that Carnivale was so focused on whales that cheaters employing simple scams would fly under the surveillance radar.

Two Boswell boys were playing Three Card Poker and sat next to each other at the table. As the boys looked at their cards, each stole out a card using a move called a gambler's palm, brought his hand beneath the table, and switched it for his brother's card. A few tables away, two of the other Boswell boys were performing the same scam at a different Three Card Poker game.

The Boswell boys were well trained. Not once did Billy see their thumbs wiggle when they palmed their cards, nor did their bodies sway when they switched cards beneath the tables.

The other three members of the clan were female and were scamming the slot machines. This was a smart play, as the majority of slot players were female.

Modern technology had made slot machines vulnerable. A light wand jammed into the coin hopper would cause a machine to overpay. Or zapping a machine with an electromagnetic pulse would make the random number generators become not so random in picking winners.

The Boswell ladies were working a new scam. Whenever they inserted a dollar bill into a slot machine, it registered as a hundred dollars in credit. Billy had never seen this scam before, and he guessed there was a special coating on the one-dollar bill that tricked the machine's internal mechanisms. Leave it to Victor to come up with something new.

The Boswell ladies weren't greedy; smart cheats never were. Each of the ladies cashed out after winning a few grand, walked to the cage with their winning slips, got their money, and took a leisurely stroll toward the elevators. Once upstairs, they'd turn over their winnings to Victor, who managed the cash. Every crew operated this way, including Billy's.

The last Boswell lady to cash out was a girl with a silver ring through her nose and purple streaks in her hair. Facially, she bore a strong resemblance to Victor.

Billy followed her onto an elevator. She had her head buried in her cell phone and was unaware she was being tailed.

The passengers got off on different floors. Billy stood in the corner and stared at the blank face of his Droid. Victor's daughter still hadn't noticed him. Good cheats had eyes in the back of their head; this girl wasn't using those on the front of her face.

On the twenty-seventh floor, the doors parted and the girl got out and took a sharp right. The thick red carpeting muted Billy's footsteps as he trailed behind her.

At the end of a hallway, she halted and removed a plastic key from her purse. Billy tapped her on the shoulder and she spun around. You had to be twenty-one to gamble in a casino, and she hardly looked it. Her eyes studied his clothing, trying to determine if he worked security.

"Leave me alone or I'll scream," she said.

"That's a cute scam with the dollar bill," he said.

"I don't know what you're talking about."

"You just won two grand playing with the house's money."

Fear tinged the corners of her eyes. "I don't know what you're talking about."

"I need to speak with your father."

"My father isn't here."

"Your father is in that room counting all the money your family just stole. Go tell him Billy Cunningham wants to say hello."

"Who the hell *are* you?"

"A friend. I'll wait right here."

THIRTEEN

Victor's daughter didn't believe Billy was a friend of her father's. The more likely scenario was that Billy was an undercover cop about to put the squeeze on her family. Undercover cops were notorious for catching cheaters inside casinos and extorting them. The girl fumbled keying the door, her hand trembling.

Billy waited in the hall, admiring the plush carpets. The color scheme was ugly as sin, just like every other casino in town. Urban legend had it that the owners purposely made their carpets unappealing to force patrons to look up when they walked through the casinos.

The door reopened and Victor's daughter waved him in to the room. She'd relaxed, and she chained the door behind him. "You saved my father's life. I thought your name was familiar."

"Sorry to scare you like that. What's your name?"

"Katrina. My friends call me Kat."

"Help me out, Kat. Your older brother. His name's Nico, right?"

"That's right. Did you make his scam, too?"

"I did. Your brother had a casino chip strapped to his knee and was using it to fool the RFID detection device in the betting circle."

"I'm impressed. How long you been scamming?"

"Fourteen years. I wasted the first sixteen years of my life."

Kat laughed and led him into the suite's living room. The rest of the clan was standing in front of their chairs and eyed their guest suspiciously. Gypsies had been persecuted for centuries and were inherently suspicious of strangers, no matter what their intention. Nico stood in front of a couch. His eyes sparked with recognition.

"I thought you looked familiar downstairs."

"Hello, Nico. Is your father around?"

"What's this about? Is there a problem?"

"There may be one soon. You don't want to be scamming this casino."

"Why not?"

"The shit's going to hit the fan, and you don't want to be standing in the way."

"My father's in the bedroom taking a nap."

"Wake him up. He'll want to hear what I have to say."

"Don't order me around."

"Do it anyway."

"You're an asshole, you know that?"

"You won't feel that way after you hear what I have to say."

Nico left the living room in a huff. The others members of the Boswell clan continued to stare at their visitor. Back when Billy was hustling knockoffs in Providence, he'd made the acquaintance of several Gypsies and had gotten to know their story. As legend had it, a Gypsy woman had been part of the mob that had gathered the day Jesus Christ was to be crucified. Something in Christ's face had touched the Gypsy woman's soul. Seeing four copper nails lying on the ground, she'd tried to steal them but managed to grab only one, leaving one nail for Christ's feet and two for his hands. Three days later when Jesus rose from the dead, he blessed the Gypsies and gave them permission to roam the earth and steal without fear of retribution.

This was the legend the Gypsies lived by. Stealing was okay so long as no one got murdered. There were other rules as well, but that was pretty much the gist of their code. It was pretty screwed up, but Billy supposed everyone had to believe in something.

Nico returned to the room. "My father's awake and wants to see you."

"Nice to meet you," Billy said to the other members of the clan.

He tipped an imaginary hat before following Nico down a hallway.

- - -

Victor Boswell sat in a recliner inside the master bedroom with his legs propped on the footrest and a glass of scotch in his hand. Victor was pushing seventy and had a receding hairline and aquiline nose that could have belonged to a prizefighter. He was a vain son-of-a-bitch and sported a fresh part in his hair.

"That's a hell of a disguise," Victor said. "Care for a drink?"

"I'm good. How's the leg holding up?" Billy asked.

"Not so great. That fucking gaming agent crippled me for life. What's his name?"

"Frank Grimes."

"Right. Grimes. Did they fire that asshole?"

"Believe it or not, he's still got his job."

"I would have sued the bastards if I didn't hate lawyers so much. Have a seat and make yourself comfortable."

Billy took a chair to Victor's left, while Nico sat on his father's right. Nico was next in line for the throne, but until Victor retired or kicked the bucket, Nico was a lotion boy and had to follow his father's orders.

"I'm guessing this isn't a social call," Victor said.

"Afraid not," Billy said.

"Let me guess. You're working a scam and spotted us doing the same. You picked this joint because the people running it are too preoccupied with the rich assholes, which is the same reason we picked it. It's a candy store." Victor rattled the ice cubes in his glass. "Am I warm?"

"You're on fire."

"And you want us to leave because you're afraid it will mess up your deal."

"Right again."

"There's room enough for both of us, don't you think? I mean come on, how many times have you ripped off a joint and spotted another crew working the floor?"

"This is different. You need to pull up stakes."

"Why should we do that?"

"I'm going to burn the lot."

Victor looked at Billy differently. "No kidding. You can really do that?"

"It took a while, but I figured out a way."

"I'm impressed. And you think the gaming board will take a hard look at the surveillance tapes and see my family working the floor and come after us."

"They're going to come after someone, that's for sure."

Victor turned in his chair to gauge his son's opinion. The look on Nico's face said the kid had gotten lost in the conversation. Victor said, "It's an old carnival expression. It means to rip off a town so badly that another carnival can never work it. Burn the lot."

"I know what it means," Nico said, even though he didn't. "I can't believe you'd go along with this crap. We were here first. Let him leave."

Victor shifted his gaze to their guest. "Nico has a point. We were here first."

"I'm built in. I can't leave," Billy said.

"What—they think you're a whale?"

"That's right. I established a fake identity and the casino has comped me and my crew into a sky palace. If I walk out, it's going to look suspicious. Look, this scam I'm working needs to be pulled this weekend. Once it happens, there's going to be a full-blown investigation. You don't want your faces on the surveillance tapes."

"Fuck no!" Nico exploded.

"Nico, watch your mouth," his father warned.

"I said fuck no, and I mean fuck no. We're not pulling up stakes. This is the best score we've had in a long time. Look at all the money we've made."

Nico retrieved a floppy leather bag from the closet. With great pride he dumped their score onto the floor in front of his father's chair, the stacks of C-notes bouncing off the carpet. Money made the world go round, and there was enough in that bag to make it go around many times.

"And that's just one day's take," Nico said proudly.

Billy could not hide his disbelief. "You stole that much in one day?"

"That's right. And there's plenty more where that came from."

The picture had just gotten real clear. Still recuperating from being shot, Victor had let Nico run the operation. Wanting to impress his father, Nico had told his family to rip Carnivale off blind, not knowing all the alarms it would set off. Billy hated to break the bad news to Nico, but he had no other choice. The cheater's code required him to help any cheater in trouble, and right now the Boswell clan was in enough trouble to earn them a long stretch in the pen.

"I hate to tell you this, but you need to shut this operation down and check out of the hotel," Billy said.

"Screw you," Nico said.

"Nico, this man is our friend," Victor said.

"He's no friend of mine."

Nico was a lost cause, so Billy addressed Victor. "Do as I say. For your own good."

"Why? What did we do wrong?" Victor asked.

Billy pointed an accusing finger at the stack of green on the floor.

"That's wrong," he said.

- - -

"Come here, I want to show both of you something."

Rising, Billy went to the window and drew back the blinds. Blazing neon from the Strip invaded the room and bathed the young hustler in lurid rainbow hues. Victor slowly came out of his chair and leaned against his son to get his balance before hobbling over to the window. Nico reluctantly followed his father but kept his distance from their guest.

The view was southerly. In the distance an airplane landed on one of McCarran's four runways. Billy pointed at a cluster of buildings in an industrial park beside the airport.

"We all know about the Nevada Gaming Control Board's Technology Division," Billy said. "Their job is to monitor the state's slot machines and video poker games. If we steal a jackpot, gaming agents are sent to investigate."

"We've heard of them," Nico said. "So what?"

"A few months back, I ran into a hustler named Maggie Flynn who I knew from the old neighborhood. Maggie was working as a snitch for the gaming board and having an affair with none other than Frank Grimes."

"Small world," Victor said.

"In a moment of weakness, Grimes told Maggie that the gaming board had set up a computer lab near the airport whose sole purpose was to protect the integrity of the state's video games and slot machines," Billy said. "You can see the top of the building from here. It has a red security light. There's also a twenty-four-hour guard."

Victor's breath fogged the glass. "Shit, I see it. Nico, take a look."

Nico stared as well. "What does this have to do with us?"

"Let the man tell his story," Victor snapped.

"The lab houses the source codes for every piece of game software approved in Nevada," Billy explained. "Every new piece of software is brought to the lab and examined before being put into play. Is the random number generator random enough? Does the video poker game pay out at the advertised rate? The lab has to give the game the *Good Housekeeping* seal of approval before it gets put into a casino."

"So tell us something we don't know," Nico said.

"Show some manners," his father said.

Billy was having a hard time understanding why Victor had chosen Nico to succeed him. Nico was a hothead and didn't have any manners, while his father was the epitome of cool and class. There had to be another reason, only Billy wasn't seeing what it was.

"According to Maggie Flynn, the lab has a new addition," Billy said. "It's called a central server, CS for short. CS is a massive computer that's wired in to every slot and video poker machine in town. It monitors jackpots."

Billy paused to let the words sink in. Victor turned from the view to stare at him.

"Say that again."

"CS monitors jackpots and looks for statistical deviations. Every casino has a 'loser list' of bad games that lose money. It can take a casino days to find these games and figure out what the problem is. Sometimes the games have a wiring problem or sometimes there's cheating taking place. CS finds these games in nanoseconds and alerts the casino."

"Nanoseconds?" Victor said, swallowing hard.

Billy clicked his fingers. "Just like that."

"Is the casino onto us?" Victor asked.

"No doubt. CS has already alerted the casino that their slot machines were compromised. Security will review the surveillance tapes to spot who's responsible. It's only a matter of time before you'll get a knock on your door. You want my advice, blow out of here right now."

"Do we retire the scam?" Victor asked.

"No. You can take it to another casino, just keep your winnings reasonable. Otherwise CS will sniff you out."

Victor addressed his son. "Tell your sisters and cousins to pack their clothes; we're checking out tonight."

Nico turned from the window. "How many fucking slot machines are there in this town—a hundred thousand? You expect me to believe one fucking computer can instantly tell when one of them is getting scammed? Fat fucking chance. Pretty Boy is yanking your chain."

"Billy wouldn't lie to us."

"Yes, he would."

"Do it anyway," his father said sternly.

Nico didn't move. This wasn't going to end well, and Billy stepped away from the window and headed for the door.

"Thanks for the heads up," Victor called after him.

"Anytime," Billy said.

FOURTEEN

Billy rode an empty elevator downstairs. He was glad to have that out of the way. He'd warned Victor and that was all the cheater's code required him to do. His mentor, a cigar-chomping gangster named Lou Profaci, had taught Billy the cheater's code, and he'd lived by it ever since. Many younger cheats didn't follow the code, believing it was an old set of rules that no longer applied. Nothing could have been further from the truth. Rules were important, especially when it came to thieving.

The rule about not ratting out another cheat was a good example. Some younger cheats thought it was okay to roll on their partners when they got arrested, mistakenly believing it was better to send a friend to jail than to go to jail themselves. But the cheat who squealed lived in a different kind of prison, one where he had no friends or people he could trust.

Upon reaching the lobby, Billy headed straight to the casual clothing store where he'd bought his disguise. The pretty college-age girl who had waited on him was still on duty.

"Back so soon?" she asked.

"Short trip. I need my old clothes back."

"I threw them away. Just kidding. They're behind the register."

From behind the counter she retrieved the clothes he'd come into the store wearing. He followed her to the dressing rooms where she unlocked one of the doors with a brass key dangling from her belt. He brushed against her as he entered the stall. She didn't seem to mind.

"What's with the key?" he asked.

"They dock my pay if anything gets stolen," she explained.

"That hardly seems fair."

"You're right. It's not fair at all."

"Does that bother you?"

"Only when I think about it."

Billy was always on the lookout for new recruits, and this young woman was a perfect candidate. She was young, she was attractive, and she didn't have an arrest record—otherwise she wouldn't be allowed to work in a casino. She also had a chip on her shoulder and would rip off the store if the opportunity presented itself. Those were all important things in his line of work. When he came out of the dressing room, he placed the clothes he'd worn to see Victor onto the counter.

"What do you want me to do with these?" she asked.

"Throw them out. What's your name?"

"Brianna, but you can call me Brie."

"Can I give you a ring sometime?"

"Only if I give you my phone number."

Brie gave Billy her number, and he logged it into the contact app on his cell phone.

"I like sushi and I'm off on weekends," she said.

"My name's Billy. Nice meeting you."

"Same here, Billy."

He walked out of the store and returned to the five-thousand-dollar blackjack game. The pit boss had held open his seat at the table, hoping he'd return. As he sat down, a cocktail waitress appeared like a genie coming out of a bottle.

"Drink, sir?"

"Rum and coke with a twist of lime."

"My pleasure."

Drink in hand, he played blackjack while keeping an eye on the elevator bank. It wasn't long before he spotted a female member of the Boswell clan walk past dragging her suitcase. More members soon followed, their departures spaced minutes apart. Leaving separately was smart, as hotel employees working the front desk were less likely to remember them.

Victor was next to last to leave and limped out on a metal cane. Like a captain staying on a sinking ship, Victor had waited for each of his family to get out before leaving himself.

Each member of the clan was accounted for except Nico. Billy wondered what the holdup was. The longer Nico stayed inside the hotel, the greater a risk he faced for himself and his family. Finally, Nico emerged from an elevator. Instead of heading toward the registration desk, Nico crossed the casino floor and sat down at a slot machine.

Billy had eyes like a hawk, and he watched Nico slide a crisp one-dollar bill into the machine's bill feeder. A hundred dollars' worth of credit appeared on the machine's LED display. The crazy bastard. Hadn't he heard a word Billy had said? Or was this Nico's way of being disrespectful to his father? It was a dumb move and would only lead to bad things.

Nico was going to get caught. Billy would have bet his condo on it. The sixty-four-thousand-dollar question was, was Nico smart enough to deal with the bust when it happened?

Part of cheating was getting caught. It happened to even the best cheats. Like the old-timers were fond of saying, if you ain't getting caught you ain't cheating. But getting caught didn't necessarily mean going to jail. Lou Profaci had taught him that as well.

- - -

Lou ran an illegal casino in the basement of a Catholic church that was a big moneymaker. It was a bustout joint, the various games rigged so the suckers couldn't win. Even the drinks were a rip-off, the liquor watered down.

One night, Lou had told Billy to act as lookout and stand on the church's roof. The church was in a seedy neighborhood and surrounded by a security fence. The only access point was the front doors. If the cops staged a raid, it would be through the front of the building.

Just past midnight, six police cruisers rolled up with their headlights off, and a small army of cops piled out. A lone streetlight made the silver badges pinned to their overcoats twinkle like Christmas ornaments. Two of the cops marched up the church's front steps and began to break down the door with a battering ram while the others lined up behind them with guns drawn.

Billy flipped on a walkie-talkie and found it was dead. Throwing open the exit door, he ran down a stairwell to the basement. The church was two hundred years old, and the creaky wood steps sounded ready to explode beneath his feet. From the front of the building came a litany of curses. Lou had chained the door, and the cops were having a hard time breaking it down.

Billy burst into the packed casino. Lou had dressed the room up nice, putting down carpeting and hanging pretty light fixtures. The joint oozed class, which was more than you could say about most establishments in Providence.

"Vice squad!" Billy called out.

Women grabbed their handbags off the backs of chairs while their husbands scooped up their chips and deposited them in their jacket pockets.

Lou marched to the back of the room, where he pressed a button on the wall. Sliding doors opened, and the crowd passed through underground tunnels that had been dug as part of the church's involvement in helping black slaves escape to Canada in the 1800s. When the last person had departed, Lou shut the sliding doors.

Lou's crew folded the roulette, blackjack, and craps tables into hideaways in the wall like Murphy beds. One moment an illegal casino had filled the basement, the next it was gone like a puff of smoke. Lou grabbed a handful of black books from the closet.

"Can you sing?" Lou asked Billy.

"As good as the next guy," Billy said.

Lou handed him a book and opened it up to a page with a bookmark. "Start singing, kid."

It was a hymnal, the page open to "Onward, Christian Soldiers." Billy started singing and the other members of the crew joined in.

The door burst open and the cops swarmed in. The sergeant in charge took one look at the devout collection of men singing the good Lord's praises and howled his displeasure.

- - -

Lou always had an escape plan; that was what allowed him to stay one step ahead of the law. Billy would have bet good money that Nico didn't have an escape plan. Nico was inexperienced and had let his father deal with those types of details.

Nico continued to scam the slot machine. Slot machines were calibrated to pay small jackpots every nine or ten pulls. It was this intermittent reinforcement that got players addicted and made them continue to play. Nico racked up several thousand in winnings and appeared oblivious to the danger he was putting himself in.

Billy's cell phone vibrated. He got out of his chair and walked away from the table before taking it out. Pepper had texted him.

`You need to come upstairs`

`Problem?` he texted back.

`Wang's creeping me out`

He'd spent enough time dealing with the Boswells. He retrieved his chips and tossed the dealer a generous tip.

"Thank you, Mr. C.," the dealer said.

Nico was still on his suicide run. Billy came up behind Nico's chair and bumped it. Nico glanced over his shoulder at the offending party.

"You need to beat it before the gaming board busts you," Billy said.

"Screw you," Nico replied.

"You're being an idiot. Leave, for your family's sake."

"They already split. You scared them."

Nico didn't get it. If he got busted, the gaming board would review the past few days of surveillance tapes and see him in a coffee shop or poolside with his family, and they'd track down the others by tracing cell phone calls or credit card purchases.

A cocktail waitress asked Nico if he needed a drink.

"Get me a beer," Nico said. "My friend doesn't need anything. He's just leaving."

They were done. Billy took out his wallet and dug out a business card, which he stuck into Nico's face.

"Take it," he said.

Nico squinted to read the lettering. "Who's Felix Underman?"

"My defense attorney. Use my name when you call him. He'll return your call faster."

"You don't scare me. Get lost."

Billy headed across the casino knowing Nico would soon get busted. The question was, how soon was soon? If the gaming board was busy, it might take them a day or two to spring into action. That was all Billy would need to pull his scam and get out.

At the elevator banks, he encountered DeSantis. VIP hosts did most of their work at night as they ran around tending to their wealthy clients. Seeing Billy, DeSantis ended his call and made his cell phone disappear into his pocket.

"Good evening, Mr. C. Quitting early tonight?" DeSantis asked.

"You've won enough of my money for one day. I'll be back tomorrow."

"The hotel has eight gourmet restaurants. Let me know if you'd like to do lunch, and I'll make arrangements for you and your friends for a private dining room."

"Thanks."

"And golf. Three Fazio golf courses at your disposal. Just give me a tee time."

"I'll do that."

Billy got into an elevator as DeSantis continued to pepper him with bribes. As the doors closed, he received another text from Pepper.

`U coming or not`

`On my way`, he wrote back.

FIFTEEN

Pepper awaited him in the foyer. She had changed into stonewashed jeans and a tight-fitting UNLV Rebels T-shirt and wore a deep frown.

"Hi honey, I'm home," Billy said.

"Where you been hiding? We were getting worried about you," she said.

"I ran into some old friends. So what's the problem with our neighbor?"

"Wang invited us over for brunch tomorrow morning." Pepper dropped her voice. "I want to know what his deal is. This guy's over the top."

"What did he do, send you a mash note?"

"Come here and I'll show you."

The smell was overpowering as they entered the living room. Every table, chair, and inch of floor space was covered in flowers. Not your usual variety of freshly cut roses and tulips, but a breathtaking assortment of orchids, hydrangeas, and chrysanthemums. Misty stood in the corner of the room. Like Pepper, she had on her unhappy face.

"Why are you looking at me like that?" Billy asked.

"You're not being level with us," Misty said. "Is he, Pepper?"

"No, he's not," Pepper said. "We went outside to take a swim and when we came back in, these flowers were here along with this note." She pulled a piece of paper from her pocket and gave it to him. "It says, 'It is destiny that our paths have crossed in a city of improbable chances. I am looking forward to getting to know each of you better.'"

"So he's enamored with you. Big deal."

"He wants sex, right?"

Pepper and Misty had forgotten that the sky palace was bugged. He pointed to the doors leading outside and moments later stood with them by the railing, where it was safe to talk.

"I told you before, sex isn't part of the equation, unless you want it to be," he said.

"Boy, I've heard that one before," Misty said. "Look, Billy, if you want us to tag-team this guy, just say so, and we'll go downstairs and buy a box of rubbers and pay him a visit. We don't have a problem fucking his brains out, but you've got to tell us in advance so we can be prepared. We're not whores who can turn it on for any customer, okay?"

"This isn't about sex," he said.

"Right," they both said.

He blew out his lungs in exasperation. Pepper and Misty had to get it out of their heads that Tommy Wang was trying to get them in the sack. Going inside, he picked up a potted chrysanthemum from the coffee table and returned holding it in his hands. "Wang didn't come to Vegas to have sex or to see floor shows. He's here to gamble in the casinos, and that's all he came here to do. A Chinese bad guy named Broken Tooth is paying for his trip and expects him to win millions of dollars and bring it back home. If Wang doesn't, he'll end up getting hurt."

"As in killed?" Misty asked.

"Yes, as in killed."

"You're kidding me. Is Wang a gangster?"

"No, but Broken Tooth is, and he runs the 14K Triad, which is the most powerful crime syndicate in China. Wang somehow convinced

Broken Tooth to lend him a few million bucks so he could beat the casinos in Las Vegas. Wang came to Vegas six months ago thinking he would double the money, go home, pay off Broken Tooth, and live happily ever after. Well, it didn't work out that way. The casinos busted him and Wang went home broke."

"I thought you said he was the most fortunate man in China," Pepper said.

"He is. Some other jokers also borrowed money from Broken Tooth and lost it all in Las Vegas. When Broken Tooth found out, he had his men put bullets in their heads. For some reason, Wang got spared the ax, and Broken Tooth sent him to Vegas to win his money back."

"Can he do that?"

"With our help he can. I read a story about Wang on the Internet and decided he was the perfect cover for our heist, so I arranged for us to get put in a sky palace next to his. I also knew that having you wear those jadeite necklaces would get him jumping."

"Why?" Pepper asked.

"Because Wang is your typical Chinese gambler who sees symbols in everything. Take this chrysanthemum. The Chinese believe this plant attracts good fortune, same with the other flowers. Wang sent it to you in the hopes you'll bring him good luck."

"So we're just two big rabbit's feet," Misty said.

"Two beautiful rabbit's feet," he said. "When you get together with Wang, you'll pull the stunts we worked on in Lake Tahoe and make Wang think he can't lose."

"Is this guy going to win the money for us?" Misty asked.

"Yup. Tommy Wang's our agent. He just doesn't know it."

"So that's how you're going to get the money out of the casino," Pepper said. "Wang's going to take it out for us."

"In a manner of speaking, yeah."

"How do we get our cut once that happens?"

"I can't tell you that."

"Are you going to murder him?"

"Come on, you know me better than that."

"Then how are you going to get it from him? He's not going to just fork it over."

"I can't tell you that. But you have my word, no one gets hurt except the casino."

Pepper and Misty thought it over.

"I'm cool with that," Misty said.

"And we don't have to fuck him," Pepper said, just to be sure.

"Tommy Wang doesn't expect you to fuck him, and neither do I. It's not on the menu."

"This has got a lot of moving parts. Are you sure it's going to fly?" Pepper asked.

"There are always risks when you steal. This scam is worth the risk ten times over. What do you say we have a drink and call it a night? On me."

Pepper and Misty both laughed. The tension had left their faces, and they'd returned to being their beautiful selves. The scam wouldn't fly without them, and Billy was going to do everything possible to allay their fears and keep them happy.

"What are you drinking?" he asked.

"Vodka and cranberry juice," Pepper said.

"Same here," Misty said.

"Coming right up."

As they went inside, a crashing sound made Billy jump. He stared at the foyer, convinced the police had broken down the door and were coming to arrest him.

SIXTEEN

The police didn't come barging into the sky palace. Billy breathed a sigh of relief and took a moment to collect himself. The crashing sound happened again. Pepper didn't act like anything was out of the ordinary, nor did Misty.

"The suite has a private bowling alley," Pepper explained. "The guys are playing. Are you okay? You look really stressed, Billy."

It had been a long day, and Billy needed to get his mind on other things. He went behind the bar and fixed their drinks, including a rum and coke for himself, came around, and served them. They clinked glasses and the crashing sound happened again.

"You bowl?" Pepper asked.

"Since I was a kid. I'm the best bowler in the world," Billy said.

"Travis thinks he's the best bowler in the world," Misty said.

"Let me at him." Drink in hand, Billy followed Pepper and Misty down a hallway that he didn't remember being on the original tour. "Who you backing?"

"My money's always on you, Billy," Pepper said.

They entered a single-lane bowling alley. It resembled a dance club with glow-in-the-dark paint and shape-shifting lasers throwing images across the ceiling. On the wall was a cupboard with striped bowling shoes.

Travis had a handful of cash that had recently belonged to Cory and Morris, and the big man watched Billy lace up with a suspicious eye.

"I didn't know you bowled," Travis said.

"It's been a few years. How much a game?"

"A hundred bucks. How many points do you want me to spot you?"

"None. Make it two hundred."

"Come on, Billy, I play in a league. I'm good."

"You're chopped liver. Two hundred a game, winner take all."

"You're on. You want to take some practice throws?"

"Of course I want to take some practice throws."

Billy found a ball to his liking and held it against his chest. Half a lifetime ago, he'd been the best bowler in his hometown, maybe the best in the state of Rhode Island, the sound of the rubber-solid ball exploding off the maple tenpins so loud and dominating that it scared other bowlers and gave him a huge edge. He had a motion like nobody else, with a high backswing that created a deep knee bend and a hook that demolished the pins and his opponents as well, the noise as loud as a cannon going off. The ball flew down the lane. Bang, a strike.

He threw two more balls with the same results.

"Aw, shit, look at you," Travis said.

"Ready when you are," Billy said.

Travis lost the first game by eighty pins. The big man didn't know how to play the outside or the inside of the lane or how to work the angles.

"Why didn't you tell me you were a ringer?" Travis asked.

"You didn't ask. Keep your head still when you release the ball."

"Thanks for the pointer."

The next game, Billy took it easy and won by thirty points. It hadn't been that long ago when he'd been making a grand a week playing illegal action games in Providence, his action backed by local wise guys. He would have gone right on bowling for dollars only he didn't want to spend his life associated with guys named Tony the Ant or Three

Fingers Louie, so he'd hung up his bowling shoes and sold his ball at the local pawn shop.

Beaten, Travis slapped the cash into Billy's palm. "I should have known."

"Live and learn. Hey, by the time this weekend is over, you'll have enough money to build your own bowling alley."

"Man, that would be a blast."

"I need your help with something."

"Sure, Billy, name it."

Pepper and Misty had gotten bored and left, as had Cory and Morris. Except for Gabe off in the corner of the room, it was just the two of them. Billy lowered his voice anyway.

"The ladies are getting antsy. Keep an eye on them for me."

"The Chinese guy has them spooked, huh?"

"He's harmless, only they don't know that. They think he's a stalker."

"That's not good."

"No, it's not. Tommy Wang's our ticket to the big time. If Misty and Pepper run away from him, our lives of luxury will have to be put on hold."

"I won't let them out of my sight."

"Thanks, man."

Travis said good night and left, leaving Billy alone with Gabe. The jeweler sat on a stiff wooden bench absorbed with his cell phone. He made a distressed sound and ran his hand through his thinning hair. Billy took the spot beside him on the bench.

"I can't get a hold of my house sitter," Gabe explained. "I called his cell phone and he didn't pick up. He didn't pick up when I called the landline at my house, either."

"This is the ex-military guy across the street with the heart problem."

"Good memory. Nate's always been Mister Reliable. My gut tells me something's happened to him, you know, with his heart. I want to go check on him."

"We don't have a car, remember?"

"I could cab it."

"I've got a better idea. Call one of your other neighbors, ask him to go over and bang on your front door, see what the deal is. If I remember correctly, Nate has a hearing problem. He's probably got the TV jacked up so loud he can't hear the phone."

"That's a good idea. I'll call my neighbor Elsie. She's an insomniac."

"I'm going to hit the sack. Ciao."

"I heard what you said to Travis. Are the girls going to bail on us?"

"Not if I can help it."

Billy went to the living room to fix a nightcap. Bowling with Travis had brought back a lot of memories, and he made the drink extra strong and took it onto the balcony. Growing up in Providence had been the pits, more so when he'd become a thief. It was a poor, half-ugly city without enough good scores to go around. Local gangsters took it personally when another thief crossed into their turf, and guys were always getting whacked over chump change.

The slider opened. Gabe appeared by his side, breathing hard.

"I just got off the phone with Elsie. My place was broken into tonight," Gabe said. "My front door's open and the foyer's trashed. Nate's car is still in the driveway."

"Any sign of him?"

"None. Elsie wants to call the cops. I told her not to do that. I need to get over there."

"Yes, you do. I'll go with you."

Billy went to his bedroom and got his leather jacket from the closet. Gabe's house was chock-full of sophisticated forgery equipment that he used to manufacture the gaffs they used for their scams. Possession of crooked gambling equipment in Nevada was a felony, and the last people Gabe wanted poking around his house were the Metro LVPD. Gabe awaited him in the living room and looked scared out of his wits.

Billy knew the feeling.

SEVENTEEN

Nobody who worked in Vegas made jack.

Not the blackjack dealers who stood on their feet eight hours a day and relied on tips to get by. Or the statuesque showgirls who balanced ten pounds of feathers on their heads and took home less than a schoolteacher. Or the front-desk receptionists who worked twelve-hour shifts and had nothing to show for it at the end of the month.

When Billy had first arrived in Vegas, he'd taken one look at the opulent casinos lining the Strip and assumed that everyone in the gambling industry was making big bucks and living the good life. The casinos generated billions, and it seemed logical the money would get spread around.

He'd been wrong. Nobody made shit. The greedy casino owners didn't share their food and there was no trickle-down effect among the employees who kept the joints running. Like Medieval times, there was a handful of kings and a kingdom of slaves, and anyone foolish enough to think they could change things had a lesson coming to them.

The same was true of the town's other businesses. Like the cab companies. Vegas taxis generated twenty-five million rides a year, yet the owners of the cab companies forced their drivers to work inhuman hours to meet revenue targets. As a result, cabbies often resorted to cheating their customers to make a buck.

"That was our turn," Billy said through the partition.

"I know where I'm going," the driver said.

"So why did you pass our turn?"

"You think I'm long-hauling you?"

"Damn straight I do."

The driver said nothing, his eyes glued to the four-lane stretch of road in front of him.

"The nerve of this fucking guy," Gabe said under his breath.

Billy put his face to the glass. "Say good-bye to your tip, pal."

The driver's eyes grew wide in his mirror. "I live on tips, man. Have a heart."

"I live here, and you're taking us for a ride."

"You're a native? Why didn't you say so?"

"I just did. Now, turn the cab around."

Their driver did a one-eighty in the middle of busy Las Vegas Boulevard. Less than sixty seconds later the cab was idling in front of Gabe's sprawling ranch house. Gabe's neighborhood had taken a serious hit during the recession, and half the houses on the block were empty. It was like living in a ghost town, and Gabe often talked about pulling up stakes once property values rose. Billy passed a crisp twenty through the partition for the ten-dollar fare.

"Keep the change," he said.

The driver took the money with a smile and handed Billy his card.

"Call me if you need a ride," the driver said.

The driver had major cojones. Billy liked that, and he pocketed the card.

- - -

Billy and Gabe headed up the front path. The house had lights in the windows and the AC unit purred. The notion that something bad had happened to Nate hung over them like a dark cloud. They halted at the front porch. Billy tested the front door and found it locked.

"I thought you said the front door was open," Billy said.

"I told Elsie to lock it. I don't need to get robbed twice tonight," Gabe said.

"Is that Nate's car parked in the driveway?"

"Yeah, that's his car."

Nate drove an aging Kia with a roof burned orange by the desert sun. Billy walked over to the car and peered through the window to see if Nate was by chance asleep in the front seat. Nate's bad heart often got the better of him and he'd napped in his car many times.

"He in there?" Gabe asked.

"Afraid not."

"I've got a bad feeling about this."

Billy returned to the front porch and Gabe handed him the key. As Billy opened the door, a rustling noise snapped his head. Gabe's neighbor Elsie emerged from the shadows wearing an oversized pair of jeans and a floppy sweatshirt. Elsie ran the neighborhood watch group and made it a point to know everyone's business.

"Gabe, is that you?" she asked tentatively.

"It sure is. How you doing, Elsie?" Gabe said.

"I've had better nights. Who's that handsome fellow with you?"

"This is my friend Billy. Billy, this is Elsie. Any sign of Nate?"

"I haven't seen him. Are you sure you don't want me to call 911?"

"Positive."

"I think you've been robbed. What if they rob me?"

"With that big dog of yours? It's not likely, Elsie."

"I want to call the police, just to be on the safe side."

"Let us deal with this, okay?"

"You got something against the police?"

Gabe stiffened at his neighbor's line of questioning. Billy could feel it and wondered if Elsie felt it as well.

"I don't have anything against the police," Gabe said. "I just don't want to waste their time over something that's probably not important. Okay?"

Elsie took a moment processing this remark. A flashlight in her hand came to life and she walked away without uttering a word. Billy's eyes had adjusted to the darkness and he watched her go. "Go walk her home," he said under his breath.

"She knows her way home," Gabe said.

"She didn't buy your line about the dog. She's going to call the police. Look, she's pulled out her cell phone and is punching in a number."

"Jesus Christ—she is. I'll be right back."

Gabe hustled across the front lawn in pursuit of his neighbor. Normally, Billy would have waited for Gabe to come back before venturing inside the house, but they were on a job and every minute away from the job was a risk. He needed to get this done and go back to Carnivale to resume his charade of pretending to be a whale.

He entered the house. A busted lamp lay on the floor in the foyer.

"Hey Nate, where you hiding?"

No response. He shut the door behind him.

"Nate? You here?"

He treaded down the hallway into a spacious living room. It had taken a while, but Gabe had finally broken down and decorated the place. Instead of hiring an interior designer, Gabe had tapped his inner adolescent and filled the rooms with an elaborate model train set. Hundreds of yards of tracks snaked through model villages, up steep hills, across suspension bridges, and through underground tunnels. There were miniature people as well, tending to gardens, walking dogs, and driving tiny cars with the tops down, their faces painted in happy smiles. It was a fantasy world where every detail was perfect. He found a remote and pushed the start button. A train came out of a tunnel tooting its horn, its cars filled with passengers. A sound snapped his head. Like a cough, but weak, gasping for air. He followed it to the rear of the house. The study door was ajar and a light burned inside. He pushed the door open with his foot.

"Nate, you in there?"

He entered cautiously. The study had a desk covered with photos of Gabe's girls, a PC, and a printer. He walked around the desk to find Nate sprawled on the floor. Or at least he thought it was Nate, his face so battered that it was hard to tell who it was.

He knelt down and tried to give comfort. Nate's nose was flattened and two of his front teeth were missing. Dried blood caked his nostrils and blood dripped from one of his ears. Nate's eyelids fluttered and he tried to speak, but nothing came out.

"For the love of Christ," a voice said.

Gabe rushed into the study, his eyes filled with tears.

"You still have that bottle of Glenlivet I gave you?" Billy asked.

"I think so," Gabe said.

"Go get it."

When Gabe returned he was holding the whiskey and a glass. Gabe poured a liberal shot into the glass and passed it to Billy. Billy poured the whiskey into Nate's mouth and got half of it on Nate's chin. Nate's eyelids snapped open and he sparked to life. Nate gave Billy a puzzled frown before seeing Gabe and breaking into a sad smile.

"I didn't tell them nothing," Nate gasped.

Gabe knelt down. "About what?"

"You know," Nate said.

"No, I don't."

"The cheating. I didn't tell them about the cheating."

Billy looked at Gabe, wanting to kill him. Rule #1 was never to talk about work. Not to friends or family or anyone else.

"I didn't tell him. Honest, Billy," Gabe said.

"I figured it out myself," Nate said, filling in the blanks. "I saw the equipment in the garage and knew you were scamming the fucking casinos. Good for you."

Nate's eyelids grew heavy. Another liberal dose of whiskey revived him.

"Who did this to you?" Gabe asked.

"Two guys tricked me into letting them in," Nate said. "Wanted to know where you were. I told them to fuck off and they beat me up. I didn't tell them nothing."

"Thanks, man," Gabe said.

Streams of bright red blood poured out of Nate's nostrils like water coming out a spigot. Nate was going down fast and there was nothing they could do to stop the slide. Billy had held the dying before and knew the drill. He drew Nate's head into his lap, not caring if the blood stained his clothes, his only concern to give comfort to Nate as he passed to the other side.

He said a silent prayer. As strange as it sounded, he still believed in Almighty God, the heavenly father the only policeman he cared about. Someday they'd have a nice chat about all the bad things he'd done, but he wanted to believe that day was far off, and until it happened he would go right on scamming and jamming and filling his pockets with other people's money.

Nate stopped breathing and his head flopped to the side.

Gabe bawled like a little kid. Billy crossed himself and let a moment pass.

"Call the others," he said.

"You mean Cory and Morris and Travis?" Gabe asked.

"Yeah. We need to bury your friend."

Gabe tried to process what Billy was saying. "Bury him where?"

"In the desert, where do you think?"

"Why not a funeral home?"

"We take him to a funeral home, they'll want to see a death certificate. The only way we get one of those is to bring in the cops. Not happening."

"I don't want—"

"I don't care what you want. Your friend's getting plopped in the ground. If we call the cops, how do we explain what happened or the cheating equipment in your house? We can't." He paused. "Now, call the others."

Nate shook his head. "Oh man, this is so wrong."

"Do it anyway."

"I need to think about this."

"Think about what?"

"What you're saying to me. It's not right. Nate deserves better, you understand what I'm saying? He served in Vietnam and all that shit. He deserves a proper funeral."

Still kneeling, Billy grabbed the lapels of Gabe's shirt and shook him hard. When that didn't get the reaction he was looking for, he slapped him across the face, using enough force to snap Gabe out of the dangerous place his emotions were taking him to. "Don't you dare question me again. Because if you do, I'll fire your sorry ass and find someone else to replace you."

"Don't say that, Billy. You're all that I've got."

"Then do what I tell you and call the guys."

Gabe rose on rubbery legs. Out came the cell phone, on which he made a call to Travis. In a trembling voice he asked Travis to get to his house as fast as he could and to bring Cory and Morris with him. Ending the call, he wiped the tears from his eyes.

"They're on their way," he said.

"Go outside and wait for them."

Gabe shuffled out of the study while Billy got to his feet. He decided it would be best to use a bedspread to wrap the dead man in. As he headed for the door, he noticed the PC on Gabe's desk was powered up, the screen burning ever so brightly.

He nearly got sick. Their scam at Carnivale was there for all the world to see.

EIGHTEEN

Billy used the mouse on Gabe's computer to scroll through the pages. It was all there. The script he'd written, the simulations they'd run, even his crude hand drawings showing where his crew would sit at the table as the Carnivale scam went down.

His face grew flush and he started to get angry. He'd spent the better part of a year hatching this scam, and he considered it one of the finer things he'd ever created. And here it was, sitting on Gabe's computer like a screen saver.

This wasn't supposed to happen. Gabe's PC was encrypted with antihacking software created by a company called Aurora, and so were Gabe's laptop and tablet. Billy's computers were encrypted with the same software. He'd made the investment in case the scam went south and their computers were confiscated by the gaming board.

So how had Gabe's PC gotten hacked? It didn't seem possible, unless Gabe had forgotten to shut it down before leaving for Lake Tahoe, allowing the bastards who had murdered Nate to see the Carnivale scam upon entering the study.

He forced himself to calm down. At the end of the day, it didn't matter how the scam had ended up being exposed on Gabe's computer. It was there, and Nate's killers had seen it.

But had they understood it? Most criminals were dumb as rocks and didn't have the mental bandwidth to understand a casino scam. But there was also the chance that Nate's killers had printed out a copy with the idea of taking a closer look later on.

He shuddered at the thought. With a printed copy, Nate's killers could blackmail Billy and his crew and ruin their lives.

With a shaking hand, he clicked on the computer's control panel and found the printer drive. By default, a computer's printer dropped a job once it was completed. But there was an option in the printer driver that kept a record of all jobs. If Gabe had enabled this option, then his answer was awaiting him in the print queue.

The print queue appeared on the screen. The last print job had occurred one hour and six minutes ago. Sixteen pages had been printed.

The Carnivale scam was also sixteen pages long.

Nate's killers had made a copy.

"Fuck me," Billy swore.

He shut down the computer. Beating a casino out of a monster score had nothing to do with stealing and everything to do with manipulating the odds. The best scams shifted the odds a few precious percentage points and tilted the game away from the house's favor into the cheater's favor. The play at Carnivale was such a scam. This Saturday, with the help of Tommy Wang, Billy and his crew would bleed Carnivale's casino until it was as dead as a crash victim sitting beneath a twenty-car pileup. It was as sophisticated a play as any that had been pulled in Vegas in a long time, and it was in danger of going up in flames.

He stared into the void of the darkened computer screen. Perhaps Nate's killers were smarter than the average scumbags and knew they'd hit the mother lode. Every crook was looking for a monster score. It was what drew criminals to Vegas, and he wouldn't be surprised if Nate's killers showed up in the next few days, hoping to cash in.

He went into the hallway and entered Nate's older daughter's bedroom. When he returned to the study he was holding the bedspread off a queen bed. He laid it across the floor and began to roll up the dead man.

Gabe returned and stood in the doorway. "Travis is here."

"Did he bring Cory and Morris with him?"

"They're in the car. What are you doing?"

"What does it look like I'm doing? Did you tell them?"

"I told them Nate got murdered and we had to bury him. Look, can we talk about this?"

"No. You got any lime?"

"What do you want a lime for?"

"I didn't say I wanted a lime. I said I wanted lime, the kind you use in the garden. We need to cover his body with it so the coyotes don't dig him up."

Gabe covered his mouth with his hand. "Can't we at least . . ."

"At least what?"

"Clean him up? He looks fucking awful."

"Sure. Go get a towel."

Gabe got a wet washcloth from the bathroom and handed it to Billy.

"Why you looking at me like that? What did I do?"

"You left your computer on. The guys who did this saw the scam and made a copy."

Gabe teetered on an imaginary tightrope. "Are you sure?"

"Either that, or you left the passwords out. Doesn't matter. They got the scam."

"I'm sorry, Billy. Really, I am."

"Save the apology for later. Go get the guys. We need to bury your friend."

"You going to fire me?"

"Look, we'll talk about this later, okay?"

"Sure, Billy."

Taking a deep breath, Gabe righted himself and left the study. Something told Billy that this fuckup would change Gabe for the better and make him start cleaning up his tracks. But they still needed to have a serious sit-down. If Gabe screwed up again, he was history.

He cleaned up Nate's bruised and battered puss. The beating had left a permanent frown in Nate's once cheerful demeanor. There was no good reason to kill a man this way. Not when you could pump a bullet into the back of your victim's head. Killers who used their hands to inflict pain had an agenda born from a lifetime of rage that could never be satiated, and there were enough of them running around Vegas that decent people kept their doors dead-bolted at night and a loaded handgun on the bedside table.

Nate's chin had taken a particularly hard shot. As the caked blood came away, a perfectly round indentation the size of a dime remained in the skin. One of his killers had been wearing a ring that he'd used to stamp poor Nate's face.

Billy's memory kicked in. He'd seen that stamp years ago on the face of an innocent child who'd been stolen from her daddy and whose kidnappers had roughed her up for no good reason. He'd always believed the kidnappers had been run down and killed. Even in a town as mean as Vegas, you didn't hurt little kids without paying the price.

He was wrong, and the stamp on Nate's face proved it. The little girl's kidnappers were still alive. Travis appeared in the study doorway along with Cory and Morris.

"What took you so long?" Billy asked.

"We went to the airport and rented a car. Is he dead?"

"As a church social. Put him in the trunk."

- - -

Vegas was defined by the Strip's six and a half miles of casinos. Venture away from the glitter, and the town quickly became Dullsville, with the same chains, quick-serve restaurants, and boring subdivisions as the rest of the country.

Gabe's street backed up onto a subdivision that had gone bankrupt during the recession, the lots plotted but never built upon. Billy decided to bury Nate in one of these lots. It was a risk, for someday the land might get developed and Nate's bones unearthed. But time was short, and they needed to get back to Carnivale before their absence caused problems.

With the headlights off, Travis drove the rental across the bumpy terrain and braked at the indicated spot. Billy took a look around to make sure there weren't any homeless people camping out or teenagers getting high.

"Let's get this over with," he said.

From the rental's trunk Billy removed a shovel he'd found in Gabe's garage. It was a moonless night, the glow of the casinos blotting out the stars. They took turns digging, each man shoveling frantically for five minutes before letting the next take over. Billy went last, believing that he should never ask one of his crew to do a job that he wouldn't do himself.

"What was that?" Gabe whispered fearfully.

Billy stopped digging and put his ear to the wind. "I don't hear anything."

"Sounds like a dog. What if it starts barking?"

"There is no dog. It's your imagination."

Gabe shone the flashlight app on his iPhone in the direction of the noise. His arm was shaking, the flashlight's beam dancing. "I could have sworn I heard something."

Billy tossed the shovel to the ground and climbed out of the grave. With Travis's help, he removed Nate's body from the trunk and carried it over to the shallow hole, where on the count of three they both let go. It landed with a dull thud, as inglorious an end as one could imagine. There would be no graveside eulogy or headstone. Nate would simply disappear, never to be heard from again. Billy felt bad about it, but he'd get over it.

They sprinkled lime over the body before refilling the hole with dirt. Gabe did not help them. Instead, the jeweler continued to point his flashlight into the void.

"Let's get out of here," Billy said.

Travis, Cory, and Morris piled into the rental. Travis was behind the wheel and fired up the engine. Gabe didn't move from his spot.

"Get in the car," Billy said.

"There's something out there watching us."

"Come on, you need a couple of stiff drinks."

"I saw green eyes glowing in the dark. There were two pairs."

"Sure you did."

Billy grabbed Gabe by the arm and began pulling the jeweler toward the rental. It was like trying to move a mountain, and he motioned to Travis for help. Travis inched the rental toward them and came to a gentle stop. Billy opened the passenger door and began to shove Gabe in.

"Come on, man, get in the fucking car, will you?"

"I swear to God, there's something out there watching us," Gabe said.

A black-tailed jackrabbit jumped out of a hole and darted past the two men. Gabe let out a startled yelp. Billy laughed and slapped Gabe on the back.

"It was just a rabbit."

"No it wasn't. Look over there."

From out of nowhere a pair of gray coyotes ran past the rental. One of the coyotes was mature and full grown, the second just a teen and learning how to hunt. They'd been hiding in plain sight, and they ran down the jackrabbit and tore it apart.

Vegas was overrun with coyotes. They hung out in the foothills and descended into the subdivisions at night. They killed house pets when the situation was right, hopping the fence and doing the grab-and-go with Spot or Precious. Everyone knew about them, including the sheriff and local game wardens, and no one did a damn thing to stop the killing.

Billy had never fathomed that. Back where he came from, packs of animals that killed were gotten rid of, the quicker the better. But not in Sin City. Here, coyotes did their killing and people looked the other way, just like he was doing now. Someday, he might understand how the locals rationalized the coyotes' presence, but he didn't see himself ever accepting it.

It was too damn savage, even for him.

NINETEEN

"Who'd you rent this junker from?" Billy asked.

"Dollar. They had the cheapest rates," Travis said.

"Drop off the car and we'll cab it back to the hotel." Billy shared the backseat with Gabe, who was still shaken up. "You need to get a couple of stiff drinks into you."

Gabe had started talking to himself. Billy feared that Gabe had perhaps suffered a nervous breakdown. Going to the emergency room was an option, except Gabe might start blabbing about stuff better left unsaid. Billy blew out his lungs.

"Stop looking at me like that," Gabe said.

"Exactly how am I looking at you?" Billy asked.

"Like you're going to pump a bullet in my head and dump me on the side of the road."

"You think I'd do that to you after all we've been through? Come on, man, get real. We're family, always will be."

"I still don't like the way you're looking at me."

"So I'll look out the window if it makes you feel better."

Gabe's cell phone was ringing, and he pulled it out to stare at Caller ID. "It's Elsie." Gabe took the call and listened for a few moments while scrunching up his face. Something changed in him, the lost expression turning into one of deepening rage. Ending the call, he tucked the phone away and addressed Travis. "Drive back to my place."

Gabe didn't give the orders when they were on a job. Billy gave the orders.

"What are you doing?" Billy asked.

"My neighbor has a security camera on her garage."

"So what?"

"She has a video of Nate's killers. I want to see it."

This was getting out of hand. Billy gave the orders and the crew followed them; for it to be any other way wouldn't work. Travis stared into the backseat in his mirror. Travis had been scamming casinos before Billy recruited him and understood how the thieving game worked better than the others. Travis knew that Gabe was skating on thin ice, and that if Gabe kept acting out of turn, his days of running with Billy's crew were over.

Billy dipped his chin. He also wanted to see this video. Hopefully, it contained a clear picture of Nate's killers and would let Billy be prepared in case they came calling.

Travis did a nifty U-turn and drove back to Gabe's subdivision.

- - -

Most in-home security cameras were pieces of junk that took grainy video that looked like it had been shot through a Coke bottle. These cameras did little more than provide their owners with a false sense of comfort and had never deterred a serious thief.

The device attached to the overhang of Elsie's garage had been made in the good old US of A and was anything but cheap. A high-end three-megapixel bullet camera with digital signal processing and a wide lens, it had built-in infrared illuminators that recorded in stunning clarity even in total darkness. Intended to protect Elsie's property, it also afforded an excellent picture of Gabe's residence across the street, which was how it came to record Nate's killers a few hours ago.

The security camera came with a software program that now resided on the hard drive of Elsie's MacBook Air. Holding fresh mugs of coffee that Elsie had presented to them as they'd entered her house, Billy and Gabe sat at the dining room table and stared at the laptop's screen. Gabe's front lawn was visible on the video, as was his driveway and house. Nothing appeared out of the ordinary.

"They'll be up in a second." Elsie hovered behind their chairs. "They're a couple of real bad hombres."

As if on cue, an American-made car came into the picture, moving slowly. The car's interior light was on, revealing two men occupying the front seats. The one riding shotgun shone a flashlight at Gabe's mailbox, reading the address.

The car braked and parked at the curb.

"That's them," Elsie said breathlessly. "The Bobbsey twins, all grown up."

The two men got out of the vehicle. They were the same height and weight, and both wore denim jackets and had ponytails. The driver walked with his shoulders hunched forward as if he'd spent his life with the wind at his back. His partner was younger and had the flashlight. Billy's eyes grew wide. It was the same pair of animals who'd trashed his condo earlier that night. The creepers. What were they doing at Gabe's place?

The creepers walked up the front path and stood on the front porch. The one with the flashlight pressed the bell. The door opened and Nate's shiny face appeared. The younger one said something that brought Nate's guard down. Nate let them in and shut the door.

The poor bastard never saw it coming, Billy thought.

"Does the video show them coming out of the house?" Billy asked.

"It most certainly does." Elsie reached between their chairs and tapped a quick command on the keyboard that sped the video forward fifteen minutes in time. "Here you go."

"Thank you."

The video resumed. Nate's killers came out of the house and walked down the path to their car. The younger one was drinking a bottle of beer, which he drained and dropped in the grass before climbing into the passenger seat. The older one was holding a doughnut, which he held in his mouth while unlocking the car and getting behind the wheel. The car started up and drove out of the frame.

Billy's mind raced. When the creepers hadn't found him at his condo, they'd gone to Gabe's place in the hopes that Gabe would tell them where he was. Only Gabe wasn't home, so they'd pummeled poor Nate. That explained their motives, but not much else. Like who the hell they were and why they were so bent on hunting him down.

Billy liked to think he'd done a good job of hiding his tracks. Neither his car nor his condo was registered in his own name, nor was his contract with his long-distance provider or the cable company. They were all registered under aliases.

He'd also kept his ties to his crew hidden. Each member got paid in cash after a job was done so there was no paper trail. And he and his crew rarely socialized outside of work and kept their personal lives separate from their professional ones.

Which left a lot of burning questions that he didn't have good answers to. Like how did these animals know where he lived or that Gabe was a member of his crew? And how did they know where Gabe lived? Billy didn't have a clue. But he sure needed to find out, because these guys had enough information to become permanent problems.

His mug was empty. He glanced over his shoulder at their hostess. "May I have a refill?"

"Certainly," Elsie replied. "Gabe, how about you?"

Gabe said nothing. The images on the screen had done a number on his head, and Gabe looked ready to jump out of the nearest window.

"He'd like some more," Billy said.

"Coming right up."

Elsie took their mugs and headed off to the kitchen. When she was gone, Billy gently jabbed Gabe in the ribs, breaking the jeweler out of his trance. "Go talk to your neighbor and tell her that the guys in the video are friends of yours," he said.

"What?"

"You heard me. Otherwise she's going to call the police and report them, and we don't want that."

"What should I say?"

"Tell her they're a couple of guys who worked for you when you owned the jewelry store, and that you told them to drop by whenever they happened to be in town."

"You want me to cover for those fucking guys?"

"Yes. I'm going to run them down."

"How the hell are you going to do that?"

"Stop questioning me, will you? Go talk to your neighbor."

"I want to know."

Billy started to steam. He had a temper, and sometimes it got the better of him and made him do things that he later regretted. He hoped that wasn't where things were headed with Gabe. "Do what I tell you, you stupid shit."

"Don't talk to me like that. I'm old enough to be your father."

"You think I don't know that?" He paused and silently counted to three. "Look, if your neighbor calls the cops, it will start an avalanche of shit that we won't be able to stop."

"You shouldn't have slapped me."

"Is that what's bothering you, that I slapped you?"

"Yeah."

"Get over it."

"I can't get over it. You wounded me, you little fuck."

Gabe's eyes had turned hard and Billy thought he understood. You could take anything away from a man except his pride. Robbed of his pride, a man often acted out and did stupid and irrational things. Billy had caused this problem, and only he could fix it.

"I was wrong. I'm sorry, man."

"You mean that?"

"Of course I mean it. I'm sorry, and that's the God's honest truth."

Gabe's face went soft and he returned from the dark place he'd gone to.

"Don't do it again, okay?"

"Do what?"

"Slap me. In the face."

Billy wasn't going to make a promise to Gabe that he wouldn't keep. He ran the show, and he would do whatever was necessary to keep his crew in line, even if it meant getting rough with them. "Go talk to your neighbor."

"You're not . . ."

He shook his head. "No," he added for emphasis.

Gabe started to protest but bit his tongue instead. Billy did not tolerate dissent when they were on a job, and Gabe knew it as well as anyone. But that didn't make things right between them, and Gabe headed off to the kitchen without uttering another word.

It was the first smart thing the jeweler had done all night.

TWENTY

Travis pulled the rental into the Dollar lot and parked in the drop-off area. While he went inside to settle the bill, Billy waited for the courtesy bus with Cory and Morris. The desert sand did not hold the heat, and an icy breeze knifed through his thin shirt.

"Where's Gabe?" Billy asked.

"He's inside using the john," Cory said. "What's the deal with him? He's acting weird."

"How so?" Billy asked, wanting to get Cory's take on Gabe.

"He keeps mumbling under his breath; can't make out what the hell he's saying," Cory said. "That guy we buried was a friend of his, huh?"

"They were tight." Billy stole a glance over his shoulder. The rental office was empty except for Travis at the counter haggling with the reservationist over the bill. You could never be too careful, so he lowered his voice. "I want you to keep an eye on Gabe. If he starts acting funny or makes a crack out of turn, you need to shut him down."

Cory and Morris traded concerned looks.

"Shut him down how?" Cory asked.

"Tell him to shut up. Do it nicely. If he keeps blabbering, grab a bottle and smack him over the head. Don't kill him, just knock him out."

Cory swallowed a lump in his throat, as did Morris. They were spooky that way. Like a pair of twins, they shared many mannerisms and weird tics. Billy stared into each of their faces.

"Did you just hear what I said?"

Cory and Morris both nodded.

"Remember, the sky palace we're staying in is bugged. If Gabe says something out of line and it gets picked up by a hidden mike, Carnivale's management will hear about it. If that happens, they might posse up on us."

"Posse up?" Cory said.

"It's a hustler's expression. What's worse than getting caught cheating? Do you know?"

"There's something worse than getting caught?" Cory said.

"You bet. Any idea what it is?"

Cory and Morris didn't know. They were still relatively new to the cheating game, and Billy had to remind himself there were plenty of things they were clueless about.

"Having a casino suspect you're a thief," Billy said.

"That's worse than getting caught?" Morris asked.

"Much worse. If a casino suspects you're a thief, they'll start spying on you until they figure out what you're doing. Everyone in the casino will watch you, from the bellboys to the cocktail waitresses to the blackjack dealers. Everything you do will be recorded and later scrutinized by the techs in surveillance. Hustlers call this a posse up. Trust me, you're better off getting caught cheating because all the casino has is one video, and those don't always stand up in court. But if the casino thinks you're dirty, they'll build a case until they have more than enough evidence to send you to prison."

Cory and Morris were starting to get the picture. If Gabe talked stupid inside the hotel and security caught it, they'd all go down, and they'd go down hard. Travis came outside holding the rental bill.

"How much did you get her down?" Billy asked.

"Twenty bucks. She agreed not to charge for the last hour."

"Nice going."

The worst jobs in Vegas took place between midnight and 8:00 a.m. They called it the graveyard shift because the people who worked it resembled the walking dead and were often bitter souls. It did not take a lot of work to get them to shave a few dollars off a bill.

"Go find Gabe. I think he's inside taking a leak. I'm getting worried about him."

Travis stiffened. "Something going on with him?"

"I'll tell you later. If he's on his cell phone, take it from him."

"You serious?"

"Yeah. I don't want him talking to anybody right now."

Travis didn't look thrilled with the assignment but kept his mouth shut and entered the car rental building. Travis made more than the others because the sleight-of-hand he performed inside the casinos had taken years to perfect and deserved greater compensation. As a result, he lived in a four-bedroom house in a brand new development in nearby Henderson and had two nice cars parked in the garage. Travis was living the good life and so was his family, and the big man wasn't about to screw it up.

The courtesy bus pulled up to the curb and the door opened with a mechanical hiss. A gruff driver told them to get in.

"Hold on a minute, my friend's still inside," Billy told the driver.

"Your friend can grab the next bus," the driver said.

"When will that be?"

"Half an hour."

"Can't you wait?"

"Nope."

Billy stepped up to the open door. "What if I say please?"

"Your charms are lost on me, brother," the driver said.

Everyone in Vegas had a price. The question was, how much money was it going to take to make this driver stay a few extra minutes? Billy glanced at the driver's run-down Nikes. You could tell a lot about a person's financial situation by their shoes. Billy had learned that on the mean streets of Providence. Just look at a guy's shoes, and you'll know if he's a player. Plucking a fifty from his wallet, he stepped up into the bus and tucked it into the driver's breast pocket.

"Be a friend. My buddy needs to catch a plane," he said.

"I could lose my job," the driver said.

Billy pulled out a twenty and added it to the fifty in the driver's shirt.

"That's not enough," the driver said.

Billy removed a ten from his wallet. Another trick from his Providence days. Pay a bribe in decreasing amounts. It sent out a psychological message that you were reaching the end of the road. He stuffed the ten into the driver's pocket.

"Are we good?"

"We're good," the driver said.

"Thanks, man, I really appreciate it."

Billy went inside the building. Cory and Morris were standing with Travis, who was banging on the restroom door. Billy told Travis to step aside, then put his mouth to the door. In a low voice he said, "Open the door or you're fired."

The door swung in. Gabe glared at him, cell phone in hand.

"Damn it, I'm talking to my kid," Gabe said.

Billy took the cell phone from Gabe's hand and stared at its face. Gabe's daughter's name and phone number were displayed in the upper corner on the screen. He raised the phone to his face, said, "Your father will call you later," and killed the connection.

"Why did you do that?" Gabe said angrily.

"I told you, no phone calls."

"She called me. We haven't spoken in days. Goddamn it, Billy . . ."

"No calls on a job. That's the rule, and you broke it. If you mouth off to me one more time, you're history. Understand? One more fucking time, and you can go back to engraving teenagers' initials into charm bracelets in a kiosk at the mall."

Tears formed at the corners of Gabe's eyes. Gabe was losing it, his emotions unraveling before Billy and the rest of the crew. He was becoming a liability and could drag them all down if they let him. There were ways to deal with this, and none of them were pretty. Billy entered the stall and yanked a piece of toilet paper off the roll, which he handed to him.

"Thanks," Gabe said, blowing his nose.

TWENTY-ONE

The rental bus idled at the curb as Billy and his crew came outside. It was a good thing the driver hadn't left, because if he had, Billy would have tracked him down and put a hurt on him, the mood he was in right now. They got in and the bus departed.

The driver drove them to ground level of the main terminal. They crossed at the pedestrian walkway and got in line for a cab to take them back to Carnivale. It was past one o'clock in the morning, but you would never have known it by the eager tourists standing in line, the money they'd brought to gamble burning a hole in their pockets.

Billy kept his eyes on Gabe. He'd always been afraid of a situation like this; if a member of his crew had a nervous breakdown while they were inside a casino doing a job, their cover would be blown, and they might end up going to jail. Cheaters got treated harshly by Nevada's penal system and were purposely exposed to hardships that other prisoners rarely saw. At the front of the line, Billy addressed the dispatcher.

"We're together. Can we get a van to take us to Carnivale?"

The dispatcher called for a van on his walkie-talkie. Ending the call, he said, "Van will be here in a minute. Where's your luggage?"

It was an honest question, and Billy knew that if he didn't give the dispatcher a feasible answer, the dispatcher would remember Billy and his crew. The key to cheating was not to be remembered by anyone you came in contact with. This included dispatchers on taxi lines.

"Airline lost our luggage," Billy said.

"Which one?"

"United."

"Figures. They lose a lot of luggage. Stand over here. Your van will be up shortly."

"Much appreciated."

Soon they were driving down the Strip in a van better suited for a bunch of preschool kids, with stiff seats and no interior lights. Billy sat in the back beside Gabe. Bursts of harsh neon from the casinos penetrated the tinted glass and did a grotesque number on Gabe's weary features. They came to a red traffic light and the van braked hard.

"Driver's taking us the long way," Gabe said under his breath.

"I know," Billy said.

"Are you going to call him on it?"

"No. Let him think we're tourists. I don't want him remembering us."

Gabe shot him a puzzled look.

"We just buried your friend," Billy whispered. "If somebody saw us and called the cops, they're going to come looking for us. That means we have to fly under the radar until we get back to Carnivale. Then we can go back to our job."

"Gotcha." Gabe paused to watch a long-legged hooker sashay past. Prostitution was illegal in Clark County, but you would never have known it by the amount of talent trolling the sidewalks. There had to be a big convention in town to draw this many working girls.

"Can I have my cell phone back?" Gabe asked.

Billy shook his head. Gabe dropped his chin and stared dejectedly at the floor.

"I'll give it to you later," Billy said.

"Sure you will," the jeweler said.

"You don't believe me?"

"No."

"Then what?"

"You're going to kill me. I'm a fucking liability, so you're going to get rid of me."

"Stop saying that."

"Then stop thinking it, because you are."

"We'll finish this conversation later."

The van dropped them off at Carnivale's main entrance a short time later. They made it upstairs to their penthouse digs without encountering their pesky VIP host or any fawning hotel staff willing to accommodate their every need. They were back in fantasy land, where nothing was real and everything was being paid for, provided Billy dropped a few million at the tables.

The bar in their suite was stocked with aged bourbons and whiskey and had a wine cooler filled with labels from the south of France. Billy popped the tops of three Stellas and fixed two stiff drinks. He left the beers on the bar for Travis, Cory, and Morris, who hadn't uttered a word since leaving the car rental return, and headed outside to the pool with the drinks in hand. Gabe stood at the railing with the wind blowing back his thinning hair.

"Here, it will make you feel better," Billy said.

Gabe sipped the drink and winced. "That's strong."

"Stronger the better." He knocked back his drink and Gabe did the same. Down below, the Strip pulsed and shook with a life all its own. "I'm not going to kill you. I'm not saying it didn't cross my mind, but I wouldn't do that to you. We'll get through this. Okay?"

"You're giving me a second chance?"

"Yeah. Just do what I tell you, and this will work out."

"You ever kill anybody you worked with? Be straight with me."

"No. But some guys in Providence I knew did."

"Why?"

"They were running a peek store in the rec room of a guy's house. The wall had neon beer signs as decorations, which work like one-way mirrors. There's a guy on the other side of the wall, looking through a Budweiser sign and reading the cards in the suckers' hands during poker games, which he texted to his partners at the table. The guy doing the reading tells his partners he wants a bigger cut. They balk, so this dope starts broadcasting what's going on. The dope wouldn't stop, so one night the others got him drunk and rolled him down Neutaconkanut Hill. The guy hit his head on a rock and died."

Gabe leaned against the railing, his face cast in stone. "What about those animals who killed Nate? Do we just forget about them?"

"We're going to pay those guys back. I'm going to run them down. Then I'm going to fuck them every which way but Sunday."

"You know who those bastards are?"

"Let's just say I know how to find them. The rest will be up to you."

"Me?"

"Yeah, you."

"What are you talking about, Billy?"

Billy slapped Gabe's shoulder. He'd given the situation serious thought during the taxi ride and had decided that he needed to get Gabe out of Carnivale. The fact that Gabe was distraught didn't mean Gabe wasn't valuable to him. Gabe had been born to hustle; he had larceny in his heart and knew how to manipulate the truth. Those were valuable commodities in the grifter's world, and Billy was not about to roll Gabe down a hill anytime soon.

"You're going to play Sherlock Holmes for me," Billy said.

"I am?"

"Yeah. Think you're up for it?"

Gabe was probably the smartest member of Billy's crew. He knew that Billy was going the extra mile for him, and a liquid smile spread across his face.

"I'll do whatever you want, Billy."

"Get some sleep, and I'll connect with you later."

"Done," the jeweler said.

TWENTY-TWO

Most contract killing in Vegas was handled by outsiders. The casinos had started this practice in the 1950s when the mob ran the town, and it continued to this day.

When someone needed to get whacked, a killer was hired from East LA or Mexico to do the dirty work. The killer usually used a gun and shot his victim in his driveway or a parking lot at night, then hit the highways in his car, never to be seen again.

Nate's killers were different. They were local and had lived in Vegas for a while. Three things had led Billy to this belief. The first was their American-made car. It was a junker, and it didn't appear capable of making the trek from LA or south of the border.

The second was the killers' willingness to visit Gabe's neighborhood after dark, with its unlit street signs and maze-like layout. Even with a GPS system, Gabe's place was hard to find. Billy knew this for a fact, as he'd gotten lost visiting Gabe several times.

The third reason was the perfectly round impression one of the killers had left on Nate's chin, no doubt the aftermath of a punch. Billy had seen that perfectly round impression before, and it was going to lead him to tracking down Nate's killers.

It was 2:00 a.m. when the cab pulled into the Casino Grand Bay. Billy entered and went straight to the house phones. The casino was packed with drunk conventioneers and dolled-up hookers who made their living servicing them. He picked up a phone and an operator came on.

"I need to speak to Harlan Ritz."

"May I tell him who's calling?" the operator asked.

"Billy Cunningham. I'm an old friend."

The operator put him on hold. Billy had scammed every casino in Vegas multiple times, except for the Grand Bay, which he'd scammed only once. The one time he'd taken the joint down, a strange thing had occurred. He'd had an attack of conscience.

Thieves weren't supposed to have attacks of conscience. When a bad thing happened on a job, a thief was expected to look the other way and go about his business.

Billy was different. Every so often, a sharp splinter in the chest made him help a stranger. It was a by-product of having attended a strict Catholic school, where the nuns had beaten into him the importance of helping others, even if it meant sticking his own neck out.

Like a few years ago at the Grand Bay. They'd been ripping off the craps game by Travis controlling one of the dice so it fell a certain way, every time. By betting the right combinations, Cory and Morris won 80 percent of the time. The play was blatantly obvious, but with Misty and Pepper using their ample charms to distract the dealers, it never failed to get the money.

As Travis got set to roll the dice, a guy wearing a two-thousand-dollar suit flew past the table holding a garbage bag. The door to the cashier's cage opened, and the guy went inside.

"Hold on," Billy whispered.

"Something wrong?" Travis asked.

"Not sure."

Inside the cage, the guy in the suit was tossing stacks of money into the bag. Casinos didn't let employees handle money this way, which meant the guy owned the joint. Billy wondered if there would be enough money left in the cage to pay them off. If not, the cage manager would issue an IOU, but no cheater in his right mind had ever accepted one of those.

"We're done," Billy said under his breath. "I'll catch up with you later."

Billy made a signal to kill the play. His crew would now purposely lose a few bets and return some of their winnings before leaving. It was the best way to take heat off the scam.

- - -

Billy's curiosity was killing him as he headed to the cage. Taking a handful of chips from his pocket, he pushed them through the bars and gave the pretty female cashier a wink. Behind her, the owner continued to throw money into the bag. He was built like a greyhound and had short black hair silvering at the temples.

"Mr. Ritz, can I help in some way?" the cage manager asked.

"Mind your own business," the owner snapped.

"Have you called the police?"

"No. Go back to work. I've got it under control."

The owner left the cage dragging the bag, his destination the elevator bank across the casino. Billy followed him. He wanted to know who he was dealing with, and he used his Droid to pull up an old news story on the Internet about Harlan Ritz. Ritz had gotten his start selling beer, built his distributorship into the largest in the southwest, sold it to a foreign conglomerate for a small fortune, and used the proceeds to build the Grand Bay.

And now Ritz was in a world of trouble. The kind of trouble that made him clean out the cage and not call the police. Life-altering trouble.

As Ritz reached the elevator bank, his cell phone rang.

"I'm here," Ritz answered. "Yes, I've got your money. No, I don't have the whole amount. There was only nine hundred thousand in the cage."

The caller said something to Ritz.

"I know where that is. I'll be there in one hour," Ritz said.

The caller tried to end the call.

"I want to talk to her. I don't care if that wasn't part of our deal. I'm not giving you the goddamn money if I can't talk to her." Ritz went silent and his eyes welled up. He suddenly snapped to attention. "Honey! It's Daddy. You hang tight. I love you, baby."

The caller came back on the line.

"I understand. No police. Just don't kill her," Ritz said.

The kidnapper ended the call. Ritz put the cell phone away before noticing Billy.

"You look like you can use some help," Billy said.

"Get lost," Ritz said.

Successful people were good at making money. Ritz knew how to run a casino, and that was probably all he knew how to do. Ritz's daughter was going to end up vulture food if Billy didn't step in. "You want to see your daughter again, don't you?"

Ritz swallowed hard. "Of course I want to see her again. Who are you?"

"I'm just a guy who cares. I can get her back, but you've got to listen to me."

Harlan Ritz's trust was not easily gained, and he spent a moment sizing Billy up. Billy didn't look like the Good Samaritan type, but when a person was drowning, he couldn't be too picky about who threw him a life preserver.

"You'd better not be screwing with me," Ritz said.

"I'm not screwing with you."

"What the hell. All right."

- - -

Ritz's penthouse office was a mess. Daily spreadsheets showing the takes from the various table games and one-armed bandits engulfed the desk. Every penny won in a casino appeared on a spreadsheet at day's end, the flow of money as closely watched as a bank teller's transactions. Those numbers were known to a close-knit group, including Ritz, his CFO, a head bookkeeper, and the managers of the day, evening, and graveyard shifts, whose salaries and bonuses were dictated by the profit the casino made during their shifts. Every casino's hierarchy was structured this way, the bond among those at the top as strong as family. Ritz wasn't going to be happy to learn that one of his inner circle was his daughter's kidnapper.

On the desk sat a framed photo of a little princess with dimples and golden blonde curls. The Gerber baby, all grown up.

"What's her name?" Billy asked.

"Carley," Ritz said.

"You raising her yourself?"

Ritz scowled at him.

"No wedding ring, no picture of your wife."

"You're very observant. My wife died a few years ago in a car accident."

"Sorry to hear that."

Ritz removed a painting from the wall to reveal a biometric wall safe. The safe sprung open after his fingertips touched the door's optical scanner, and he removed a handgun, which he checked to make sure it was loaded before strapping it on a leather holster.

"You going to a gunfight?" Billy asked.

"Stop making jokes."

"The kidnappers will be watching you when you drop the money. If they see you're packing, they might get scared and snuff your kid. Lose the gun."

"Why would they get scared? Isn't this what they do for a living?"

"No. They're amateurs."

"How the hell do you know that?"

"They called you at work. A smart kidnapper calls his victim while he's at home and corners him. It's how the game's played. Lose the gun."

"For the love of Christ. You're a criminal, aren't you?"

"Now that you mention it, I am."

"What were you doing in my casino, robbing me?"

"I didn't steal that much."

"I should shoot you right now, you know that? How much did you steal from me?"

"About ten grand."

"Jesus Christ. I need a miracle, and I get you instead."

"You could do worse. Now, lose the gun, or I'm out of here."

"What do you have against guns?"

"They draw the police, and I don't particularly like cops."

Ritz had a decision to make. He could make the drop with Billy or go it alone. He returned the gun and holster to the safe and picked up the garbage bag filled with money.

"I don't know why I'm listening to you," the casino owner said.

- - -

Ritz's ride was a sleek BMW 760Li sedan. The soundtrack from a Disney movie came out of the Bang & Olufsen speakers, leading Billy to assume that Ritz had been with Carley not that long ago. Billy wanted to ask Ritz how the abduction had happened, just to confirm his earlier suspicion that a trusted employee was the culprit, but decided not to go there just yet.

Billy drove east on Flamingo to Memorial Highway while Ritz stared out the window at the blur of passing headlights. At Ritz's instructions, he pulled into a strip shopping center and drove around back to a dumpster that was the designated drop. Parking a hundred feet away, he killed the engine.

"Why park so far away?" Ritz asked.

"Because they need to see you," Billy said.

"So they're watching us. Is my daughter with them?"

"She's somewhere else. Get out of the car and take your time walking to the dumpster. Do the drop and return to the car. No fast movements, and don't even think of taking out your cell phone. Once you're in the car, I'll drive you back to your casino."

"How do I know they're not going to kill her once they have the money?"

"If the people who kidnapped your daughter had planned to kill her, they would have done it after they abducted her and not let a bond form. They didn't do that. You'll get her back."

"How the fuck do you know all of this?"

"I hang with bad people. Now, get moving, before they get suspicious."

Beneath a gibbous moon, Ritz slow-walked to the dumpster, lifted the lid, and heaved the bag of money inside. Billy used the opportunity to have a look around. The land behind the strip center was arid and flat, and he guessed the lookout was perched on the top of a flat-roof garage a half mile away, watching with a pair of infrared binoculars while talking to his partner on a cell phone, the partner holed up in a motel with the blindfolded kid. Once they got their hands on the ransom, they'd count it, and when they were satisfied Ritz had held up his end of the bargain, they'd let the girl go. The kid would be traumatized, but Daddy had enough dough to hire a good shrink and get her straightened out.

Ritz returned to the car. He was sweating bullets and breathing hard.

"Good job." Billy eased the car out of the spot.

- - -

The call came fifty minutes later. The kidnappers had dumped Carley in a vacant lot next to the Ellis Island Casino on Koval Lane. Billy again did the driving.

Ritz found his daughter sitting on the ground, dirty and bleeding from the mouth.

"They hurt her," Ritz cried, cradling his child in his lap.

Billy glanced at the kid as he drove back to the Grand Bay. One of the kidnappers had popped her in the jaw, the blow leaving a perfectly round impression in the skin that resembled a man's ring. This treatment told Billy that the kidnappers had a score to settle with Ritz, and he was surprised that Ritz hadn't already figured this out.

"You know a good doctor who makes house calls?" Billy asked.

"What's wrong with the hospital?" Ritz asked.

"The doctors will want to know who beat her up. If you tell them the truth, the police will want to know why you dealt with the kidnappers yourself. Word will get out you were blackmailed, and that will make you look weak. You need to keep this quiet."

Ritz clutched his daughter to his chest. "I don't know of anyone. Do you?"

"The guy I use is named Ibarra. He runs an urgent care clinic on Flamingo and doesn't report his clients' injuries to the police."

"Is he any good?"

"I haven't heard of any of his patients dying."

"Call him."

Soon they were in Ritz's office watching Ibarra shine a pen light in Carley's eyes. Ibarra reeked of cigarettes and cheap booze, which he didn't try to hide. He gave Carley a sedative and the little girl drifted off to sleep on the couch. Ritz stuffed enough money into Ibarra's hand to buy his silence and walked him to the door. Billy remained by the couch and gazed down at the little girl. She looked like an angel, and he wondered what kind of animal would punch a defenseless kid in the face. Ritz edged up beside him.

"So what do I owe you?"

"You don't owe me a thing."

"I wasn't born last night. Name your price."

"How much is your daughter's life worth?"

"You trying to blackmail me?"

"Just asking a question."

"She's worth more than everything I own. I think it's time for you to go."

Billy went to the door with the intention of not looking back. But his conscience wouldn't let him. He needed to explain the deal to Ritz, otherwise the kidnappers would steal Carley again, only this time she'd end up buried in the desert with petrified wood for a headstone.

"The people who did this work for you. I thought you should know that," he said. "I figured it out when you were on the phone with them. You told them you could come up with only nine hundred thousand, which wasn't what they asked for. More like a million, right?"

Stunned, Ritz nodded.

"But they accepted the figure because they already knew how much money was in the cage. They asked for a million, hoping you might have mad money stashed in your office. When you told them you had only nine hundred, they didn't balk. They *knew*."

Ritz blinked, the gears shifting in his head. "It was Fister."

"He work for you?"

"Used to run the day shift. I caught him stealing and termed him."

"Sounds like he's the one. Don't be so nice to him this time around."

Ritz thought about what Billy was saying and nodded.

"I need to run. See you around," Billy said.

Ritz's attitude changed, and he walked Billy to the elevators in the hall. The elevator doors parted, and Billy got in and punched the button for the lobby.

"You still haven't told me what I owe you," Ritz said.

"Let me get back to you," Billy said.

- - -

The operator came back on the line, snapping Billy out of his daydream.

"Mr. Ritz said he'll send someone down for you."

Billy hung up. Moments later a security goon wearing an ill-fitting suit appeared. As they went up in the elevator, the goon appraised Billy as if taking his measurements.

"Something wrong?" Billy asked.

"Mr. Ritz said you're a cheat, and that I should remember what you look like."

"You used to work security at the Luxor."

"How did you know that?"

"We met about a year ago. My crew rang a cooler into a blackjack game and took the joint for thirty grand. You were working security, and I stood right next to you, talking football while my crew switched six decks on the dealer and cleaned you out. Remember me now?"

Next stop was Ritz's corner office. Ritz was packing a few extra pounds but didn't look much different. A chair and drink were offered. Billy was soon swirling cubes in a glass of bourbon. Ritz parked himself on the edge of his desk and raised his glass in a silent toast.

"How's your daughter doing?" Billy asked.

"Just turned twelve going on twenty-one," Ritz replied. "I put her in a private boarding school, just for the peace of mind. She seems to like it. So what can I do for you?"

"Do you have a photo of her?"

Ritz shot him a funny look before handing Billy a framed photograph off the desk. It showed Carley in a field hockey uniform and wearing braces. Billy was able to make out the faint outline of the scar that one of her kidnappers had put on her jaw for no good reason other than being subhuman. He handed the photo back.

"When I left your office three years ago, I assumed you were going to have the guys who kidnapped your kid whacked. Why didn't you?"

"What are you talking about?"

"The kidnappers are still around."

Ritz stared at the floor. Billy bore down on him. "A guy named Fister was behind your daughter's kidnapping. Fister had a partner. Why didn't you have those assholes whacked?"

"How I handled Fister and his brother is none of your business."

"Yes, it is. Those two bastards murdered a friend of a friend of mine. Punched him in the face and left the same impression on his chin that they left on your daughter's face." Billy paused. "You let them go, and I want to know why."

Ritz went to the picture window behind the desk and fixed his gaze on a distant point. Billy came up beside the casino boss. "You owe me, man. I saved your kid."

Ritz took a swallow of his drink before replying. "That night after we got Carley back, I got my gun out of the safe and grabbed my head of security and two guards I trusted. We drove to Fister's house and let ourselves in. Fister and his brother were inside counting the ransom money. We had them dead to rights.

"I asked Fister which one of them had punched Carley. Fister said that he and his brother had planned the kidnapping but had hired two pros to carry it out. They'd paid the pros fifty grand, which had come out of the ransom money. I made Fister give me their names."

Ritz stopped talking. A line of sweat had formed above his upper lip.

"Then you killed them," Billy said.

"Yeah. Shot them in the head and got rid of their bodies. Then I set my sights on the other two. Their names were Haney. A father and son who did jobs for the casinos."

"You mean killings?"

"That's right. They've been around a long time."

It was no secret that the casinos rubbed out cheaters who kept coming back and robbing them. Hollywood had shown the practice in movies and it had been written up in books, yet it still went on, the cheaters' bodies deposited in shallow graves on the outskirts of town.

"I wanted to pay the Haneys back, so I talked to another casino owner I know," Ritz said. "My friend told me the Haneys were off limits. Seems they're connected to a lot of bad stuff. If this bad stuff were to ever come out, the whole town would go up in flames. Those were my friend's exact words."

"So you left them alone."

Ritz nodded.

"Is that why you put your daughter in boarding school? Because they're still around?"

"It was part of the reason, yes."

Billy had heard enough. He was going to have to tread carefully with the Haneys, but that didn't mean he wasn't going to pay them back in spades for what they'd done to Nate.

"I've got to beat it. Thanks for the drink."

The security goon was in the hallway as Billy left Ritz's office. The goon rode with Billy to the lobby and marched him through the bustling casino, as if believing Billy's skills might cause a few errant chips to fly off the tables and land in the young hustler's pockets.

"I'm going to remember you," the goon said.

"Sure you are," Billy said.

TWENTY-THREE

It was three thirty in the morning when Billy entered the sky palace at the Carnivale to find Cory and Morris in the living room playing gin rummy and Travis parked in front of the flat-screen TV, watching a soccer match from another part of the world. He assumed Gabe and the girls were in bed, getting their beauty rest. He clicked his fingers and pointed at the slider. He needed to talk to Travis, Cory, and Morris away from the prying ears of the hidden mikes planted in the walls, and the three men rose from their chairs and followed him outside to the pool area.

"How's Gabe been acting?" Billy asked.

"He calmed down, hit the sack about an hour ago," Travis said.

"You still have his cell phone?"

Travis produced Gabe's cell phone from his back pocket.

"What about the phone in his room?" Billy asked.

"I took it out," Travis said. "Gabe fixed himself a stiff drink and said he wanted to be alone. I went in and talked with him for a while. He's back to normal."

"You sure about that?"

Travis hesitated, hearing the challenge in Billy's voice. "Positive, Billy. Gabe's his old self again. I wouldn't have left him alone if he wasn't."

"I told you to watch him. Next time, do as I fucking tell you. That goes for all of you. When I say something, I want you to follow it to the letter. Am I making myself clear?"

Billy didn't chew out his crew very often. When he did, he didn't mince words. Travis swallowed hard and mumbled, "Yeah," under his breath. Cory and Morris simply nodded.

Going inside, Billy walked down the twisting hallway to Gabe's bedroom. The suite was a maze, and he came to the room he thought was Gabe's and rapped lightly on the door.

"Come on in, we're all friends here," a female voice said.

He twisted the knob and stuck his head in. "Hi. I was looking for Gabe."

"You can come in anyway," Misty said.

Misty and Pepper sat on the king bed in their birthday suits, practicing the backgammon scam they planned to pull on Tommy Wang tomorrow. Most scams were designed to part suckers from their money. This scam did the opposite and would make Wang think he had the Midas touch. Selling the play to Wang wouldn't be easy, but Misty and Pepper had rehearsed the scam enough times in Lake Tahoe that Billy felt confident they could pull it off.

Billy let out a wolf whistle. Misty and Pepper had stopped doing porn years ago but hadn't stopped getting naked whenever it suited them, their bodies tan and desirable.

"Want to jump in the sack, big boy?" Pepper said teasingly.

Any other time he would have said yes. They'd had threesomes before and the memories were still fresh. He pointed at the bathroom door, and they followed him into the tiled room where he shut the door and spun on the faucets before speaking again.

"You ready for tomorrow?" he asked.

"As ready as I'm ever going to be," Misty said.

"Me, too," Pepper said. "Gabe dropped by a little while ago and watched us play. He said we had the mechanics down pat."

Billy raised his eyebrows in alarm. If Gabe had slipped up and spoken out of turn, the hidden mikes in the wall would have picked it up. "Did he actually say that?" he asked.

"In so many words," Misty said, sensing his alarm. "He didn't give us up."

"You sure?"

Misty and Pepper both nodded.

"Glad to hear it. How's Gabe behaving?"

"He lost his best friend tonight and is taking it hard," Misty said.

"You think he's depressed?"

"Yeah. Wouldn't you be?"

"I'm pulling him off the job. Gabe isn't acting right. If he makes a crack out of turn and the mikes pick it up, we're finished. Besides, I've got another job for him to do. Remember the guy on TV with my name who got murdered? Those killers were actually looking for me. They went to Gabe's house earlier tonight and beat Gabe's friend to death. I'm going to have Gabe track them down. It will give him something to do, keep his mind off things."

"Who's trying to kill you? One of the casinos?" Pepper asked.

Her question gave Billy pause. He had stolen millions but had purposely spread out the stealing so no one casino felt too much pain. He couldn't think of a single casino that had lost so much money that they'd go to the trouble of hiring a pair of hit men to take him out.

"I don't know who's behind it," he said. "I'm hoping Gabe can figure it out. Gabe has an old friend in the police department who can help."

Billy spun off the faucets. Back in the bedroom, he said good night.

"Come back if you feel lonely," Pepper said.

- - -

Billy found Gabe lying fully dressed on the bed, popping pieces of caramel popcorn into his mouth while watching college baseball on the flat-screen TV. Gabe was addicted to college sports the way most men were addicted to pussy; the more he got, the more he wanted.

"Hey, boss," Gabe said.

Billy pulled up a chair. He picked up the remote from the bed and jacked up the TV's volume. Gabe sat up and threw his legs over the bed. Billy motioned him closer. Gabe leaned in, and Billy brought his lips next to Gabe's ear. "I made Nate's killers. They're a father and son duo named Haney. I want you to use your source in the police department to track them down."

Gabe brought his mouth next to Billy's ear. "You want me to call Bennie?"

"Yeah. You guys still tight?"

"Tighter than a gnat's ass."

Back when Gabe owned a jewelry store, he'd employed an off-duty black cop named Benjamin Wright to dissuade thieves from robbing the place. Bennie now worked undercover with the Metro LVPD and was wired into the police department's inner workings and its secrets.

"Call him and get a line on the Haneys before they try to take me out again," Billy whispered.

"What am I going to say?" Gabe whispered back. "I can't just come out and ask him who they are. He'll get suspicious."

"Make up a story. Rehearse it before you call him."

"All right. When do you want me to leave?"

"Now."

"You really want me gone, don't you?"

"You're not doing me any good here."

Gabe packed his things and together they took an elevator downstairs. The casino was still jumping but the rest of the place was a tomb, and they walked to the front entrance without encountering another soul. Outside by the taxi stand a yellow cab idled at the curb. The driver hopped out and put Gabe's suitcase in the trunk.

"Airport?" the driver asked.

"Yeah. Delta terminal," Billy said.

The driver loaded Gabe's suitcase and got back behind the wheel. It was a necessary precaution for Gabe to cab it to the airport, and from there, for him to take another cab to his house. Billy and his crew were pretending to be out-of-towners, and that charade needed to be continued, even with people who didn't directly work for the casino.

Billy started to go back inside. Gabe touched the young hustler's sleeve.

"I'm not getting something," Gabe said. "How did the Haneys know where I lived? I'm the one member of the crew who nobody ever sees. How did those fucking guys find me?"

The words hit Billy in the head like a lead pipe. Gabe was the invisible member of the crew and had been used only a handful of times in actual scams, usually when they were shorthanded. Gabe should have been the least vulnerable member of Billy's crew, and not susceptible to contract killers paying him a surprise visit late at night.

Billy thought back to the surveillance tape Gabe's neighbor had shot of the Haneys as they'd pulled up to Gabe's house. The son had been holding a piece of paper with an address. Whoever had hired the Haneys had given them Gabe's address.

Right then, Billy realized he knew who the Haneys' employer was. The cab's meter was running, and he said, "Driver's running up the fare. Go home. I'll call you tomorrow."

"Am I safe in my house?" Gabe asked.

"Yeah, you're safe. Remember, it's me they're after."

"I think I'll sleep with a gun under my pillow, just in case."

"You do that."

Gabe got in and the passenger window came down. "This is a cop, isn't it, Billy?"

Of course it was a cop. Only a cop would have the resources to connect Gabe to Billy, and then to gain access to Gabe's home address. Billy had pissed off plenty of law enforcement during his time in Vegas, but none so badly that they wanted him dead. Except for one guy. This guy had a history with Billy that had turned personal, and that was never a good thing.

"Yeah, it's a cop," Billy said.

"What are you going to do?" Gabe asked.

"To be forewarned is to be forearmed."

"You're going to pay him back."

Not a question but a statement of fact.

"I'll think of something. Now, go home and get some sleep," Billy said.

"Will do, boss."

- - -

The taxi peeled away. As Billy headed back inside, he spied Maggie Flynn and Jimmy Slyde coming toward him. Mags was dressed in a low-cut blue dress and looked good enough to eat. The gaming board had put Mags on their Most Wanted List and distributed her photo to the casinos, but that hadn't stopped her from coming back and ripping off suckers. Some people were born to steal, and Mags was one of them.

He ducked behind a concrete pillar that was part of the hotel's facade. Mags stood at the curb while Slyde hailed a cab. She was so close that Billy could smell her perfume. The last time he'd seen her, they'd been sharing a bed in a funky hotel in Venice while plotting their future together. It had seemed like a fairy tale, until Mags had told him that she wanted to join his crew so they could take down casinos together.

Billy had gotten scared. Mags was risking her freedom every time she set foot inside a casino. She didn't seem to care, but Billy cared, not just for his own safety but also his crew's. His crew was the closest thing to a family he'd ever had, and he wasn't going to let the love of a woman put them in jeopardy. So he'd split without saying good-bye.

A cab pulled up. Slyde opened the back door and Mags got in. Her dress went up her leg, exposing her thigh. The breath caught in Billy's throat.

He stepped out from his hiding place and watched the cab fade into the night. There was a name for what he was feeling. Euphoric recall. Remembering the amazing stuff while forgetting the bad. Putting a label on it didn't change how he felt. Mags had stolen his heart, and if the opportunity ever presented itself to win her back, he'd grab it. He didn't know if the outcome would be any different, but it was certainly worth a try.

TWENTY-FOUR

-FRIDAY, ONE DAY EARLIER-

If there was any part of a man's body that gave him away, it was his mouth.

A man couldn't control his mouth, at least not all the time. Get a man upset or nervous, and the corners of his mouth would turn down, while the tip of his tongue licked his lips like a dog anticipating a piece of steak. When a man's mouth behaved this way, it was called a tell.

Pavlov, ring that bell.

This wasn't the only part of a man's anatomy that betrayed him. Flaring nostrils or a bobbing Adam's apple were also tells, and so was accelerated breathing. Every poker player worth his salt knew how to read these tells. It was part of the game.

Mags had learned how to read tells while playing poker in the back room of Lou Profaci's factory on Providence's south side. Lou manufactured Rolex knock-offs and counterfeit "brand-name" clothes that fell apart the first time they were laundered. To move product, Lou employed a team of hustlers who were given a defined territory. Mags had been part of that team.

On rainy days, the team played cards in the factory's back room. Everyone in the game was a hustler, yet no cheating was allowed, as Lou did not tolerate his people stealing from one another. It was in these games that Mags had learned the art of reading tells. She was the only female in the game and her pretty face was a weapon. If she really wanted to get an opponent's defenses down, she'd unbutton the top of her blouse and flash some hardware.

When Mags had first come to Vegas, she'd tried to read her opponents and discovered that Vegas poker players knew about tells, and they wore ball caps and shades to hide their faces. Reading tells in Vegas didn't work, so Mags had stopped doing it.

That had changed with the arrival of Jimmy Slyde. Slyde's little magic pills had taken her ability to read tells to another level. While under their influence, nothing escaped her.

If that wasn't enough of an edge, the pills expanded her memory and allowed Mags to remember how her opponents played every single hand during the course of a game. She'd always enjoyed ripping off suckers, but this was an all-new high, the adrenaline coursing through her veins so fiercely that beads of sweat broke out on her forehead and her hands got clammy.

And like any great high, all she could think about was doing it again.

- - -

Mags was taking another sucker to the cleaners when her cell phone buzzed. Her purse was slung over the back of her chair and the vibration carried through the frame. She stole a glance at the gold Piaget strapped to her wrist. Eight in the morning. No one ever called this early.

"You got a plane to catch?" a voice asked.

It was the mark. A banker named Dolan with a penchant for challenging the town's best poker players in games of heads up. Dolan liked to play early in the morning when most poker players were asleep, as it gave him an edge. Dolan also wore a secret device strapped to his leg that vibrated every ten seconds. This let Dolan time his opponents' bets, which was another surefire way of reading tells. These tricks had allowed Dolan to beat some of the town's sharpest players, but they hadn't worked on Mags. She'd already taken thirty grand from him and expected to have the rest of his bankroll in short order.

"Who said anything about catching a plane?" she said.

"You looked at your watch. You weren't planning on leaving, were you?"

"A fun party like this? Not on your life."

"Good, because I'm planning on winning my money back," Dolan said.

"Is that so," Mags said.

"That's right, little lady. You can't win every hand. It's not mathematically possible."

Dolan was already starting to make excuses, a sure sign of a sore loser. In the beginning he'd been charming, but that had worn off once Mags had started beating him.

"What if I *was* going to leave?" Mags asked.

"You can't. We've got rules around here."

"What rules are those?"

"The rule that says you have to give me a chance to win my money back."

"Never heard of it."

"Don't get cute with me. It's part of the game."

Mags rose and grabbed her purse. She had no intention of leaving but wanted to rattle Dolan's cage. "Nice playing with you."

Dolan spun around in his chair. "Tell her to sit down."

Slyde stood at the bar sipping a Bloody Mary while looking resplendent in an Ermenegildo Zegna silk suit with a cashmere vest. They were playing in the soon-to-be-demolished Riviera in a suite with cheap furnishings and threadbare carpeting.

Slyde shrugged as if to say, *What do you want, man?*

"That's bad action," Dolan said. "If she leaves, I'll tell the concierge."

Slyde twirled the celery in his drink. The Riviera's concierge was taking a cut off the game and Slyde didn't want Dolan talking bad to him about Mags.

"Mags, why don't you give this gentleman a chance to win his money back?"

"Why should I?" Mags said.

"Because it's the sporting thing to do," Slyde said.

Men were all the same; gracious when they won, assholes when they didn't. Dolan was cheating yet had the nerve to cry foul. Mags decided to go straight for the jugular.

"Double the stakes, and I'll stay," she said.

"You serious?" Dolan said.

"I'm always serious about money."

"You're on." To the hired dealer, Dolan said, "Shuffle up and deal."

Mags returned to her seat and assumed the position. Elbows on the table, chin resting on her hands, eyes locked on her opponent's face. Dolan's breathing became accelerated when he was dealt a strong hand, and it was enough of a tell to beat the banker out of every cent he had. She told herself her mystery caller could wait.

- - -

Forty-five minutes later, she had all of Dolan's bankroll. As she raked in the final pot, the banker leaned over the table and forcefully grabbed her wrist.

"You cheated me."

"Get your hands off of me, or I'll call hotel security," Mags said.

Dolan released her. "I'm going to search you, find out how you won."

"You'd like putting your grubby hands on me, wouldn't you?"

"You're wearing something."

"You really think I cheated you?"

"Damn straight. Nobody's that good."

"I'll tell you how I won. You broke your nose once, didn't you?"

Dolan was stunned. "Playing football. How'd you know?"

"You have a deviated septum. Every time you have strong cards, you shut your mouth and breathe through your nose. It sounds like a train whistle. That's how I knew."

Dolan's cheeks turned bright red. Mags couldn't help it and started laughing. It was out of line to laugh at someone you'd just taken to the cleaners, but she couldn't control herself when she was flying high on Jimmy's magic pills.

Dolan slapped her across the face.

"Fuck you," the banker said.

Dolan's entourage sat on a couch getting wasted on champagne and blow. Two friends from back home and a pair of black call girls. Their heads collectively snapped.

Mags had grown up with five brothers and could hold her own in a fight. Her fist caught the tip of Dolan's chin and the banker's eyes rolled up into his head like hurricane shutters. His head bounced on the table during his journey to the floor. His entourage surrounded him, the hookers trying to wake him up. The last thing the hookers wanted was to get caught in a suite with a corpse.

Dolan's eyelids fluttered. Mags rubbed the spot where he'd slapped her.

"Asshole," she said.

Slyde had seen enough. He grabbed the money off the table, threw the dealer a tip, and hustled Mags out of the suite to an elevator.

"Goddamn it. Didn't I tell you never hit a sucker?" Slyde said.

"He slapped me," Mags said.

"I don't care if he squeezed your titties. You can't touch 'im."

"Well, I did. Fuck it. I need some coffee. I'm crashing."

Coming down off Slyde's little white pills was becoming harder, and they retreated to a dumpy coffee shop off the hotel lobby where Mags drank a carafe of coffee before she began to feel normal again. Slyde had lost his patience and lectured her.

"You can't keep this bullshit up. If Dolan tells the concierge how badly you trimmed him, the concierge will stop setting up games for us. Worse, he'll tell the other concierges in town, and they'll stop calling us, too."

"What did I do? Besides beat his sorry ass?"

"You gave him bad action. That's the kiss of death in this town. The casinos grind the suckers down and take their money real slow. The suckers go along with it because they think they have a chance. That's the illusion that everybody sells. Even guys like me."

"So what should I do? Let the suckers win a few hands? Stretch it out?"

"That will work. Think you're up to it?"

"Sure. But you're going to have to give me extra pills to take. They're not lasting as long. I don't want to lose my edge during a game."

"I've got plenty of pills. But you've got to promise, no more bad action."

"You've got my word."

They got up to leave. Mags made a detour to the lady's room and splashed cold water on her face at the sink. The pills were messing up her head, but she wasn't about to stop taking them. The allure of winning tens of thousands of dollars, night after night, was far too great. Her cell phone beeped in her purse. She'd forgotten about her mystery caller and retrieved a lone voice message. The sound of Billy Cunningham's voice cut her like a knife.

"I need to talk to you. Call me," Billy said.

Mags leaned against the hand dryer and swallowed hard. No "I'm sorry about Venice" or "Hey, Mags, I should have called." Had Billy forgotten that he'd dumped her like a sack of garbage after promising her a job running with his crew? Mags hadn't forgotten, and she'd been waiting for the opportunity to return the favor. She pulled up his number and called him back.

"Hello, stranger."

"How you been?" Billy asked, as if nothing had happened.

"I'm doing great. What's up?"

"Sorry to bother you, but I need your help. Can I buy you breakfast?"

"Sounds urgent."

"It is."

Billy was in trouble; Mags could hear it in the timbre of his voice. And in his desperate state he'd decided that dear old Mags could fix his problem. And maybe Mags could fix it, or maybe she could make Billy's situation get a whole lot worse.

"I'm game," she said.

"Great."

Billy gave her the address of a local breakfast spot and said he'd meet her there in an hour. Mags said okay and hung up. She left the restroom to find Slyde waiting for her.

"What were you doing, taking a shower?" he asked.

"I didn't know we were in a rush," Mags said.

"We are now. We got trouble."

Slyde jerked his thumb over his shoulder. Standing by the elevators was a three-man EMR team pushing a gurney. One of the medics held a flesh-colored cervical collar. The elevator doors parted and the team pushed the gurney into the car.

"What are they doing here?" Mags asked.

"I overheard them talking. They're here for Dolan," Slyde said.

"What's wrong with him?"

"You hurt the guy."

"Guess I don't know my own strength. What's that thing that guy's holding?"

"It's a horse collar. You broke Dolan's neck."

"Is that bad?"

"Yeah, it's real bad."

"Fuck him. Let's blow this dump."

TWENTY-FIVE

The best breakfast spot in town was at the Egg & I on West Sahara. Mags got there early and talked the hostess into seating her at a secluded booth behind the mural that took up most of the wall. She ordered the signature banana nut muffin and a pot of coffee.

She was blowing the steam off her third cup when a yellow cab pulled up to the front door and Billy hopped out. She'd been screwed over by plenty of guys, but none as royally as Billy. She'd stuck her neck out and saved Billy from getting arrested during a heist, and Billy had repaid her by taking her to a swanky hotel and fucking her brains out while promising Mags she could join his crew, and the two of them would cheat Vegas's casinos together.

It hadn't quite worked out that way. When she'd woken up the next morning, Billy was gone, in his place some money laying on the pillow. She'd never felt more betrayed in her life.

So she'd come back to Vegas holding a grudge. She was going to pay the little fucker back for the whore's treatment and for breaking his promise to her.

Billy spotted her and came over to the booth. He sported a neat goatee with his hair parted on the opposite side and was dressed like a young executive. Working a scam in one of the casinos and using a false identity, she guessed. He slid into the booth and flashed a smile. Men were stupid that way. They thought time healed all wounds. It didn't.

"Thanks for coming," he said.

"Anything for you," she said.

"You still mad about what happened in Venice?"

"I got over it. I like the goatee. It makes you look older."

"Can I steal some of your coffee? I'm running on fumes."

"Help yourself."

He took a clean mug from the next table and poured a cup. He looked exhausted and more than a little worried, and she guessed there was a good reason that he'd called her. But he wouldn't get to it right away. First he'd talk bullshit and prime the pump. The smart ones always did.

"I hear you're running with Jimmy Slyde these days," he said.

"Good news travels fast," she said.

"You need to be careful with that guy. He's a user."

"Slyde uses me, I use him, and in the end we both get what we want. Isn't that how most business relationships work?"

"Slyde's different. He'll chew you up and spit you out. He'll hurt you bad."

Mags almost said, *"Worse than you?"* but she bit her tongue instead. A long moment passed between them. It was Billy who started the conversation going again.

"How's your daughter doing? Her name's Amber, right?"

Mags blew the steam off her mug. "That's right. She's doing okay, I guess."

"She ever graduate from college?"

"Last month, top of her class. Believe it or not, she wants to be a cop, maybe try to get into the FBI academy one day. Wouldn't that be a hoot."

"You make it back home for her graduation? You told me you were going to."

Her mug hit the table hard and she gave Billy a look that would have sent most men to their graves. Mags had flown back to Providence on a red eye, gone to her daughter's graduation, and left that night. Too many painful memories to stay any longer.

"Why do you care?" she asked.

"Because I know how much she means to you. When we were in Venice you told me the gaming board tracked you down by tapping your daughter's phone. They knew you were going to call her. That says a lot."

Mags had done a hard landing from the drugs she used to beat Dolan that morning. So hard that she was having a tough time keeping her eyes open and staying focused. She drank more coffee before replying. "To answer your question, I went back to see her graduate and took her out to lunch. I've never been more proud of anything in my entire life."

"You did right by her."

"I sure did."

Billy reached across the table and took her hands as if they were made of glass and would break if he dropped them. "Do you know why I dumped you in Venice? Because I was afraid we'd get caught scamming a casino, and my crew would get busted and go down, and I wasn't going to let that happen. My crew means as much to me as Amber means to you, and I won't let anything harm them. Does that make sense?"

"I guess."

He pulled his hands away. "You had any contact with Grimes since you came back?"

During a period of her life that Mags would have rather forgotten, she'd worked as a snitch for the gaming board and had been under the thumb of Special Agent Frank Grimes, who she'd also had an affair with. Both relationships had ended in less than spectacular fashion.

"Haven't gotten around to calling him. Why?" she asked.

"Grimes hired a pair of guys named Haney to whack me. They went to a friend of mine's house last night and murdered someone staying there."

"Jesus. How do you know Grimes was behind it?"

"Has to be. The Haneys went to my apartment at Turnberry Towers, which isn't in my name, yet somehow they knew I lived there. They also knew where a member of my crew lived. Grimes is the only person with that information, and he has a motive."

"Payback time."

"Exactly. Normally, I'd leave town and let the dust settle. But I'm working a scam and I'm not going to walk away from it."

"Must be a big score."

"Biggest of my life."

"What's the play?"

"I've got a whale playing anchor for me at Carnivale. The whale is built in with the casino, so they won't get suspicious when he takes them down."

Using an anchor to rip off a casino was one of the cleverest scams around. The anchor was usually a rich sucker who regularly lost big bucks at a casino and was not considered a threat by casino management. The cheaters would convince the sucker to play a particular game in the casino that happened to be rigged. The sucker would play the rigged game and take down the casino for an enormous score. Because the sucker had a history of losing, the casino wouldn't make a fuss, believing they would make the money back down the road. The term *anchor* came from the fact that the play was rock solid and always got the money.

Billy was about to make a gigantic score, and Mags wasn't going to be there by his side. She felt a tinge of sadness and glanced out the window into the parking lot.

"Stop being angry at me," he said.

"Who said I was angry at you?"

"It's written all over your face. I shouldn't have run out on you without explaining the deal. It was a shitty thing to do, and I'm sorry. Once this job is done, I'll make it up to you."

She fixed her gaze on him. "Did you have to leave money on the pillow like I was a whore?"

"I wasn't going to leave you stranded." He paused. "It was all the money I had."

"You gave me *all* your money?"

"I kept two hundred bucks for myself, and that's the God's honest truth. I'll make it up to you. We'll go to Acapulco and I'll show you the best time you've ever had."

His eyes said he was telling the truth. But his eyes had also said he was telling the truth when he'd taken her to Venice, and look how that had turned out. Men made promises that they never intended to keep. It was part of their genetic makeup to screw over the opposite sex.

But Mags wasn't going to tell him that she didn't trust him anymore.

"All right, you win," she said. "When this is over, you get to whisk me off my feet and treat me like a princess. Now, what do you want me to do?"

"I want you to call Grimes and tell him you heard a rumor that he put a contract out on my life. Tell Grimes everyone in town knows about it. That should make him call off the Haneys."

"When do you want this done?"

"As soon as you can. I don't want the Haneys ruining things."

"I'll call him when we're done."

"You're the best."

"I bet you say that to all the girls."

"Just you." He took her hand and brought it up to his face so he could kiss it. "Call me after you talk to Grimes, okay?"

"You bet."

"And promise me you'll be careful with Jimmy Slyde."

"Don't worry about Slyde. I've got him covered."

Billy slipped out of the booth and came up beside her chair. Gave her a smooch on the lips that made her go flush before he walked out of the restaurant. In the parking lot, he summoned a cab on his cell phone that soon appeared and whisked him away.

She gazed out the window long after he was gone. The things he'd said sounded genuine, and she had to remind herself that Billy was a cheat, and that the only people he was true to were his crew. No one else counted. And since she wasn't a member of his crew, the promises and apologies and hand-holding and expressions of concern were nothing but air.

She took out her cell phone and hit the photo gallery icon. A graduation photo of Amber appeared and Mags found herself getting choked up. She'd never hidden that she had a daughter from the hustlers she worked with, yet Billy was the only one who'd asked after her. Billy cared about Amber, and he still cared about Amber's mother.

She pulled up Frank Grimes's number and started to call him. But her finger wouldn't push the icon to make the call go through. Grimes had abused her and she still had nightmares about it. Just thinking about him turned Mags's stomach upside down.

She drank more coffee and tried to clear away the cobwebs. She wanted to do right by Billy but could not bring herself to reconnect with Grimes.

She had an idea. She'd send Billy a text message, telling him that she'd connected with Grimes, but that Grimes had refused to call off his dogs.

She typed up the message. Her eyes fell on the very last words she'd written. *I love you.* She was setting herself up again to be hurt, and she quickly erased them.

Be careful, she wrote instead.

TWENTY-SIX

A line of tour buses painted in blinding Day-Glo choked the entrance to Carnivale's casino. These were not ordinary tourists, but blue-haired geezers whose idea of a swell afternoon was to piss away their Social Security checks playing the nickel slots.

Billy sat in the back of the cab trying to pull himself together. Seeing Mags had been rough, and he'd yet to calm down. Mags was a walking time bomb and would eventually blow herself up, yet his feelings still ran deep for her, and he guessed they always would.

He didn't like that Mags was running with Jimmy Slyde. Slyde had hurt a lot of people, including many women. Slyde's reputation was of someone who couldn't be trusted. When the scam at Carnivale was finished, he planned to look Slyde up and have a chat with him. If Slyde knew that Billy had a thing for Mags, he would be less inclined to screw with her.

The old folks tottered into the casino on canes and walkers. Casinos didn't care who they ripped off, and that included the elderly. Every day, thousands of geezers played the slots while eating box lunches supplied by the casinos. That would have been okay if the games were fair, only they weren't fair. Slot machines were legalized stealing, the odds of hitting a jackpot worse than being struck by lightning. The old folks didn't have a prayer, and by midafternoon they'd be back on the buses without a dime to show for their efforts.

This was going nowhere. Billy tossed the driver some bills and hopped out.

He hiked up the entrance breathing the buses' dirty exhaust. Near the front doors, his cell phone vibrated. Mags had texted him. Grimes won't call off the Haneys. I tried. Be careful.

He put the phone away. He'd doubted whether things would ever be right between them again, and he decided there was still hope. Maybe he'd surprise her and take her to Hawaii instead of Acapulco.

He went inside and stuck his head into the casino. A sea of blue hair sat at banks of slot machines, grinding away. Elderly day care, courtesy of your friendly neighborhood casino.

An elevator took him to the sky palace where he found Pepper and Misty in the living room, preparing for their breakfast with Tommy Wang. Both wore sundresses that accentuated their tan bodies, their makeup so expertly applied it turned them into movie stars. He reminded himself that the sky palace was bugged, and that he needed to watch his tongue.

"Morning, ladies."

"Morning, Billy," they both said.

Misty was giving the miniature TV camera and battery pack concealed inside her purse a final check. The battery pack was flashing green, indicating it was fully charged.

"All set?"

"We sure are," Pepper said.

At the minibar, he poured three glasses of mineral water, two of which he presented to them. They clinked glasses in a toast.

"Here's to pleasure themes and get-rich schemes," he said.

"I'll drink to that. How's Gabe doing?" Misty asked.

"Gabe's fine. I sent him home last night."

"You didn't fire him, did you?"

"Whatever gave you that idea?"

Pepper and Misty traded looks. One of the others had said something. It was a bad way to start a job, and he said, "Whatever happened with Gabe is behind us. Understood?"

"We were just worried, that's all," Misty said.

"Gabe is like family," Pepper chimed in.

"Stop worrying. Gabe is gold," Billy said.

They looked relieved. Although Billy ran the crew, Gabe was still the old man, and the others looked up to him. When their glasses were empty, Billy walked them to the door. Through the fabric of Pepper's sundress, he spied a skin-colored patch taped to the small of her back. It looked like a bandage, but in fact was a receiver antenna that would transmit the signals sent out by the camera hidden in Misty's purse. The camera was able to transmit signals for up to a mile, but that was in an open field. The casino's walls were thick and would severely limit the camera's range. The antenna taped to Pepper's back guaranteed a clear picture.

"Wish us luck," Pepper said.

"Good luck." He dropped his voice. "Remember, I'll be watching."

- - -

Billy went to his bedroom and retrieved his laptop. Then he escaped to the balcony deck and sat on a lounge chair by the pool. Las Vegas had perfect weather most of the year, the achingly blue sky so sharp it was hard to look at without shades.

He powered up the laptop and typed in a command. He looked no different than anyone else hanging by a pool, the only difference being, he was about to mastermind the biggest rip-off the town had seen in decades.

The feed from Misty's camera filled the laptop's screen. Misty and Pepper were inside Tommy Wang's sky palace, chatting with their host.

Misty had put her purse on a coffee table, allowing Billy to watch everything that took place. The camera was a precaution that Billy felt was necessary. If Wang sensed he was being conned, he might call security. Or, he might get angry and physically hurt Pepper and Misty. If either of those things happened, Billy would have a chance to react and save them.

On the screen, Wang popped a bottle of bubbly and served his guests. There were fresh-cut flowers on every table and a spread of food befitting a king. Beautiful women were considered good luck in Asia, and Wang was pulling out all the stops to impress.

Pepper and Misty ate it up. Not that long ago, they'd been living in a trailer park with a couple of pound pups, and now here they were, getting the star treatment in the ritziest digs in town. Being a thief had its perks, especially in Vegas.

Pepper and Misty made small talk as they sipped their champagne. They had reached the crux of the con, for it was now that Wang needed to be convinced to play an innocent game of backgammon with his guests. If Wang didn't take the bait, the scam wouldn't fly.

Wang took the bait. Of course he'd play backgammon with Pepper and Misty. Wang called the concierge, and a few minutes later, a backgammon game was delivered to his suite.

A coffee table was cleared and the backgammon game set up. Billy could no longer see what was going on, and he sent Misty a text and told her to move her purse.

Misty got the text. She picked up her purse and placed it on another table, pointing it so Billy could see the backgammon board. Signaling between cheaters had gotten a whole lot easier with the advent of cell phones.

Billy leaned back in his lounge chair. The only thing he enjoyed more than pulling a scam was watching another cheat pull a scam. In this case, the cheats happened to be his students, which made the play that much sweeter. He settled in for the ride.

TWENTY-SEVEN

Backgammon was one of the world's oldest board games. The game consisted of a board, two sets of fifteen checkers, two pairs of dice, a doubling cube, and two dice cups.

The object of the game was simple. The checkers were moved by a roll of the dice, with a player winning by removing all of their checkers before their opponent.

The game was a combination of skill and luck. An inexperienced player might win a round or two, but over the long run, an experienced player would come out ahead.

Billy had a good reason for choosing backgammon to scam Tommy Wang. It was similar to a popular Chinese board game called *Coan ki*, and there was a strong likelihood that Wang had grown up playing *Coan ki* and already understood the game's fundamentals.

Misty went first and rolled the dice. Then it was Wang's turn. It soon became obvious that Wang was an experienced player, and that Misty had little chance.

Wang won, and they started a new game. Misty suddenly began to cough. She'd worked on the cough for weeks until it sounded real, and cause for alarm.

Wang's smile vanished.

Misty pointed at her throat as if choking.

Wang went to the bar to fix a glass of water. Misty used the opportunity to scoop up the four dice on the board and replace them with four gaffed dice hidden in the pocket of her sundress. The gaffed dice were loaded with motion-activated transmitters and could be made to electronically roll various combinations that appeared fair but weren't.

Misty passed the real dice to Pepper. Rising from her chair, Pepper went outside onto the balcony, where she pitched the stolen dice over the railing. Bye-bye evidence.

Wang brought Misty a glass of water. Misty took a swallow and pretended to recover. Wang's smile returned and he sat back down. The game resumed.

Backgammon scams were common and often took place beside hotel swimming pools. In these scams, the sucker initially got taken for chump change, with the bets growing in size with each subsequent round. The losses quickly added up, with the sucker eventually losing a sizable amount of money.

The con they were playing on Wang was different. In this scam, Wang was going to win, and made to believe he was the luckiest bastard on the planet. Billy didn't think there were two people more capable of pulling this off than Pepper and Misty.

The sun came out from behind the clouds, the glare catching the computer's screen. Billy shifted his lounge chair and the picture came back into focus. He watched Misty lose the next game against Wang.

"You're amazing!" Misty exclaimed.

The feed had no audio, yet Billy still knew what Misty was saying. This was because every line was scripted, with nothing left to chance or improvisation.

"I give up," Misty said to Pepper, following the script. "See if you can beat him."

Pepper and Misty switched chairs.

"Let's play," Pepper said.

Wang went first and tossed the dice onto the board. The dice showed a four and a two, totaling six. Pepper pointed at the dice.

"Another six! That's amazing!" Pepper said, following the script.

The game resumed. Wang continued to throw sixes, along with eights and nines. Each time these numbers came up, Pepper stopped the game to point it out.

Wang's lucky numbers—six, eight, and nine.

It all looked innocent, and Wang didn't have a clue he was being conned. Had Wang turned his head, he would have noticed that each time he threw the dice, Misty was tapping an app on her cell phone that caused the gaffed dice to roll a certain way.

But Wang didn't turn his head. He was too enamored with the drop-dead, redheaded beauty sitting across from him. Pepper had sent an arrow through his heart, and Wang was smitten. Billy couldn't have been happier, and he went inside to grab a Coke from the bar.

When he returned to his chair, the scene on his laptop had changed. The backgammon game was over, and Wang was pouring the last of the champagne into the flutes.

Wang lifted his flute in a toast. His face was flush with the euphoria that came from winning. It didn't matter if it was a friendly game of cards or a contest with a million bucks on the line. Winning produced sensations that were better than any drug, even better than sex.

Wang had swallowed the bait. Now Pepper and Misty needed to reel him in.

- - -

Pepper didn't think the backgammon con could have gone smoother. The weeks of practicing up in Lake Tahoe had paid off. Billy was smart that way; he left nothing to chance.

They moved to the sitting area in the suite's living room and sat on couches covered in exotic animal hides. Wang fixed a plate of delicious finger food, which he graciously offered.

"You're the luckiest person I've ever met!" Misty exclaimed. "Isn't he?"

"You're telling me," Pepper said. "I've never seen anyone roll dice like that. You didn't cheat us, did you?"

Wang was taken aback and placed the plate of food down on a coffee table. "Cheat? I would never cheat."

"Never?"

Wang shook his head.

"So you're a square john," Pepper said.

"What is a square john?" Wang asked.

"A truly honest person. Someone who wouldn't cheat, even when the opportunity's staring him in the face. There aren't many of them in this town."

Wang laughed softly. "Count me as one. You could say good fortune is on my side."

"You mean you're lucky," Pepper said.

Wang shook his head. "Luck is when you find money in the street, and that can happen to anyone. Good fortune is a gift from the gods. When good fortune shines down upon a person, it is that person's responsibility to recognize it and seize the opportunity."

"Is good fortune shining down on you?" Pepper asked.

"Yes," Wang said with emphasis.

"How can you tell?"

Wang started to answer but hesitated. He wanted to tell them but hadn't worked up the nerve. Pepper leaned over, put her hand on his thigh, and gave it a squeeze.

"You can tell us. We're your friends."

"Very well. A gangster named Broken Tooth sent me to Las Vegas because he believes good fortune has shone down upon me. My mission is to win ten million dollars, which a group of unlucky Chinese gamblers lost in the casinos here several months ago."

"Does he really have a broken tooth?" Pepper asked.

"Yes. He is very ordinary looking, except for his broken tooth. I believe this is why he's chosen not to have it fixed."

"Why does Broken Tooth think you can win ten million dollars?" Pepper asked.

"It is a long story," he said solemnly.

"Can you do it?"

"I most certainly am going to try."

Pepper stole a glance at Misty. So that was why Billy had picked Tommy Wang to rip off Carnivale's casino. Wang was a man on a mission, and that mission was to win big.

"What's going to happen if you lose?" Misty asked.

"Then I will be shot. Broken Tooth is not a forgiving man," Wang said.

The tiny meatball on the toothpick Pepper was nibbling no longer tasted so good, and she placed it on a napkin. Pepper had decided that she dug Tommy Wang. He was soft-spoken and had impeccable manners, and she admired those qualities in a man. She wanted to ask Wang why he didn't just cut bait and run; she guessed there was more to the story than he was telling them.

"How do you know when good fortune is shining down on you?" she asked, wanting to change the subject. "Do the skies open up and you hear a voice?"

"It is subtler than that," he replied. "There are signs in everyday occurrences that indicate when good fortune is happening. Take the backgammon game we just enjoyed. I rolled the numbers six, eight, and nine more times than the other numbers. In China, six means wealth, eight means prosperity, and nine means long-lasting. These are signs that good fortune is smiling down on me."

Which was why Billy rigged the backgammon game for those numbers to come up, Pepper realized. To get Tommy Wang to think he couldn't lose.

"There is another reason," their host said. "You are here."

"You think we're part of your good fortune?" Pepper asked.

"Yes. The first time I met you, you were wearing lucky jade. And now the luckiest numbers appear on the dice each time I roll them. You are bringing me good fortune."

Pepper feigned surprise and looked at Misty. Then she looked back at Wang.

"Wow," she said.

Wang went to the bar and popped another bottle of champagne, which he brought to the table. He refilled their flutes to overflowing and stared at Pepper with a smoldering fire burning in his eyes. Pepper had stopped thinking men were special about the time she'd started making porn movies, and she was more than a little surprised when she felt her knees weaken.

"I have a favor to ask," Wang said.

"Name it," Pepper said.

"I would like you to accompany me to the casino tonight. Both of you. I would be honored if you said yes."

Going on a date with Tommy Wang was not part of the plan. Pepper glanced at Misty, who already had her cell phone out and was typing in a text. Before they accepted Wang's offer, they needed to run it by Billy. While they were on a job, nothing happened without Billy's approval.

Which was why the words that came out of Pepper's mouth surprised her.

"You're on," Pepper said.

TWENTY-EIGHT

Special Agent Frank Grimes was having a crappy day. First he'd woken up to find the coffeemaker on the fritz. Then over breakfast he'd sparred with his wife over his late hours. Upon arriving at work he'd discovered his desktop had crashed. He didn't think it could get any worse until he'd gotten a text from Junior Haney saying things hadn't gone according to plan last night. That didn't sound good, so he'd gone outside to the parking lot and climbed into his Jeep Cherokee before calling Junior on his cell phone.

"What do you mean, things didn't go according to plan?" Grimes said.

"We went to Gabe Weiss's house like you told us to, only Gabe wasn't home," Junior replied. "Another guy was there, house-sitting. My father beat the guy into telling us where Gabe was."

"Your father beat him up? How bad?"

"Bad enough."

"Bad enough to kill him?"

"Probably."

Grimes shook his head in disgust. The Haneys had now snuffed two innocent men, and Grimes wondered how high the body count would get before this was over.

"Guy was in rough shape when we left," Junior continued. "Yeah, my father probably killed him. He gets that way sometimes, you know?

His mind snaps and he loses total fucking control. Something good did come out of it, though. We know where Cunningham is."

"How do you know that?"

"It was on Weiss's computer. Cunningham's staying at the Carnivale."

"So go get him."

"We plan to, but we need your help. You know, fake ID."

"Consider it done. Where are you now?" Grimes asked.

"At a hookah bar," Junior said.

"At eleven o'clock in the morning?"

"It was my father's idea. He wanted a smoke."

"Give me the address, and I'll be over as soon as I can."

- - -

The gaming board employed nine hundred special agents whose job was to catch cheats and thieves. When foul play inside a casino was suspected, a gaming agent would come to the casino disguised as an employee and spy on the suspected cheat. Disguises ranged from cocktail waitresses to culinary workers or maintenance people.

Grimes took the elevator to the basement where these disguises were stored. He requested two disguises for a fictitious sting from the clerk on duty. The clerk fetched a pair of olive green maintenance men uniforms and two clip-on ID badges, which he made Grimes sign for.

Grimes returned to the parking lot and put the disguises into his vehicle. He left the parking lot and was soon driving south on I-15. Traffic in Vegas was unpredictable, with no rhyme or reason to its patterns. Twenty-five minutes later, he'd gone exactly eleven miles.

He took Exit 30 and let his GPS guide him. He'd thought whacking Cunningham would be child's play for the Haneys, and it bothered him that they'd now killed a couple of innocent people. But he wasn't going to lose any sleep over it. Because of Cunningham, he'd been denied two promotions and hadn't seen a raise in years. As a result, he was driving a car with a hundred thousand miles, his oldest kid was going to a community college, and his wife worked retail. He didn't care if he had to kill half the population of Las Vegas; if it meant putting Cunningham's lights out, it would be worth it.

He entered a deserted strip center and parked. The hookah bar was also a notary. What a novel idea. Puff on a hookah while having a document stamped. He grabbed the disguises and went inside. The place was decorated like a rec room with cheap rugs on the floor and gaudy wall decorations. The Haneys sat at a corner table, puffing on a hookah. Or at least the elder Haney was. Junior was drinking coffee and looked like he'd just rolled out of bed.

Grimes didn't know that much about the Haneys except Wilmer was from Texas and had worked for the Dallas mob before moving to Vegas and marrying a pretty blackjack dealer, who was Junior's mother. As the story went, Wilmer had confessed the horrible things he'd done back in Dallas to his wife one night, and the wife, upon learning she'd married a monster, had downed a bottle of sleeping pills. Grimes pulled up a chair and dropped the disguises on the table.

"These will get you into the Carnivale," Grimes said.

Junior checked out the disguises. "Maintenance men?"

"That's right. You don't look like management."

"That supposed to be a joke?"

"Just calling it the way I see it."

"My father and I have a question. You said you worked for a Strip casino. Which one?"

Grimes had told the Haneys he worked security for a Strip casino. He hadn't wanted them to know he was with the gaming board for fear they'd extort him down the road.

"MGM Grand," Grimes said.

"The MGM owns a bunch of casinos, don't they?"

"Their parent company owns twelve casinos," Grimes said.

"Is the Bellagio one of them?"

"Yes, it is. Did Cunningham scam the Bellagio?"

"Now that you mention it, he did. We found evidence that Cunningham scammed the Bellagio for a major score, and the casino doesn't know about it," Junior said.

"Define major score," Grimes said.

"A hundred grand."

"That's nonsense. Management at the Bellagio would have to know of the theft. The loss would show up on the spreadsheets at the end of the shift."

"Cunningham figured out a way to keep the losses hidden."

"And you and your father know how."

"Yes, sir. Saw it on the computer in Gabe Weiss's house."

Grimes's job performance was based upon how many scams he uncovered during the course of a year, and the Bellagio scam might very well be his ticket to a bonus.

"How much do you want for this information?" Grimes asked.

"Five hundred bucks," Junior said.

"That's a little steep."

"Forget about it, then."

"No, I'll pay." Grimes paused, trying not to act too anxious. "So what is it?"

"You've got to pay to play. There's an ATM in the bar next door. We'll wait."

Grimes paid a visit to the seedy bar next door and made a withdrawal from his personal checking account. Most bars in town had a couple of slot machines and, as a result, also had ATMs. He returned to the table and slapped the bills onto Junior's hand.

"This had better be on the level," Grimes said.

"It is." Junior added, "You're going to like this."

- - -

Grimes thought he knew every conceivable way of stealing from a casino. Listening to Junior explain the Bellagio scam, the special agent realized he was wrong.

By Nevada law, casinos were required to follow a set of strict procedures regarding keeping inventory of chips. Chips were as valuable as money and tightly regulated.

Chips were kept inside the casino cage, which was monitored 24-7 by security cameras. To prevent a casino from running out of chips, casinos were required to keep more chips inside the cage than were actually needed. The largest denomination was black hundred-dollar chips. Every casino had hundreds of thousands of dollars of unused black chips in their cages. These chips sat in the back of the chip drawers and were rarely touched.

The heist at the Bellagio had occurred during a long holiday weekend. Cunningham and his crew had come into Bellagio's casino and bought fifty thousand dollars' worth of chips at the cage. Then they'd visited one of the Bellagio's gourmet restaurants and eaten dinner.

Their meal done, they'd returned to the cage and spilled the chips they'd bought earlier through the bars to the cashiers. It was a lot of money, and the cashiers had jumped.

At that moment, the cage manager had opened a drawer containing black chips and begun replacing real hundred-dollar chips with stacks of plastic fakes hidden in his pockets.

"So the cage manager was involved in the scam," Grimes said.

"He sure was," Junior replied.

Cunningham's crew had pulled this stunt eight different times over the long weekend, and it had gone off without a hitch. The cage manager had hidden the stolen chips in a gym bag in his locker, which he'd later brought out and given to Cunningham.

To launder the chips, Cunningham had used a gang of strippers from a local men's club. Strippers often received chips as tips, and the girls had come into the Bellagio over a period of several weeks to cash in the stolen loot.

"When did this heist take place?" Grimes asked.

"Last Fourth of July weekend," Junior said.

The Bellagio was required to keep the surveillance tapes for twelve months, so a video of the heist still existed. Cunningham and his crew had probably worn disguises and would be hard to identify. But the cage manager could be identified and tied to the theft.

Grimes felt himself getting excited. He'd pay a visit to the Bellagio this afternoon and review the surveillance tapes. Once he had his evidence of the cage manager switching in the fake chips, he'd bust the creep and sweat him until he got a confession. Making a thief's life miserable was the best part of his work, and his day didn't seem so gloomy anymore.

Grimes rose from his chair. "Call me when you whack Cunningham."

"You'll be the first to know," Junior replied.

- - -

Through the hookah bar's tinted front window, they watched Grimes pull away in his Jeep Cherokee. Junior picked up a rubber tube connected to the hookah and filled his lungs with sweet-tasting smoke called shisha. "Bowl's almost empty. Want some more?"

His father grunted yes.

"We need a refill," Junior called to the back.

The Turkish owner appeared and handed Junior a hand-printed menu. Junior picked a concoction called baja blue, just for the hell of it. Soon he and his father were puffing away.

"Do you think he knows we're playing him?" Junior asked.

His father grunted no.

"Then here's to getting rich together," Junior said.

Junior and his father had decided not to whack Cunningham. They'd been whacking cheats for twenty years and had saved the casinos plenty, yet had little to show for it. That was about to change. Tomorrow afternoon, Cunningham and his crew were going to take down the Carnivale for a major score, and the Haneys were going to get a big fat cut.

The Haneys' allegiances had shifted. The casinos were no longer their friends. Billy Cunningham was their friend, and was about to afford Junior and his father a lifestyle that up until this point in their sorry lives they'd gotten glimpses of only by watching TV. Beautiful homes with manicured yards, sports cars designed like rocket ships, oceanfront Mexican villas. It was in their grasp if they played their cards right.

"Had enough?" Junior asked.

His father grunted that he'd had enough.

Junior settled the tab and scooped up the disguises. The money they made off Cunningham's scam would buy more than just pretty stuff. It would give Junior the means to get his old man straightened out. It was no fun living with a person who never spoke and barely communicated with his own son. Maybe with the right doctors, the walls would come down and his father would start acting normal again. Junior certainly hoped so, as there were things about his past that he knew nothing about. Like his mother, who'd died when he was an infant. The faded snapshots showed a pretty, smallish woman with dancing eyes. Where was she from? Did she have brothers and sisters? Maybe Junior had cousins out there who he might connect with. Anything was possible.

Junior also wanted to hear about his father's life in Dallas. There was a history to his father's violent ways, a secret scorched deep in the recesses of his soul, and Junior wanted to know what had driven his father to make so many brutal choices in his life. It was no fun not knowing his family's history. No fun at all.

They went outside to the parking lot. A door was about to be opened, and Junior realized how excited he was.

"I'll drive," he announced.

His father grunted okay and threw him the keys.

TWENTY-NINE

Billy was sitting by the pool when he got a text on his cell phone from Misty.

`Pepper's having lunch with Wang. You cool with that?`

He nearly toppled out of his lounge chair. When you were running a con, you never got too close to the mark. It was the first lesson he'd taught Pepper and Misty when he'd recruited them.

`Tell Pepper no`, he typed back.

`She already said yes`, Misty answered.

The laptop was balanced on Billy's lap, on its screen the live feed from the hidden camera in Misty's purse. Tommy Wang and Pepper were no longer in the picture anymore.

`Get back here. Both of you`

`Yes, boss`

He shut down his laptop and opened the slider into the suite. As the crew's captain, it was his job to keep each member in line. One weak link was capable of breaking the entire chain, and he would not tolerate Pepper going off script. He walked down the hallway to the foyer. He wanted to be waiting when Misty and Pepper returned so he could read Pepper the riot act. Nearly canning Gabe last night had been brutal, and he wasn't looking forward to this. The door opened and Misty entered.

"Where's Pepper?" he asked.

"She decided to stay," Misty replied.

"Why didn't you grab her, make her leave?"

"How? It wouldn't look right."

Billy reminded himself that the sky palace was bugged. They hadn't said anything incriminating, and he motioned for Misty to follow him outside to the balcony.

"Is Pepper out of her mind? If she slips up, we're finished."

"Don't worry," Misty said reassuringly. "Pepper has Wang eating out of her hand."

"I know. I was watching, remember?"

"You sound pissed off."

"I am pissed off. Pepper broke the rules."

"Come on, Billy, it's not that bad."

"Don't go there."

Misty placed her arms on Billy's shoulders as if to hug him. Then she gave him a flirtatious little smile intended to calm him down. It didn't work.

"Go get Pepper, and bring her back here. I mean it. Right fucking now."

She lowered her arms. "You going to can her?"

"It crossed my mind."

"How about me?"

"It depends how this conversation ends."

"Jesus, Billy. Why are you acting like such a prick? You having a bad day?"

"Who said I was acting like a prick?"

"I did. What's come over you?"

He took a deep breath. Having breakfast with Maggie Flynn had done a number on his head. He'd thought his feelings for Mags would have faded but had discovered the opposite was true. It was a hard thing to deal with, so he was taking his frustration out on Misty.

"Sorry. I've had a rough morning. Now, go find Pepper."

"What should I say?"

"Tell Pepper the boss needs to speak with her. And don't take no for an answer."

Misty looked worried. She and Pepper were a team. They'd appeared in porn movies together and cheated casinos together, and they also jointly owned a house and one day hoped to start a business. If Billy decided to cut Pepper loose, Misty would surely follow.

He opened the slider and ushered Misty off the balcony.

"Go get her," he said.

- - -

Billy stayed on the balcony and tried to calm down. There were times when he wished he worked solo and didn't have to deal with the headaches that employees brought.

Besides making his crew a lot of money, he'd managed to keep them out of jail. Every cheat in town had done time, except for his crew. Their records were spotless, and Billy liked to think it was because of the way he ran his operation.

His cell phone vibrated. Caller ID said DeSantis. Probably calling to find out why Billy wasn't downstairs in the casino losing money. He took the call.

"Mr. C., how's it going? Is everything to your satisfaction?"

"No complaints so far."

"We haven't seen you in the casino today."

"I was just heading down to play some BJ."

"Would you like the same table as yesterday? I can also arrange for the same dealer."

"Why not."

"I'll have a seat reserved for you at the thousand-dollar table. See you soon."

Billy went inside to change into his gambling clothes. Casinos were not subtle when dealing with whales. A good example was the whale staying at Caesars who'd requested a call girl be sent to his suite. When the whale didn't appear in the casino the next morning, a pair of security guards went to the suite, broke the door down, and dragged the call girl out in her lingerie.

Billy had still not gotten the sky palace's layout down. At the hallway's end he came to a door and stuck his head in. Cory, Morris, and Travis sat in the private theater, gorging on burgers. Playing on the big screen was the remake of *Ocean's Eleven* in which George Clooney and his fun-loving gang steal millions from the Bellagio's vault, the only problem being that Vegas casinos keep their money in banks, just like everyone else.

"Where'd you get the food?" Billy asked.

"Room service. Want us to order you some lunch?" Travis asked.

"I'm going downstairs to play blackjack."

Billy found his room and changed into a pair of white silk slacks, a Dolce & Gabbana T-shirt, and a Brunello Cucinelli sports jacket with a pocket square. He appraised himself in the full-length mirror and decided he looked like a player. He met up with Misty in the living room.

"Where's Pepper?" he asked.

"I don't know where they are," Misty said.

"Did you try her cell phone?"

"I called and texted. She didn't pick up. I'm sorry, Billy. This isn't like her."

"Is she in love?"

"It's starting to feel that way."

He told himself not to get angry. It had been his idea to have Pepper and Misty con Wang at backgammon, knowing their charms would win over the Chinese gambler. If Pepper and Wang had fallen in love as a result, he had only himself to blame.

"Can Pepper handle this guy?" he asked.

"Yeah, she can handle him."

"Then we'll have to hope for the best. I need to hit the casino. Care to join me?"

"Sure. Are you still angry at Pepper?"

"I'll get over it."

- - -

With Misty draped over his arm, Billy entered Carnivale's casino. It wasn't noon, yet the suckers filled the green felt tables, wagering money on games they had no chance of winning but believed they could. It was the American dream turned upside down, with the little guy never having a chance. DeSantis hovered nearby like a stalker.

"Ready to play some blackjack, Mr. C.?"

"Isn't that why we're here?" Billy replied.

"How are you doing in the chip department?"

"I'm a little low, Eddie."

Billy signed a chit for a half million dollars' worth of chips at the cage. Next stop was an empty chair at the five-thousand-dollar table. His ass hadn't hit the seat when the dealer announced, "Place your bets, please."

"Call me if you need anything," DeSantis said.

"I'll do that," Billy said.

Billy needed to make up for lost time and slid ten thousand in chips into the betting circle. The average BJ game saw eighty-five hands dealt an hour, with the players losing 52 percent of the time. If he continued to bet ten thousand a hand, the casino would realize a seventeen-thousand-dollar-an-hour return.

Misty hovered behind Billy's chair. It was a strategic position, as it would discourage other players from trying to strike up a conversation with him. Casinos often employed retired cops to roam the floor. These cops had a gift for grift and were good at spotting thieves. The less talking done to strangers, the better.

"Would you care to sit down?" the dealer asked Misty.

"No, but thanks anyway," Misty said.

- - -

An hour later, Billy was down thirty-five grand.

Based upon his calculations, the loss should have been half that amount. Which could mean only one thing. He was being swindled.

Casinos weren't supposed to swindle their customers, but it happened. Sometimes, a slot machine got put on the floor that didn't pay out. Or a pit boss tore up several high-valued cards in a blackjack game under the excuse that a drink had spilled on them. This was the proper procedure, so long as the cards were replaced. When the pit boss didn't, it was cheating.

Billy had a photographic memory, and he replayed each hand that had been dealt to him in an effort to determine when the swindle had taken place. It took a little while, but he found it. The casino was card counting and using the information to alter the game.

Most casinos card counted their blackjack games. Either the pit boss did the counting or a computer in the surveillance room was used. If a player betting five dollars a hand suddenly bet $500, the casino would check the count to determine if the player was a counter.

Carnivale was using the information differently. They were counting the game at Billy's table and telling the dealer to reshuffle whenever the cards' composition favored the players. High-valued cards favored the players; low-valued cards favored the house. As a result, Billy wasn't getting many high-valued cards, nor were the other players. Carnivale was keeping the high-valued cards out of play.

The dealer was doing the dirty work. Billy noticed a flesh-colored plastic earpiece. He'd assumed it was a hearing aid but now wasn't so sure.

He excused himself from the table to take an imaginary phone call. Walking back to the table, he glanced at the dealers working the other blackjack games.

They were wearing earpieces as well.

He played a few more hands and lost every one. His face burned. Misty began to massage the muscles in his neck, which were as tight as knots.

"You okay?" she whispered in his ear.

"They're scamming us," he whispered back.

"So that's why I'm not seeing any aces. Shall we alert the gaming board?"

"Very funny. Let's get some lunch."

He gathered up his remaining chips and rose from the table. He considered not tipping the dealer but decided against it. In Carnivale's eyes, he was a sucker, and he needed to keep up that impersonation for as long as he could. He tossed five black chips to the dealer.

"Thank you, Mr. C. Come back soon," the dealer said.

- - -

Billy took his time leaving. If Carnivale was cheating their customers at blackjack, there was a strong likelihood management was scamming the craps, roulette, and baccarat games as well, and he and Misty took a long walk around the casino.

"Uh-oh. Looks like trouble," Misty whispered.

They had stopped to watch a craps game. Casinos that cheated at dice often employed shaved dice that rolled fewer winning combinations than normal. Billy looked up from the game to see a small army of security goons rushing down the aisle toward them.

"Don't move," he said.

They held their ground as the goons rushed past.

"What was that about?" Misty asked.

"Beats me. What are you in the mood for?"

"Pizza. I hear the hotel has a great pizzeria."

"Italian it is." He took out his cell phone and called DeSantis. "I need the best table at your pizzeria in two minutes. Is that going to be a problem?"

"Not at all, Mr. C. How was your blackjack game?" their host asked.

"I lost. Later."

They began the long march to the lobby where the hotel's restaurants were located. Every casino was designed to make their patrons do a strenuous amount of walking, hoping their legs would tire and they'd sit down and play a few hands.

At the end of their walk, they again crossed paths with security. The goons had gotten their man and were dragging Nico Boswell from the casino. The goons had roughed him up; Nico's shirt was torn, and a sickening stream of blood gushed out of his nose.

Billy's stomach churned. The goons were going to back-room Nico in a windowless cell where they'd take turns slapping him around and intimidating him. Only after the goons had inflicted more pain and instilled the fear of God in Nico would they turn him over to the police.

As the goons hustled past, Nico looked right at Billy. The poor kid was scared out of his wits, and his eyes begged for help. The goon in charge slapped Nico in the back of the head.

"Keep moving," the goon said.

THIRTY

Carnivale's pizzeria was named Serious Pie. The hostess escorted them to a corner table away from the other diners and handed them menus.

A waiter took their drink order. Billy ordered mineral water for the table. The waiter left and Billy rubbed his face with his hands.

"You know the guy who just got busted?" Misty asked.

"Was it that obvious?" Billy asked.

"It was to me."

"How about the goons?"

"They're too dumb to notice stuff like that. Who is he?"

"His name's Nico Boswell. His family's been scamming the casinos for years. Roulette, craps, BJ, they've even taken down slot machines. They're legends."

"Are they here, too?"

"No. The family left yesterday. Only Nico hung around."

"What's going to happen to him?"

Billy looked over the menu. The filet mignon meatballs looked tasty, only his appetite had gone away. The casinos didn't rough up patrons they suspected of cheating unless they'd gathered enough videotape evidence to put them away. The waiter returned to the table, and Misty ordered a thin crust veggie pizza while Billy went for the house salad.

"You didn't answer my question," Misty said. "Is he going down?"

The easiest way to deal with unpleasant subjects was not to think about them. He shrugged as if to say *I don't know.* Misty squeezed his arm.

"Why do you care?" he asked.

"Pepper and I talk about it all the time," she said. "You've done a great job of keeping us out of jail, but it might happen someday. Better to hear about it ahead of time."

"Nico's going down," he said. "His family was working a slot-machine scam. The gaming board has technology that detects when the slots are losing too much money, and they found out and nailed him."

"Will he do time?"

"Three to five if he's got a good lawyer. Five to seven if his lawyer sucks. They'll lock him up in Ely, which is where most cheats get put."

"Why Ely?"

"It's the worst prison in the state, so the judges throw cheats there to teach them a lesson. The cellblocks are run by gangs, and the gangs run card games. If you're a cheat, you're expected to deal the game so your gang wins. It's no fun if you get caught."

"What do they do?"

Billy mimed getting his throat slit. Misty let out a little shriek.

"That's horrible. Can you help this guy?" she asked.

"I already warned his family. Nico didn't listen."

"That's not what I asked you. Can you help him?"

He took a breadstick from the basket and broke off a piece. The cheater's code required that Billy attempt to help Nico if he could. "I could try, but it would put us in jeopardy. If the casino finds out that I know Nico, they might get the wrong idea."

"What if he gets scared and gives you up?" Misty said. "He could strike a deal with the district attorney and roll on you. Then we'd be royally screwed."

Billy munched on the breadstick while giving Misty a hard stare.

"I saw it on a TV show once," she explained.

"Nico's relatives are Gypsies. He's not giving me up."

"What about the cheater's code? Doesn't it say that we're supposed to help other cheaters if they get in trouble? That guy needs your help, Billy."

Billy lived by the cheater's code and had drummed it into every person who joined his crew. If a cheat got jammed up by the law, other cheats were expected to help out by both moral and material support. Their lunches came and Misty dug into her pizza.

"How's it taste?" he asked.

"Too much garlic but not bad. Want a slice?"

"No, I'm good."

He watched her eat. Misty was right; he was obligated by the code to help Nico despite the bad blood between them. The problem was, he didn't have much time. Once the casino turned Nico over to the police and a report was filed, all bets were off.

"A penny for your thoughts," Misty said.

"It's doable," he said.

"You can spring him?"

"I think so."

"How?"

"I'll call our VIP host and ask him to talk to management."

"You mean DeSantis? Can he do that?"

"If I ask him, he just might."

Misty didn't understand. Billy leaned in close and explained. "Remember the fight between Mike Tyson and Evander Holyfield at the MGM Grand?"

"Is that the fight where Tyson bit off Holyfield's ear?"

"That's the one. Everyone was betting on Tyson to win so needless to say they lost their shirts. After Tyson was disqualified, the spectators spilled into the casino and several fights broke out. Then a gangbanger pulled a gun and fired into the ceiling."

"I remember that. There was nearly a riot. So what's this have to do with Nico?"

"That night, a famous basketball player was playing blackjack in the MGM's casino. This basketball player was known to drop a million bucks when he came to town.

"The basketball player had two buddies with him. As the gangbanger shot up the casino, everyone hit the floor, except the basketball player's buddies. They stayed in their chairs and helped themselves to chips from the dealer's tray. The next day, the theft got spotted when the MGM reviewed the surveillance tapes. Guess what happened."

"The MGM called the police."

"Nope. They called the basketball player instead."

"They kept the theft hush-hush? Why, were they afraid of the publicity?"

"Hardly. The MGM was afraid they might lose the basketball player's action if they busted his two friends, so they gave the friends a pass."

"Is your credit line as big as the basketball player's was?"

"Bigger."

"Will Carnivale let Nico go if you ask them?"

"They might. It depends upon how convincing my story is."

"What are you going to say?"

"I'm going to tell DeSantis that I just saw an old high school chum of mine getting hauled off the floor, and would they be so kind as to let him go."

"You're not going to mention that Nico was cheating."

"No, that would be telling them too much. Always keep your lies simple."

"You think it's going to work?"

"Let's find out."

Billy called DeSantis's number on his cell phone. He had already lost a sizable amount of money at Carnivale's blackjack tables, which made him gold in management's eyes. But was it enough of a loss for management to let Nico skate? He was about to find out.

"Hey, Mr. C., how you doing?" DeSantis answered cheerfully.

"I've got a favor to ask, Eddie," Billy said.

"Name it, Mr. C."

"I just saw an old friend of mine having a chat with your security. They pulled him out of the casino and are holding him. I was hoping they might be convinced to let him go."

DeSantis coughed into the phone. "Any idea what your friend was doing?"

"I'm sure it was no big deal. His name's Nico Boswell. We were best friends in high school, used to go out on double dates. I'd hate to see anything happen to him. Do you think you could pull some strings and make this go away? It would mean a lot to me, Eddie."

"Let me see what I can do, Mr. C. Back to you in twenty."

"You're a star, Eddie."

THIRTY-ONE

Misty finished her pizza and then ate Billy's salad. She had lost weight in Lake Tahoe and it showed in her cheekbones. The stress that came when planning a big job was always huge. Billy had also lost weight and found hair in the shower's drain. There was no question that stealing was bad for your health. It also wrecked marriages and led to alcoholism and drug abuse. These were bad things, yet he wouldn't have traded the lifestyle for the world. Let the lawyers and doctors have their country clubs and swollen bank accounts. Every time he took down a casino, he experienced more thrills than those fuckers saw in a lifetime.

"So what do you think? Will the casino let Nico walk?" Misty asked.

Billy shrugged. Twenty minutes had passed since he'd talked to DeSantis and asked for Nico to be let go. DeSantis had promised to call back, and Billy didn't know if the lack of communication was a good sign.

"Hard to say," he said.

"What's your backup plan if they don't?"

"Who said I had a backup plan?"

"You always have a backup plan. That's why Pepper and I decided to join your crew when you recruited us. You're one step ahead of everybody else."

"And I thought it was my boyish innocence and charming good looks."

"Ha-ha. So what is it?"

"I'll threaten to leave and go back to the Rio."

"Is losing a good customer enough to make them do it?"

Billy nodded. He'd done the math on Carnivale. They were a publicly traded company on the New York Stock Exchange, and according to their most recent 10K filing with the SEC, the parent company spent $1.35 billion on Carnivale's yearly operations. Dividing that number by 365 days, and then dividing that number by twenty-four hours, broke down to $154,000 per hour. It was a huge nut, and hopefully enough to cloud management's judgment.

The rules were different inside a casino. Their customers broke the law every day by bringing prostitutes to their rooms, but rarely were the police called. And if a customer connected to a whale got caught stealing, the casino just might look the other way.

His cell phone vibrated on the table. He flipped it over and stared at its face.

"Guess who," he said.

"Sweet-talking Eddie DeSantis?" Misty asked.

"You got it. What do you want to bet they're going to let Nico go?"

"What kind of odds are you giving me?"

"Fifty-fifty."

Misty shook her head. "I'd never bet against you."

"How about all the tea in China?"

"You're on, hot shot."

- - -

"You're a genius," Misty said as they crossed the casino.

"Remember, Nico's an old high school buddy. We wrestled together," Billy said.

"Why'd you pick that sport?"

"Because neither of us is big enough to have played anything else."

They came to the casino cage. DeSantis stood in front of the cage, talking to his bosses on his Bluetooth. Behind him stood a frightened Nico with two brutish security guards.

Seeing Billy, Nico blinked.

How cute, Billy thought. Carnivale's security hadn't told Nico what the deal was. Instead, they'd sent him onto the casino floor with the guards. These same security people were now watching via the eye-in-the-sky, wanting to see how Nico reacted when Billy appeared.

Without missing a beat, Billy embraced Nico as if he were his long-lost brother.

"I told them you're an old friend. Act like one," he whispered in Nico's ear.

"Got it," Nico whispered back.

The embrace ended, and Billy introduced him to Misty.

"Nice to meet you," Nico said.

"Billy's told me so much about you," Misty said.

"All of it's lies," Nico said with a good-natured laugh.

"So what seems to be the problem?" Billy asked.

"The casino thinks I was cheating." Nico's tone turned serious. "I didn't do anything wrong, and that's the God's honest truth."

Nico was protesting his innocence. That could mean only one thing. Security did not have enough evidence to turn him over to the police just yet. If they had enough evidence, Nico would have kept his mouth shut and said absolutely nothing.

"My friend isn't a cheat," Billy said to DeSantis.

"I'm sorry, Mr. C., but the casino felt it was necessary to pull your friend off the floor," DeSantis explained. "The casino believes he was passing fake chips and had a real chip taped to his leg to trick the reader in the table. Security searched your friend when he was at the table. They found a broken piece of elastic and a black chip lying beneath his chair."

"That stuff could have been left by anyone," Billy said.

"We believe it was taped to your friend's leg."

Billy put his arm around Nico's shoulder and drew him close. "I've known this man for most of my life. We went to school together, and we wrestled together. He does not cheat or steal. If you don't let him go, I'll leave and never come back."

DeSantis hesitated. Management was speaking to him through his Bluetooth.

"My bosses inform me that they'll give your friend a pass, provided he doesn't play in our casino again," DeSantis said.

The gods had spoken. Nico was a free man. The pair of butt-ugly guards didn't look thrilled with the arrangement. Fuck 'em, Billy thought.

"Thanks, Eddie," Billy said. "I appreciate you looking out for me."

"That's what I'm here for," DeSantis said. "Don't hesitate to call if I can be of service."

- - -

"You okay?" Billy asked when DeSantis and the guards were gone.

"They slapped me around. Nothing I haven't been through before." Nico stuck his finger into his mouth and ran the tip over his teeth to see if any were broken. "I'm good."

"Glad to hear it. Let's take a walk."

"I need to get out of here. In case you didn't notice, these people don't like me."

"You need to hang around for a little while," Billy said. "I told the casino we were buds. It's going to look suspicious if you take off. Remember, I'm staying here."

"What about my clothes?"

"I'll get you some new threads. Follow me."

Nico didn't like it. As they passed through the casino, he eyed the exits.

"Stop that. It looks suspicious," Billy said.

"You think security's watching us?" Nico asked.

"Of course they're watching us. It's what they get paid to do."

The casino's overpriced men's store was called The Cuban Connection. Nico changed his torn clothes for a billowing white silk shirt and black silk pants.

"These are a little pricey," Nico said.

"Everything's comped. You like carnival games?" Billy asked. "The casino has an arcade in the basement with pinball machines and video games. We can hang there and talk without being overheard."

"You think they've got food? I'm starving to death," Nico said.

"We'll get you fed," Billy said.

Misty had said little since they'd rescued Nico and now broke her silence. "If you boys don't mind, I think I'll go lie by the pool and work on my tan."

"Any word from Pepper?" Billy asked.

"Pepper sent me a text, said everything's cool," Misty said.

"She didn't elope with Tommy Wang, did she?" Billy asked.

"Not yet." To Nico she said, "Nice meeting you."

"You, too," he said.

- - -

To reach the arcade, they needed to take a special escalator. As they headed toward it, Billy noticed how dejected Nico was acting. His troubles with the casino were over, but his troubles with his family were just beginning. He was going to have some explaining to do and might lose face with his father. That could lead to Nico's role as heir apparent being stripped away.

Billy didn't want that to happen. If Nico got sent to the minors, it would cause a disruption in the Boswell family, a disruption that Billy would always be associated with. That association would be a negative one, and it would ruin any chance of them doing business together.

To survive as a thief, you needed a crystal ball to see into the future. Billy's crystal ball was telling him that he needed to give Nico something to take home to his father, a nice little present that would put Nico in a good light and cement Billy's own reputation with the family.

They took the escalator into the basement. Music started to play, and Nico pulled out a cell phone and glanced at caller ID. "My father's looking for me, wondering where I am."

"Does he know you got busted?" Billy asked.

Nico shook his head. "My old man's never been caught cheating a casino, if you can believe that. He's going to blow his top when I tell him what happened."

Nico let the call go to voice mail.

Maybe not, Billy thought.

THIRTY-TWO

Carnivale's arcade was designed like a carnival midway and had air hockey, Skee-Ball, bumper cars, and an assortment of pinball machines. There was also a Dairy Queen, and Nico ordered a flamethrower cheeseburger with steak fries and a hot fudge sundae. They took a table outside the restaurant near a family with a bunch of wild kids. The kids were making enough noise to make it impossible for an undercover security guard to eavesdrop on their conversation.

"Help yourself," Nico said. "How long you been grifting?"

Billy took a fry to be sociable. "Started when I was sixteen. How about you?"

"Same age. Who turned you out?"

Grifters were not born; they were made. An aspiring grifter would apprentice with a seasoned pro and learn the ropes before getting turned out on his own. "I made my bones with a guy named Lou Profaci. One day, Lou gavc me a test, said if I passed he'd give me my own turf. I had to steal a lousy buck from a restaurant."

"Restaurant people are sharp. How'd you pull it off?"

"I'd run into the restaurant holding some bills. I'd go up to the cashier and say, 'Lend me a dollar. My father doesn't have change to pay the cab driver. He'll pay you back with dinner.'"

"Did it work?"

"No, they told me to beat it. I eventually came up with an angle that sold the play."

"What did you do?"

"I'd hail a cab outside the restaurant. The cab would pull up, and I'd open the back door and say, 'My parents will be right out.' Then I'd run inside and tell the cashier that my father needed a buck to pay the driver. The cashier would give me the buck, no questions asked."

"Sweet."

"How'd you make your bones?"

The burger with the fancy name was a memory. Nico picked up the ice cream sundae and jabbed it with a spoon. "I made my bones with the rug scam. You know it?"

Billy shook his head.

"We were living in Chicago. My father and uncle would drive around in a van with a rug in the back and pull into the driveway of a nice house. They'd take the rug out and go to the front door. My father would ring the bell while I'd hide in the bushes. The owner would come out, and my father would offer to sell the rug for two hundred bucks. The owners always said yes. This was one beautiful rug.

"My father would offer to take the rug inside. As he and my uncle carried it in, I hid behind it. Once I was inside, I ran around stealing stuff. The next part was tricky. My father would tell the owner the actual price for the rug was two grand. The owner would pitch a fit, and my father would say the deal was off. My father and uncle would cart the rug out of the house, and I'd leave the same way I came in." The ice cream was gone, and Nico licked the spoon. "That was my test. All of the kids pulled the rug scam, and I came out on top."

"You were the fastest," Billy said.

"I was the fastest, but that wasn't the reason."

"You stole the good stuff, and the others didn't."

"That's right. My haul was always the most valuable. That was why my father decided I should run the show one day. I knew what to steal."

"Is your father thinking of retiring?"

"He doesn't want to, but his health sucks. I'll be running things soon." Nico gingerly touched his stomach.

"You okay?"

"Fucking guard punched me in the kidneys. I'll piss blood for a few days. I'm sorry I didn't listen to you and leave when my family did. I learned my lesson."

"You going to tell your father what happened?"

"I have to. Our family doesn't hold back."

"He's not going to be happy."

"I still have to tell him. Those are the rules."

Billy nodded. Now he understood why Victor had chosen Nico to run things. The kid knew not to lie when the situation demanded the truth, no matter how painful the truth might be. You couldn't teach a person a quality like that. It was something you were born with.

"I'll give you something to lessen the pain. You play pinball?" Billy asked.

"I'm the best pinball player in the world. Ten bucks a game?"

"You're on, tough guy."

- - -

Many hustlers used fronts to launder their money. Bars, restaurants, and Laundromats were excellent fronts, as they did most of their business in cash. The Boswells used a bowling alley as a front that had a game room with pinball machines. Nico had grown up playing and could have beaten most people with his eyes closed, his feel was so good.

They played a game called Theater of Magic. It had all the prerequisite bells and whistles and gave out a lot of extra balls. To his credit, Nico didn't rack up the score and make Billy feel stupid. Hustlers called this playing below speed, and it was a common tactic in pool halls. Playing below speed kept the sucker in the game without letting him win.

"How good are you at foosball?" Billy asked.

"Nobody beats me at foosball," Nico declared.

Billy was a better than average foosball player, and they split games. As they knocked the Ping Pong ball around the table, Billy explained how the Carnivale scam worked and how Nico's family could profit from it. It was a new angle, and at first Nico didn't get it.

"Is that really possible?" Nico asked.

"Yes, sir," Billy said.

"You'd better explain it to me again. I'm missing something."

Billy went over the Carnivale scam a second time. The scam had a unique element. People not involved in its execution could profit from its outcome, provided they were in the know. That was not true for most casino scams, where only the cheats came out ahead. In that regard, the Carnivale scam was more like a fixed horse race. If a bettor knew which horse was going to cross the finish line first, the bettor could profit by placing a wager.

Nico got it this time. The Boswells could make a huge score, without incurring the risk normally involved with taking down a casino.

"That's fucking beautiful," Nico said.

"I thought you'd like it," Billy said.

THIRTY-THREE

Billy beat Nico at foosball and won back the money he'd lost at pinball. Billy loved to win and so did Nico, and Billy had a feeling this was the beginning of a beautiful friendship.

They left the arcade and took the escalator to the main floor. Billy walked Nico through the casino and outside to the valet area. He did not want security to have a change of heart and back-room Nico again. That wasn't going to happen if Nico was by his side.

The uniformed valet said, "You need a taxi?"

"My friend's going to the airport," Billy said.

"No luggage?" the valet asked.

"No, he travels light."

The valet stepped off the curb and blew his whistle. A line of yellow cabs was parked just off the entrance. The vehicle in front started its engine and drove forward.

"How did you know I was going to the airport?" Nico asked.

"Your car's parked there, isn't it?" Billy said.

"Who told you I had a car?"

Most hustlers who worked Vegas came by car, parked at McCarran, and cabbed it into town. Having a car at the airport gave the hustler the freedom to leave at the drop of a hat.

"Lucky guess," Billy said. "Is your father's health really that bad?"

"He never fully recovered from being shot by that fucking gaming agent," Nico said. "My father should stop working, only he can't. Stealing's in his blood. Mark my words, he's going to be rigging a slot machine when his heart gives out."

"There are worse ways to go."

"Tell me about it."

The cab kissed the curb. Nico stuck out his hand.

"I owe you one," Nico said.

"Yes, you do," Billy said.

- - -

Billy returned to his special chair at the five-thousand-dollar blackjack table and lost more money. The odds were stacked against him and his stacks of chips shrank before his eyes. To ease the pain, a flirtatious cocktail waitress kept the drinks flowing. The pit boss also got in the act and offered to have a masseuse work the knots out of his back while Billy got fleeced.

Billy played along, but it wasn't easy. Back in the carnival days, suckers would get a piece of chalk run down their back, which was where the expression "a mark" came from. Billy was the mark here, and every person working in the casino seemed to know it.

His cell phone vibrated. He pulled it out and saw a text had arrived. As he started to read it, the dealer cleared his throat. The dealer was an older man dressed in an embroidered guayabera in keeping with the casino's Cuban theme. His name tag said Roland.

"Cell phones are not permitted at the table," Roland said.

Billy picked up the last of his chips and pushed his chair back from the table. "Let me ask you a question, Roland. I've played more than a hundred hands and didn't get a single blackjack. What do you think the odds are of that happening?"

Roland's cheeks burned. On average, a player received a blackjack every seventeen hands. The odds of Billy not getting a blackjack were next to impossible, unless the house was cheating.

"Pretty high," Roland admitted.

"Try astronomical. Tell the pit boss thanks for the massage."

He left the table, steaming. Casinos that ripped off their customers were called bust-out joints and, if caught, could lose their license. Yet bust-out joints rarely got shut down. Instead, the corporations that owned the casinos were made to pay a paltry fine and clean up the games. In that regard, the rules were different when it came to cheating. Hustlers got thrown in jail, while the corporations got slapped on the wrist.

He forced himself to calm down before reading the text. It was from Misty.

`Big trouble. You need to get upstairs.`

Either Pepper had run off with Tommy Wang or Cory and Morris had gotten high and said something stupid that the hidden mikes had picked up.

He called Misty's cell phone and got patched in to voice mail.

"Call me," he said.

No job ever went exactly as planned. But this job had a dark cloud hanging over it, and a little voice inside his head told him it might be time to cut bait and run.

A new text message appeared. Misty had sent him a photo taken on her iPhone that showed Travis, Cory, and Morris tied to chairs with duct tape slapped over their mouths. There was also a pistol in the photo, and it was pointed at Travis's head.

`Hurry`, the accompanying message read.

He hurried to the elevators. He asked himself who'd be brave enough to come into a casino in broad daylight and kidnap his crew at gunpoint. Only one name came to mind. The Haneys.

He got into the elevator and swiped his key against the security plate. He told himself not to panic, that he'd been in worse jams and managed to come out on top. If he kept his wits about him, he could save his crew from getting hurt.

As he went up, sweat poured down his face, and he could barely breathe.

- - -

The sky palace was as still as a funeral home. He shut the door and heard his shoes squeak on the tile as he entered the living room. The younger Haney was behind the bar fixing himself a drink. He was about five-ten, wiry, and dirty, as if he'd just rolled out from beneath a rock. He wore a maintenance man's uniform with the Carnivale logo stitched over the pocket and had a laminated badge around his neck. A black handgun lay on the bar.

"You must be Cunningham," the younger Haney said.

Billy told himself that he needed to play this one beat at a time. He brought his fingers to his lips and saw the younger Haney's eyebrows arch.

"Watch what you say. Place is bugged," Billy whispered.

"Your girl said as much. Want a drink?"

"A water would be good. What's your name?"

"Jack, but everyone calls me Junior. Nice to meet you."

"Not really," Billy said.

Communication was defined by small gestures. By offering to fix Billy a drink, Junior was saying he wished to talk business. Had that not been the case, Junior would have knocked Billy to the floor and pistol-whipped him, just to demonstrate who was boss.

A glass of water appeared on the bar. Billy took a long swallow. Junior drank a Jack and Coke with no ice. He had third-world body odor and two rows of bad teeth. Crime paid in varying degrees, dependent upon the criminal's level of skill and sophistication. Thieves and con men were at the top of the totem pole, hit men at the bottom.

Junior slid his gun off the bar. "Where's a good place to talk?"

"By the pool. But first, I want to see my people."

"You can do that when we're done."

Billy dropped his voice. "Did you hurt them?"

Junior shook his head.

"Do I have your word on that?"

Junior's eyes flashed and he nodded. Billy was in no position to be challenging him, except Junior wanted something, and Billy wasn't going to play ball without setting ground rules.

"Let me hear you say it," Billy said.

"We didn't hurt 'em. Now, let's go outside," Junior whispered.

A moment later they were standing by the pool with the midday sun burning their necks.

"Where's my crew now?" Billy asked.

"In that fancy little movie theater. My father's babysitting them."

The same father who had nearly taken a hammer to Jo-Jo's skull and had helped beat poor Nate. They claimed that 1 percent of the population was sociopaths. The number was higher in Las Vegas. A lot higher.

"So what do you want?" Billy said.

"Peace, love, and understanding, and a lot of fucking money." Junior laughed at his own joke. "We were hired to murder you. We had every intention of doing that until we found the files on your friend Gabe's computer describing the scams you've pulled. You're a clever little shit, but you already knew that."

"Glad you think so," Billy said.

"The scam you're pulling on this joint is a case in point," Junior went on. "You're going to steal ten million buckeroos and by the time the casino figures out what you've done, it will be too late for them to do anything. That gets an A-plus in my playbook."

"You know, you're a lot smarter than you look," Billy said.

Junior cracked a smile. "Folks tell me that. They're surprised that I can string a few words together into a sentence. My old man's smart, too. He just doesn't talk."

The crazy ones usually don't, Billy thought.

"So here's the deal. We want to form a partnership with you. In exchange for us not killing you, we want a cut of your haul from this job."

"How big a cut you want?"

"Twenty percent."

"Two million bucks."

"That's right. Million for me, a million for my father."

Most lowlifes would have asked for half the cut. Junior was either being sensible and avoiding any unnecessary negotiating. Or he was playing Billy.

"How do I know you won't kill me when the job's over so you can collect the payment from whoever hired you?" Billy asked.

"That actually crossed our minds," Junior said. "You see, our client really hates you and wants you dead immediately, so we're going to oblige him."

Billy's stomach tightened. "You're going to kill me?"

"Hell no. You're our meal ticket, pal. What we're going to do is lie to our client and tell him we killed you. Then he'll go away. Once that's out of the way, there's no reason to kill you."

"How about my crew? Will you leave them alone as well?"

"Sure. This is a partnership. What's done is done."

"Then let's do it."

They shook hands, sealing the deal. Junior was giving Billy a cold, hard stare, as if trying to burrow a hole into Billy's soul and read his thoughts. Billy did his best to keep a poker face. He didn't believe Junior was telling the truth. The Haneys had killed Nate, killed some guy with the misfortune of having the same name as Billy, and popped a defenseless little girl in the face, and that was just the stuff he knew about. They were sickos, and Billy would have bet good money that they were planning to kill him and his crew once they had their money. They'd even picked out where the execution would take place and where they planned to bury the bodies. It was how killers thought. Leave no witnesses.

So Billy played along to buy some time. But all he really wanted to do was shove a sharp object into Junior's ragged face and throw the sick bastard over the balcony so he could get acquainted with the pavement thirty-six floors below. Let the police try to figure out which floor Junior had fallen from. Good luck, boys.

"So who hired you to kill me?" Billy asked.

"He says he works security for one of the casinos, but I think he's lying."

"Why do you think that?"

"We've done jobs for casinos before. The heads of security always wear nice suits and silk neckties. They're into cuff links and monogrammed shirts. They don't make big salaries but they're hoping for a promotion, you know what I mean?"

"They're aspirational," Billy said.

"That's a nice word. Aspirational. Our client's not like that. His clothes are cheaply made. He doesn't have dreams. That tells me he's a cop, maybe a gaming agent."

Junior had just described Special Agent Grimes down to his ugly socks. Billy feigned surprise. "Your client's a gaming agent?"

"That was my read on him. He got us these uniforms and badges."

"Does that bother you? He could turn around and bust you."

"Not going to happen. We're on good terms with the gaming board."

The hairs rose on the back of Billy's neck. No one had ever accused the men who ran the Nevada Gaming Board of being choir boys. Their agents had been caught falsifying evidence against suspected cheaters in court and illegally tapping the phone lines of defense lawyers. One agent had also gotten caught stealing jackpots from slot machines using the board's own laptops. Bad stuff, but nothing compared to what Junior was telling him.

"You've done jobs for the gaming board?" Billy asked.

"You ask too many questions," Junior said.

"Just curious. Those guys are always chasing me."

"And now one of them wants you dead. Any idea who he is?"

Billy was not about to give up that piece of information, and he shook his head.

"Give me your cell phone number," Junior said.

"What for?"

"Just give it to me, and stop asking so many questions."

Billy recited the number. Junior logged it into his cell phone.

"I'm going to be calling you for updates," Junior said. "We'll meet up in a few days when you're done and work out how we're going to get paid."

"Sounds like a plan," Billy said.

"You're a sneaky little bastard, so don't even think of double-crossing us."

"You don't take checks?"

"That's a good one. I'll have to remember to tell my father that."

The wind had shifted, and the foul smell coming off Junior was turning Billy's stomach. As Billy tried to turn away, Junior clamped his hand on the young hustler's shoulder.

"One more thing," Junior said.

"What's that?"

Billy never saw the punch coming. It snapped his head and flashbulbs exploded before his eyes. Junior broke his fall and carefully laid him out on the concrete deck.

THIRTY-FOUR

While the casinos hated cheats, they hated the people who caught them even more.

The small army that made up the enforcement division of the gaming board was the most powerful law enforcement agents in Nevada. Gaming agents had the power to enter a casino at will, review surveillance tapes, and interview employees. No advance warning was given, and neither a search warrant nor a subpoena was needed.

Gaming agents also had the power to freeze a game. If a slot machine wasn't paying out correctly, a gaming agent would hook a laptop into the machine and run a software program against the machine's random-number-generating chip. This inspection was done while other patrons were watching, and it often hurt business.

Gaming agents could also freeze table games. If the payout from a blackjack game or roulette table deviated from normal percentages, a gaming agent had the authority to have the equipment carted away on dollies and taken to a lab for inspection. This was also done in full view of patrons and usually resulted in bad publicity for the casino.

Grimes had decided to bust the Bellagio's cage manager on the casino floor. Grimes did this without consulting with Bellagio's management so they wouldn't be prepared for any fallout. It promised to be nasty, which suited Grimes just fine, as the special agent disliked casino people about as much as he hated cheats.

Grimes had brought three agents to assist him. Their names were Braun, Morrell, and Dawson. Grimes had told them to dress down, and each agent wore jeans and untucked shirts to hide their guns. Grimes wore a suit so everyone knew he was in charge.

Their suspect was named Nicky Corr. Grimes had gotten Corr's work history from the sheriff's department, which kept a file on every casino employee. Corr was thirty-six years old and had a bachelor's degree from UNLV's school of hospitality.

Corr had been in the Bellagio's employ for ten years. He had started as a lowly security guard before becoming a cashier and eventually being promoted to cage manager. Corr's work history was spotless, until now.

Corr was presently inside the cage, managing the cashiers. Grimes parked himself in front of a slot machine across from the cage so he could watch Corr in action. He displayed a nervous energy that Grimes believed was a fear of getting caught. The evidence of Corr's misdeed was in the chip drawers, and it was eating a hole inside him.

Braun, Morrell, and Dawson also sat in front of slot machines, pretending to be Iggys, or ignorant tourists. Grimes clicked his fingers, and they sprang to life.

"Let's nail this asshole."

Grimes marched over to the cage door and banged loudly. Braun, Morrell, and Dawson flanked him, their badges pinned to the belt loops in their jeans.

The door sprang in. Corr stood there, gums flapping.

"Nicky Corr?" Grimes said.

"That's right. Who are y-you?" Corr stammered.

"Special Agent Frank Grimes, Nevada Gaming Board. You're under arrest for ripping off the cage this past Fourth of July. Please step back."

The gaming agents entered the cage. Corr was cuffed and read his rights, while Braun, Morrell, and Dawson opened up the chip drawers and conducted an inventory of the counterfeit black chips that Corr had substituted for real chips over the July Fourth weekend. The cashiers stayed at their windows, trading whispers.

"There's more than a hundred grand in fake chips here," Braun announced.

"Did you really think you'd get away with this?" Grimes asked.

"It was worth a shot," Corr said under his breath.

A phone hung on the wall. Grimes picked it up and got patched through to the casino's general manager. Grimes explained what had happened and suggested that a substitute cage manager take over to make sure none of the cashiers got any bright ideas. The GM started to ask a question and Grimes hung up on him.

"I'm taking this douche bag downtown," Grimes said. "Can you guys manage without me?"

"It'll be hard, but we'll manage," Braun replied.

- - -

Grimes escorted Corr through the Bellagio's busy casino.

"Can't you spare me the walk of shame and take me out the back door?" Corr asked.

"Not on your life," Grimes said.

Corr dropped his head as they marched past the blackjack pit and other table games, but he could not avoid his fellow workers' hostile stares. Through the front doors they went to where a KLAS news team had set up camp. Grimes occasionally threw the media a bone to get good press. KLAS was his favorite, and they usually sent a pretty reporter to interview him. Today it was a comely redhead named Kelly Ringer who stuck a mike in Grimes's face.

"Special Agent Grimes, can you tell us the name of your suspect and what he's accused of?"

Grimes gave Ringer the gritty details while Corr stared at the ground. A cameraman circled, trying to get a close-up of the guilty man's face.

"Get that camera away from me," Corr snapped.

"Stop talking," Grimes said.

"Have a heart. I've got three little kids," Corr said.

"They have my condolences," Grimes said.

Silent tears streamed down Corr's face. Grimes finished the interview and told a valet to bring up his Jeep Cherokee. By the time his vehicle came up, Corr was racked with sobs. Grimes opened the back door and ordered Corr to get in. As Grimes walked around to the driver's side, his cell phone rang. Caller ID said JH.

"Give me some good news," Grimes answered.

"I just sent you a text. Take a look," Junior Haney said.

"Is this going to make my day?"

"You could say that."

Grimes hung up and retrieved Junior's text. That's just beautiful, he thought. Kelly Ringer hadn't strayed far and Grimes tried to contain his excitement. He called Braun on his cell phone. "There's been a change of plans. I need you to take Corr downtown and book him."

"I'll be right out," Braun said.

- - -

Leaving the Bellagio, Grimes drove to a bar called the Stateside Lounge where he knocked back a shot of whiskey and a beer chaser. It was exactly the jolt to the system that he needed. The bartender sold him a miniature bottle of mouthwash and he left.

Next stop was his boss's office on the second floor of the gaming board's headquarters. Bill Tricaricco, director of field agents, was a fifteen-year veteran whose job Grimes someday wished to have. Grimes blew into his hand to make sure the smell of whiskey was gone before rapping on Tricaricco's door.

"It's open. Come on in."

Grimes entered to find Tricaricco at his desk multitasking. Eyes on his laptop, his thumb tapping a text message on his smartphone while chatting with a field agent on his Bluetooth. Tricaricco's primary job was to catch cheats. It was thankless work; for every cheat they caught, five more slipped away. Tricaricco twirled his finger. He was Italian and talked a lot with his hands. Grimes pulled up a chair and positioned it so he faced his superior.

"Good morning," Grimes said.

Tricaricco spoke to his Bluetooth. "Let the guy walk. But make sure you distribute his photo to the other casinos. He sounds like the kind who will show up again." Tricaricco pulled the Bluetooth from his ear and tossed it on the desk. "How did it go at the Bellagio?"

"We've got the cage manager dead to rights."

"You said Cunningham was behind the heist. Will the cage manager roll on him?"

"Not necessary."

"Come again?"

"Cunningham's dead."

Tricaricco sat up straight in his chair. He was wired in to the police and was the first to hear when cheats and other miscreants met unhappy endings. "Who told you that?"

"No one," Grimes said.

"Then how do you know Cunningham's dead?"

Grimes produced his cell phone and retrieved the photo of Cunningham lying on the ground in a pool of blood that Junior Haney had sent him. He passed it across the desk and showed the photo to his superior.

"Son of a bitch," Tricaricco swore. "You didn't do this yourself, did you?"

"I used the Haneys."

"You hired them to kill that little bastard? What made you do that?"

"Remember what you told me that time we got drunk together? You said there's the law of the land and there's the law of the jungle. Well, the law of the jungle just caught up with Billy Cunningham. He won't be bothering us anymore."

Tricaricco stared at the grisly photo and could not help but smile. "I'd like to blow this up and frame it. Guess that's not such a smart idea."

"Want me to send it to you?"

"Hell, no. I'll just keep it in my memory." Tricaricco passed the cell phone back to Grimes. His face became serious again. "Did you cover your tracks on this?"

"Yes, sir. I didn't give the Haneys my real name, and I paid them in cash."

"But they have your cell phone number, and that's traceable," Tricaricco said.

"This isn't my cell phone," Grimes said. "I lifted it off a slot cheat we busted at the Mandalay Bay. I plan to wipe my fingerprints off it and toss it in the trash."

"You feel confident the killing can't be traced to you or to the gaming board."

"Yes, sir," he said.

"Does Cunningham have family? Or a girlfriend?"

"I ran a background check. His father's dead and his mother's in prison—what a surprise. He's slept with half the women in town but doesn't have a steady girlfriend. No one's going to go to the police and demand an investigation. He'll just be forgotten."

"What about his crew? Can they cause us problems?"

"Cunningham's the brains behind the operation. With him out of the picture, the rest of his team will just fade into the sunset."

Behind the desk was a bookcase. Books had become a thing of the past, and its shelves were bare, save for a small wooden box. The box was shrink-wrapped in plastic and needed a penknife to be opened. Tricaricco passed it to his guest.

"Good job, Frank. Help yourself."

It was a box of Arturo Fuente Opus X Belicoso XXX cigars, possibly the best line of smokes in the world. The only casino in town that carried them was Caesars and the prices were insane. Grimes removed one and sniffed it. The smell was sublime. Tricaricco produced a fancy lighter in the shape of a gun.

"Can we smoke here?" Grimes asked.

"We can do whatever the hell we want," Tricaricco said.

Soon the office was engulfed in a haze of purple-blue smoke. The world was filled with winners and losers. This was what it felt like to be a winner, Grimes realized.

"What did the Haneys charge you?" Tricaricco asked.

Grimes told his boss the figure without revealing that he'd paid it twice.

"That's pretty steep. You've got a kid in private school."

"Actually, two of my kids are in private school," Grimes said.

"Private school's expensive. I should know—all three of my kids went to one. Here's what I want you to do. Expense the cost of the hit. Spread it over a few months of reports. Come up with something creative, and I'll sign off on it."

The words were slow to sink in. Grimes had been a special agent with the gaming board for more than a decade. He liked the work and the power it afforded him, yet he'd always felt like he was missing out. Now, finally, he understood how the department worked. He'd sworn to uphold the law but was also expected to stop thieves and cheats from ripping off the town's casinos. And if it became necessary to break the law to do his job, so be it.

"Thanks, Bill, I really appreciate it," Grimes said. "There's something I wanted to ask you. What's the deal with Old Man Haney? Why doesn't he ever talk?"

"His name's Wilmer, and he doesn't have a tongue. He cut it out himself."

"That's disgusting. Why did he do that?"

"Wilmer was a hit man for a crime syndicate in Dallas. The syndicate wanted a rival killed, so Wilmer planted a bomb in a car outside a restaurant. Unfortunately, it was the wrong car, and Wilmer ended up killing his own parents. Not long after that, he moved to Vegas and married a pretty dealer and had a kid. One night, Wilmer got drunk and confessed to his wife what he'd done. Instead of forgiving him, his wife ODed on sleeping pills and checked out. Wilmer got so upset that he cut out his tongue. Used a pair of scissors is the story I heard."

"He murdered his own parents? How does he live with himself?"

"By not talking, I guess."

Grimes's mouth tasted like ash. He placed the cigar into a promotional ashtray from one of the casinos on the desk. Everyone had a history, but there were some better left not spoken about, and he found himself wishing he'd hired someone else to whack Billy Cunningham.

THIRTY-FIVE

Jimmy Slyde had decided to take Mags home after the bad scene at the Riviera. Mags needed to lay low for a while and get reacquainted with Netflix. In a few days the dust would settle, and he'd take her out again to scam another rich sucker.

Slyde was sitting at the intersection of Tropicana and the Strip when he got a phone call from the concierge at the Palazzo. There was a high-stakes card game taking place in one of the hotel's Lago suites and an empty chair at the table had Mags's name on it.

Slyde mulled it over. Their arrangement had nearly run its course, and he didn't see himself fronting her much longer. Better to get the money while he could and end things on a high note. He told the concierge at the Palazzo okay and ended the call.

The next intersection was Hacienda. Slyde spun the wheel, performed an illegal U-turn, and headed back into town. Mags came out of her slumber with a start.

"I thought you were taking me home," she said.

"Change of plans. There's a big game at the Palazzo."

"I'm done. No more scamming for today."

"There's a lot of money on the table. I'll get you some coffee, wake you up."

"My mind's all mush. The pills wore off."

"I'll give you some more. It's easy work. You can't say no."

Mags glared at him. "My hand hurts from belting that asshole. I want to go home."

Some tender loving care was in order. Slyde took Mags's hand and kissed her swollen knuckles while he drove. "Come on, baby, you can do it."

"How come you're nice to me only when you want something?"

"I'm always nice to you, baby. You just appreciate it more sometimes."

"Is that what it is."

"You know I wouldn't steer you wrong. Once we're done fleecing these suckers at the Palazzo, I'll take you home and put you to bed. What do you say?"

Mags withdrew her hand and stared at the road. "All right, but you'd better give me those pills. I ain't worth shit to anybody right now."

- - -

The Palazzo was an all-suite joint tucked between the Wynn and Venetian on the north end of the Strip. Every hotel in town had a special amenity that it advertised to death in order to make itself stand out. For the Palazzo, it was the fact that the resort was eco-friendly.

Eco-friendly was an oxymoron in Vegas. The town was committed to the waste of the region's precious resources and had been since the first casino had been built seventy years ago. Millions of watts of power were wasted every time the Strip's neon lights came on, while excessive watering of golf courses and landscaping had sucked dry the nearby Colorado River.

The Lago suite was nothing to write home about. Nineteen hundred square feet of furniture covered in animal prints and a bunch of dull wall coverings. A green felt poker table occupied the living room's center, and around it, five chairs. A Hollywood producer named Rand Waters sat at the table with two flunkies. Waters was pushing sixty but played a younger man, his sleeveless muscle shirt displaying a pair of well-toned arms. Waters had produced so many hit TV series over the years that even Mags knew his name.

Introductions were made. Mags had played poker with Hollywood hotshots before and knew the drill. It was all about enhancing the star. Waters was the star, and everyone present was expected to fawn over him like the next coming of Christ.

The hired dealer shuffled and dealt the round.

"Where are you from, Mags?" Waters asked.

"Providence," Mags replied.

"I visited there once. A lovely town."

"You should get your eyes checked," she said.

Waters laughed. A split second later, the flunkies joined in.

"Have you ever acted? You could be on TV," Waters said.

"I thought we were here to play cards," Mags said.

"Fasten your seat belts, boys. We're in for a ride," he said to the flunkies.

The game was no-limit Texas Hold 'Em. Mags decided not to give Waters bad action and purposely lost the first few hands. It was apparent that the flunkies had an agreement with Waters and would drop out whenever Waters had good cards and bet aggressively. Hustlers called this playing cousins.

In most poker games that Mags had played in, cell phones were turned off. That was not the case with Waters. The TV producer's iPhone lay on the green felt next to his chips and was constantly beeping, buzzing, and vibrating. Play was stopped if the call was deemed important, and Waters would talk to the caller while Mags and the flunkies twiddled their thumbs.

After the fourth interruption, Mags decided she'd had enough. Waters needed to be cut down to size. Her opportunity came the very next hand. She got dealt two aces, a pair of bullets. Waters also had a pair. Mags knew this because Waters had gotten a pair earlier, and his breathing had become accelerated. Waters's breathing was accelerated now, and Mags put him on a pair of jacks.

Mags raised five grand.

Waters came over the top and raised Mags ten grand.

Mags went for the kill and shoved her chips forward. "I'm all in."

Waters turned white. His jacks were good, but were they good enough?

"That's a very a-aggressive bet," Waters stammered.

"You can always muck your hand," Mags suggested.

"Should I?"

"I would if I were you."

Waters stared at his cards. He was out of his element, and he knew it.

"I call," he said.

They flipped their cards faceup. As she'd suspected, Waters had jacks. The dealer dealt the flop, then fourth and fifth street. Mags's aces held up, and she raked in the massive pot.

"You're awfully good," Waters said.

"Beginner's luck," Mags said.

"You're a natural. Let me give you a screen test."

"I've never acted in my life. I wouldn't know what to do."

"Just be yourself. I know talent when I see it, and you've got talent. Doesn't she?"

"The camera will eat her up," one of the flunkies said.

Mags had not expected this to turn into a casting call. Slyde stood on the other side of the suite talking on his cell phone. His face was filled with worry, and he motioned to her.

"Excuse me, gentlemen, I'll be right back," she said.

- - -

The suite had a game room with the prerequisite pool table and pinball machine. Slyde shut the door behind them. "That was the concierge at the Riviera. You broke Dolan's neck."

"Is he alive?"

"Barely. The C2 vertebra is broken in two places. They call it the hangman's fracture because that's what breaks when a person gets hanged. Dolan is at the emergency room at the hospital, about to go into surgery. He's already talked to the cops and is pressing charges."

"But he struck me. It was self-defense."

"Dolan's buddies told the cops that you attacked him. The two hookers are backing up the story."

"Are the police looking for me?"

"Yeah. You want to go talk to them, give them your side of the story?"

"Are you out of your fucking mind? I'm not allowed to set foot in a Vegas casino, remember? The police will put me into a cell and throw away the key."

"Then what do you want to do?"

"I need to talk to a lawyer."

"A lawyer's going to tell you what I'm telling you. You have to talk to the police."

Mags leaned against the wall and hugged herself. Her world was suddenly caving in and she didn't know what to do. "Will you go with me?"

"Go with you where?" Slyde asked.

"To the police. I need you to back up my story."

"Me and the police don't get along."

"For the love of Christ, you're all I got, Jimmy."

"Fuck it. All right, I'll back you up."

Slyde was lying to her. Mags could tell by the soft tone of his voice and the subtle narrowing of his eyelids. Slyde was going to drop Mags and run like hell. The betrayal was enough to make her head explode, and she wanted to scratch his eyes out.

"You prick," she said.

Slyde pretended not to hear and walked out of the game room. He had his parking slip out and was calling downstairs to the valet for his car to be pulled up.

"Wait for me, you piece of shit."

Mags hustled after Slyde across the suite. Upon reaching the door, she felt a hand on her arm. Waters stood next to her wearing his best Tinseltown smile.

"You can't leave now," Waters said.

"Afraid so," Mags said.

"But I just ordered lunch from room service."

"You'll have to give me a rain check."

"I was serious about what I said. Give me the chance, and I'll make you into a star."

"That's some pickup line."

Slyde was halfway down the hallway, hustling toward the elevators. If Slyde got on and the doors closed, Mags knew she'd never see him again.

"Got to run. Been a pleasure," she said.

Waters shoved a business card into her hand.

"Call me anytime," the Hollywood producer said.

THIRTY-SIX

"Look, he's waking up," Misty said.

Billy spent a moment getting his bearings. He was lying on a couch in the sky palace with his crew assembled around him. John Legend played on the room's sound system, the volume loud enough to make it impossible for the hidden mikes to make out their conversation.

"Are those crazy bastards gone?" he asked.

"They split a while ago," Misty said. "You had us worried. I was going to call the house doctor, but Travis said not to, that it would set off too many alarms."

Billy took a moment to wipe the caked blood from his nostrils. Getting punched in the face was an occupational hazard, and he checked for broken bones or chipped teeth. Everything felt normal except for the swelling above his upper lip. He could live with that.

He shifted his attention to his crew. Cory and Morris looked like scared rabbits, while Travis and Misty showed more concern than fear. Pepper was still AWOL, and he wondered if she'd gotten hitched to Tommy Wang in one of the town's el cheapo wedding chapels.

"Any word from Pepper?" he asked.

No one replied. Of all the problems he was dealing with, Pepper could wait.

Travis said, "Your jaw's swollen. Misty's got pain pills for you to take."

Misty handed him four Ibuprofen and a glass of water. Billy downed the pain pills and leaned his head back on the cushion.

"Hey, Billy, listen. We think it's time to get out of Dodge," Travis said. "Can we do that without blowing your cover?"

Billy thought about it. If they left Carnivale early, he could wire the casino the money he'd lost at blackjack. It would be a hit to his bank account, but his false identity would remain intact, and Carnivale's management would be none the wiser.

He started to tell Travis yes, then killed the words coming out of his mouth.

"We can't leave," he said.

Travis's face crashed. "How come?"

"We have new partners. I don't think they'd like us leaving before the job's done."

"You struck a deal with those guys?"

"Keep your voice down. The reasons those guys didn't whack you is because I agreed to give them a piece of the action. If they don't collect, they'll go to the police and give them the folder they printed off Gabe's computer that explains the scam."

"So we're stuck."

"Afraid so. We can't bail."

Travis looked defeated. The big man found a chair and dropped himself into it. "Those guys are killers. It's just a matter of time before they take us out."

"That's not going to happen. When the job's over, I'll deal with them," Billy said.

"How you going to do that?"

"I said, keep your voice down."

"Does it matter at this point, Billy?"

It was starting to feel like a mutiny. If Travis bailed, the others would also leave, and the scam would fall apart. Worse, they'd probably stop working for Billy and join other crews in town that scammed casinos, of which there were many. Billy was not about to let that happen. The crew was his baby, and he would do whatever was necessary to keep them together, even if that meant telling them things about himself that he'd preferred not come out. Pushing himself to his feet, he went to the bar and grabbed a handful of cold beers out of the fridge for the guys and a wine spritzer for Misty.

"Let's take this outside," he said.

- - -

The pool area had a coffee table and five chairs made of cast iron so they wouldn't blow away. Billy passed the drinks around. The wind was blowing from the northwest, and screams from the Stratosphere's death-defying rooftop rides filled the air.

"I'm about to tell you some stuff that can't be repeated," he said.

"Got it," Travis said.

Cory and Morris sipped their beers and nodded agreement.

"This conversation won't go any further," Misty said. "Now, tell us how you're going to stop these motherfuckers from murdering us after the job's over."

Misty had never been one to beat around the bush. Billy removed his wallet and placed it on the table. The billfold had a hidden compartment, and he folded it back and removed a stiff white business card. The card had the United States Department of Justice's distinct blue and gold seal, which included the words *Federal Bureau of Investigation*.

Misty got to see the card first. "Well, lookie here. Ken Shapiro, Special Agent, Las Vegas Field Office. He even gave you his private cell number. You know this guy?"

Billy acknowledged that he did indeed know an FBI agent named Ken Shapiro.

The others examined the card as well. Travis handed it back.

"What's the connection?" the big man asked.

"I did a job for the FBI," Billy said. "A gang of North Korean cheats was ripping off casinos in town. The scam required that a dealer be involved. The dealer got caught and offered to rat out his partners in exchange for immunity. The North Koreans didn't like that, so they slit the dealer's throat. Shapiro contacted me and asked that I help the bureau figure out how the scam worked, so they could nail the North Koreans and put them away."

"Did you?"

Billy nodded. Part of the cheater's code specified that a cheat never expose another cheat to the law. Billy had broken the code, and he needed to explain to his crew why.

"You were in the military, weren't you?" Billy asked.

"Army. I did a tour of Iraq," Travis replied.

"My father served in Vietnam, and my grandfather was in Korea. I grew up believing that if your country comes calling, you should say yes. Shapiro told me the North Koreans' blackjack scam was bringing in a million bucks a week and that the money was being sent directly back to the mother country. It was enough money for that little fucker with the funny haircut to build a nuclear bomb. When I heard that, I decided I'd better help him. Later that night, I went in disguise to a casino and watched the North Koreans in action."

"They could have killed you," Misty said.

"I played the Iggy. They didn't have a clue."

"So what was the scam? Is it something we can use?" Cory asked.

"The North Koreans were marking the edges of all the high-valued cards with luminous paint," Billy said. "One of the gang had a camera with a red filter in the sleeve of his jacket. After the decks were shuffled, the dealer placed the cards on the table, and the guy with the camera took a high resolution shot of the cards, and the filter picked up the luminous marks.

"The picture was sent to a computer across town, where another member of the gang analyzed it and determined when the high-valued cards would be dealt. This information was sent to the gang through inner-canal earpieces, and they bet accordingly."

"You said the dealer was involved. How?" Travis asked.

"The dealer's job was to give the camera enough time to take a clear picture," Billy said. "That required stalling on the dealer's part. It was the scam's only flaw. The FBI busted the North Koreans the next day. They also nailed the guy with the computer and found information on other gangs cheating the Native American reservation casinos. It put a real dent in Kim's bankroll. And for that act of selfless patriotism, Shapiro told me to call him if I ever had an emergency."

"Which you'll do to stop the Haneys from murdering us," Travis said.

"That's right. I know of several jobs the Haneys have pulled. I also have Gabe digging up dirt on them. When we're finished scamming the Carnivale, I'll contact Shapiro and pass along the information. Shapiro will bust them and add another feather to his cap."

"What's going to stop the Haneys from turning over the information they found on Gabe's computer to the gaming board?" Travis asked.

"I'll ask Shapiro to destroy the folder," Billy said.

"He'll do that for you?"

"Damn straight he will. I risked my neck. He owes me. Any more questions?"

There were none. Billy looked each of them in the eye before speaking again.

"Are we good?"

"I'm good," Travis said.

"Me, too," Cory said.

"Fine here," Morris said.

Misty reached across the table and touched Billy's wrist. "Thank you for telling us this. It means a lot to us."

Cory and Morris went back inside the sky palace. Travis followed moments later. Misty started to rise from her chair and Billy cleared his throat. The sound stopped Misty in her tracks and she sat back down.

"So where is she?" Billy asked.

Misty shook her head, pretending not to understand.

"Pepper. Where is she?" Billy asked.

"I don't know where she is," Misty replied.

"You have the nerve to fucking lie to me, after what I just told you? You and Pepper live together, eat together, and probably take showers together. Don't you dare tell me you haven't heard from her, because I know you have. Now, where is she?"

Misty dropped her hands in her lap and started to reply, but no words came out. Her allegiance was to Pepper and always would be. Her chair made a harsh scraping sound as she stood up. Standing at the balcony, she pointed due north.

"Pepper's over there, on the rides."

"You're kidding me."

"No, I'm not."

In the distance was the Stratosphere, a casino hotel known for its terrifying rooftop rides. Billy envisioned Pepper and Tommy Wang riding the roller coaster as it whipped around the needle-shaped building, their screams piercing the air like a pair of high school kids on a date.

"Is she in love with him?" Billy asked.

"What do you think?"

"I think she is."

"You just might be right."

Misty returned to her chair, leaving Billy to wonder if they'd ever hear from Pepper again. Love did strange things to people. He'd found that out the hard way with Maggie Flynn. All he could hope was that Pepper didn't have as hard a landing as he'd had.

THIRTY-SEVEN

The date had almost not happened. Tommy Wang offered to buy Pepper a drink in one of Carnivale's fancy, high-priced cocktail lounges, and Pepper nearly turned him down. Tommy was the mark, and it wasn't smart to get too close to people you conned.

But Pepper hadn't done that. Instead, she'd accepted, and off they'd gone. She liked Tommy; he was gentle and caring, attributes rarely found in men who gambled large sums of money in casinos. Billy had said that Tommy had nearly died at a gangster's hands, and Pepper had a feeling there was more to the story. Lurking behind Tommy's soulful eyes was a secret, and Pepper was determined to unlock that secret and make him share it with her.

As they took the elevator down to the hotel's first floor, Tommy pointed through the elevator's tinted glass walls at the needle-shaped spire of the Stratosphere casino.

"Have you ever ridden on the roller coaster on the top of that building?" he asked. "I hear the screams from my balcony. It sounds wonderful."

The Stratosphere's rooftop roller coaster had a unique construction, its chairs attached to a giant teeter-totter. After taking a trip around the building at breakneck speed, the coaster unexpectedly pitched over the hotel's edge and dangled nine hundred terrifying feet above the ground. These were the screams that Tommy heard from his balcony at the Carnivale.

"Don't tell me you've never ridden a roller coaster," Pepper said.

"When I was a little boy, my family visited the Shijingshan Amusement Park in Beijing, but I was not tall enough to get on the roller coaster," he explained. "I had to stay behind while my brothers and sisters rode on it. It was a very sad day."

"We need to fix that."

"Will you go on the roller coaster with me?"

A hint of fear had crept into his voice. Maybe the story wasn't entirely true; maybe Tommy had been too afraid to get on the ride with his siblings.

"You bet I will," Pepper said.

- - -

The roller coaster docked and Pepper pulled Tommy off. His legs had turned to jelly and silent tears ran down his cheeks. Grown men did not weep uncontrollably on amusement rides, and Pepper realized there was something seriously wrong with her date.

Most men were broken; what you saw on the outside was a well-constructed facade meant to impress the opposite sex. Pepper decided she could deal with it. Tommy was her ticket to the big time, and she was more than happy to prop him up until they took down Carnivale.

She took him to the Air Bar on the 108th floor of the Stratosphere. The place was empty and she grabbed a corner table with a panoramic view of the Strip. Tommy sat slumped in his chair with his chin resting on his chest. Pepper dabbed away the wet spot on his mouth with a napkin.

"Is your friend okay?" the waitress asked.

"The ride freaked him out. Better bring us two shots of whiskey," Pepper said.

"He's not the first one. I'll bring you water, too."

The waitress's heels clacked across the checkered tile floor. Pepper pulled herself close and gave Tommy's cheek a gentle slap. "You still with me, cowboy?"

His eyelids fluttered. "Hi."

"Hi yourself. How do you feel?"

"I will be all right. I'm sorry if I embarrassed you."

"Don't worry about it. If you don't mind my asking, what were you were bawling about?"

"What is bawling?"

"Crying, as in real loud."

"I had a flashback and saw my dead parents."

This was getting heavy. The waitress returned with their drinks. Pepper placed a shot glass against Tommy's lips and poured.

"That burns," he said.

"It's supposed to. Here, drink some water."

He sipped from the glass. "Much better."

"You want this other shot?"

Tommy declined. Pepper slammed back the second shot. Nothing set the world straighter than whiskey. "If you don't mind my asking, what made you have a flashback?"

"I thought I was going to die."

"Come on, it was just a flipping ride."

"I had a bad experience not long ago and have not been the same since."

Pepper didn't like the sound of this. What if Tommy experienced another flashback when they were ripping off Carnivale and started crying his head off?

"Want to talk about it? I'm the world's best listener," she said.

"I would prefer not."

Tommy was holding back. Had they been at the sky palace, she would have thrown him on a couch and screwed him. Porn had taught her how to make a man open up, the layers as easy to peel as an onion. Because they were in a bar, she did the next best thing and stroked his thigh. "I like you. You're one of the coolest guys I've ever met. Come on. Tell me."

Aroused, he sat up straight in his chair. "I need more whiskey," he said.

Pepper snapped her fingers and their waitress hit the table.

"Give us another round," Pepper said.

- - -

"My country is different than yours," Tommy said after he'd had another drink. "We believe that life is a wheel that never stops turning. A person can step on, or step off, at any time. No matter what the person does, the wheel keeps turning. Does that make sense?"

Pepper didn't know what the hell Tommy was talking about.

"I guess," she said.

"The wheel is the only thing that truly matters. When a Chinese person gambles, he isn't really concerned about winning or losing. He does it for the action and the excitement that comes from stepping on the wheel. If he loses all his money and steps off the wheel, no big deal, because he can always step back on the wheel another time."

"I get it. The wheel's a higher power," Pepper said.

"Exactly. The wheel is a higher power. Back home, I am an accountant for a large manufacturing company, and I handle a great deal of money. Several months ago, I attended a conference with other accountants from my company. One night, a group of us got drunk and came up with a scheme. We would each borrow money from the bank accounts we managed and spend a weekend gambling in Macau. One of the accountants had a system to win at blackjack that he claimed was unbeatable. So we did it."

There was a name for people who played systems: losers. Pepper knew where this was heading but decided not to ruin Tommy's story. "What happened?"

"We won big and caught the attention of a gangster named Broken Tooth, who is tied to the Macau casinos. Broken Tooth offered to stake us ten million dollars to beat the Las Vegas casinos with our system. We agreed, and a few weeks later tried our system here. Unfortunately, it did not work the second time, and we lost everything."

"What happened when you got home?"

"We went to Macau and broke the bad news to Broken Tooth. He did not act upset, but offered to buy us lunch. We went to a restaurant and realized it was empty. Broken Tooth's men lined us up in front of a wall and aimed pistols at us. That was when my dead parents appeared to me. They were so ashamed of what I'd done."

Tommy became filled with grief and stopped talking. Pepper gave his leg a squeeze. "And then?"

"Broken Tooth said, 'Fire!' and his men obeyed. I shut my eyes and heard the sound of bullets ripping flesh and bodies hitting the ground. And all I could think was, why am I still standing? I opened my eyes and saw the other accountants lying dead around me. I didn't understand what had happened. Only later did I learn the truth."

He again fell mute. Pepper handed him her untouched shot.

"Drink this."

"I am already drunk."

"Do it anyway."

He obeyed, and knocked back the drink.

"So why didn't you die?" she asked.

"Broken Tooth's men made a mistake and shot the accountants standing to either side of me, but failed to shoot me. Broken Tooth started laughing and asked me if I had an angel sitting on my shoulder. I told him I had two angels, my dead parents."

"Do people believe in angels in your country?"

"Oh yes. When you go to a cemetery, you'll see people putting food on a tombstone and burning fake money so the angel has what he or she needs in the afterlife." He wiped his mouth on his sleeve. "Broken Tooth said good fortune was smiling down on me, and he ordered me back to Las Vegas. If I won the lost money back, all would be forgiven."

"Broken Tooth staked you a second time? That's crazy."

"You are right. It's impossible to beat the casinos. I might as well go home now."

Tommy slumped in his chair, a beaten and broken man. She nearly kicked herself; she was supposed to be boosting Tommy up to believe he couldn't lose. Instead, she'd forced him to take a bad trip down memory lane. There was an easy way to fix that. She got on the Internet on her cell phone, pulled up the Stratosphere's website, and made a reservation for a deluxe room with a king bed. There were plenty of different priced rooms to choose from, not that it mattered. They were all the same once you turned the lights out.

She dragged him downstairs and booked the room. Took an elevator to the 17th floor and pulled him into the room, where she stripped off his clothes and made him lie on the bed. He started to pass out and she slapped him across the face. Her clothes came off next.

"You are more beautiful than I imagined," he said drunkenly.

"You're pretty hot yourself," she said.

She switched off the lights and climbed aboard. The splashy TV spots for the Las Vegas Convention and Visitors Bureau boasted about the great shows, great food, and great golf, but what really made the town great was the amount of fucking that went on. Thousands of women made their living turning on tourists, including street walkers, call girls, bar hookers, strippers who turned tricks, girls who trolled the casino floors, and brothel babes. Prostitution was illegal in Vegas, but the cops looked the other way, and for good reason. Fucking turned cowards into heroes and weaklings into supermen. Without it, the casinos would never have survived.

The sex brought Tommy out of his funk. The color returned to his cheeks and his smile grew ever so wide. He made a spot for her on his pillow, and Pepper snuggled up beside him. Her cell phone was blinking on the night table and she picked it up.

Billy had sent her a text.

```
We need to talk
```

Billy had to be steaming by now. He had spent a long time planning this heist and invested a lot of money, and he had a right to know what she was up to. She wanted to tell him to cool his jets, everything was okay, while not coming off as being disrespectful.

"Is something wrong?" Tommy asked.

"My boss is looking for me," she said.

"Is that bad?"

"He doesn't like it when I wander."

"Is he in love with you?"

Pepper shook her head. The sex she'd had with Billy had nothing to do with love. Billy had known that and so had she, and they'd both been comfortable with the arrangement.

Tommy combed his fingers through her thick hair. He didn't act drunk anymore, just glad to be alive. That was when she realized this was the real thing.

She sent Billy a reply.

```
Call you later
```

THIRTY-EIGHT

Billy sat in a chair on the balcony holding an ice pack to his swollen lip. He'd been punched in the face before, and the resulting bruises were memorable for the shapes they'd taken. Some resembled foreign countries, others barnyard animals. The bruise inflicted by Junior Haney looked like a purple pig, and it also hurt like hell.

His cell phone vibrated. Pepper had replied to his text. He shielded his eyes to read her reply. `Call you later.` He showed the message to Misty before putting the cell phone away.

"I'm sorry, Billy," Misty said.

"You need to talk to Pepper, explain what's going on."

"I'll try. She's never acted like this, and I've known her for a long time. I guess . . ."

"Go ahead and say it. She's fallen head over heels for this guy."

"It sure seems that way."

"You surprised?"

"You bet I'm surprised. Aren't you?"

Billy shrugged. Vegas was a tough town for relationships. He'd dated plenty of women, and the majority had told him they didn't believe in love and thought it was a bullshit emotion. Pepper had said pretty much the same thing to him, yet had run off with the first guy who'd treated her right. "You need to call her and tell her to get back here," he repeated.

"What if she blows me off?" Misty asked.

"If she gives you crap, tell her that I checked Tommy Wang out. He's taken."

Misty's mouth dropped open. "You're kidding me."

"The guy has a wife and kids back home. Tell Pepper that when you talk to her."

"Jesus Christ, that will kill her."

Water was dripping down his face from the melting ice pack. He'd never been good at being a prick, and he relented. "All right, then try this. Tell Pepper I have tickets to see Bruno Mars at the MGM tonight, and since Gabe won't be coming with us, she can invite Tommy Wang to join us. You can spring the news to her there."

"You want me to tell her?"

"Someone's got to, and it isn't going to be me."

Misty called Pepper on her cell phone. Billy was close enough to hear Pepper's voice when she answered. Pepper sounded half-asleep, which could mean only one thing: she had slept with the mark. Misty placed her cell phone against her chest.

"Pepper wants to know what time she needs to hook up with us."

"Show starts at eight. Tell her to meet us there fifteen minutes before."

"Got it."

Misty relayed the information and ended the call. She looked relieved, and Billy was happy to have that behind them. He needed to head downstairs and lose more money in the casino, and he rose from his chair and went to the slider. He'd already had enough surprises to last a lifetime of jobs. As he started to pull back the slider, Misty came up beside him.

"You didn't make that up about Wang having a family, did you?"

Sometimes Misty surprised him. Misty thought she understood men because of all the porn she'd done, but in reality, she didn't know the first thing about them.

"What do you think?" Billy said.

"Oh shit," she said.

- - -

Billy put on fresh clothes and appraised himself in the bathroom vanity. His face looked a little rough for wear but would pass muster. Plenty of guys who came to Vegas stayed up all night drinking and gambling and looking like death warmed over the next day, and he didn't think his rough appearance would draw many stares. Heading downstairs in the elevator, he got a call from Gabe. He'd found himself missing Gabe and hoped the jeweler had recovered from last night's meltdown.

"How's it going?" Billy answered.

"I hear the Haneys paid you a visit," Gabe said.

"Who told you that?"

"Travis called with the bad news. Are they really blackmailing us?"

Billy didn't think the Carnivale's elevators were bugged, but that didn't mean their conversation wasn't being listened to. Anyone with a few hundred bucks could buy equipment at a spy store that would let them eavesdrop on private cell phone conversations.

"Let's talk about this later, okay?"

"I've got the goods on them. My friend with the police came through. Where do you want to meet?"

There it was again—Gabe telling Billy what to do. Billy said nothing, wanting Gabe to read the silence and understand that he was treading on thin ice with his employer.

"That is, if you're free," the jeweler said.

"I'm not free, but for you, I'll make the time," Billy said.

"You won't be disappointed."

"I need to clean my clothes. I'll meet you in thirty minutes."

"Your clothes? What are you talking about?"

"Figure it out."

- - -

In a city with more surveillance cameras than people, The Laundry Room was a unique watering hole, and did not have any electronic surveillance. The bar was hidden behind a secret door in East Fremont, and a visitor needed to text a secret number to gain entry. Once inside, a strict set of rules applied: no standing at the bar, no loud voices, and photographs and selfies were prohibited.

Billy took a table. Up at the bar, two hustlers he was friends with were discussing a job. Billy could tell as much by the way their shoulders were hunched over and the conspiratorial tone of their voices. Gabe slid into a seat and stuck his hand into the bowl of gourmet popcorn on the table. His eyes were bloodshot from lack of sleep and he was wearing yesterday's clothes.

"This is delicious. You want some?" Gabe asked.

"No thanks. Too spicy for me," Billy said.

"Your face is puffy. Did the Haneys really beat you up?"

"That's ancient history."

"You're not really going to partner up with them, are you?"

Billy dropped his voice. "I'm going to screw the Haneys once the job is over."

A waiter in a starched shirt and bow tie took their orders. Gabe ordered a dirty martini, Billy the house special called the Ransom Note. When the waiter was gone, Gabe started talking. "My friend Bennie with the police department didn't want to talk about the Haneys. He said they were bad news and warned me to stay away from them. When I insisted, he hung up on me."

"This isn't starting out very well."

"It gets better. I called Bennie back and reminded him that I paid him off the books all those years he guarded my jewelry store. I told him that if he didn't help me, I'd report him to the IRS for unreported income and they'd put a lien on his house."

"How did that go over?"

"Like a fart in church. He cursed me out, then caved."

"Nice going."

"Thanks. So here's the skinny. Bennie told me that the police have linked the Haneys to several dozen unsolved murders. The father's a mute and crazy as a loon, and he likes to beat his victims to death or stab them with an ice pick. The father leaves evidence at every crime scene, yet he and his son have never been brought up on charges."

"Teflon-coated."

"Exactly. I asked Bennie why, and that's when it got hairy."

"How do you mean?"

"Bennie said that what the Haneys did could ruin the city, and that if I went around shooting my mouth off, I'd end up getting eighty-sixed."

Their drinks arrived. Gabe took a gulp of his martini and wiped his mouth on his sleeve. In Vegas getting eighty-sixed meant you'd get taken eight miles out into the desert and get buried six feet down. For a cop to have shared this little piece of information meant that the Haneys weren't just Teflon-coated, they were bulletproof.

"So what did these jokers do, whack Jimmy Hoffa?" Billy asked.

"No. They murdered Cal Branche."

"You're kidding me."

"Bennie swore it was true."

There were plenty of unsolved murders in Vegas, and most were forgotten as quickly as a losing Keno number. But the killing of Cal Branche on a cold February night a decade ago hadn't been forgotten. The papers still ran stories on the anniversary of the crime, and Branche's family continued to offer a substantial reward for the killer's arrest.

Billy had met Branche once. He'd just landed in town and was washing dishes while looking for a crew to run with. Upon leaving work one night, he'd encountered Branche in the parking lot. Branche was soft-spoken and friendly, and had suggested Billy join the local culinary workers' union, of which Branche was president.

The next day, Billy had asked his coworkers about Branche and heard good things. Nevada was a right-to-work state, yet Branch had persuaded nearly all of the culinary workers to join the union. This power had let Branche negotiate steady increases in wages and benefits with the casinos. As a result, culinary workers could buy houses and send their kids to college.

Everyone had liked Cal Branche.

"Who paid for the hit?" Billy asked.

"Bennie said a group of casino owners was behind it," Gabe said. "Branche wanted the casinos to offer health-care insurance for the culinary union members. The casinos claimed it was too expensive, so Branche said he'd negotiate a deal with a local hospital chain to provide medical care to culinary employees that the casinos would split the cost of."

"It sounds like Branche outmaneuvered them."

"Exactly. The casinos couldn't turn his deal down without looking bad. That's when the casino bosses decided to put a contract out on him."

"And the cops knew about this."

Gabe stole a glance at the pair sitting at the bar. Satisfied they weren't eavesdropping, he removed a square of paper from his breast pocket, unfolded it, and passed it across the table.

"You tell me," Gabe said.

It was a newspaper article written a few days after Branche's decomposed body was discovered by a hiker beneath a pile of rocks in the desert. The article stated that a father-son duo named Haney had been detained by the police as suspects, and later released. The article also stated that because of Branche's connections to the casinos, the gaming board had interviewed the Haneys. At the bottom of the article was a photo of Branche taken in better times. Tan and Hollywood handsome, he sported a pencil-thin mustache and a thick mane of silver hair. In his hand was a cigarette, which he held a few inches from his lips.

"So the cops and the gaming board kept a lid on it," Billy said.

"That's right. Gives a whole new meaning to the name Sin City, don't you think?"

- - -

Billy paid their tab. He did not speak again until they were outside. The Fremont District was a missed opportunity, a broiling-hot concrete and asphalt ravine filled with clip-art neon signs, jaundiced banners, and clusters of gangly palms, the sidewalks littered with human debris.

"You did a good job. I'm proud of you," Billy said.

"Thanks, Billy. That means a lot to me."

"I need to run. When this is over, I owe you a steak dinner."

Gabe took out his car keys. "You're not pissed at me for what happened last night?"

Last night seemed like another lifetime ago, and Billy shook his head.

"I was in a bad way. I won't do it again, and that's a promise," Gabe said.

"Do what?" Billy said.

Gabe broke into a smile. Billy had always assumed that once Gabe had enough money, he'd open up another swanky jewelry store inside a Strip casino and go back to being legit. But the tone of Gabe's voice told Billy that wasn't the deal at all. Gabe liked the thieving life and was in it for the long run.

"I'm out of here. Now, go home and get some sleep," Billy said.

"Did you ever meet Cal Branche?" Gabe asked.

"Once. He came to a restaurant where I was washing dishes, tried to get me to join the union. He seemed like a decent guy."

"Cal was a great guy. He was also a customer of mine. He used to come into my jewelry store and buy stuff. He went to UNLV on a scholarship and played hoops for two seasons until he blew out his knee."

"Is that why he walked with a limp?"

"Yeah. After he got murdered, his wife came in and asked me if I could produce receipts of Cal's stuff so she could file a claim with her insurance company. She told me her husband's killers had picked his body clean before they'd dumped him. Watch, gold chain, his rings, they took everything except his driver's license so the police could identify him. His wife was so upset, she started crying right in the store."

"They took his wedding ring?"

Gabe nodded. He was roiling inside, the memory ripping him apart. Two drunks staggered out of the Beauty Bar and hurtled past as if running a three-legged race.

"What kind of person does something like that?" Gabe asked.

"The Haneys aren't people," Billy said.

"What do you mean?"

"People are expected to play by certain rules, even bad people. Ones that don't are no better than animals. Now, go home and get some sleep. You need it."

Billy started down the sidewalk. He heard the sound of Gabe's size twelves crunch the concrete and turned around.

"I'm sorry, Billy, but I've got to know."

"You've got to know what?"

"Are you going to fuck these guys? Please tell me yes. Then I'll be able to sleep."

Billy was good at many things. Fucking people was one of them. The key was to never let them see it coming. Gabe knew that better than anyone but still felt the burning need to ask.

"I'm working on it," Billy said.

THIRTY-NINE

Jimmy Slyde sat on the couch in Mags's condo. Fading sunlight streamed through the blinds as the day came to a close. On the flat-screen TV, Judge Judy read the riot act to a couple of born losers. Across from him, Mags sat in a chair holding a tumbler of vodka. Slyde had filled the glass to the brim in the hopes that it would bring her down and she'd be able to sleep. So far, that hadn't happened, and it had seemed to rev Mags up to another RPM level, her mouth going nonstop.

"That fucking guy wants to turn me into a movie star, can you believe that? I should have told him how I starred in a musical in high school, *Once Upon a Mattress*. I played the wicked queen Aggravain. Everyone said I was great."

"What guy?" Slyde asked.

"Rand Waters, the guy we swindled earlier. He's a big-shot TV producer—I've seen his name in the credits of lots of shows. He gave me his card, told me to call him."

"You going to do it?"

"Maybe. I don't know. What do you think?"

What Slyde thought was that he needed to get Mags out of Vegas before the police hauled her pretty ass off to jail for breaking Dolan's neck. The problem was, where was he going to stash her? Sending her to LA to hook up with this Waters character didn't sound like such a bad idea.

"I think you'd be great," Slyde said. "All you have to do is memorize some dopey lines and act natural in front of the camera. That can't be too hard."

"What if I suck?"

"If you sucked, this Waters guy wouldn't have given you his card."

"I've got talent, huh?"

"Loads of talent. That's why you're so good with the grift."

Mags raised the tumbler to her lips and drank. She didn't seem to notice that half the drink went down her face as she stared into space. "It's like lying, huh? Just one big pretend."

"That's right. One day, I'm going to be telling people that I knew you back when. You know what I'm saying?"

"Yeah." She smiled dreamily. "Should I change my name to something more theatrical?"

"What's wrong with the name you got?"

"I never liked Maggie. Makes me sound like a fucking bird."

"What you got in mind?"

"I always liked the name Loretta. It's different."

Slyde's cell phone was vibrating, and he took it from his pocket. Caller ID said Jumping John Houghton, the concierge at New York New York, was trying to track him down. Everyone called him Jumping John because he couldn't stand still.

"If it isn't my old buddy, Jumping John. How you been?" Slyde answered.

"How soon can you get over to Champagne's Café? We need to talk," Jumping John said.

"You got a job for me, or is this a social gathering?"

"This is about your lady friend. The shit's about to hit the fan."

Slyde glanced at Mags. She was zoned out and hadn't heard a word. He stuck the phone against his chest, said, "Hey Loretta, I need to take this," and left for the kitchen.

- - -

"Everybody's scared out of their minds over this Dolan thing," Jumping John said.

"Who's everybody?" Slyde leaned against the fridge.

"The other concierges in town you do business with."

"It didn't happen in their casinos."

"Doesn't matter. We still do business with you. Get your ass over here."

"Don't talk to me like that."

"I'll talk to you any fucking way I want to. This situation needs to get fixed."

"Fixed how?"

"That's what we want to discuss. Your ass is in a sling, Jimmy. Shit flows downward, and you're going to be on the receiving end of some serious shit. Now, get over here."

Jumping John had picked the wrong person to threaten. Slyde drew a Ruger SP101 from his pants pocket and spun the chamber to make sure it was fully loaded. Then he pressed the button on the front of the grip and a red laser beam appeared on the wall above the kitchen sink.

"Champagne's Café. That's the place with velvet walls," Slyde said.

"That's it," Jumping John said.

"I'm leaving now."

- - -

Champagne's Café was on Maryland Parkway and never closed. Slyde had tried to have a meeting there once and had nearly suffocated from the cigarette smoke. The parking spaces in front were taken, so Slyde pulled around and parked in the space next to the back entrance. He was three steps from going inside when the barrel of a gun was pressed against his spine.

"Don't move," a voice said.

"That you, Jumpster?" Slyde asked.

"Yup. Put your hands against the wall."

Jumping John patted Slyde down and removed the Ruger from his pocket. The concierge pushed Slyde toward a black stretch limo parked in the rear of the property.

"We going for a ride?" Slyde asked.

"Nope. It's just a precaution. Now, get in," Jumping John said.

Slyde straightened the knot in his tie before climbing into the limo. Three other concierges who Slyde did business with sat on the opposing leather seat. There was Lee Grant, the concierge at Circus Circus, Dave Allmand, the concierge at the Aladdin, and Mike Roche, the concierge at the Palms. Each man was dressed identically: tailored silk suit, dark vest, and silk necktie. Each also had a stiff drink in his hand. Jumping John followed Slyde into the limo and shut the door behind him.

"He was carrying this." Jumping John displayed the Ruger.

"You expecting a gunfight?" Grant asked.

"I always carry a gun. You can never be too careful these days," Slyde said.

The limo fell silent. Slyde had a history with the four concierges that preceded Maggie Flynn. With Grant, it was concealing a high-resolution camera inside an AC vent so they could cheat the owner of a baseball team in a high-stakes poker game; with Allmand, Roche, and Jumping John, the scam had been using taped delays of horse races to fleece their high-rolling customers at the casino's sports books. The four concierges were in deep with Slyde, a decision they now regretted.

"Do you want a drink?" Jumping John asked.

"Beer's good," Slyde said.

Jumping John served him a can of Sin City IPA. Slyde popped the top and drank. Had the beer come in a bottle, Slyde would have broken it and used the edge to slice their throats.

"We have a problem, Jimmy," Jumping John said. "Dolan told the police the poker game at the Riviera was rigged. Dolan implicated you, Maggie Flynn, and me. I've already spoken to the police and told them I had nothing to do with it. We know you won't squeal, which leaves Maggie."

"I'm taking Mags to LA. She's going to disappear," Slyde said.

"For how long?" Jumping John asked. "The gaming board banned her from setting foot in a casino, yet she still came back. The woman has a problem."

Slyde wasn't going to argue with Jumping John there, and he sipped his beer.

"The police told me Maggie's facing multiple charges for breaking Dolan's neck and for cheating him at cards," Jumping John said. "She's going down hard. We're afraid she might cut a deal with the DA and implicate us."

"Mags isn't a rat. She won't talk," Slyde said.

"Of course she'll talk," Grant said. "She's a criminal, and will do whatever it takes to save her own skin."

"She's a cheat, and cheats have a code. She won't talk," Slyde said.

Grant looked at Slyde like the black hustler had lost his mind. The other concierges were giving him similar looks. In their world, there was no code that people lived by, just a loose set of rules that got bent and twisted to suit the individual's needs.

"Do you know what the courts will do to us if Mags talks?" Roche asked.

Slyde wanted to tell Roche that getting screwed was the price you sometimes paid for breaking the law, but he didn't think Roche or the others would appreciate the sermon.

"Not only will we go to prison, but the state will take away our houses, our cars, and drain every last cent from our bank accounts," Roche said. "They'll destroy us and our families. We'll be ruined."

"We can't let that happen," Allmand said.

"No, we can't," Grant agreed.

"Are you getting the picture, Jimmy?" Jumping John said. "Mags is a liability. She needs to disappear."

"Permanently," Grant added.

Allmand and Roche nodded agreement. The decision had been made; now a sap needed to be recruited to carry out the dirty deed. Slyde crushed the empty beer can between his palms. "You want me to ice her?"

The four concierges nodded. That was exactly what they wanted.

"What happens then?"

"The investigation will stall, and the Riviera's insurance company will cut Dolan a check for his medical expenses," Jumping John said.

"You're saying that with Mags out of the picture, the dust will settle, and everything goes back to normal."

"That's right," Grant said. "We want you to make the crazy bitch disappear. It's the only solution."

Slyde blew out his lungs. He had no qualms about killing, and in fact had killed in the past. But killing Mags was different. She'd made him a lot of money and still had a few good scores left in her. Slyde wanted to ask them what would happen if he said no, but he thought he already knew. They'd put their hands on him and squeeze the life out of his body, and then they'd track down Mags and do the same to her. That was why they'd all had a stiff drink before Slyde arrived. To work up the courage. Seen in that light, Slyde didn't have any other choice.

"I'll take care of it," Slyde said.

Their business was done. Jumping John opened the door and Slyde climbed out of the limo. Slyde straightened his jacket and walked to where his car was parked. He had a thought and went back to the limo. The tinted back window came down.

"Forget something?" Jumping John asked.

"My gun," Slyde said.

"I'll mail it to you," the concierge said.

FORTY

The clunker in Gabe's driveway didn't look familiar. It was an American model manufactured by Chrysler that hadn't caught on. Gabe parked behind it and got out. Through the driver's window he spied fast-food wrappers and beer cans lying on the floor of the backseat.

"There you are. I was beginning to worry about you."

Gabe looked up to see his neighbor Elsie coming down the front path.

"Whose car is this?" he asked.

"It's your friends' car," his neighbor replied. "I hope you don't mind, but I let them in with the spare key you gave me. I went out for my afternoon walk and saw them sitting in your driveway in the broiling hot sun. I thought it was the neighborly thing to do."

"What friends are you talking about?" Gabe asked.

"The ones from last night who I thought were burglars. You said they were your friends, remember? Please don't tell me I'm imagining this."

Gabe processed what Elsie was saying. The front door of his house opened and Junior Haney stepped out. The younger Haney waved to him like an old buddy.

"You let them in," Gabe said under his breath.

"Is that okay? I'm happy to ask them to leave."

Gabe didn't think Elsie asking the Haneys to leave was going to work. This was his problem to deal with. "It's fine. I'm sure they were very appreciative."

"They most certainly were. Although the older one is very odd. Does he have problems?" Elsie placed a finger to her temple. "You know, up here?"

"He's just quiet," Gabe said. "Let me go say hi. Thanks for helping out."

"You're more than welcome. Have a nice day."

Steaming, Gabe marched up the path. The younger Haney was holding the remote to the train set. Gabe ripped it from his hand.

"What do you want?"

"Your neighbor's a sweet old gal," the younger Haney said.

"I said, what do you want?"

"Me and my father got to thinking. Your boss, Billy, is a cheat, and cheats can't be trusted. So we decided to move in with you while the scam at the Carnivale was going down. Sort of like insurance, if you know what I mean."

"You're a piece of shit, and so's your father."

"In case you didn't know it, we're business partners, so start acting nice."

It was all Gabe could do not to put his hands around the younger Haney's throat. He entered the house and marched down the hallway into the living room. His prized electric train set was racing around the track, and he punched the remote and watched the train screech to a halt. A tiny replica of himself stared up from the engineer's car.

"This isn't starting out well," the younger Haney said. "My name's Jack, but everyone calls me Junior. It's nice to meet you."

Gabe bounced the remote off Junior's chest in a rage. Junior's pleasant demeanor evaporated, and he lifted his shirt to expose the gun tucked behind his belt.

"Do that again, and I'll shoot you," Junior said.

"You killed my friend last night. Why did you do that?"

"I didn't lay a hand on him. My old man goes off his rocker sometimes. Don't ask me why."

"Your father kills people, and you don't know why?"

"It's just his nature," Junior said.

Gabe retrieved the remote from the floor and tossed it on the train table. Billy was planning to put the screws to Junior and his deranged father once the Carnivale job was over. Revenge was a plate best served cold, and Gabe told himself to be patient.

"Is your father here?" Gabe asked.

"He's in the garage playing with your toys," Junior said.

Gabe's stomach tightened. The garage was his workshop, the work tables filled with different cheating gaffs that would someday be used to take down the casinos. He spent much of his time there and could count on one hand the number of outsiders he'd allowed to see it.

"I'd like to meet him."

"Happy to. You first," Junior said.

Access to the garage was gained through the kitchen. Gabe pushed the door open and entered the attached two-car garage. Bright fluorescent lights illuminated the concrete-floored room. The elder Haney stood at a worktable, examining the gaffed Keno game.

"Pop, this is Gabe Weiss," Junior said.

The father looked up. He had a raptor-like face and soulless eyes. An inhuman grunt escaped his parched lips.

"What did he say?" Gabe asked.

"He wants to know the deal with the Keno game," Junior said.

Gabe decided to play along and moved toward the worktable. Gabe still had a jeweler's eye and spotted the glittering diamond Bezel Rolex on the old man's wrist. There was no doubt in Gabe's mind that this was the same diamond Bezel Rolex that he'd sold to Cal Branche a decade ago. Cal Branche's body had been picked clean after his murder, and Gabe wondered how many pieces of Cal's jewelry the father was wearing.

It got him angry just thinking about it.

Gabe shifted his focus to the Keno game on the worktable. Keno was for suckers, the odds of winning so astronomically high that practically no one ever did. Eighty numbered Ping-Pong balls sat inside a circular glass enclosure called a bubble. At the press of a button, a blower sent air into the bubble that mixed the balls in a random fashion.

Numbers were drawn by pressing a lever that opened a plastic tube, causing the balls to lift into a V-shaped device called the rabbit ears. Players made wagers by circling numbers on blank Keno tickets. If a player's circled numbers matched the drawn balls, they won.

Keno was considered impossible to cheat, since no human hands ever touched the balls. Billy had a method in mind, and one day he'd given Gabe a box of sewing needles hardened with a titanium nitride coating. Within a few hours, Gabe was able to gaff the balls in a way that was invisible to the naked eye.

A blank Keno ticket lay next to the machine. Next to it, a golf pencil. Gabe picked up the ticket, circled ten boxes, and placed the ticket facedown on the table.

"It's showtime," Gabe said. "This Keno game looks legit but is rigged and can make you a fortune, if you know what the secret is. Allow me to demonstrate. Please start the game."

The elder Haney started the machine. The blower made a soft whirring sound as the balls flew around the bubble.

"Does that look fair to you?" Gabe asked.

The elder Haney pressed his face to the bubble. A grunt escaped his lips.

"My father says yeah," Junior said.

"Press the lever, and start picking the winners," Gabe said.

The elder Haney hit the lever. One by one, balls traveled up the gooseneck and filled the rabbit ears. The game was stopped after twenty balls had made the journey.

"You know how the game works?" Gabe asked.

The elder Haney grunted yes.

"How about you?" Gabe asked.

"Sure, I've played before," Junior said.

"Good. Take a look at my ticket, and see how many winners I picked."

Junior picked up the ticket and compared the circled numbers to the numbers on the twenty balls in the rabbit ears.

"He got eight winners," Junior told his dad.

"Which would make me approximately a grand, depending upon the casino I'm playing in," Gabe said. "A thousand bucks on a ten-dollar investment. You can't beat that."

The elder Haney snatched the ticket out of his son's hand and looked at the numbers Gabe had chosen. Gabe had fooled him, and the crazy bastard didn't like being fooled. Throwing the ticket to the floor, the elder Haney picked up a screwdriver lying on the table.

Gabe stepped back, bumping into the son.

"Please don't hurt me," Gabe said.

The elder Haney didn't have malice on his mind. Instead, he took apart the machine with the screwdriver and dumped the twenty balls out of the rabbit ears onto the table. He held each ball up to the light, bounced it on the floor, and when none of those tests proved adequate, grunted another unintelligible command to his son.

Junior left the garage. Soon he returned holding a large glass of water. The old man dunked the balls in the water. Each one floated innocently to the top.

The Haneys were no longer watching Gabe. That was good, because he'd gotten a text from his daughter, telling him she was driving to Vegas to talk to her father about her relationship with Cory. Gabe could not let his daughter be around these animals.

He asked himself what Billy would do. Billy was the champ when it came to dealing with tough situations. Billy often said that the best way to deal with an enemy was to make him a friend. It's worth a shot, Gabe thought.

"How'd you like to see the Keno scam in action?" Gabe asked.

The elder Haney stopped the water test. His eyebrows went up.

"We rigged the Keno game at Palace Station," Gabe explained. "What do you say we head over there, grab a steak dinner, and win ourselves some money."

The elder Haney considered it and grunted to his son.

"My father wants to know if you'll explain the scam to us," Junior said.

"Of course," Gabe said. "Let's go."

- - -

Palace Station was what locals called a sawdust joint. It was a half mile off the Strip and featured cheaply priced rooms, mediocre food, and lousy floor shows. Keno cost a dollar a ticket and could be played in the Grand Cafe over dinner.

The only steak on the menu was a chewy New York Strip smothered in onion strings with a scoop of lumpy mashed potatoes on the side. While the Haneys chowed down, Gabe filled out the Keno tickets that a pleasant waitress brought to their table. Every seven minutes, the winning numbers were flashed across an LED display over the marble-top bar. By the time the Grand Chocolate Cake desserts arrived, Gabe had won $600.

"How come you don't bet more?" Junior said. "If you bet more, you win more."

"Because it wouldn't pass the smell test," Gabe said. "If I just waltz in here off the street and win thousands of dollars, the alarms will go off and security will be all over me like a cheap suit."

"Why's that? Aren't people supposed to win?"

"Not at Keno. The house has a thirty percent edge. The players aren't expected to win, and they rarely do. If you're going to scam a Keno game, you need to steal the money in drips and drabs. Hustlers call scams like these ATMs. You withdraw the money when you need it."

"How long can you work a scam like this?"

"For as long as you want."

"Years?"

"Sure. Provided the house doesn't change the balls, which they rarely do."

The father leaned over and whispered in his son's ear. Gabe still hadn't figured out what the old man's deal was. There was a rage burning inside of him unlike anything Gabe had ever seen, and he wondered if the old man had been in the burning deserts of Iraq or Afghanistan. Men were not born hating their fellow man; they became that way.

"We want this scam for ourselves," Junior said. "You understand what I'm saying? You give us this as part of our deal with you."

Gabe didn't have a choice, but he wanted something in return. "My daughter is coming over to my house. I'll give you the Keno scam if you stay away."

The elder Haney whispered in his son's ear. Junior nodded.

"You have yourself a deal," Junior said.

An invisible weight lifted from Gabe's shoulders. On a paper napkin, Gabe wrote twenty numbers with the golf pencil. Done, he passed the napkin across the table.

"Every time you play the game, bet on these numbers. Do that, and you'll always win."

Junior stared at the napkin. "You had these committed to memory, huh?"

"You bet. That's part of being a cheat. Commit as much as you can to memory, and there's less evidence if the cops come calling. I'd suggest you do the same." His daughter would be at his house soon, and Gabe rose from the table. "Remember, don't win too much in one sitting. And when you do come back here, do it during a different shift. That way, it's less likely an employee will remember your faces."

The father again whispered in his son's ear. Junior rose from the table and followed Gabe out of the café and through the casino. They had brought separate cars, with Gabe having parked with the hotel's valet. As they were waiting for Gabe's car to come up, Junior spoke.

"You still haven't explained how it works."

"The winning balls are normal, but the losing balls aren't," Gabe said. "They've been punctured with sewing needles. When the blower is turned on, the losing balls eventually drop because the air pushes through the holes. Only the winning balls are capable of entering the gooseneck."

"How did you rig the balls?" Junior asked.

"A young guy in our crew got a job at the factory where the Keno game is manufactured," Gabe explained. "The balls are stored in plastic sleeves. When no one was looking, our guy punctured the balls through the plastic with a needle. Our guy then got a hold of a work order and saw that Palace Station had ordered a new Keno game. After that, it was easy."

A uniformed valet brought up Gabe's Infiniti SUV. The Infiniti was the first purchase Gabe had made after joining Billy's crew. Sixty grand, cash. Every time Gabe got behind the wheel he was reminded that he'd made the right choice in becoming a thief.

"I've got to run," Gabe said.

"You do that," Junior said.

As Gabe climbed behind the wheel, he realized how frightened he was. These animals had killed Nate for no sane reason, and they would kill him too if the mood struck them. A loud rapping sound snapped his head, and Gabe lowered the passenger window.

Junior stuck in his head, his face a vicious snarl.

"Don't go thinking that this changes things between us," Junior said. "You're a cheat, and cheats can't be trusted. If we catch one whiff that you or Cunningham are trying to double-cross us, we'll beat Cunningham to death and make you watch. Then we'll find your daughter, tie her to a tree, and rape her, and make you watch that, too. That's a promise you can take to the bank."

Junior pulled his head out.

"Have a nice night," he said.

- - -

Gabe did not see the highway as he drove home. Or if he did see it, the pavement did not register in his brain, the images of the Haneys torturing his daughter poisoning his thoughts. His car's sound system was connected to his Droid via Bluetooth, and he called Billy by speaking Billy's name into the speaker positioned above his head. The call went to voice mail.

"Call me back when you get this," Gabe said, his voice cracking. "And do it fast."

FORTY-ONE

At seven o'clock, the stretch limo pulled in to the MGM's valet area, and Billy and his crew got out. Even though the Bruno Mars show didn't start until eight, Billy had attended enough events at the MGM to know to arrive at least an hour early.

Billy exited the limo with Misty glued to his side. Misty wore a red sequin miniskirt and a low-cut blouse designed to cause whiplash wherever she went. Cory and Morris followed, wearing the slacker uniform of jeans and untucked shirts. Travis came next, dressed in a sports shirt and blazer and holding what looked like a beer. The big man never drank when on a job, and the bottle contained water. Last but not least was Eddie DeSantis, who, along with attending to Billy and his crew, would be scouring the crowd for new whales to steal.

"Follow me," DeSantis said, the tickets fanned in his hand.

You couldn't survive in Vegas and not have a theme. For the MGM Grand, it was all about the magic of Hollywood. A rectangular movie screen the size of a football field flashed larger-than-life images of a dancing Bruno Mars as they passed the front desk.

DeSantis walked through the casino and they followed. Every Vegas hotel made visitors pass through their casinos first, in the hope that a person might drop a few dollars. It was about as subtle as parking a hooker at the front door, and it worked.

They entered an area called the District and passed the usual array of overpriced shops and restaurants before reaching the Garden Arena entrance. A line of people waited to get in.

"Let me see if I can grease some wheels here," DeSantis said.

Their host went to the front of the line. Travis edged up next to Billy.

"The first job I ever pulled with you was here. Remember?" the big man asked.

"Like it was yesterday," Billy replied.

"How much did we pull down that night?"

"A hundred large."

"That's right. I thought I'd died and gone to heaven."

Every casino had a flaw that could be exploited. For the MGM Grand, that flaw was its entertainment venues. There were several, including a lavish Cirque du Soleil production, a nightclub with rotating DJs, and a magic show featuring illusionist David Copperfield.

Billy enjoyed a good magic show, and one evening had taken a date to see Copperfield. His date had heard about a new illusion where a female volunteer was made to float over the crowd. His date had told Billy she hoped Copperfield picked her to levitate.

To their disappointment, Copperfield did not perform the trick that night. After the show, Billy and his date had a drink at one of the casino's bars, and his date had expressed her disappointment to the bartender. The bartender had explained that the illusion had caused the magic show to run over its allotted time limit, which cost the casino money at the tables.

A light bulb had gone off over Billy's head. Each show inside the MGM had a set time limit that the performers were expected to follow each night. By adding a new illusion to his show, Copperfield had taken away time when customers were expected to be inside the casino losing their hard-earned dough. It wouldn't have mattered if the trick were the greatest illusion ever created. It was costing the MGM, so it had to go.

Billy had done his homework, and he learned that the concerts staged inside the Garden Arena followed the same formula. Each concert was expected to be one hour and thirty minutes in length, and not a minute longer. Musicians weren't allowed to add encores even if the fans pitched a fit. It was written into their contracts.

For Billy, the information was worth its weight in gold. Each time a concert let out, a sea of people swarmed down the hallway into the casino, causing momentary confusion. You couldn't have asked for a better distraction to take down a casino.

The night of Travis's baptism, Billy's crew had switched six decks off a blackjack table for six decks in a prearranged stack. Hustlers called this ringing in a cooler. Travis's role was to take the decks off the table right as the concertgoers flooded the casino and the dealer turned her head to watch them rush past. At the same time, Billy had removed the stacked decks from an arm sling he was wearing and put them on the table. The scam had gone off without a hitch, allowing them to then rip off the game for a hundred grand.

"I'm hungry," Misty said. "Why don't you buy me some yogurt."

"Your wish is my command," Billy said. "Hey guys, I'm buying."

A Blizz frozen yogurt store was located next to the arena entrance. The yogurt was self-serve and came in a variety of flavors. Misty chose cookies and cream, Cory and Morris pistachio and pomegranate. Both wore sloppy grins, and Billy wanted to give them hell for being high on the job, but he had too many other problems right now. They left the store.

"I just got a text from Pepper. She'll be here with Tommy soon," Misty said.

"How soon is soon?" Billy asked.

"Pepper said they were a few blocks away."

Pepper had been gone since noon. In a town that moved as fast as Vegas, that was enough time to get married, have a couple of kids, and break up. DeSantis appeared.

"There you are," their host said. "We need to get to our seats."

"Two from our party are running late," Billy said. "I hope that isn't a problem."

"Just let me know when they get here, and I'll come out for them."

"Sounds like a plan," Billy said.

Whales did not wait in line. DeSantis had bribed the ushers working the concert, and their host led them up to the entrance, where they were whisked inside and led by the ushers down an aisle to their third-row-center seats. Other concertgoers craned their necks as their party passed, assuming Billy and his crew were somebody special. We are somebody special, Billy thought. *We're the best fucking hustlers in all of Las Vegas.*

At one minute before eight, the house lights dimmed. The sold-out house let out a cheer. Misty squinted at her cell phone and said, "Pepper and Tommy are here."

DeSantis was roaming the arena in his never-ending hunt for whales. Billy sent him a text and asked him to get Pepper and Tommy. DeSantis replied with a thumbs-up emoji.

At exactly eight o'clock, the curtains parted, and Bruno Mars and his band took to the stage. Their first number was the award winning "Locked Out of Heaven," and the crowd stood on its feet and roared. Pepper and Tommy Wang slipped into their seats, their faces flush from lots of alcohol and plenty of sex. Pepper wore a leather miniskirt and a red silk blouse. The clothes looked new, and Billy guessed Tommy had paid for them.

When the song was over and the crowd had returned to their seats, Billy touched Pepper on the wrist. She glanced nervously his way.

"Glad you could make it," Billy said.

- - -

Bruno Mars put on a great show, and Billy let himself get lost in the music and dancing. The performance lasted exactly one hour and thirty minutes, and when the crowd was hoarse from yelling for an encore that would not come, they began to file out of the arena.

DeSantis stood in the aisle awaiting his party. Their host had not sat down during the show, preferring to roam the front rows of the arena. Now that Bruno Mars was done, it was back to business, and DeSantis flashed Tommy Wang a big smile.

"I didn't forget about you," DeSantis said to Wang. "Are you ready to have your wildest fantasy fulfilled, courtesy of the Carnivale?"

Wang was still riding the high of having spent the afternoon in Pepper's company and clapped his hands together excitedly. "I am booked at the Joint?"

"Yes, you are," DeSantis said. "Tommy Wang and the High Rollers are going to set the town on fire. The limo's waiting out front."

"We leave now?"

"Correct. We could walk to the Hard Rock, but superstars should arrive in style."

"When do I go on?"

"At eleven."

"That doesn't give us much time. Can't it be later?"

DeSantis gave his client a friendly pat on the arm. "Don't get cold feet on me. It wasn't easy selling this to Hard Rock's management. They don't let just anybody appear at the Joint."

"Then I'll be ready. Can my friends come?" Wang asked.

"Sure. The more the merrier," DeSantis said.

Wang turned to face Pepper. "It would be my honor to invite you and your friends to hear me sing at the Hard Rock tonight. Please say yes."

Pepper reacted like she was sixteen and being asked to her first prom. To Billy she said, "This sounds like a blast. Come on, Billy, what do you say?"

All eyes fell upon the boss. Billy did not want to go to the Hard Rock. He'd ripped the place off so many times that security had taken the precaution of not only hanging an unflattering photograph of him on the wall of the surveillance room, but of also running a continuous loop of surveillance video of Billy scamming the casino on a flat-screen TV. He was on the Hard Rock's Most Wanted List, and if security caught him on the premises, there would be hell to pay.

But if Billy didn't go, he would hurt Tommy Wang's feelings. And that might affect their ability to use Wang to take down the Carnivale tomorrow.

Damned if he did, damned if he didn't.

"Sounds like fun. I'm game," Billy said.

FORTY-TWO

The distance between the MGM Grand and the Hard Rock was exactly 1.3 miles. Billy knew this for a fact, since he'd once run it while being pursued by the Hard Rock's security staff.

"Do we really want to be stepping into the Hard Rock?" Travis whispered.

Billy and his crew were in the limo. In the opposite seat sat the two lovebirds. Dance music was playing over the limo's sound system and Tommy Wang was feeling no pain.

"Don't have much choice," Billy said under his breath.

Tommy Wang pulled the opened bottle of Dom Pérignon from an ice bucket and refilled Billy's flute. "Here's to our new friendship."

Billy saluted him. "So what kind of songs do you sing?"

"I like rock 'n' roll. Rolling Stones and Led Zeppelin are my favorites," Wang replied.

"Do you sing in a band back home?" Billy asked.

"No band," Wang said, shaking his head.

"You sing solo?"

"I sing in the shower," Wang said with a laugh.

Billy's face burned. They were going to the Hard Rock to hear Wang sing karaoke. Travis gave him a poke in the ribs with his elbow.

"Maybe we can duck out when no one's looking," the big man whispered.

"Right," Billy said.

- - -

The Joint at the Hard Rock was a mixed bag. Classic acts like Peter Frampton and Cheap Trick played there, but there were also pole-dancing competitions and fetish balls. Billy hoped that DeSantis had reserved them a private suite to avoid mixing with the rest of the crowd, and to his chagrin discovered that DeSantis had them sitting in reserved seats on the main floor.

"You know what they say. Closest to the stage wins," DeSantis said.

DeSantis took Wang backstage to get ready. The featured act was Jimmie Vaughan and the Fabulous Thunderbirds, with Tommy Wang and the High Rollers serving as warm-up. Billy had attended concerts at the Hard Rock before he'd become persona non grata and knew that the crowds were young and hard-drinking. The moment Tommy Wang let out a bad note, they were going to eat him alive.

Pepper sat at the end of the aisle. She had not made eye contact with him. Billy pulled the rubber band off his wrist and sent it her way. Most hustlers wore rubber bands on their wrists and used them to tie up their bankrolls in case they got robbed. The hustler would toss the bankroll over a wall or beneath a parked car, and then retrieve it later on. He'd never had to use his rubber band, but he wore it under the belief that it was better to be safe than sorry.

The rubber band landed in Pepper's lap. She glanced his way.

"Did Misty talk to you?" Billy asked.

"About what?" Pepper asked.

Misty hadn't told Pepper the bad news. Billy rose from his seat.

"Let me buy you a drink," he said.

"Sure, Billy," Pepper said.

The Joint had two bars. Each had a long line of patrons waiting to buy drinks. Billy waved a hundred-dollar bill and a bartender took his order. Glasses in hand, he moved away from the bar for some privacy. Pepper reluctantly followed.

"I've got a couple of things I want to say to you," Billy said. "First you had no right putting Misty in the middle of this situation. If you want to run off and fuck some guy, that's your call. But don't use your best friend as your messenger."

Pepper stared into her drink. "Sorry."

"Here's the second thing. Who's the easiest person in the world to con?"

Pepper shook her head.

"Take a guess."

"A rich sucker?"

"A rich sucker is the second easiest person in the world to con. Rich people think that because they're successful in business, they're smart, when in fact most of them are chumps. The easiest person in the world to con is another grifter. Know why?"

Pepper shook her head again.

"Grifters think they know all the angles. Any time you think you know all the angles, your ass is going to get paddled. Like your ass got paddled today."

Pepper's lower lip began to tremble. "What are you talking about?"

"Tommy Wang conned you this morning, and you fell for it, hook, line, and sinker."

"He conned me? How?"

"Figure it out yourself."

Pepper's mind raced as she played back her day with Tommy Wang. Pepper was going to figure it out eventually, and when she did, it was going to sting worse than a nest of hornets.

"Now, here's the last thing I want to tell you," Billy said. "When this job is done, you have a decision to make. Do you want to stay with the crew or not? If you leave, no hard feelings. If you stay, you're going to have to play by my rules, because I will never tolerate a fucking stunt like this again. Do you understand?"

Pepper's face had turned to stone. "He's married, isn't he."

"Took you a while."

"Don't be so goddamn smug. Is he?"

"Married with kids."

"How many?"

"Two."

"Teenagers?"

It took Billy a moment to catch Pepper's drift. If the kids were nearly grown, then maybe she could live with the deception. Anything else, no.

"The kids are still in diapers," Billy said.

A tear ran down her cheek. "He told me a story about that gangster Broken Tooth executing him and some accountants, only he miraculously got spared. Was that bullshit, too?"

Billy handed her his napkin. "That part's true. The bullet meant for Wang hit the guy standing next to him. Broken Tooth decided it was a good omen, and he sent Wang back to Vegas."

The house lights flickered and the packed room let out a cheer. Up onstage, four long-haired musicians strolled out and got reacquainted with their instruments. Billy had seen them before in clubs around town playing warm-up for name acts. They had a tight sound and soon the crowd was moving as one to the beat.

Pepper faced the stage, her eyes throwing daggers. Hell hath no fury like a woman scorned, and Billy knew Pepper would pay Wang back for the deception. Maybe she'd get him drunk and send him back home with an obscene tattoo stamped on his ass, or maybe she'd get her hands on his cell phone and initiate a dialogue with Wang's wife. Pepper had a creative side to her, and Wang was in for a royal screwing.

"Whatever you're planning has to wait until the job is finished," he said into her ear.

"You're no fun," Pepper said.

"Ladies and gentlemen, welcome to the Joint inside the beautiful Hard Rock Hotel and Casino," a man's voice boomed over the P.A. "Our feature act this evening is straight from Austin, Texas—Jimmie Vaughan and the Fabulous Thunderbirds. But before we bring out Jimmie and the band, please give a big Hard Rock welcome to Tommy Wang and the High Rollers."

The band broke into a cover of the Rolling Stones's "Satisfaction." Tommy Wang bounced onto the stage, waved to the crowd, and grabbed the mike off its stand. His eyes were glassy and he looked loaded. Billy braced himself for the worst.

- - -

When it came to live entertainment, no one did it like Las Vegas. The comics were always funny, the magicians never failed to blow your mind, and the bands and singers always delivered the goods. Crummy acts were given a bus ticket and never invited back.

The lyrics coming out of Wang's mouth sounded professional and in perfect pitch, as if Wang had been singing in front of packed houses his whole life. At first Billy wondered if Wang was lip-synching, but ruled that out when Wang coughed into the mike. Something else was going on here, and he wondered if Wang had been lying about his singing prowess.

When the song ended, there was lots of applause and foot stomping. Wang bowed to the crowd, and they ate it up and cheered.

"He's not bad," Billy said.

"He didn't sound like that in the shower," Pepper said.

"He sang for you?"

"He sure did. He thinks he's a celebrity."

"His voice sounded different?"

"Try fucking awful. You would have thought a cat was being strangled."

The band broke into Bruce Springsteen's "Born to Run." Wang picked up where he'd left off, and he belted out the lyrics without missing a beat. Billy prided himself on knowing all the angles, and it was going to bug him until he learned the secret behind this stunt.

DeSantis stood on the main floor to the left of the stage. Beside the VIP host was an overweight roadie with long flowing hair wearing a tie-dyed T-shirt. Billy told Pepper he'd be right back and sifted his way through the crowd to where DeSantis stood with the roadie.

"Having fun, Mr. C.?" DeSantis shouted into Billy's ear.

"Not bad. So what's the deal here?" Billy asked.

DeSantis played dumb while the roadie ignored him.

"I have it on good authority that Wang can't sing worth a damn," Billy said. "I want to know how you're making him sound so good. There's got to be a trick."

DeSantis touched his Bluetooth. One of his bosses was talking to him. "Excuse me, Mr. C., but another client just arrived, and I need to go take care of his party. Troy, why don't you explain how your magic box works. I'm sure Mr. C. will be intrigued."

With that, DeSantis hurried away. Troy was punching numbers on the screen of an iPad. Billy spotted a thin gold watch on Troy's wrist and other expensive jewelry. Most roadies didn't make squat, and Billy decided Troy wasn't your run-of-the-mill stagehand. Billy pointed at the innocuous black box sitting on the edge of the stage.

"Is that your magic box?" Billy asked.

"Guilty as charged," Troy said.

"What does it do?"

"It makes the old new again."

"What are you, the Riddler? Come on, tell me."

Troy answered without taking his eyes off the stage. "Most of the acts that play this town are oldies. Elton John, Cher, Diana Ross, Olivia Newton-John. Problem is, audiences don't want to hear what these singers sound like today; they want to hear what they used to sound like. So I invented the magic box."

"You're altering their voices."

"That's a simple way to put it. It's called a pitch-shifter. Take your friend up on the stage. The pitch-shifter raises or lowers your friend's less-than-stellar voice to perfect pitch while the band plays. The pitch-shifter also compares your friend's rendition to the original version and smooths out any clams."

"What's a clam?"

"A bad note."

"Is this your invention?"

"Pitch-shifters have been around. Mine just happens to work better than anyone else's."

"So you rent your services and laugh all the way to the bank."

"You're a sharp guy, Mr. C."

Up onstage, Tommy Wang belted out his final number, Grand Funk's "We're an American Band." Wang was about to wear out his welcome, and a polite round of applause followed him off the stage. Troy shut the cover on his iPad and slipped the tablet under his arm.

"Audiences leave my shows happy," Troy said. "It might be a computer trick, but who the hell cares? At the end of the day, I make people feel good, and that's all that matters."

Billy understood exactly what Troy was saying. If you made suckers feel warm and fuzzy, they'd empty out their wallet for you.

"Nice meeting you, Mr. C.," Troy said.

"Same here," Billy said.

Billy sifted his way through the crowd back to his group. Two ugly-looking dudes, one small and built like Mighty Mouse, the other tall and muscular, blocked his path.

"Remember us?" Mighty Mouse said.

Billy never forgot a face, especially when it was someone who wished him harm. Their names were Snap and Guido, and they were enforcers employed by a Vegas bookie named Tony G who did his business while playing golf at the Mandalay Bay. Not that long ago, Billy had fleeced Tony G during a round, and when the enforcers had put up a fuss, Billy sent a putter into Snap's face that shattered his nose, and then used the same putter to damage Guido's testicles.

"Our boss wants to talk to you," Snap said.

"Tell him some other time," Billy said.

Guido dropped his hand on Billy's shoulder. "Try right now, Pretty Boy."

"My business with your boss is over. We had an agreement."

"Is that so? Well, I guess he forgot," Guido said.

The criminal underworld of Las Vegas was no different than anywhere else. When a pair of thieves struck an agreement, it was as good as a contract signed in blood. For Tony G to be reneging on the promise he'd made to Billy was unthinkable.

"You're making a mistake," Billy said.

"We'll let Tony G be the judge of that. Get moving," Guido said.

Snap went first. Billy followed, while Guido brought up the rear.

FORTY-THREE

Bookies were as important to Las Vegas's economy as hookers, and just as illegal. When a gambler placed a bet with a bookie, he did so knowing that if he won the bet, he would not have to pay a penny in taxes to Uncle Sam. That reason alone made bookies a bargain.

Tony G specialized in sports betting, both college and pro, which was huge in Vegas. Billy had heard that Tony G handled $100 million a year in bets, most of it on football, with more than 20 percent of that taking place during the Super Bowl.

Tony G was sucking on a Corona as Billy and the enforcers entered the luxury box on the upper level of the club. The luxury boxes had a panoramic view of the general admission area, and Billy guessed the bookie had been spying on Billy and his crew since they'd come in.

"Have a seat," the bookie said.

Guido shoved a stool under Billy's ass. Billy sat down and said nothing. Tony G guzzled his beer and made his guest wait. The bookie was shaped like a bowling ball and had a mat of white fur growing out of the V in his polo shirt.

"That's a cute disguise you're wearing," Tony G said. "I wouldn't have recognized you except for the cowlick in your hair. Dead giveaway."

"You and I had an agreement," Billy said.

"Guido, make our guest show some respect."

Guido slapped Billy in the head. Billy's head snapped and he saw stars.

"You scammed me out of three hundred grand with a rigged horse race," Tony G said. "Brought in a Brazilian ringer at a track in California and suckered me into accepting a huge bet on it to win. Normally, I'd say, live and learn, but not with the likes of you. I want my money back, every last cent. And if you don't give it to me, I'll call security and tell them there's a known cheat in their nightclub. You understand what I'm saying?"

The bar in the luxury box was covered in dead soldiers. Tony G had been pounding the beers and when he saw Billy come into the Joint, he'd gone on tilt and decided to pay Billy back. Billy had to believe that if Tony G wasn't drunk, he wouldn't be acting this way. It was out of character and bad form, and bookies prided themselves on looking good in this town.

"You're going back on our agreement," Billy said, making it a statement.

"That's right," Tony G said.

"Why don't you drink some coffee and think this over."

"What are you saying, you little rat-shit fuck—that I'm drunk?"

"Drunk as a skunk is more like it. We had an agreement and you shook my hand on it. What's done is done. No hard feelings."

"Fuck you," Tony G said.

"No, fuck you."

"Put the hurt on this little asshole. Make sure you mess up his face."

The enforcers sprang to life. Billy leaped off his stool, grabbed it by the legs, and swung the stool around his head so the enforcers stayed back. Tony G was enjoying himself, and he sucked down his beer and tossed the empty bottle into a wastebasket, where it shattered.

"Stand down," Tony G said.

The enforcers returned to their neutral positions. Billy wasn't fooled and kept the stool on his shoulder. He retreated to the door and opened it with one hand.

"We'll see you outside in the parking lot, won't we, boys?" Tony G said.

- - -

When it rained, it poured. Billy hadn't truly understood what that expression meant until now. Leaving Tony G's luxury box, he headed straight for the restrooms located on the side of the theater. There would be people there, so he'd be safe from the enforcers for a little while.

He locked himself in a stall and had a seat. Ran his hands through his hair and tried to think. He prided himself on his ability to wiggle out of tight jams. Usually, he did it with his mouth, but this situation was calling for a different approach.

His cell phone vibrated and he took it out of his pocket. Gabe calling. He needed a friendly voice to talk to, and he answered the call.

"Hey," Billy said.

"Didn't you get my text?" Gabe said. "The Haneys were in my house when I got home this afternoon. The crazy father found the Keno scam in my garage."

"Don't tell me you showed it to them."

"What the hell else was I supposed to do? They're both crazy as loons. I took them to the Grand Cafe at Palace Station, and we played the Keno game and they won and that's how I left them. I'm sorry, Billy. There was nothing else I could do."

An irate patron knocked on the stall door. "Hurry up, will you?"

"What did they want?" Billy asked.

"They don't trust you, so they came to my house and got Elsie to let them in," Gabe said. "They plan to watch me until the scam at the

Carnivale is done. They threatened to kill me and my daughter if we try to screw with them."

Billy's mind was racing, a plan forming in his head. It just might work, and he said, "How long ago did you leave them?"

"Did you hear what I just said—they threatened to kill my kid!"

"So buy your kid a ticket to New York and book her into a hotel," Billy said. "I told you before that I was going to handle these monkeys, remember? Now, answer the fucking question. How long ago did you leave the Haneys at the Grand Cafe?"

"About an hour and a half ago."

A thin smile formed on Billy's lips. "And you taught them the Keno scam."

"That's right. I gave them the winning numbers."

"Perfect. Go to bed, and get some sleep."

"I don't feel safe at my house, not with those animals running around."

"Then stay at the Holiday Inn. I'll call you later."

The patron banged on the door. "Have a heart; I'm going to explode."

Billy ignored the dying man's pleas. Using Google, he located the phone number at the Grand Cafe at Palace Station and was soon sweet-talking the hostess into paging the Haneys.

"What do your friends look like?" the hostess asked.

Like they just crawled out from beneath a rock, Billy almost said.

"Have you seen *Sons of Anarchy*? They could have acted in it," he said instead.

"I'm looking at them right now," the hostess said.

"You're amazing," Billy said.

The hostess put him on hold. A moment later, Junior came on the line.

"Having fun?" Billy asked.

"How'd you track us down?" Junior asked suspiciously.

"Gabe told me where to find you. I've got a job for you."

"You don't say. What have you got in mind?"

"How much would you charge me to beat the shit out of some guys with tire irons?"

- - -

Jimmie Vaughan and the Fabulous Thunderbirds didn't need a pitch-shifter to rock the house. They'd been playing the blues for forty-plus years and could have knocked out every song in their set in their sleep. Standing in front of the stage with his crew, Billy let himself get lost in their music and forgot his problems for a little while.

The show ended with the band playing a rousing version of "Texas Flood." Then the house lights went up and the crowd filed out. Billy turned his attention to the luxury boxes at the back of the theater. Tony G and his unfabulous enforcers had come to the Joint to hear live music, just like Billy, and there was a chance that Tony G's threat was nothing more than hot air. But there was also a chance it was real, and that Guido and Snap would physically harm Billy once he ventured outside the Hard Rock to the parking lot.

So Billy had hired the Haneys for protection. It had felt strange, but he didn't see that he had any other choice. He'd struck deals with the devil before, and he knew the drill. Like sand shifting in the desert, the Haneys' allegiances were dictated by opportunity and little else.

DeSantis appeared at the front of the stage. "Some show, huh? The limo's outside waiting to take everyone back to the Carnivale."

Billy didn't want to leave the Hard Rock just yet. Traffic in Vegas was unpredictable, and he wanted to give the Haneys enough time to travel across town.

"The valet area will be jammed," Billy said. "I say we hang around for a little while and do some gambling."

"I have never gambled here. Is it nice?" Tommy Wang asked.

"They've got a special room for high rollers called The Peacock with a bar made of glowing onyx. There's nothing like it in town."

"Does that sound good to you?" Wang asked Pepper.

Pepper smiled. Behind her eyes, a slasher film was playing, and Tommy Wang was getting cut to pieces over and over.

"Whatever you want," Pepper said.

The Joint was nearly empty. As Billy and his crew and Tommy Wang started to leave, DeSantis pulled Billy to the side. "I don't mean to put a damper on things, Mr. C., but my bosses are tracking your play, and you're a few hours behind today. I need to get you back to Carnivale so I can justify all these great perks I've given you tonight."

"The valet area will be jammed. I don't do lines," Billy said.

"Nor should you have to. The limo is parked in a roped-off area of the parking lot. All the high rollers get their limos parked there. That way, they can leave without waiting."

"You want me to walk through a parking lot? Is it secure?"

"Of course it's secure, Mr. C. Now, if you don't mind, I need to get you and your friends back to the mother ship."

Parking lots in Vegas were never a safe bet. They were poorly lit and rarely had enough security cameras. That was why gamblers wore rubber bands around their wrists or resorted to carrying concealed weapons to protect themselves. But if Billy balked about returning to the Carnivale, DeSantis's bosses might decide Billy wasn't worth all the free goodies and ask him to leave. If that happened, the scam would collapse, and their big payday would disappear.

"You're sure it's secure," Billy repeated.

"Trust me, Mr. C. You're in good hands," DeSantis said.

- - -

The valet area outside the Hard Rock was a mob scene, with too many people and not enough cabs. DeSantis escorted Billy's group down a sidewalk to the roped-off parking area, where a VIP limo awaited them. Billy hustled along, trying to hide his growing apprehension. Guido and Snap were no ordinary enforcers. Guido was a bodybuilding champion while Snap fought mixed martial arts. Each was strong enough to break one of Billy's arms faster than an Olive Garden bread stick.

DeSantis lifted the rope, and his crew climbed beneath it. Billy went last, his eyes fixed on a pair of shadows next to the building. He hated this shit. Every criminal group had rules and arrangements that they followed. This was especially true in Las Vegas, where a thief was not expected to step on another thief's toes or disrupt his business.

The shadows came to life and moved toward him. It was Guido and Snap, and their hands were missing. Billy blinked before he realized both were wearing black leather gloves.

"Excuse me, but this is a restricted area," DeSantis said.

Guido placed the palm of his hand on the VIP host's chest and gave him a push.

"Get lost, homeboy," Guido said.

DeSantis wasn't paid to be a hero and retreated. Billy's crew stood on the other side of the rope, unsure of what was going on. Billy held his ground and tried to stay cool.

"Step over here," Guido said.

"You sure about this? You didn't do so well the last time," Billy said.

"The more you talk, the more this will hurt," Snap said.

"You strung more than five words together," Billy said.

Guido lifted the rope and motioned with his hand. Billy said, "I'll be right back," and ducked under the rope. Guido and Snap led him back to the sidewalk where Tony G stood puffing on a fat stogie. The bookie blew smoke into Billy's face.

"I've been looking forward to this," Tony G said.

"Does this mean our arrangement's over?" Billy asked.

"We never had an arrangement," the bookie said.

"So you lied to me."

"You're funny."

"I just want to know where we stand."

"You talk too much, doesn't he, boys?"

"Want us to knock out his teeth?" Guido asked.

"That would be a good start," Tony G said.

The cavalry had arrived and not a moment too soon. Billy removed a monster wad of cash from his pocket and peeled off a handful of C-notes.

"You think you can bribe your way out of this?" Tony G said.

"It's not for you," the young hustler said.

The Haneys materialized out of the shadows. They had come loaded for bear, with Junior wielding a Louisville slugger, his old man a tire iron. Billy started walking backward until he bumped into Junior, while never taking his eyes off Guido and Snap.

"Took you long enough," Billy said.

"Fucking traffic," Junior said.

Billy stuffed the money into the breast pocket of Junior's denim shirt and walked away. The sickening sounds of shattering bones followed him across the parking lot to the waiting limo. DeSantis held open the door for him.

"You okay, Mr. C.?" the host asked.

"Never better," Billy replied.

FORTY-FOUR

-SATURDAY, THE KILLING-

Billy awoke Saturday morning believing the worst had passed. So many things had gone wrong over the past two days that he'd lost count. But now here he was, about to steal more money off a Vegas casino than any thief had in a long time.

The sky palace had a private gym, and he spent a half hour pedaling an exercise bike while gazing at a muted TV bolted to the ceiling. Billy was not the first cheat to take a Vegas casino for a multi-million-dollar score. Several crews had already done this by rigging blackjack games and slot machines. The casinos had chosen not to publicize the losses, fearful that other cheats would think they were candy stores. A casino lived by its reputation, and if cheats thought a casino were an easy target, they'd pick it clean like a vulture.

He worked up a sweat and ordered breakfast on an iPad that was wired into the hotel's kitchen. By the time he'd finished his shower, a butler had delivered the food to the dining room. Two organically grown eggs over easy, three strips of fat Canadian bacon, a basket of steaming rolls, fresh OJ, a pot of Jamaican coffee, and a bowl of fruit with delicacies flown in from the four corners of the world.

Travis joined him, fresh from his swim. Billy put a piece of bacon and a roll on the bread plate, and then passed it Travis's way.

"Thanks, Billy. You get any sleep?"

"I slept like a baby. How about you?"

"Not so great. Too much on my mind."

Travis looked like death warmed over. That was not unusual in Vegas on a Saturday morning, where most people looked like *The Walking Dead* stand-ins. What worried Billy was Travis's state of mind. Travis was the only member of Billy's crew who had worked for a casino, what people in the business called a gamer. Travis had dealt craps, blackjack, and roulette, and had a deep understanding of how casino people thought.

Travis had taught Billy many things. One of the most important was that most casino employees hated their jobs and worked on autopilot. As a result, these employees were easily fooled. But, if an employee sensed a customer was cheating, the employee would sound the alarm, not wanting to get blamed if the game lost money.

Travis was Billy's second pair of eyes inside the casino. Billy needed for Travis to be sharp, and he poured him a cup of coffee. The big man's eyes grew wide as the caffeine hit his bloodstream.

"What is this—rocket fuel?"

"It's called Blue Mountain. It's what Jamaicans drink to offset all the ganja they smoke. Speaking of which, what's the deal with Cory and Morris? Are they still toking?"

"Not around me."

It was the kind of answer that let Billy draw his own conclusions. Cory and Morris had been flying high at the Hard Rock, but Travis wasn't going to break the code and say so.

"If I get a whiff, they're done," Billy said.

"You said that the last time you caught them," Travis said.

"Well, this time I mean it."

"You're the boss."

Billy wiped his plate clean with a piece of bread. After his mother went to prison, Billy's father had taught himself to cook and prepared the family meals. It had been a struggle, and to show his appreciation, Billy had wiped his plate clean after every meal.

Finished, Billy went outside to the pool. Travis refilled his cup and followed.

"So what's the deal with Pepper? Is she in love with Wang?" Travis asked.

Billy shushed him with a finger to his lips. "Be careful. Voices carry."

"Is she?" Travis whispered.

"She was. Not anymore. He's married."

Travis sipped his morning joe. "Love is for suckers."

"You think so?"

"Yes, indeed. I found out the hard way. Got married when I was thirty, thought it would last forever. We were on the rocks in five years. Couldn't get away from each other fast enough."

"What happened?"

"We got blinded by love, thought it would solve our problems. What a joke."

"You don't believe in love?"

"Not anymore. Live and learn."

"What about Karen? Don't you love her?"

"It's different with Karen," Travis said. "We knew each other in high school, double-dated a few times. After the divorce, I looked her up, found out she was also divorced and raising two kids on her own. I know this sounds screwed up, but I don't love her. We're just good friends. I feel . . ." Travis struggled for the right words. "I feel safe with her."

"Does she love you?"

"I never asked her. How about you? Do you believe in love?"

The conversation had turned awkward. Billy went to the railing and gazed down at the swirling mass of humanity thirty-six floors below. If love was for suckers, then he was the biggest sucker of all. He'd fallen head over heels for Maggie Flynn before he was shaving, and the feelings had yet to fade away. It didn't seem to matter that Maggie was on a suicide run and might one day destroy herself; Billy still carried a torch for her and always would.

Travis shouldered up beside him.

"Do you?" the big man asked.

"Sometimes," Billy said.

"Don't worry, you'll get over it."

From the adjacent sky palace came the sound of shattering glass, followed by an angry woman's voice that sounded a lot like Pepper.

"Another one bites the dust," Travis said.

- - -

You couldn't be a beautiful woman living in Las Vegas and not have been cheated on at least a couple of times. It was one of the harsh realities of residing in a gambling town.

Pepper had been cheated on enough times to know the drill. Catch the bastard red-handed and shove the evidence in his face. If the bastard started lying, rip out his tongue.

Pepper and Tommy Wang had slept in, had sex, then ordered breakfast. A uniformed butler wheeled the meal into their bedroom and popped a bottle of bubbly. They ate the meal in bed and giggled each time a crumb fell between the sheets.

When the meal was over, Wang slipped out of bed. As the bathroom door clicked shut, Pepper took his cell phone off the night table and scrolled through the apps. She found the photo gallery and felt the breath catch in her throat. She'd wanted to believe that Billy had gotten it wrong, but Billy rarely got things wrong. Wang's wife and two children were on prominent display with dozens of photos of family outings. The wife was petite and pretty and the kids were absolutely darling. It was all Pepper could do not to scream.

Pepper slipped out of the covers and fixed herself a mimosa. Wang came out of the bathroom and saw her standing naked by the bed and got the wrong idea. The glass barely missed his head.

"You dirty bastard!" she said.

A saltshaker was next, followed by a half-filled coffee cup. Wang's reflexes were good, and he expertly dodged the projectiles.

"What did I do?" he begged.

"You lied to me."

"I would never lie to you."

The best shots were the least expected. She pretended to calm down and Wang lowered his guard. The sugar bowl flew out of her hand and bonked him cleanly on the forehead. A smart man knows when he's beaten, and Wang wisely grabbed a bathrobe and retreated to the other room. Pepper wrapped herself in a bedsheet and followed, holding the evidence in her hand.

"Why didn't you tell me you were married and had a couple of rug rats?" she said.

Wang sat on a chair in the living room, nursing his forehead. "What are rug rats?"

"Kids. And a wife. They're all over your cell phone."

"I am divorced," he said without flinching.

"Like I haven't heard that one before," she said.

His face took on a forlorn expression. "My wife served me with papers after I became associated with Broken Tooth. She told me I had shamed my family, and the only honorable thing to do was sign them. So I did."

Pepper knew bullshit when she heard it, and she also knew the truth. She knelt on the floor next to the chair, still wrapped in the bedsheet. "Look at me," she said.

Her lover shifted his eyes. "Yes?"

"Did you love her?"

"Very much."

"So why did you sign the divorce papers?"

"Because she no longer loved me, and I wished to protect my children."

"But you weren't killed by Broken Tooth's men. You lived."

"Yes, I lived."

"So did you contact your wife and try to patch things up?"

"I spoke to her once over the phone. My wife said that my being spared did not erase the shame I had brought upon my family." Wang gazed fondly at the smiling photos stored on his cell phone. "All I have left are these."

Pepper thought she just might cry. She took Wang's head in her hands and kissed him on the mouth the way a good man was meant to be kissed. His face was filled with hurt, and she found herself wishing she could take back the last fifteen minutes and flush them down the toilet.

"Want to go another round with the champ?" she asked playfully.

His eyes lit up. "That would be wonderful. But first I have a question."

"What's that?"

"Is your boss a criminal? He strikes me that way when we are together."

Pepper let out a strained laugh. Wang's sky palace was also bugged, and hotel security had just heard Wang cast a shadow over Billy's reputation.

"Whatever gave you that idea?" she asked.

"He never seems to relax. Is someone after him?"

This was getting hairy. Back in Lake Tahoe they'd rehearsed for this very scenario, Billy being of the belief that there would always be problems on jobs, and the only way to handle them was to prepare a story ahead of time and commit that story to memory.

"Billy's a hedge-fund manager. He gets insider information on companies, and then he buys their stock, waits for it to go up, and dumps it. They say that behind every fortune is a crime. Well, Billy's committed a hundred crimes, and they're all perfectly legal."

"I see. We have many men like him in my country as well."

"I bet you do. Ready when you are."

Smiling happily, Wang escorted her back to the bedroom.

FORTY-FIVE

Jimmy Slyde knew his place on the food chain. It was down at the bottom, one notch above the pimps and streetwalkers. This was partly due to the shade of Slyde's skin, but more because he was a street person, with no formal education except the school of hard knocks.

This lack of pedigree didn't mean that Slyde couldn't drive a European sports car or have a closet of designer suits. Slyde could own all the toys he wanted, and no one in Las Vegas would have cared. What Slyde couldn't do was think he was anything more than a common thief.

Thieves took orders, and Slyde had been ordered by the concierges of four major Vegas casinos to get rid of Maggie Flynn. The orders could have come from anyone of power—GMs, pit bosses, floor managers—and Slyde would have obeyed them. If Slyde didn't, his days in Sin City would be over, and he'd be forced to leave town. That was how things worked in the desert. If you didn't play the game, you were done.

Mags lived in the Stone Ridge development on the southeast side of town. Slyde pulled into her narrow driveway and lowered his window to listen for any signs of life. Most of her neighbors had day jobs and did not come home until the sun went down.

Slyde took the takeout from Kapit Bahay off the passenger seat and got out. Mags had a thing for Filipino fast food, and he'd brought a disposable Styrofoam plate filled with chicken adobo and lumpia plus two unsweetened iced teas.

He went to the front door and knocked. "Daddy's here. Open up."

The door swung in. The pills had worn off and Mags looked like hell.

"You shouldn't have," she said.

"Nothing but the best for my girl."

"You better not have forgotten the special sauce."

"Got that, too."

Mags chained the door behind him. Her condo was furnished with dumpy furniture knock-offs. It was a familiar refrain. Years of scamming and nothing to show for it. Slyde handed her the bag, and Mags went into the kitchen to put the food on real plates.

"Make yourself at home," she said.

Slyde took a seat at the head of the dining room table. In the table's center was a stack of playing cards still in their boxes and wrapped in plastic. They were not ordinary playing cards but had come from a number of well-known casinos. There were decks from Mandalay Bay, Bellagio, Circus Circus, the Venetian, Aria, and Monte Carlo.

Slyde examined the bar codes on the boxes and determined the cards were real. The casinos went through extraordinary procedures to safeguard their cards that included special markings on the boxes and storing them in warehouses where the security was as tight as Fort Knox. But that hadn't stopped the town's cheats from getting their hands on a deck, marking it, and finding a clever way to ring those marked cards into a game at the casino where the cards came from.

If it wasn't bolted down, the cheats would take it out of a casino, rig it, and bring it back. This included dealing shoes, roulette wheels, and even slot and video poker machines. An employee or two was usually involved and were bribed to look the other way.

Mags served Slyde a plate of food. She sat down next to him and started to eat.

"Dolan isn't doing so hot. There's a fifty-fifty chance he'll never walk again."

"So?" Mags said.

"You broke his neck, Mags. Don't you remember?"

"Serves him right for smacking me in the face."

Slyde guessed the pills had wiped out her memory from last night, and that she'd forgotten there was an outstanding police warrant with her name on it. She was so far gone it wasn't funny.

"What's the deal with the cards?" Slyde asked.

"I talked to Rand Waters last night. He wants me to come to LA and take a screen test. I'm going to play the part of a lady hustler and perform a scam."

"No shit. What scam you got in mind?"

"It's called Hey Baby. You know it?"

"That's a new one. How's it work?"

"Take out a deck and I'll show you."

Slyde peeled the plastic off a deck of Aria playing cards and removed them from the box. The back design was lattice red with the casino's distinct logo on both ends.

"You know how to muck a card?" Mags asked.

"I've been mucking since I was in diapers, baby."

"Muck one of the aces and stand behind my chair. Bring the deck with you."

Slyde removed the ace of spades from the deck and palmed it in his right hand. He rose from his chair and moved around the table until he was behind Mags's chair. She placed her fork onto her half-finished meal and shoved the plate to the side.

Slyde gave her the Aria deck. From it, Mags removed the ten of hearts and the six of spades, and dropped the two cards facedown on her place mat.

"A lot of casinos have gone back to letting players touch their cards during blackjack," she said. "They stopped for a while because of all the cheating that was going on, but now the casinos have decided to go back to their old ways."

"Got to keep the customers happy," Slyde said.

"Let's pretend I've been dealt these cards. You're standing behind me, pretending you're my boyfriend. You've got the ace palmed, and your hand's resting on my chair."

"Easy enough," Slyde said.

"I take a look at my cards and see I've got a stiff. So I palm out the six like this."

Mags picked up the two cards and glimpsed them. Slyde watched her expertly steal out the six of spades and drop her hands into her lap. Years of practice and self-denial had gone into that little move, and Slyde realized that Mags had skills he'd yet to tap into. Like an unfinished meal, she was going to be thrown away before she was done.

"What happens to the six?" he asked.

"My open purse sits on the floor between my legs. The six gets dropped into the purse, which I close with my feet. It's the perfect cleanup."

"So what do I do?"

"That's the good part. The moment the six leaves the table, you say, 'Hey baby, you've got blackjack.' Your hand picks up the ten and adds the palmed ace. You turn them faceup and toss them on the table. The surveillance cameras don't spot a thing."

Slyde gave it a try. He picked up the ten while adding the ace concealed in his hand, and tossed the two cards faceup onto the table. "Hey baby, you've got blackjack," he said.

"That wasn't so hard, was it?" Mags said.

"Piece of cake."

Slyde returned to his seat. Mags knew all the angles and wasn't afraid to steal the watch off your wrist, and Slyde told himself he needed to get this over with before he changed his mind. He stuck a straw into his iced tea and took a sip.

"Shit. I ordered sweetened, and this is unsweetened. You got any sugar?"

"Coming right up."

Mags went into the kitchen to fetch the sugar. When she was gone, Slyde removed a vial of sleeping medicine from his pocket and dumped it into Mags's tea. She returned with the sugar bowl and Slyde made a big deal of adding a heaping teaspoon to his drink. Lifting his cup, he offered a toast.

"Here's to Hey Baby," he said.

- - -

Mags resumed eating. Her eyes did not leave Jimmy's face. Back when she was a little girl, her mother had taught her about intuition. Her mother believed that intuition was the messenger of fear and was a woman's best defense. Right now, Mags's intuition was telling her Jimmy wasn't being square with her, and she tried to figure out why.

She'd known Jimmy for a few months, and like most men she'd known, Jimmy was as predictable as a wasp on speed. Jimmy played the same rap music when he drove, wore the same cologne, and ordered the same items off the menu when in a restaurant. Nothing ever changed.

Mags put her fork down. She'd found the thing that was bothering her. Jimmy always took her out to eat. Not once had he brought takeout to her place. So why had he this time?

Her mouth had gone dry, and she picked up her tea. Floating on the top of her drink was a tiny bit of white powder. She nearly screamed. The son of a bitch had spiked her drink. But why? If he'd wanted to sleep with her, all he had to do was ask.

She gave her guest a hard stare. His forehead was covered in sweat. Sex wasn't on his mind, far from it. He was here to harm her. That was why he'd mentioned Dolan—to justify killing her.

She bunched up her napkin and rose from the table. Jimmy's eyes rose as well.

"Something wrong?" he asked.

"My stomach's bothering me. I'll be right back."

She ran down the hallway to her bedroom and locked the door. Entering the bathroom, she locked it as well, then sat down on the toilet seat. She wished like hell she owned a gun. She'd considered purchasing one but never had, fearful she might one day use it on herself.

Out came her iPhone. She couldn't call 911: It would only lead to her getting arrested for breaking Dolan's neck and thrown in jail. There were her girlfriends, but they worked during the day in the casinos and would probably urge her to call the cops.

She had run out of road, and she stifled the cry in her throat. Crying was for losers, and she told herself she wasn't a loser. A knock on the door made her jump.

"You okay in there?" came Slyde's voice.

"How the hell did you get into my bedroom?" she shrieked.

"I carded the door. I thought maybe you were sick."

"Get out or I'll call the police!"

"You ain't calling the police. Open the door, Mags."

"I said get out, before I blow your brains out, you dirty bastard!"

"You don't own a gun. You told me that the first time we met. Now, unlock the door and make this easy on yourself."

"You fucking bastard!"

Slyde's shoulder hit the door, causing the hinges to sag. Mags frantically typed out a text on her cell phone. There was only one person left who could save her from Slyde, and that was Billy. She'd come back to Vegas to punish him, but now she realized that was only because she had feelings for the little shit. Her cell phone slipped from her fingers and hit the floor. Fear had started to take hold, and she heard her mother's warning that no man could be trusted.

Slyde's shoulder hit the door again. A large splinter appeared in its center.

Mags grabbed the cell phone off the floor and hit send.

FORTY-SIX

Billy was a big fan of reality TV, and he regularly taped episodes of *Survivor*, *Big Brother*, and anything involving the Kardashians. The shows were supposed to be real, yet the episodes were in fact scripted, with each line of dialogue written to obtain the maximum impact.

Cheating a casino was a lot like an episode of a reality TV show. The scam had a script with lines of dialogue for each participant. If each participant adhered to the script, the scam would run without a hitch. If a participant deviated from the script and made a crack out of turn, the scam would unravel faster than a roll of toilet paper in a hurricane.

It was all about the script, and no one was better at writing them than Billy.

- - -

At noon, his crew assembled in the sky palace's living room. Cory and Morris were showing no ill effects from their night on the town and wore jeans and polo shirts. Travis had gone upscale, dressed in khakis and a blazer with mother-of-pearl buttons. Misty wore a miniskirt and silk blouse and looked like a runway model.

The script began with Billy addressing his crew.

"Afternoon, everyone. Ready to have some fun?"

His crew responded with an enthusiastic yes.

"Then let's go."

His crew followed Billy out of the sky palace. Billy walked across the hall and knocked on the front door to Wang's digs. "Hey Tommy, it's Billy. Rise and shine, my friend."

After returning from the Hard Rock, they'd had several rounds of drinks in a bar called Havana Nights, and Billy and Wang were now on a first-name basis. Wang opened the door wearing a bathrobe. He had just rolled out of the sack and his hair looked like a bird's nest.

"Good morning, Billy. How are you?" Wang said.

"I'm doing great. Sleep well?"

"Very well. And yourself?"

"Like a log. I'm heading down to the casino to do some gambling. Care to join me?"

Wang's grin disappeared. Wang had been sent to Vegas to win back the money he'd lost, yet so far he'd avoided the casino like the plague. DeSantis had to be all over him, just like he was all over Billy. Billy had to believe that Wang was scared of losing everything again, and the dire consequences he'd face upon returning home.

"I woke up feeling lucky. You know that feeling?" Billy asked.

Pepper appeared at Wang's side. She wore one of Wang's long-sleeve dress shirts and nothing else. Her hair was also a bird's nest. She gave Wang's arm a loving squeeze.

"I think so," Wang said, sounding a little shaky.

"Of course you do," Billy scolded him. "You wouldn't be here if you didn't. It's what separates the winners from the losers. So let's go win some money."

Wang still wasn't sold. "I must get dressed. I will join you later."

"Take your time. I'll see you downstairs. You like to play roulette?"

Pepper let out a squeal, then spoke her line. "I love roulette. It's my favorite game."

"I like roulette, too," Wang said.

"I'll save you and Pepper a seat at the table," Billy said.

- - -

Albert Einstein once said that the only way to win at roulette was by stealing chips off the table. Einstein figured out what countless gamblers before him had discovered the hard way. Roulette was for suckers, the odds of winning so impossibly high that nearly no one ever did.

Billy placed a call to DeSantis during the ride down in the elevator.

"Hey, Eddie, how's it going?" he said.

"Good morning, Mr. C. How are we doing today?"

"I'm heading down to the casino to win some of my money back. Would it be possible for you to open up a roulette table for us?"

"I'd have to ask my bosses, Mr. C."

"I've got seven people in my party, so there should be seven chairs at the table."

"I'll call you right back, Mr. C."

"I hear a hint of hesitation in your voice, Eddie."

"I need the approval of the casino floor manager. It's his decision."

"Tell the floor manager that if he says no, I'll go play someplace else."

"Understood, Mr. C. Let me work some magic."

"You do that, Eddie."

Nevada's casinos were required to follow rules regarding their daily operations. These rules included dealer procedures, handling money, and requests from customers. If a casino broke these rules, it could lead to a strict fine or suspension of their gaming license.

These rules didn't apply to whales. Whales could ask for whatever they wanted, and often did. If a casino refused to honor a whale's request, the whale would leave, and millions would fly out the door. As a result, a whale's request was rarely turned down.

Billy felt certain that Carnivale would open up a roulette table for him. In fact, he would have been willing to bet money on it.

The elevator doors parted. They made a detour at Starbucks and ordered drinks. Billy went for a mocha Frappuccino with whipped cream and a cherry on top, while everyone else got the brew of the day. As they left the shop, Misty filched the cherry and popped it into her mouth.

"Thief, thief," he said.

"So sue me," Misty said.

Weekends saw a swelling of visitors from Southern California, and Carnivale's casino was filling up. The roulette area had four tables and was sectioned off by a thick velvet rope.

DeSantis was there to greet them. The host unlatched the velvet rope and ushered them over to a table with seven chairs positioned around it. Their croupier was a handsome Latino dressed in a cream-colored jacket. Standing next to him was the game's banker.

"Mr. C., let me introduce you to Rafael, your croupier."

"Nice to meet you, Rafael," Billy said.

"The pleasure is mine, Mr. C.," the croupier replied.

Rafael gave the wheel a vigorous clockwise spin and sent the little white ball in the opposite direction. The ball raced at blinding speed around the wheel's tilted circular track before losing momentum and falling into one of the numbered pockets. In keeping with the Carnivale's Cuban theme, the wheel was an old-fashioned design called a high-profile that featured pockets slightly deeper than their newer counterparts.

"A seven. That's my lucky number!" Pepper exclaimed.

Tommy Wang and Pepper joined Billy's crew at the table. Wang wore a black short-sleeve shirt and black trousers that seemed to be a uniform among Asian gamblers. Pepper wore matching leather pants and jacket that showed off every curve.

A cocktail waitress took their drink orders. Billy leaned over and whispered in Pepper's ear.

"I heard glass break earlier. You get things worked out?"

"What do you think?" she said with a wink.

- - -

There were two variations of roulette, French and American. The French version had a zero on the wheel along with the numbers one through thirty-six. The addition of the zero gave the casino a 2.7 percent edge.

In the American version, there was a zero and a double zero along with the one through thirty-six. The addition of the double zero gave the house a whopping 5.26 percent edge.

In keeping with the tradition of ripping off its customers, the Carnivale's wheel was the American version with the higher edge.

Being an accountant, Wang quickly noted the higher house edge.

"This is a risky game," Wang confided to Billy.

"The bigger the risk, the greater the reward," Billy said.

Roulette players used special plastic chips that had no value away from the roulette table. These chips came in a variety of colors, with different colors assigned to players at the table. Once a player had his chips, he was allowed to decide what denomination he wanted his chips to be. The croupier then placed a chip on the rail with a marker on top to indicate each player's chip value. The whales went first.

"Five thousand a chip," Billy said.

Wang hesitated. He had obviously not wanted to start at such a high amount. Pepper dropped her hand on Wang's thigh and gave it a squeeze.

"The same," Wang echoed.

Billy's crew declared their values, which ranged between ten dollars and a hundred.

"Place your bets," the croupier said.

The table had an electronic board, which displayed the last twenty numbers the ball had landed on. This was done as a courtesy to the players to let them see if their lucky number had recently come up. The numbers were meaningless, but players still consulted them.

It was showtime. Pepper removed a slip of paper from her purse and placed it on the table. This was the crux of the scam, for if Pepper didn't deliver her lines correctly, Wang would feel a breeze and realize the whole thing was a setup.

"Tommy, look," she said. "Your numbers have all come up. That's good luck."

Wang appeared to be confused. He stared at the slip of paper and shook his head.

"Don't you remember? These are the numbers that came up when you won at backgammon yesterday. *Your lucky numbers.*"

So much had happened since yesterday morning that Wang had all but forgotten about his amazing prowess while playing Pepper and Misty at backgammon. A spark of recognition flickered in his eyes and Wang shifted his gaze to the electronic board. "Your lucky numbers were six, eight, and nine," Pepper said. "Look at all the different numbers with six, eight, and nine that have come up. It's a lot more than the others!"

The numbers six, eight, and nine were scattered across the board. They hadn't come up more than the other numbers, but Pepper made it sound like they had.

"Bet on anything with those numbers in them, and you'll win," she said.

Wang took her advice and made a five-thousand-dollar street bet on the numbers twenty-six, twenty-eight, and twenty-nine. If the little white ball landed on one of those three numbers, the house would pay Wang $55,000.

Billy made a split bet on the numbers eighteen and nineteen. His crew made bets on the other numbers on the board that contained

Wang's lucky numbers. Hopefully, one of these numbers would hit, and the session would start out right. If none of Wang's lucky numbers hit, no big deal, but it would be nice to start out with a winner.

Rafael spun the wheel and sent the little white ball in the opposite direction.

"Good luck, everyone," the croupier said.

The wheel slowed and the ball hit the pocket walls before finally settling on number twenty-six. The table erupted and Wang jumped out of his seat. He grabbed Pepper by the shoulders and gave them a squeeze.

"You were right. They are lucky!" Wang told Pepper.

Pepper looked shocked. This was not in the script, and she glanced at Billy for some sort of explanation.

Dumb fucking luck, Billy mouthed silently.

- - -

It was all going according to plan until Billy got the text from Mags. He hadn't been able to get Mags out of his mind since his talk with Travis that morning. Mags was the most messed-up woman he'd ever known and might very well ruin him someday, yet he didn't care.

Out came his cell phone. His eyes scanned her text.

`Slyde trying to kill me`

Billy turned in his chair so his back was to the table, and he called her.

"You've got to help me," she begged, choking on her tears.

Billy heard a terrific banging sound in the background. "Where are you?"

"Locked in the john in my bedroom. He's breaking down the door."

"Call the cops, for Christ's sake."

"The cops want to arrest me. Billy, you've got to help me."

A tap on Billy's shoulder snapped his head. Rafael stood behind Billy's chair wearing a stern look. "I'm sorry, Mr. C., but phone calls are not permitted at the table. House rules."

"Take a hike," Billy snapped.

"Mr. C., you must put your phone away."

"You heard me. Get lost."

"I'll have to call the floor supervisor."

"Do that, and I'll leave."

Rafael hesitated. Roulette was closely watched, with one surveillance camera devoted to the wheel and a second to watching the layout. Whatever decision the croupier made was being filmed and would later be dissected by management.

Rafael decided to punt, and he returned to his spot by the wheel.

"Place your bets," Rafael announced, as if nothing had happened.

Mags screamed into the phone. "He's going to kill me."

"Hang on, I'm coming."

Billy got out of his chair so quickly that it toppled backward onto the floor. He had stopped thinking coherently and no longer cared how his actions looked. Even though he'd walked out on her, Mags had always been a part of his future; someday, he saw them patching things up and embarking on a life of crime together. Improbable, yes, but not impossible. And now Jimmy Slyde was taking that future away from him.

"You still keep a key under the flower pot?" he asked.

Another scream and the line went dead.

- - -

His crew lifted their eyes as one. They knew something was amiss but could have no idea what it was. With his right hand, Billy brushed imaginary lint off the left sleeve of his sports jacket. Hustlers had their own sign language; brushing the sleeve meant everything was George, or okay, and that the play should proceed.

Wang gazed up at him. "Is everything all right?"

"I have a fire to put out. I need to get on my computer," Billy explained.

The line made perfect sense. Computers were forbidden inside a casino, so it was necessary for Billy to leave the casino in order to get on one.

"Travis, I need to speak with you for a minute."

Travis rose from his chair and followed Billy across the bustling casino floor. Once during rehearsal in Lake Tahoe, Travis had played Billy's part, and he hadn't screwed it up.

"You're the captain now. Take over for me," Billy said.

"I think I still remember the lines. Where you going?"

"I can't tell you that."

"When will you be back?"

"I don't know."

"No offense, Billy, but how the hell am I supposed to run a scam when I don't know how the fucking thing works? You never told me."

They had reached a short hallway that led to the hotel's entrance. DeSantis was at the end of the hallway, coming toward them. Security had seen Billy making the phone call at the roulette table and alerted management, who'd sent DeSantis to straighten things out.

"I'll tell you later. Just follow the script, and Wang will win," Billy said.

"No, he won't," Travis protested. "Wang's lucky numbers aren't coming up enough. He's ahead now, but he'll lose in the long run."

"Trust me. Just follow the script. All will be revealed in due time," Billy said.

"Jesus Christ. You sound like Yoda in *Star Wars*."

Billy gave Travis a gentle push, and the big man hustled away. Billy headed down the hallway, meeting DeSantis in the middle. Billy did not slow down, forcing DeSantis to do a snappy about-face and follow him.

"Is everything okay, Mr. C.? I heard there was a problem at the table."

Billy's mind was racing. The lie he told had to be convincing. "One of my associates got drunk last night and smacked a bouncer at a nightclub. He called me from the jail and asked me to bail him out."

"I'm sorry to hear that, Mr. C."

"Where's the jail, anyway?"

"It's in old downtown. I can get the address for you."

"Do they take credit cards?"

"I'm sure they do."

They went outside the hotel to the valet area. It was total gridlock, with a long line of people waiting for their cars to come up. The line for cabs was equally long. By now, Slyde had broken down the door and gotten his filthy hands on Mags. Mags could bullshit with the best of them, and Billy prayed that she'd somehow convince Slyde not to kill her.

"Does your hotel have a limo I can borrow?" Billy asked.

"I'm sorry, Mr. C., but the limos are at the airport picking up clients," DeSantis said.

"Listen, Eddie, the longer I'm away from the tables, the less money you make. It would be in your best interest to find me a car."

In Vegas, money talked, and everything else was just camouflage. DeSantis removed a set of car keys from his pocket and handed them over.

"Take mine," the VIP host said.

FORTY-SEVEN

It was an unwritten rule that people who lived in Las Vegas did not loan their cars to strangers. There were too many ways to get in trouble in Sin City, and giving a stranger the keys to your car was often an invitation to disaster.

DeSantis's ride was a bloodred Mustang convertible with a V-8 engine. It was a powerful machine, and as Billy drove down the sidewalk on Sahara Boulevard to avoid traffic, police sirens pierced the air. He pulled down a side street into an alley and let the sirens pass.

He returned to Sahara's sidewalks while retrieving Gabe's number on his cell phone. The call went through and Gabe picked up on the first ring.

"I'm having breakfast with my daughter. I'll call you right back," Gabe said.

"You still have that gun your wife left behind?" Billy asked.

The line went deadly still. Gabe's ex-wife had cleaned house before departing, leaving Gabe with a mattress to sleep on, his computer, a coffeemaker, and a handgun.

"You still there?" Billy asked.

"I'm here," Gabe said.

"Do you have the gun or not?"

"I've got it."

"I need you to bring it to me." Billy recited Mags's address. "Make it fast."

He reached Mags's development in record time. A black Beamer with whitewall tires was parked in the driveway, and he parked so the Beamer was boxed in and jumped out.

He stuck his ear to the front door of Mags's place and heard music playing inside. "Wicked Games" by The Weeknd, a song filled with menace where no one involved got off easy. The beep of a car horn snapped his head. Gabe idled at the curb, his window down.

"You okay?" Gabe called to him.

Billy hustled over to the car. Gabe looked both ways before passing a handgun to him.

"It's got a safety. Turn the safety if you plan to fire it," Gabe said.

Billy stuck the gun down the front of his pants. He pulled his blazer closed, hoping to conceal the weapon. "Can this gun be traced to you?"

"No. A guard who worked at my jewelry store gave it to me."

"Good. Now, make yourself scarce."

"What the hell's going on, Billy? You got a score to settle?"

"Something like that. I'll call you later with the bloody details."

"Good luck."

Gabe threw his vehicle into drive and burned out.

- - -

The spare key to the front door of Mags's condo was beneath the flowerpot. Billy let himself in and silently closed the door behind him. The powerful punch of marijuana filled the air. On the dining room table, he spied two unfinished plates of food and two iced teas.

He was sweating like a man going to the electric chair and tossed his blazer over a chair. The gun was now visible, and he moved it behind his back, the barrel kissing the crack in his ass. He wondered if he were capable of taking another human life, and realized he was about to find out.

The master bedroom was at the end of a hallway in the back. He gathered his courage before starting his walk. The smell of dope grew stronger with each step.

The bedroom door was ajar, and he opened it with his foot. Mags lay facedown on the bed, naked and unconscious. Her clothes had been torn off her body and were scattered on the floor. Jimmy Slyde towered over her, wearing red boxers and nothing else. Slyde had a six-pack and vein-popping arms. In his right hand was a tube of K-Y UltraGel, which he was in the process of smearing on the fingers of his other hand. Billy thought he just might kill the bastard.

Slyde realized he had company. The tube landed on the sheets. He came around the bed to get a better look at his unexpected visitor. "Cunningham."

"Did you fuck her?" Billy asked.

"Not yet."

"But you were planning to."

"Damn straight. She said she wanted to get naked with me. I can't turn down an invitation like that."

Mags was a beauty. She'd told Slyde that in order to buy more time.

"You're a piece of shit," Billy said.

"Don't tell me you've still got a thing for Miss Maggie," Slyde said. "From what she told me, you guys stopped being an item a while ago."

"I'm in love with her," Billy said.

"You're in love with this crazy bitch? I thought you were smarter than that."

"That's just how it is. She told me you want to kill her. What the hell did she do to you?"

"She became a liability. You know what I mean."

"No, I don't."

"Is this going to be ugly?"

"Afraid so."

Slyde's clothes were piled on a chair. Slyde reached into the pants pocket and removed a knife. He pushed the button, and a six-inch blade sprang out, the metal gleaming in the harsh bedroom light. Right then, Billy knew that it wasn't going to end until one of them was dead.

He retreated and walked backward down the hallway with Slyde in pursuit. The condo's layout was unfamiliar, and he kept bumping into walls. He waited until he'd reached the living room to draw the borrowed gun from the small of his back and pull back the safety. Slyde's reputation was for being a cruel bastard, and if Billy didn't shoot him, Slyde would kill him—probably slowly, certainly painfully—and would have no second thoughts about it.

Seeing the gun, Slyde broke into a toothy smile.

"You think I'm kidding?" Billy said.

"Your arm's shaking," Slyde said.

Billy wasn't terribly fond of guns. He'd been scamming for most of his life and never felt the need to carry one. His weapon was his wits and his ability to stay a step ahead.

That wasn't true for most cheats. Most cheats carried heat and didn't care if they capped a victim during a job or if they killed another thief who crossed them. Billy was different that way and didn't possess a killer's cold-blooded instinct. Slyde knew this. He'd sized Billy up and decided he would take his chances pitting his switchblade against Billy's gun.

"You don't have the balls to shoot me," Slyde said.

"You're not a very good judge of character," Billy said.

"You've never shot a gun in your fucking life."

"That doesn't mean I won't shoot you."

Slyde's expression was one of contempt. Billy didn't scare him at all.

"You're bluffing," Slyde said.

"Call my bluff and see what happens," Billy said.

Eight feet, maybe less, separated them. The adrenaline coursing through Billy's veins had caused a surreal slowdown of events, and he saw the tip of Slyde's knife flick back and forth with the fury of a serpent's tail. His enemy lunged forward. As Billy squeezed the trigger, he had a troubling thought. He didn't know if the gun was loaded. Only when the gun barked in his hand did Billy know. The bullet slammed into Slyde's chest and he melted to the floor. The expression on Slyde's face was one of surprise; he'd underestimated Billy and paid the price.

"Rot in hell," Billy said.

Slyde took his sweet time dying. The life slowly seeped out of his body, shutting his eyes a few centimeters at a time. And then he took a last gasp and was gone.

Billy shuddered. He'd never felt the need to take a life, and he realized he'd let his feelings for Mags cloud his judgment. Falling in love had screwed up his head, and he tried to pull himself together.

Male voices carried from outside. At the living room window he parted the curtains and looked out. A black and white Metro LVPD cruiser was parked out front. Two cops stood behind it pointing guns at the house. One was on a walkie-talkie radioing for backup.

He retreated from the window and tossed the gun onto the couch. He was about to be arrested and thrown in jail. It might take a day before his lawyer would be able to plead his case before a judge and get bail set. Twelve months of planning was about to go down the toilet. Or not.

He called Travis. Travis was still at his chair at the roulette table. Travis made Billy wait and walked away from the table before speaking.

"Where are you? We're all getting nervous," Travis said.

"Change of plans. You're now officially in charge."

"Are you coming back?"

"Not right away. I'll explain later. Just follow the script, and we'll all end up rich."

"For the love of Christ, Billy, this is insane."

"Have I ever steered you wrong before?"

"That's not the point. You're not here, and you're the whale. What do I tell DeSantis if he asks me where you went?"

"I told DeSantis I had to bail a friend out of jail. Use that story."

Travis went quiet, and Billy wondered if he'd lost him.

"I sure hope you know what you're doing," the big man said.

"Keep the faith," Billy said.

His next call was to his attorney, an aging shark named Felix Underman. Underman had represented every wise guy and mobster to run afoul of the law during the past four decades. Underman's longtime secretary, Holly, answered and patched him through to the boss.

"Hello, Billy, how are we today?" his attorney asked.

"Not so good," he replied.

"I'm sorry to hear that. What seems to be the problem?"

"I just shot a guy, and the police are going to arrest me."

"Is he dead?"

"Yeah, that's why I shot him."

"I'll meet you at the jail in an hour. Whatever you do, don't say a word to the police."

"I wasn't planning on it," the young hustler said.

The voices outside had multiplied. The backup unit had arrived. Billy told his lawyer he'd see him at the jail and ended the call. He didn't want to leave without saying good-bye, and he stepped over Slyde's lifeless body and hurried down the hallway to the master bedroom.

Mags lay unconscious on the bed in all her glory. She had to be the most beautiful woman he'd ever known. He wanted to believe the cops would treat her with respect, but that was wishful thinking. He retrieved her underwear and clothes from the floor and began to dress her.

A loud banging carried from the front of the condo.

"This is the police. Open the door," said a man's voice.

The smart move would have been to let the police into the condo. Instead, he pulled Mags up into a sitting position and tried to shake her awake. Slyde had done a number on her, and her beautiful face was covered in ugly purple bruises.

"Come on. Wake up."

The police burst into the house, yelling at the top of their lungs the way cops liked to do. Mags's eyelids fluttered, and she looked around the bedroom before settling her gaze on Billy.

"You made it," she said.

"Was there any doubt in your mind?"

She tried to smile and winced in pain. "My face hurts."

"Be quiet, okay? You need to go to a hospital."

"Where's that piece of shit Jimmy?"

"Playing poker with the devil."

"You killed him?"

Billy acknowledged that he had indeed ended the life of Jimmy Slyde. Mags leaned in and planted a kiss on Billy's cheek.

"My hero," she said.

FORTY-EIGHT

The Clark County Detention Center was nobody's idea of a good time. Located in a seedy section of old downtown, it was here that the city's miscreants were formally booked and stuck into filthy holding cells to wait for their defense attorneys or friends to bail them out.

Billy had been ground through the system enough times to know the drill. It took an hour for a clerk with a room-temperature IQ to type up the charges against him, another half hour for his fingerprints and mug shot to be taken. Everything inside the jail worked in slow motion, a preview of what his life was to become if he were so unfortunate as to go to prison.

He'd never spent more than a night in jail, but there was always a first time. He'd just shot a man to death, and his bail was going to be high regardless of how good a job Underman did convincing the judge that his shooting Jimmy Slyde was an act of self-defense.

The holding cell was a cramped space with a wooden bench and a toilet. It was standing-room- only, and Billy found a spot in the back and leaned against the cold concrete wall. An inmate with greasy slicked-back hair stuck out his hand.

"Name's Jinx Williams," the inmate said.

"What do you want?" Billy replied.

"Who said I wanted anything?"

"I did. What do you want?"

"Nothing. What's your name?"

"Billy."

"Got a last name?"

"Up yours."

"That's a funny last name."

"Have a nice day."

A spot came open on the bench and Billy grabbed it. Everyone in Vegas had a scam, including inmates in the detention center. There the scam was to get the name of a guy who'd been busted and have a friend on the outside call the guy's family, identify himself as an official at the jail, and solicit bail using a credit card.

Billy stuck his hands in his pants pockets to wait. In his right pocket was a folded square of paper. He'd turned over his valuables to the clerk during processing but had failed to turn over the piece of paper. He removed it, assuming it was a receipt, and discovered that it was the newspaper article about the murder of union leader Cal Branche that Gabe had given him. Having nothing better to do, Billy decided to read the article again.

Although Billy had met Cal Branche only once, the meeting had left an indelible impression. Vegas was a town filled with larger-than-life personalities, and Branche was one of those, with a ready handshake and a manner that bespoke trust. Branche had many admirers, and it was hard to fathom how his murder had gone unsolved for so long.

Gabe had claimed the Haneys were responsible and that the cops and gaming board were involved in the cover-up. It made sense, only there wasn't any hard proof, and without proof, it was just another conspiracy theory for people to chew on.

The night of his murder, Branche had landed at McCarran and, while claiming his suitcase, had chatted with several airline workers who recognized him. Going outside, Branche boarded a jitney that took him to his black Suburban in long-term parking. During the jitney ride, Branche called his wife to let her know he'd arrived and would be home soon.

Branche never got there. His wife waited several hours before calling the police and filing a report. Three days later, his decomposing body was found buried under a pile of rocks in the desert. A single bullet to the back of the head had taken his life. His corpse was stripped clean, except for his driver's license, which his killers had purposely left behind.

Billy stopped reading and stared into space. Gabe had said that the police and gaming board had interviewed the Haneys but let them skate. Was it a cover-up, or were the Haneys really innocent? There was no way for him to know for sure. It was a dead end, and he started to fold up the article while staring at Branche's photograph.

"Sorry, man," he said under his breath.

In the photo, Branche held a cigarette. Branche was a chain-smoker, and Billy recalled Branche offering him a cigarette the time they'd met. Billy noticed something that he hadn't seen before. On the third finger of Branche's right hand was a ring. The ring was perfectly round and contained an old coin. Not gold or silver, but maybe brass, and really old.

Billy read the article again. Branche's body had been stripped clean by his killers except for a piece of ID. All his jewelry had been stolen.

Shit, Billy thought.

- - -

Jinx Williams sat on the opposite end of the bench, trying to get a new inmate to give him his name. He saw Billy approach and stood up.

"What do you want?" the detention center hustler said.

"How'd you like to make a quick five hundred bucks?" Billy asked.

Money made the world go round. Jinx and Billy moved to the far corner of the cell away from the bars so a passing guard would not overhear them.

"Start talking," Jinx said.

"I want to make a phone call on your cell phone," Billy said.

"Who said I had a cell phone?"

"I did. You're getting names of guys who just got busted and giving them to a pal on the outside, who's calling the families and scamming them out of bail money. You need a cell phone to do that."

"You're a smart one."

"That's debatable. Do we have a deal?"

"How do I get my money?"

"My lawyer is going to show up soon. Have your guy on the outside come down and my lawyer will give him the money."

"You've got this all figured out, don't you?"

"Is that a yes?"

"Make it a grand, and you have yourself a deal."

They shook hands on it. It was how business was done between thieves—no contracts or fancy lawyers, just a man's word and the pressing of the flesh. Jinx glanced at the bars before bending over to tie his shoe. Pulling up his pants leg, Jinx removed a clamshell phone no bigger than a cigarette lighter. Standing, he passed the phone to Billy.

"Sit down on the bench, and I'll stand in front of you," Jinx said. "Keep your face close to my back so the camera in the hallway doesn't see you."

"Got it."

Billy took a seat on the bench and Jinx blocked for him. The other inmates ignored them. Billy called Gabe and got put into voice mail, and he called again. This time, Gabe answered.

"Hello?" the jeweler said suspiciously.

"It's me," Billy said in a quiet voice. "I got busted."

"Shit, Billy."

"I need your help. Is your daughter still there?"

"She left. I didn't want her here in case those animals showed up."

"That's why I'm calling. I may have the goods on them."

"Really? What did you find?"

"A piece of evidence that ties them to Cal Branche's murder. You told me earlier that Branche was a client when you owned the jewelry store in the casino."

"That's right. Cal came in all the time."

"Did you ever sell him a ring with an old coin in it?"

"Now that you mention it, I did."

"Describe it to me."

"Guard's coming, stop talking," Jinx said.

"I'll be right back. Don't go away," Billy said into the phone.

Billy slipped the phone into his pocket and crossed his arms in front of his chest. A guard entered the hallway outside the cellblock escorting a new inmate. The new inmate was drunk as a skunk and staggered as he walked. The guard opened the door and pushed the inmate in.

"Lie down on the floor and sleep it off," the guard said.

The inmate entered the cell and lay on the floor as if it were a feather bed. The guard left, and Billy removed the phone from his pocket.

"Still there?"

"I'm here," Gabe said. "I remember the coin I sold to Cal. I bought a cache of old coins that were smuggled out of Israel and turned them into jewelry. The coins came from the reign of Caesar Crispus and dated back to 300 AD. As the story goes, Crispus's wife conspired against him, so he had her burned to death in a vat of boiling oil. They were real popular and sold out right away. The ring I sold to Cal had a brass coin and was the last of the lot."

It was all adding up. But Billy had to be sure.

"Did Branche buy this ring for himself or as a gift?" the young hustler asked.

"For himself," Gabe replied.

"Are you sure?"

"I'm one hundred percent sure. Cal was wearing the ring the next time he came into the store. Told me it was his favorite piece of jewelry."

Billy had heard enough. "That's beautiful. I've got to run."

"Is there anything I can do?" Gabe asked.

"You've done plenty, man. Thanks."

Billy ended the call. Jinx had stuck his hand behind his back, and Billy deposited the phone into his palm. Jinx bent down to tie his shoe and made the phone disappear. Moments later the guard returned to the holding cell and unlocked the door.

"Which one of you gentlemen is Cunningham?" the guard asked.

"You're looking at him," Billy said.

"Your lawyer's here. Let's go."

"Nice doing business with you," Billy said under his breath. "My lawyer's name is Underman. Have your guy come down, and Underman will give him the money."

"Will do," Jinx said.

FORTY-NINE

Billy had been arrested many times in Las Vegas, and not once had the guards inside the detention center felt the need to handcuff the young hustler. Partially because Billy was small in stature and the guards were all brutes, and also because of the vibe Billy gave off.

It was no different this time, and the guard escorted Billy to the visitor's room without handcuffing him. Billy took a chair in front of a Plexiglas wall with a round hole for talking. Underman sat on the other side of the wall, tapping his fingers on his fancy alligator briefcase.

Billy sat down, and the guard retreated to the wall to stand. The room was bugged, and anything incriminating that Billy said to his lawyer would be used against him in a court of law.

Underman started to speak. Billy shushed him with a finger to the lips.

"I talk, you listen," the young hustler said.

Underman shut up. Lawyers were paid to talk, and this was going to be hard.

"You ever hear of Custer's Last Stand?" Billy asked.

Underman nodded that he had.

"Well, this is Cunningham's Last Stand, and I'm going down swinging."

"I'm in your corner," his attorney said.

"I need for you to contact Frank Grimes and Bill Tricaricco of the gaming board and set up a meeting. Tell them that I know who murdered the union leader Cal Branche, and that I want to speak with them before I give the newspapers the story."

Underman turned white as a ghost. "You know who killed Cal?"

"You knew him?"

"Very well. Cal stood up for his beliefs. That's a rarity in this town."

"To answer your question, yes, I know who murdered him."

"Well, I'm sure the gaming board will be interested to hear what you have to say. How soon do you want this meeting?"

"Right now."

"Be reasonable, Billy. It's a Saturday afternoon, and these men are probably home with their families, enjoying the weekend."

"I want the meeting right now. Tell Grimes and Tricaricco that if they don't come, I'm going to the media with the story."

A good attorney knew how to read between the lines. Underman took a moment to choose the right words before responding in a whisper. "This sounds like blackmail."

"It is."

"I'm not comfortable with this."

"All you have to do is sit in the room and listen."

"That's it?"

"And bring a radio."

"A radio? What for?"

"You'll see." Billy called to the guard that they were done. "See you soon."

- - -

Back in the holding cell, Billy got to know Jinx better. For Jinx to have a cell phone in his possession was not because the guards had missed it when they'd patted him down. He had bribed the guards to look the other way, and that took a lot of guts.

Jinx was working a sweet scam inside the detention center. Every weekend, he got himself arrested on a minor charge. Because the detention center was packed, it took hours before Jinx got to stand before a judge. He used that time to work the holding cell and get the names of new inmates, where they lived, and the names of a wife or girlfriend.

When he had five or six good prospects, he'd call his partner on the outside and give him the information. His partner would use the Internet to find the prospect's phone number, call it, and identify himself as a deputy at the jail. His partner would request a credit card number or PayPal account information so the inmate could post bail.

On an average weekend, Jinx took down five grand bilking inmates. His only fear was that he'd someday bilk the same inmate twice, and the inmate would take revenge.

"So what's your angle?" Jinx asked.

"I cheat casinos," Billy said.

"Good for you, man."

A guard appeared outside the holding cell. "Cunningham, front and center."

"See you around," Billy said.

The guard escorted Billy to a windowless interrogation room on the sixth floor. Grimes and Tricaricco were present and wore faded jeans and polo shirts and Saturday stubble on their chins. Both men stared at the young hustler like he was a ghost.

"Hello, Billy," his attorney said. "Special Agent Grimes and Special Agent Tricaricco were kind enough to interrupt what they were doing and come down."

"I really appreciate it," Billy said.

The interrogation room had a pocked wood table with four chairs. Billy and his attorney sat down on one side of the table, Grimes and

Tricaricco on the other. The gaming agents could not stop staring at Billy, their faces a mixture of confusion and anger.

"You bring the radio?" Billy asked his attorney.

Underman produced a cheap radio and set it on the table. Billy turned on the power and spun the dial to 92.3 FM, the KOMP. *Laurie Steele & the Homegrown Show* was on. Billy set the volume so it was just loud enough to drown out their conversation to the mikes in the ceiling.

"Turn that thing off," Tricaricco declared.

Billy put his elbows on the table. "No."

"I said, turn that fucking thing off, or I'll do it for you."

"You don't want the mikes to pick up what I have to say. Grimes hired the Haneys to whack me. I found out, and now you're going to pay for it."

Tricaricco looked ready for a heart attack while Grimes stared miserably at the desk.

Billy had the gaming agents right where he wanted them. He removed the newspaper article reporting Cal Branche's murder from his pocket and placed it on the table so Cal's pleasant face stared up at them. The gaming agents glanced at the article before looking away.

"Ten years ago, Cal Branche got shot in the back of the head and buried in the desert," Billy said. "At the time, Cal was trying to make the casinos pay for health insurance for their employees, which would have cost them millions if Cal got what he wanted.

"The police conducted an investigation and interviewed the Haneys, who were hanging around McCarran the night Cal came in. The gaming board also talked to the Haneys." Looking at Tricaricco, he said, "You talked to them."

"So what if I did?" Tricaricco said.

"You knew the Haneys whacked Cal, but you let them go. So did the cops. Cal Branche being dead was good for the town's casinos, so you let them walk."

“There was no proof,” Tricaricco said, clearly on the defensive. “There were more than a thousand passengers at McCarran the night Cal Branche’s plane came in. The fact that the Haneys were there doesn’t prove a damn thing.”

“The Haneys are a couple of two-bit thugs. The father gets his kicks out of punching people in the face. The father doesn’t wear gloves and neither does his son, which means they leave clues at the scene of the crime, like fingerprints and trace fibers. But the casinos told the gaming board and the police to ignore the evidence, so you did.”

Tricaricco looked ready to explode and addressed Underman. “I wasted my fucking afternoon to listen to this horseshit? You’re going to pay for this, Felix, mark my words.”

Underman was on a first-name basis with every judge in town, and not accustomed to being threatened. He started to reply and Billy silenced him with a sharp kick under the table.

“I have proof,” Billy said.

That shut Tricaricco down. Grimes had gone mute and had yet to make eye contact.

“I’d like to see it,” Tricaricco said.

“I’m guessing that after you got the call from the casinos, you got rid of the evidence that linked the Haneys with Cal’s killing,” Billy said. “But there was one clue that directly implicated the Haneys that you missed.” He jabbed the photo. “Look at his hand.”

The gaming agents leaned in to stare at Cal Branche’s photograph. So did Underman. Normally, Billy would have milked the moment to make the gaming agents squirm, but there was a scam at the Carnivale with his name on it, and he wanted to be there when it went down.

“The ring Cal’s wearing has a brass coin from ancient Rome that bears the likeness of an emperor named Caesar Crispus,” Billy said. “The ring’s a one of a kind and was sold to Cal by a jeweler in town who I happen to know. When Cal’s body was discovered, it was picked clean. Everything was gone, including that ring. Guess who has the ring now?”

"Who?" Tricaricco said, practically choking on the word.

"Old Man Haney."

"Maybe he bought it in a pawn shop."

"Tell that to the DA."

Tricaricco looked at Underman. "You went to the district attorney already?"

"That was a figure of speech. Wasn't it, Billy?" Underman said.

"That's right. Not that it didn't cross my mind," Billy said. "But I thought it would be best if I told you gentlemen first."

The interrogation room went quiet and the cheap radio's music washed over them. Tricaricco and Grimes both understood what was about to happen. The DA would see the chance to solve Cal's murder and make a name for himself. The buck would stop with the gaming board, and Grimes's and Tricaricco's lives would be forever ruined.

Grimes broke the silence. "So what do you want? Money?"

"I want you to vouch for me," Billy said.

"Vouch for you how?"

"This morning I shot a guy to death named Jimmy Slyde. Slyde's a scumbag with a rap sheet the length of your arm. I want the both of you to stand up in front of a judge and say that I was working for the gaming board as an informant, and that you asked me to keep tabs on Slyde. This morning, Slyde beat up a woman named Maggie Flynn and was about to rape her—"

"That little slut's involved in this?" Grimes said.

It was all Billy could do not to put his hands around Grimes's throat and snap his neck.

"—when I discovered him in the act. Slyde tried to stab me, and I shot him in self-defense. That's it. Get me off, and this story about the Haneys goes away."

Tricaricco chewed it over, since at the end of the day it was his decision to make. Striking a deal with the devil was risky, but it beat facing the music any day of the week.

"All right," Tricaricco said.

"You'll do it?" Billy asked.

"Yeah, I'll do it," Tricaricco said.

"I want one more thing. This bullshit has to end, and the slate wiped clean. Nothing I did to the gaming board deserved you fuckers putting a contract out on my life."

Tricaricco glanced at Grimes. "You on board with that, Frank?"

"I'm on board," Grimes said reluctantly.

"Let me hear you say it so we're all clear," Billy said.

"The gaming board will leave you alone. The slate is wiped clean," Grimes said.

"That includes anything I've done in the past."

Grimes looked like he was going to get sick, and Billy guessed that the special agent had evidence about past crimes that Billy had committed that he hoped to use to prosecute him.

"Whatever you did before is ancient history," Grimes said.

"But if we catch you cheating a casino, we're still going to bust you," Tricaricco said, the anger rising in his voice. "You understand what I'm saying, Billy? The past is the past, but that doesn't mean you get a free ride to steal."

Billy had never wanted a free ride. Free rides were for lazy bastards who thought the world owed them a favor. What Billy wanted was a set of hard-and-fast rules that both sides agreed to play by. If the gaming board caught him cheating and could prove it in court, Billy would do the time. But if the gaming board couldn't catch him, they had to leave him alone.

Billy came out of his chair. He'd said everything he was going to say. The gaming agents hesitated before also standing. Not one to be left out, Underman stood up as well.

"It's been nice doing business with you," Billy said.

FIFTY

"Any word from Billy?" Cory whispered in Travis's ear.

The big man shook his head. They'd been playing roulette all afternoon and the time had come to take down Carnivale. Travis had stepped away from the table to see if Billy had sent him a text, but there were no messages on his phone.

"So what do we do?" Cory whispered.

"Full steam ahead," Travis said.

"You sure?"

Travis said he was sure. For all he knew, Billy could be dead, or in jail, or on a plane to another country. None of those things were going to stop the crew from finishing the job. It was how the cheating game worked.

The big man rose from his chair. The script now called for Billy to speak to the croupier and stop play. But since Billy wasn't there, it was up to Travis to utter the convincing line.

"Hey, Rafael. That guy over there just insulted us," Travis said.

Rafael had been working the game all afternoon. Normally, croupiers were changed every hour, but this was not always the case when whales were playing.

"Who are you referring to?" the croupier asked politely.

"That tall guy asked if Misty was a hooker. Didn't he, Misty?" Travis said.

"Yes! I've never been more insulted in my life," Misty said.

"Please point him out," Rafael said.

Travis pointed at the group of tourists observing the roulette game. Only a small portion of people inside a casino actually gambled; the rest just stood and watched.

"It was the tall guy in the back," Travis said.

"I will ask management to have him removed," Rafael said.

"Is that all you're going to do?"

"Removing people from the casino is not my job. Place your bets, please."

Travis sank into his chair. He had failed miserably. The line would have worked if Billy had spoken it. Billy was the whale, and the casino was committed to making whales happy.

Tommy Wang slid a sizable bet onto the layout. Wang was losing his shirt and had started doubling his bets to recoup his money. The casinos called this practice chasing your losses. It was what paid for the nice light fixtures and fancy carpets.

The rest of Billy's crew also placed their bets.

Rafael spun the wheel and set the little white ball in motion. The wheel slowed down and the ball landed on double zero. Everyone lost, and Rafael swept the losing bets off the layout.

"This is no good," Wang said dejectedly.

Wang looked ready to call it an afternoon. If he walked away from the game, the scam would unravel, and all their hard work would be for nothing. Pepper sprang into action and grabbed her lover's sleeve. "Remember the backgammon game yesterday? You started out losing, and then you won everything in sight. Your luck will come back."

"I am losing too much. Soon my money will be gone, and I will have to go home."

"You'll get hot again. I can feel it."

Wang shook his head miserably. Losing had sapped the life out of him, and he looked like a broken man. Billy had taught them to work as a team, and it was Misty who saved the day.

"Rafael, can you hold our spots while we visit the bar?" Misty asked.

"Of course. Your chairs will be waiting upon your return," the croupier said.

"I need a drink. Anyone care to join me?" Misty said.

"Hey handsome, why don't you buy us a cocktail?" Pepper said.

Wang found the strength to smile. He had lost everything but Pepper's affection. With Pepper and Misty on either arm, the Chinese gambler made his way toward the bar.

Cory, Morris, and Travis stepped away from the table and went into a huddle. They'd done their best to keep Wang entertained but had run out of clever things to say. The scam was starting to feel like a movie that had run too long.

"You need to try the line again," Cory said.

"It didn't work the first time; it won't work the second," Travis said.

"It's the only play we have," Cory said.

"What would Billy do?" Morris asked.

Travis's head snapped. "Speak of the devil. Let's ask him."

Billy glided across the casino toward them. He was still in character, and he walked with the self-assuredness of a whale. Whatever reason had caused him to leave was now behind him. Seeing them, he frowned. "Why aren't you upstairs?"

"I tried the line," Travis said.

"And?"

"It didn't fly."

"Let me give it a try. Go round up the girls. We've got some stealing to do."

- - -

"Sorry about that," Billy said after his crew returned to the roulette table. "How's everyone doing?"

"I am losing badly," Wang said.

"Well, let's see if we can change that." Billy's pile of chips was right where he'd left it, and he placed four five-thousand-dollar bets on the layout. Wang hesitated, then placed his bets on the same numbers.

"Let 'er rip," Billy said.

Rafael set the wheel in motion and launched the little white ball. The wheel slowed down and the ball landed on one of Billy's numbers. It was pure dumb luck, but sometimes that was the best kind of luck to have. The table erupted and the life returned to Wang's solemn face. Billy glared menacingly at the tourists gathered behind the velvet rope.

"Is something wrong, Mr. C.?" the croupier asked.

"I just heard someone call my assistant a prostitute," Billy said.

"I'm terribly sorry, Mr. C. I will call security immediately."

"It happened before, too," Pepper said, sounding hurt.

"Are you kidding me? Did they toss the guy?"

"They didn't do a thing," Pepper said.

Billy directed his anger at the croupier. "What kind of a place is this? If I wanted my people to be insulted, I'd gamble on Fremont Street. Come on, gang, let's blow this dump before I lose my temper."

Billy and his crew exchanged their roulette chips for regular casino chips. Wang did the same. As they walked away from the table, Rafael placed a frantic call to management.

"You did it," Travis said under his breath.

"I'm just getting warmed up," Billy said.

- - -

Billy went straight to the cage. DeSantis and his boss were waiting. Casino management wasn't about to let Billy and Wang fly out the door without putting up a fight.

"Mr. C., this is my boss, Larry Lamb," DeSantis said.

Lamb extended his meaty paw. Lamb was what people in the casino industry called an office orangutan. He ate too much, drank too much, and didn't know the meaning of the word *exercise*. One day, Lamb would drop dead at his desk, and another orangutan would replace him.

Billy ignored Lamb's outstretched hand.

"I think we deserve the chance to fix this problem, considering all the things we've done for you and your friends," DeSantis said.

"We've lost a lot of money in this joint. That more than pays for the concert tickets and free meals, don't you think?" Billy said, unwilling to bend.

"Mr. C., we're going to make things right, you have my word."

"Twice my assistant gets called a hooker while playing roulette. You blew your chance, Eddie. I've had enough of your bullshit."

"But Mr. C. . . ."

"Take a hike."

The situation had turned ugly. Lamb tapped DeSantis on the shoulder, signaling for him to leave. More than likely, DeSantis wouldn't have a job when he came to work tomorrow. It didn't matter that DeSantis was a loyal employee willing to do backflips to make his clients happy. What mattered was that a whale was angry, and whales came first.

DeSantis turned his back and walked away.

Lamb jumped in and started talking. "The casino has asked me to extend its sincerest apologies for this unfortunate situation, Mr. C. We will do *anything* to make things right."

"Define anything," Billy said.

"You can play in our high-roller salon, which is closed off from the public."

"Salons are for assholes," Billy said.

"We can put you in a private suite, then."

"Not interested."

"Then how about your sky palace? We can have the equipment brought up along with the dealers. You'll be able to gamble in total comfort and privacy."

Billy brought his hand to his chin. "What about food?"

"We can have a chef prepare food in your sky palace, as well."

"How about a bartender?"

"That, too. I'd also send up a masseuse to give you neck massages while you play."

"Pedicures for the ladies?"

"Absolutely. Your wish is my command, Mr. C."

Billy nodded his approval. In a few days, after the smoke had cleared and people were thinking clearly again, Carnivale's management would conduct an internal review to determine how they'd lost so much money to one gambler. Among other things, the review would state that it was Lamb's idea to let Billy and Tommy Wang play roulette for high stakes in the sky palace, outside of the secure confines of the casino.

Playing hard to get was the name of the game. Billy turned to his crew and said, "So what do you think? Should we stay or should we go?"

Each member of his crew stuck to the script with their replies.

"Sounds good to me," Travis said.

"I'm game," Cory said.

"Me, too," Morris said.

"I'll do whatever Pepper wants," Misty said.

"Let's give them another chance," Pepper said, clinging to Wang's arm.

The moment of truth had arrived. They all looked at Wang.

"I think I would like that," the Chinese gambler said.

"It's unanimous. Wang's sky palace it is," Billy said.

FIFTY-ONE

The safest place in Las Vegas was inside a casino. Between the surveillance cameras and trained security, it was hard for a criminal to do business. Crimes happened, but only with a great deal of planning and preparation.

Outside of the casino was a different story. Customers got robbed inside hotels every day, often in the halls but sometimes in their rooms. Crafty thieves would impersonate employees to gain entry, stick a gun in a victim's face, and rob him or her blind.

There were also larger thefts committed by scammers and cheats. Bookies had set up illegal bookmaking operations in Strip hotels, then used the casino to recruit customers with the promise of better odds and no taxes to pay to Uncle Sam.

And teams of card cheats had staged games in private suites where rich suckers got fleeced by dealers trained in sophisticated sleight of hand.

Casinos were secure. The buildings that surrounded them were not.

Billy sat at the bar in Wang's sky palace drinking a Corona. The last few days had felt like a marathon; now the finish line was in sight. Pepper and Wang sat beside him at the bar, sipping rum punches made by a pleasant young woman named Star.

"Is everything to your satisfaction?" Star asked.

"Everything's perfect," Pepper cooed.

Out by the pool, a well-proportioned masseuse was giving Travis a massage. Cory and Morris were next in line and had their shirts off. Misty sat in a lounge chair, getting a pedicure from a chatty Filipino woman. Whoever said crime didn't pay wasn't doing it right.

"Hey, Larry, let's get this show on the road," Billy said.

Lamb stood in the center of the living room, a small computer in his hand. The room's furniture was gone, replaced by a gleaming roulette wheel on an antique table. Four employees had brought in the equipment and set up the game under Lamb's watchful eye.

"Just a few more minutes, Mr. C.," Lamb replied.

"You said that ten minutes ago. Hurry up."

"Good things are worth waiting for, Mr. C."

"I've heard that one before."

Lamb set the wheel in motion and spun the little white ball. The easiest way to beat the game of roulette was by exploiting a biased wheel. The wheel was a piece of furniture made of wood and metal and subject to subtle imperfections. These imperfections caused the wheel to spin out of balance, with the ball favoring one side of the wheel more than the other. A hundred and fifty years ago, a clever French gambler had broken the bank at Monte Carlo by exploiting a biased wheel, and casinos had been on the lookout for the scam ever since.

Lamb pointed the computer at the wheel and clocked its spin. He did this a dozen times. The last time, he nodded. The wheel was not biased.

"We're ready, Rafael," Lamb said.

Rafael stood like a statue by the slider. The croupier broke out of his trance and straightened his bow tie before taking his position at the table.

"Mr. C., the table is yours," Lamb said.

Billy slid off his stool along with Pepper and Wang. They took the same seats at the table as they'd had downstairs. His crew came in from outside and joined them.

"Place your bets," Rafael said.

Wang toyed with his chips and seemed uncertain how much to wager.

"Shoot the pickle," Billy told him.

Wang gave him a confused look. "You want to shoot me?"

"No, no. It's an expression. It means go for it."

"You think I should bet heavy?"

"Why not? Fortune favors the brave."

"Play your lucky numbers," Pepper whispered in Wang's ear.

Wang picked up his glass of wine and chugged it down. He let out a deep breath before placing his bets on his lucky numbers from the rigged backgammon game. Rafael set the wheel in motion and spun the little white ball.

"Good luck, everyone," the croupier said.

The hardest part of ripping off a casino was acting surprised when it happened. Most cheaters thought they should jump up and down and start yelling, but that often looked staged. The best response was a moment of stunned silence, followed by cheers and back slapping.

Moments later, Billy's crew did just that.

- - -

On August 21, 1951, Binion's Horseshoe Casino opened its doors and proceeded to lose $200,000 the first night of operation. According to urban legend, it was the last time a casino in Las Vegas had a losing day.

Until now.

Within an hour, Wang had won back the money he'd lost downstairs. The ball was falling his way, the lucky numbers winning enough times to give him a huge edge over the house.

Lamb did not seem overly concerned. Wang had established himself as a sucker, and suckers were expected to win every once in a while. It was what kept them coming back.

By the end of the second hour, Wang was up $3 million. Billy and his crew had tried to camouflage the winning by purposely placing losing bets. As their stacks grew smaller, Wang's stack had become a fortress. Wang was a different person when winning, and he banged the table with the pent-up energy of a man who'd been kept down too long.

By now, Lamb was sweating through his underwear. Thinking Wang was on an extended winning streak, Lamb tried to break Wang's rhythm and told the bartender to refill Wang's wineglass whenever it ran dry.

By the fourth hour, Wang was slurring his speech and was up $6 million.

Lamb's next move was to change croupiers. An ice princess named Nicolette took over the game, and within twenty minutes Wang had beaten her out of another million bucks.

Lamb was growing desperate. Too much money was flying out the window, and Lamb stepped away from the table and made a hurried call on his cell phone. A minute later, the promised chef appeared and offered to whip up their favorite meals.

Wang eyed the chef suspiciously. Wang knew that when the meals were delivered, play would be halted, and the Chinese gambler wasn't about to let that happen.

"What is your pleasure this evening?" the chef asked.

"Big Mac," Wang said.

"I'm sorry, but Big Macs aren't on the menu," the chef said.

"Go get one," Wang said. Then added, "With a large order of fries and a chocolate shake."

A whale was not to be denied, and the chef left in a huff.

- - -

Thirty minutes later, Wang got his Big Mac and fries and his shake. He unwrapped the food at the table and offered Pepper the first bite. Pepper was playing drunk, having dumped several rum drinks down the toilet. She took a bite and giggled.

Wang was now up a cool ten million. Lamb had brought in reinforcements, and three more office orangutans had joined the party. Like Lamb, they were corn-fed bruisers.

Sweat was doing a death march down Lamb's face. If Lamb didn't do something, the casino's bottom line would reflect a losing night, a losing week, and a losing quarter.

Lamb took the ball from the croupier and went to the bar, where he used a mallet to split the ball open. A crew of Italian cheats had swindled the Ritz in London using a transmitter concealed in a cigarette pack and a receiver embedded in the ball.

Lamb searched through the powder and frowned.

You ain't even close, Billy thought.

Wang rose from his chair. He was three sheets to the wind and could barely stand up. Billy rose as well and said, "I think we're done, don't you?"

"Not done," Wang said drunkenly.

"You want to continue to play?"

Wang pointed at the layout and to Lamb said, "One million on each lucky number. I give you a chance to win your money back."

Billy rocked back on his heels. The scam wasn't foolproof, and Wang's lucky numbers would not come up all the time. If Wang lost, Billy and his crew lost as well. But if Wang won, they'd be eating steak and lobster for the rest of their lives.

Lamb made a call on his cell. Ending the call, he said, "We'll take your action."

An exchange was made. Wang's fortress of chips became ten black chips, with each chip representing $1 million. Wang placed his bets on the layout with Pepper's help.

The wheel was set in motion and the ball spun.

"Shoot the pickle!" Wang screamed.

FIFTY-TWO

No one had ever cried when a casino lost money, except for the people who ran it. The office orangutans accompanied Wang in an elevator to the main floor of the casino. In Wang's hands was $36 million in chips. It was easily the single biggest loss a casino had ever suffered.

Billy and his crew followed in a separate elevator. Upon reaching the casino, they joined the procession while staying several steps back. It was not uncommon for casinos to steer winning gamblers to tables in the hopes of winning their money back, and Billy was going to make sure that Wang did not take any unexpected detours. Upon reaching the cage, Wang passed his thirty-six million in chips through the bars to a cashier. The cashier's jaw dropped open.

"Cash me out," Wang said.

A cash transaction report was slid through the bars along with a pen. Wang took his time filling in the necessary information.

"What happens now?" Pepper whispered into Billy's ear.

"Tommy takes his money and goes home," Billy said.

"Just like that?"

"Yup, just like that."

"But the casino has to be suspicious. He just won thirty-six million bucks."

The casino *was* suspicious. It was too much money for a player to win at roulette, or, for that matter, at any other casino game. But knowing something wasn't right and proving it were two entirely different things. Because Wang had played roulette inside a sky palace, there were no video tapes for the casino to review. Without those tapes, it would be impossible to determine the number of times Wang's lucky numbers had paid off, which happened to be off the charts. This was why Billy had worked so hard to get the game moved out of the casino.

"Misty thinks the croupiers were involved," Pepper whispered. "She thinks you taught them to spin the ball a certain way so it landed on Tommy's lucky numbers. Is that possible?"

"No."

"Misty said she saw it in an old movie."

"This isn't the movies."

"Were the croupiers involved?"

"Nope."

"Then why did the guards escort the last croupier away?"

"So the casino can give her a polygraph."

Wang was given another form to fill out. Since 9/11, the federal government required gamblers to report cash transactions more than $10,000. The casinos hadn't taken this law seriously until the MGM got shut down for noncompliance.

Cory and Morris edged up next to Billy.

"Morris thinks he figured it out," Cory whispered.

Billy liked when his crew tried to dope things out. It meant they were curious, and not just along for the ride. "Lay it on me."

"The wheel was biased," Morris whispered. "At first I thought it was weighted, but then I realized Wang's winning numbers were all over the wheel. You somehow put grooves in the wheel that made the ball drop on those numbers."

"Grooves can be seen," Billy said. "They're good if you're going to rip off the joint once, and that's all they're good for."

"I told you that wasn't how it worked," Cory whispered.

"But that's the only way it can work," Morris whispered back.

"Keep trying," Billy said.

Morris was partially right about how the scam worked. The only reliable way to cheat at roulette was with a biased wheel. Wheels could be biased by applying weights to the underside, which caused sections of the wheel to favor the ball's path. As scams went, a biased wheel was self-working. The wheel did all the work, while the cheats made all the money.

The casinos knew about biased wheels. To protect themselves, they bought their wheels from companies that guaranteed the wheel's reliability. These wheels were flawlessly balanced, with pockets uniformly surfaced and frets resistant to wear.

This didn't mean that cheats hadn't found ways to bias wheels. It happened, and usually involved an employee who biased the wheel when no one was looking. This was accomplished using a special varnish that caused the ball to slow down and fall on desired numbers.

The casinos knew these tricks. The wheel used in Wang's sky palace would be tested for special varnishes and weights. If nothing improper was found, the wheel would be sent to the gaming board lab, where it would be tested again. If the gaming board discovered even the slightest bias, it would instruct Carnivale not to pay Wang off. Wang would then be forced to take the Carnivale to court to get his dough.

Billy had taken these things into consideration when devising his roulette scam. Neither the casino nor the gaming board would find anything wrong with the wheel, and they would not have grounds to deny Wang. Tomorrow afternoon, a pair of Loomis armored trucks would pull up to Carnivale's entrance and deliver Wang his money. End of story.

Wang was done filling out the forms. The look on his face was one of relief. Wang would go back home, settle his debt with the Chinese gangster, and live happily ever after. If he were smart, he'd take up another hobby and never gamble inside a casino again.

Two beautiful cocktail waitresses appeared. Each held a tray of champagne flutes. The drinks were passed out. Lamb had on his brave face, and he offered a toast.

"Congratulations on your incredible win," Lamb said.

The three other orangutans raised their flutes and offered their congratulations.

Billy sipped his drink, smelling a rat. Wang was already liquored up; Lamb had made sure of that back in the sky palace. If Lamb kept feeding Wang booze, Wang could be convinced to return to the tables and start gambling again. If the Carnivale was desperate enough, they might rig the game and steal some of their money back. It happened.

"Get your boyfriend away from these goons," Billy told Pepper.

"Maybe I'll put him to bed. He's looking a little worn out," Pepper said.

"You're really in love with him, aren't you?"

"I'm afraid I am. Have you ever fallen in love on a job?"

Billy smiled. The first scam he'd ever pulled, he'd fallen in love with Maggie Flynn. "Stay with him. Just in case a hooker gets sent up and tries to talk him into going downstairs and gambling."

"Will do. You still haven't told us how we get our money. You going to rob him?"

"I told you in Lake Tahoe that wouldn't happen. Wang keeps the money."

Pepper nearly dropped her drink. "All of it?"

"All of it."

"What about our share?"

"That comes later."

Billy handed his empty flute to a waitress. The adrenaline that came from scamming the casino had burned off, and he was spent. He was going to remember this day for the rest of his life, not only because of the score, but because he'd killed a man and felt no regrets. He hoped he'd never have to do it again but wasn't making any promises.

He bid good night to Wang and his crew and headed for the elevators.

FIFTY-THREE

"How you two gentlemen doing?" the bartender asked.

Grimes was doing shitty, thanks for asking. The gaming agent pointed at the empty shot glass on the bar. It looked lonely, and the bartender filled it to the brim.

"How about you?" the bartender asked.

Tricaricco put his hand over his shot glass to say he was done. The bartender returned the bottle of Johnnie Walker to the shelf and took a sawbuck from the stack of bills on the bar.

"Keep the change," Grimes said.

The bartender left to wait on another thirsty customer. Grimes took a deep breath and slammed back the drink. He hadn't eaten and it hit his empty stomach like a hand grenade.

"You should get some food," Tricaricco suggested.

"Screw that. I'm heading home and hitting the sack," Grimes said. "There's no reason to rush this. I'll deal with this situation tomorrow."

They were sitting in the darkened bar in Frankie's Tiki Room, a Polynesian-themed cocktail lounge on Charleston. The evening shift at the casinos had ended and the joint was filling up with dealers looking to end the day on a high note. Tricaricco still wore the clothes he'd had on earlier in the day, as did Grimes. The gaming agents had not gone home to their families, but instead had phoned their wives to say an emergency had arisen.

"Fuck tomorrow. You'll deal with it now," Tricaricco said, barely able to control his anger. "This is your problem, Frankie boy, and you're not going to walk away from it."

"Is that an order?" Grimes asked.

"Don't be a wiseass. I'm here to help you."

"Is that why you paid for the kerosene?"

Tricaricco stopped talking and looked over Grimes's head into the bar. "A guy who used to work for the gaming board just came in. Let's get out of here before he makes us."

Grimes slid off his chair and followed Tricaricco outside. His head was spinning and the cool night air hit him like a slap in the face in the parking lot. They went to his car and he fumbled pulling his car keys from his pocket. Tricaricco took the keys from his hand.

"I'll drive, you navigate," Tricaricco said.

"You taking me home?" Grimes asked.

"No, Frank, I'm not taking you home."

"You can't make me do this."

"What other choice do you have? This is the only way it can end. Now, get in the car and we'll go get it done."

"What if I mess it up? What then?"

"You're not going to mess it up. Now, get in the car."

The alcohol had thickened Grimes's tongue and fogged his brain. He went to the driver's door before realizing that he wasn't driving. He walked around the back of the car, and before getting into the passenger side, he halted and puked his guts out on the pavement.

"You okay?" Tricaricco asked when Grimes was settled in.

"Not really," Grimes said.

- - -

Grimes had never been to the house at night and it took him a while to find it. The neighborhood south of Nellis Air Force Base was ground zero for criminal activity and drug dealing, and he knew they were taking a risk coming here.

"This is it," Grimes said.

Tricaricco parked at the curb and killed the engine. They sat in silence and watched cars pull up to different addresses and people jump out and run in, to emerge only moments later.

"I can't do this," Grimes blurted out. "I'm going to get caught. Look at how many fucking people there are out there. Someone's going to spot me."

"Do you know how many people got whacked in this neighborhood last year? Half the murders in the city happened here. It's an everyday occurrence," Tricaricco said.

"What are you saying—that no one will notice?"

"No one cares, Frank. These people are animals. Let's get this over with."

The two men got out of the car. Tricaricco popped the trunk and removed the paper bag with the stacks of hundred-dollar bills that he'd withdrawn from the branch of the Nevada State Bank where he kept his personal account. The five-gallon can of kerosene was also in the trunk and still had the sticker from True Value. He handed Grimes the money bag. "Whatever you do, don't drop it. The magazine's fully loaded and the safety's off."

"Right."

"I'll be here waiting for you. Trust me, Frank, it's the right thing to do."

"No, it's not."

Drunk and breathing hard, Grimes headed up the front path clutching the bag to his chest. He'd always wondered what it felt like to be a soldier in combat and realized he was about to find out. Before he could knock on the front door, the sickly yellow overhead light came on and the door swung in.

"It's a little late for a house call, don't you think?" Junior Haney said.

"I've got another job for you," Grimes said.

"You want us to kill another cheat?"

"Yup. Guy's been scamming us at baccarat. We want him to disappear."

Grimes opened the mouth of the bag and let Junior have a look. Money blinded people to reality and brought down their defenses. Junior motioned him inside and locked the door.

"Let's go talk with my father," Junior said.

They headed down a narrow hallway to a living room filled with cheap furniture. There were no wall hangings or framed memories of the past, nothing to suggest a life other than the one the Haneys were living right now. Wilmer Haney sat on a couch watching wrestling on the muted TV. On the coffee table were the remains of several meals served on paper plates. Grimes had decided that Wilmer was as unpredictable as a wild animal and was the one to worry about. Wilmer stopped watching TV and glared murderously at Grimes.

"He's got another job for us," Junior explained.

Wilmer grunted under his breath in a language only his son understood.

"My father doesn't understand why you aren't at home," Junior said.

"The casino where I work called me in," Grimes explained. "They caught this guy cheating us at baccarat. He's done it before, so we decided it was time to get rid of him."

Wilmer let out another grunt. On the third finger of his right hand was the antique ring that had belonged to Cal Branche. It occurred to Grimes that if the father hadn't picked Branche's body clean like a vulture after murdering him, none of this would have occurred.

"My father wants you gone. Come by tomorrow, and we'll talk about it," Junior said.

"You don't have to be hostile about it."

"Just go."

Grimes placed the money bag on the coffee table, reached in, and removed the 9mm Glock 43 pistol hiding beneath the stacks. He pointed it at Wilmer's forehead and squeezed the trigger. The bullet went straight through and popped the back of Wilmer's head like a rotten piece of fruit. Blood flew back into Grimes's eyes, momentarily blinding him.

"You motherfucker!" Junior screamed.

Grimes aimed at the sound of Junior's voice and emptied the magazine. Junior let out a bloodcurdling scream and his body crashed to the floor, taking down a lamp on the way.

Grimes staggered into the kitchen. At the sink he found a dishrag and wiped the blood from his eyes. He was disintegrating inside, the act of taking another life more horrible than anything he could have possibly imagined. Hiring Junior and his father to whack Billy Cunningham had seemed like a smart thing to do; Cunningham had ruined his career, and a payback had been in order. Now, in hindsight, he had to believe it was the stupidest thing he'd ever done.

His cell phone vibrated and he pulled it from his pocket. It was Bill.

"All done," Grimes said.

"I knew you could do it. Come out and get the kerosene so we can finish this."

It had been Bill's idea to burn the house down. The fire department did not like coming to this area of town, and by the time they responded, the Haneys' house would be an inferno, and all evidence of the crime would be gone.

"I think I'm going to pass out," Grimes said.

"Hold yourself together, Frank. It's almost done."

Grimes ended the call. In the fridge he found a two-liter bottle of Coke from which he took a long swig. The job was almost finished, but it would never end. For the rest of his life, he would dream about the suspicious look on Wilmer's face right before he shot him.

When Grimes returned to the living room, Junior was propped up against the wall, trying to peck out 911 on his bloodied cell phone.

Grimes found a butcher knife in the kitchen and finished the job.

FIFTY-FOUR

-TWO WEEKS LATER-

The day after ripping off Carnivale, Billy had driven to Santa Monica and booked a suite at the Hotel California with an ocean view and electric guitars autographed by famous rock musicians hanging on the walls. He was in a festive mood and didn't mind paying the exorbitant rates.

He'd spent the days hanging on the beach, his nights on the pier eating at Rusty's and the Albright. He took rides on the roller coaster and Ferris wheel, visited the aquarium, and did all the other touristy stuff. What he didn't do was talk to any of his crew.

His crew had also left town. Gabe was in San Diego spending quality time with his daughters; Travis had taken his family to Disneyland; Pepper and Misty were relaxing at a spa in Palm Springs; Cory and Morris had gone to the mountains to hike but were probably in Colorado smoking weed with exotic names like Pineapple Express and Martian Mean Green.

As the end of the month rolled around, Billy called his stockbroker and gave him instructions on what to do with his portfolio.

On the first day of the next month, Billy ordered room service and stayed glued to the flat-screen TV in his suite, watching the business channel. This was the day that quarterly earnings were announced. By that afternoon, Billy knew that he'd hit a home run right out of the park.

A few minutes after the stock market closed, he texted his crew.

- - -

They met up at Gabe's place a few days later. Billy splurged, ordered lunch from the Delivered Dish, and laid it out on the kitchen table. There was enough food for a small army.

His crew wasn't in a talkative mood. Kept in the dark for too long, they'd become moody and suspicious. Billy decided to start the meeting on a high note, and he walked around the kitchen and handed each member an envelope with their name printed on it.

Misty opened her envelope and shrieked. "This check is for more than a million bucks."

"That's right," Billy said.

"But that wasn't what you told us in Tahoe. You said it would be less."

"The payout was bigger than I expected. There is one downside. You have to declare the money as income on your tax returns and pay your taxes. If your accountant asks you where you got the money, tell him you made it on the stock market."

"Now I get it. You shorted them, didn't you?" Cory said.

"Those business classes you've been taking are really paying off," Billy said. "You're right, I did short them."

"For how much?"

"Seventy bucks a share."

"That's huge. How many shares did you own?"

"Two hundred thousand."

"Jesus Christ. You made a fourteen-million-dollar profit. No wonder you didn't tell us what the deal was. If word got out, you'd go to prison for insider trading."

Misty looked confused. "What the heck are you talking about?"

"Wang's win at the Carnivale happened on the last day of the company's fiscal quarter," Cory explained. "The loss forced the company to report a loss and the stock tanked."

"How do you make money from that?" Misty asked.

"I've been playing the stock market through a broker," Billy explained. "Three weeks ago, I had my broker borrow two hundred thousand shares of Carnivale stock. I told my broker to sell the shares the same day for what I paid for them, which he did. When Carnivale's stock tanked, I bought two hundred thousand shares at the lower price and returned the borrowed shares to the lender while pocketing the difference."

"Is that legal?" Misty asked.

"You bet it's legal," Billy said.

Travis wore a worried expression. The certified check hadn't wowed him like it had the others. If anything, the big man looked more than a little scared. "Look, Billy, we've all figured out that you got a gaffed wheel into Wang's sky palace. You and I both know that the gaming board's going to dissect that wheel in their lab and eventually figure out what the secret is. Once that happens, they're going to realize we were involved and come looking for us."

"They're not going to figure it out," Billy said.

"How can you be so sure?"

Gabe sat at the head of the kitchen table eating Swedish meatballs with a toothpick. Gabe had been through hell and back and it was time for Billy to acknowledge Gabe's contribution. "Because Gabe's a fucking genius, that's why," Billy said.

"Thanks, Billy," the jeweler said. "You guys want a demonstration?"

"Yeah," they all said.

"Follow me."

- - -

Gabe's two-car garage served as his workshop. Whenever a new piece of casino equipment came on the market, Billy bought one and gave it to Gabe to play with. On the workshop table sat a roulette wheel identical to the wheels used at Carnivale's casino.

"A little back story is in order," Billy said. "A year ago, I got introduced to Eddie DeSantis through a mutual friend. DeSantis had just started working at the Carnivale, and he had a real grudge with his bosses. A whale got drunk one night and raped a guest in his suite. The casino was afraid of losing the whale's business, so they made DeSantis cover it up.

"DeSantis wanted to pay his bosses back. I saw a real opportunity, so I struck a deal with him. I would go to the Rio pretending to be a whale, and DeSantis would convince his bosses that I was worth stealing and putting up in one of Carnivale's sky palaces."

"Wait a second," Misty said. "If DeSantis was involved in the scam, why were you always giving him crap? What did that prove?"

"Remember the Bluetooth earpiece DeSantis wore? His bosses were listening to him, just like Big Brother. I didn't have a choice," Billy said.

"So it was just a big act," Misty said.

"That's right. DeSantis played a role, just like the rest of you. And he also got a million-dollar payday." Billy set the wheel in motion and gave the ball a spin. "DeSantis had another role, which was to help me get a gaffed wheel into a storage room at the Carnivale. Roulette wheels are pretty sturdy and are rarely replaced. Carnivale's spare wheel was kept in a storage room with no surveillance cameras. Switching the wheel for a gaffed one was easy."

"Is this wheel gaffed?" Travis asked.

"It sure is. But you won't find the secret, no matter how hard you look," Billy said.

"You're kidding me," Travis said.

"Show him," Billy said.

Gabe went to his worktable and picked up a plastic cup filled with thin metal screws. Gabe told Travis to hold out his hand and poured a dozen screws into the big man's palm.

"Between each number on a roulette wheel is a metal separator called a fret," Gabe said. "The frets are attached to the wheel by screws made of carbon steel. Each screw has a fifty-four percent carbon and forty-six percent magnesium composition. The screws in your hand are different. They have forty-two percent carbon and fifty-eight percent magnesium. They're slightly softer, which causes the ball to land on those numbers more of the time. These screws let Wang win."

Travis shook his head. The big man had worked as a dealer and knew how thorough the gaming board was. "I hate to be a party pooper, but this won't hold up. We're fucked."

"We're fucked if the gaming board can replicate what happened in Wang's sky palace, and they can't do that." Billy took the ball out of the wheel and tossed it to Travis. "This wheel is gaffed so Wang's lucky numbers come up. We used it to test the scam. Go ahead and spin it a few times and see what happens."

Travis spun the wheel ten times in a row. The crew stood around the worktable, their eyes glued to the ball. Not once did one of Wang's lucky numbers come up. Billy said, "Let me give it a try," and on his very first spin, one of Wang's numbers won.

"How the hell did you do that?" Travis said, clearly exasperated.

"Say uncle, and I'll show you," Billy said.

"Uncle, uncle."

"Try it again, but this time, spin the wheel as hard as you can."

Travis gave the wheel a much harder spin. This time, one of Wang's numbers hit.

"Explain this to me, will you?" the big man said.

"It's all physics," Billy said. "If the wheel is spun at an excessively high speed, the ball is compelled to the line of least resistance. The faster the rotation, the harder the ball hits the frets that are firmly screwed down. At the same time, when the ball bounces against the frets with the softer screws, it meets less resistance and is more likely to come to rest."

Travis nodded, now a believer. "They'll never figure that out."

"You're right. They never will."

"How'd you get the croupiers on board?" Morris asked. "Were they part of the scam?"

"No, they were unwitting accomplices. Carnivale's croupiers are from Havana, and in Cuba croupiers are trained to spin the wheel much quicker than here in the States. If a player gets hot, the croupiers spin it even faster, thinking it will change the run of the game."

"So when Wang started winning, the croupiers helped him out by spinning the wheel even faster," Morris said.

"Yes, they did. I plan to send them very nice Christmas presents this year. Anonymously, of course."

His crew took turns trying out the gaffed wheel. It wasn't long before they were believers as well, and they drifted back into the kitchen and helped themselves to the catered food. In a few days, after they'd deposited their checks and it had sunk in, they'd be different people. Whoever had said that money didn't buy happiness had never been poor.

Everyone was happy, except for Pepper. She'd come to the meeting wearing a pair of designer shades and hadn't uttered a word, not even after getting her share of the loot. That wasn't like her, and Billy got her outside onto the lanai and shut the slider for privacy.

"You're not acting like yourself. What's going on?"

"You were right," Pepper said, her voice cracking.

"Why are you so hoarse?"

“Because I’ve been crying.”

“About what?”

“Him.”

“Wang?”

“Who else?” She produced her cell phone and displayed its face. Wang had sent her a text with a selfie taken with his wife and kids. They looked like one big happy family. “Tommy flew home, and when his wife heard he’d won thirty-six million bucks, she took him back. He sent me a Dear John text. Thanks for the memories.” Tears poured down her cheeks, and she made no attempt to wipe them away. “You told me Wang was no good, but did I listen? Fuck, no. I went and let him break my heart.”

Pepper wanted to hurt someone. She pulled out her check and started to tear it in half. Billy snatched it from her fingers, knowing she’d regret it later on. He held out his arms, and she fell into his body, laying her head on his chest.

“Goddamn men,” she sobbed.

FIFTY-FIVE

Billy knew a lot of hustlers who abused alcohol and took drugs. Stealing released endorphins that got them high; then, they took drugs or got drunk to come down.

It was a brutal cycle that always ended badly.

Billy had heard the names Sydney and Bobby Rehmar upon arriving in Las Vegas ten years ago. The Rehmars had helped hundreds of addicts by opening their home to them and helping them kick their addictions. The Rehmars didn't care if you stole for a living or if you were a brain surgeon. All they cared about was helping you get better.

The Rehmars were long gone, but their legacy lived on. Inside the sprawling Las Vegas Recovery Center on the north side of town was a pair of single-story houses called the Rehmar Recovery Residences that were dedicated to help addicts seek long-term recovery.

Sydney's residence housed eight women and was a sweet deal. It had private bedrooms, cable TV, and a pool. Billy sat on a lounge chair watching Mags tread water in the deep end. She'd been off the pills and booze for several weeks and was having a hard time adjusting.

"How do you feel?" Billy asked.

"Shitty. Go to the liquor store and buy me a fifth of vodka, will you?"

"Not on your life. Want a flavored bottled water?"

"Some friend you are. Gimme a cigarette."

A pack of Eve cigarettes lay on Mags's chair. Billy banged out a cigarette and removed a pack of matches from the plastic. Mags swam over and draped her arms over the edge. She shook her head and drops of water flew everywhere. His heart skipped a beat.

"What's wrong?" she said.

"Who said anything was wrong?" he said.

"Your face turned softer than a football in Foxboro."

He lit a cigarette and took a puff. Kneeling, he stuck it between her lips.

"When did you start smoking?"

"The moment I got here. Everybody in this joint smokes like a chimney. It's called switching addictions. You should try it. Death on the installment plan."

The way she held the cigarette made her look like a movie star. He picked up the manuscript lying next to her chair and thumbed through the pages. "What's this?"

"It's a treatment for a TV show that a producer named Rand Waters sent me. I fleeced him at poker at the Riviera, and he told me I should be on TV."

"You fleeced him, and he offered you a job?"

"Some men like to be dominated."

"What are you going to do on TV—commercials?"

"Acting in a serious crime drama on network TV. I'd be the lead. Waters is big-time, a real force of nature out in La-La Land. I read that online."

It wouldn't be the first time a thief had made it big in Hollywood. Billy opened the manuscript and started reading. The series was called *Night and Day*, the lead a thirty-five-year-old single mother of two named Becca Nightingale. The show took place in Las Vegas and centered around Becca's double life. By day, Becca was an investigator for the gaming board and solved crimes committed against the casinos by nefarious thieves and scam artists. At night, Becca put her badge away and ran with a crew of cheats who robbed the casinos blind.

Mags came out of the pool and dried herself with a towel.

"Want another cigarette?" he asked.

"You're psychic."

He repeated the ritual and placed the cigarette between her lips. "What's your motivation for ripping off the casinos?"

"We find out in the second episode that Becca's old man owned a small casino that got shut down by the corporations that owned the big joints," Mags explained. "Her old man lost everything and ended up committing suicide."

"So Becca has a grudge."

"You bet. The money she steals from the casinos, she donates anonymously to homeless shelters and charities at the end of each show."

Billy couldn't help but laugh. There was no such thing as Robin Hood, there was only Robin Hoodlum, who stole from the rich and kept all the money for himself. Mags ripped the treatment from his hands and tossed it onto her chair.

"You think they're going to make a show about a bunch of crooks?" she said angrily. "Every episode has got to have a happy ending, otherwise the advertisers won't buy into it."

"Don't be pissed. I saved your life, remember?"

"Meaning what? That things are good between us again? You're going to have to crawl on your belly through cracked glass before I forgive you, babe."

Her eyes said that she meant it. He wasn't sure what he'd come here expecting from her. A simple thanks would have been nice, or maybe a hug and a peck on the cheek.

"Why did you send me that text if you feel that way?" he asked.

"Because I knew you'd come to my rescue. Now, answer the question."

"You didn't ask me a question."

"How much is this place setting you back?"

"Fifteen grand for a month stay."

"That's pretty steep. Did they make you pay up front?"

"Uh-huh. Cash on the barrel."

She took his chin with her hand. For a moment, he thought she was going to kiss him.

"I can't pay you back," she said.

"Don't worry about it."

"So what do you want? Besides getting me back in the sack and screwing my brains out."

Mags would turn him inside out if he wasn't careful, and he went to the edge of the pool and stared at the deep blue water. "You still want to run with me?"

"What did you just say?"

"Do you still want to run with me and my crew?"

Her lounge chair made a harsh scraping sound. Mags came up beside him, the smug look gone from her face. "You little piece of shit. All I ever wanted was to run with you. And then you dumped me in Venice because you thought I'd get busted and so would your crew."

"I made a mistake. I'm sorry."

"Is that it? You're sorry. How fucking trite."

"I'm offering you a job. I want you to join me. I've got a scam in the works, and I want you to be a part of it."

"I have a job. I'm going to be an actress."

This didn't sound like the woman he knew. "You really think this will work out?"

"Let me tell you what I think. The only reason men are interested in me is because I'm good at being a thief. You, Lou Profaci, Jimmy Slyde, that's all you boys saw in me. Now Rand Waters tells me that I've got real talent as an actress. I'd be crazy not to give it a shot."

He put his hands on her arms and looked her square in the eye. "Maybe you do have talent. But how long do you think you'll want to do that? You're a thief and you always will be. You'll be bored out of your flipping mind in Hollywood. There's no action there."

She blinked. "There isn't?"

"No. You get up at the crack of dawn, put in a ten-hour day, go home and read the next day's script, back in bed by nine thirty. Is that the kind of life you want?"

Mags swallowed the lump in her throat. "No."

"You were born to steal."

"I won't argue with you there."

"Say yes, and I'll make you the happiest woman on earth."

"You mean that?"

"Yes."

"Why the sudden change of heart?"

"A guy in my crew is married to a woman he doesn't love. It made me think that you have only one true love in your life, and if you don't grab the chance, it won't come again."

Her eyes went dreamy. "Am I your true love?"

"Yeah. I want to scam casinos with you."

"Let me think about it."

"You already have thought about it. I want an answer."

"Stop being an asshole."

He was not going to let her manipulate him and started to walk away.

"Wait!" she said. "You haven't told me the play."

- - -

Billy made her sit down beneath the shade of an umbrella and parked himself beside her.

"I'm going to Sacramento tomorrow to have a sit-down with the Boswells, better known as the Gypsies. Victor Boswell wants to retire and has decided to go out with a major bang. He has a huge score that will require his family and my crew to pull it off."

"What kind of score?"

"Victor has a way to beat every casino on the Strip at blackjack. He won't tell me what the method is, but knowing him, it's a sweet play. He says we'll need an experienced card painter to pull it off. If I remember correctly, that's your specialty."

"I can't set foot inside the casinos. You know that."

"We'll disguise you, make you look like a retired schoolteacher."

"You've already thought this out."

"Every last step. No one will suspect a thing."

Her eyes danced with possibilities. Fifteen years ago, sitting in the front seat of her sputtering Toyota in a McDonald's parking lot in Providence, Mags had revealed her dream to run with a crew in Vegas. Now Billy was offering her the chance to make that dream come true.

"You've hooked me," she said.

"Is that a yes?"

"What's my take?"

His heart did that funny thing again. "Victor says we'll steal fifty million easy and split the money in half. What would you say if I gave you two million bucks to work your magic?"

"Are you serious?"

"I've never been more serious in my life."

Mags shut her eyes and hugged herself. Up until a few minutes ago, she had no money, no life, and a future as uncertain as a weatherman's forecast. "Does that make us partners?"

"If that's what you want, yes."

Her eyes opened. "If I get caught painting cards, they'll put me away for life. Go see your friend Victor and let him show you this scam. Then call me with the details."

"Is that a yes?"

"It's whatever you want it to be," she said.

FIFTY-SIX

The Boswells ran their operation out of the Lucky Strikes bowling alley on the east side of Sacramento. Billy and his crew arrived at noon in a rented SUV and parked in the deserted lot. A sign taped to the front door read **CLOSED FOR PRIVATE PARTY.**

Two hours later, Billy walked outside of the bowling alley for some privacy and called Mags on his cell phone while standing in the building's cool shade. "The blackjack scam's better than I thought," he told her. "Victor did it for us a dozen times, and I still don't have a clue how it works. We could end up owning a casino by the time this thing's over."

"You're pulling my leg," Mags said.

"I'm serious. This is the holy grail of cheating."

"Do you really think we could end up owning a casino?"

Crews of cheaters had bankrupted casinos in Monte Carlo, Biloxi, and the Bahamas, but never in Las Vegas. There was a first time for everything and he said, "I don't see why not."

"Dreams can come true, and they can happen to you, if you're larcenous at heart," she sang into the phone. "Do you have a date in mind?"

"The first Sunday of the NFL playoffs. Vegas is a zoo then."

"Sounds like a plan. Where are you taking me to dinner so we can celebrate?"

"Don't you need a pass to get out of that place?"

"I'll sneak out without telling anyone."

"Does this make us partners?"

"I believe it does."

They settled on an Italian restaurant called Geno's, and he agreed to drive to the Rehmar Residences and pick her up after his flight landed that afternoon. He ended the call thinking that a door had opened in his life. He'd been running solo a long time, and the novelty had worn off. It was time to partner up. Sure, Mags was a loose cannon, but so were most people who made their living thieving. With the right supervision and guidance, she'd do just fine.

At four he landed at McCarran, got his car from short-term parking, and broke every speed limit driving to her place. At the north end of the Strip he found a jewelry store in a strip center and overpaid for a glittering diamond necklace. He hated getting ripped off but put the feeling aside. He wanted to impress, and he didn't care what the necklace cost.

Back on the road, he called Mags and got voice mail. He left a message telling her he was running behind and would be there soon. His voice was filled with excitement and he felt like a teenager going on his first real date.

Twenty minutes later, he parked in front of the recovery residence where Mags was living, got out of his car, and spent a moment composing himself. He had robbed every casino in Vegas—some of them multiple times—and could not remember feeling so nervous.

He headed up the brick path. It was strange, but when he thought about Mags, it wasn't in the context of scamming the casinos but of them doing things together, like buying a house or taking a vacation. Stupid mundane shit that had never seemed important, until now.

He removed the jewelry box from his pocket. The pretty salesgirl had wrapped it with silver paper and a crimson bow. He took a deep breath before pressing the buzzer. A tough-looking broad with a butt dangling from her lips answered the door and gave Billy the once-over.

"Hey handsome, what can I do for you?" she asked.

"I'm looking for Mags," he said.

"Who?"

"Maggie Flynn. She's a resident."

"Hold that thought."

The door was shut in his face. Several minutes passed, and he told himself good things were worth waiting for. When the door reopened, a barefoot woman without makeup stood before him. She also found Billy enjoyable to look at.

"Aren't we a breath of fresh air," the barefoot woman said.

"I'm looking for Maggie. She's expecting me," Billy said.

"No, she's not."

"Excuse me?"

"Your girlfriend blew out of here a few hours ago. Prince Charming driving a Mercedes whisked her away. She asked me to give you this, in case you came by."

Billy's hand was trembling as he took the envelope from the barefoot woman's hand. Mags had written *Now we're even* on the front for all the world to see.

"Want to come in?" the barefoot woman asked.

"Some other time," he said.

Sitting at a traffic light, he read her note. Mags had decided to give Tinseltown a try and had convinced her daughter to fly out to LA and meet her. She was tired of the grifter's life and trying to outrun the law, and was giving up cheating for good. She ended the note by telling Billy that he would always be in her heart but that it was best if he just let her go.

So this was how it felt to get dumped. It was a new experience, and he didn't like it. He told himself he'd get over her, but deep down inside, he knew that was a lie. Mags was his first love, and he would always regret not getting it right the first time.

His heart was aching as he shredded the note and tossed the pieces out the window as he burned down the highway. In the rearview mirror they danced like butterflies on the dark pavement.

ACKNOWLEDGMENTS

I would like to thank the following people for their contributions to this book. Russell Barnhart, for writing *Beat the Wheel*, the definitive work on beating the game of roulette. Kjersti Egerdahl and Kevin Smith, whose story ideas and editorial contributions are always welcome. My wife, Laura, for being my biggest fan. And a very special thanks to the crew of cheaters I met in Las Vegas who agreed to let me tell their story.

ABOUT THE AUTHOR

James Swain is the national bestselling author of eighteen mystery novels and has worked as a magazine editor, screenwriter, and novelist. His books have been translated into many languages and have been chosen as Mysteries of the Year by *Publishers Weekly* and *Kirkus Reviews.* Swain has received a Florida Book Award for fiction, and in 2006, he was awarded France's prestigious Prix Calibre .38 for Best American Crime Writing. When he isn't writing, he enjoys researching gaming scams and cons, a subject on which he's considered an expert.